Desire & Sacrifice

Duncan Wood

To My Beloved Sons,

In the story of my life, you are the most beautiful chapters. I love you with a depth that words can barely capture.

With all my heart and soul,

Dad

Chapter 1

That Damned Beep

The young man twisted and turned in his bed as he slept, a light patina of sweat on his forehead as he wrestled with this all-too-familiar dream. He felt himself running down a long hallway, his rubber soles squeaking on the glossy floor. His breathing was heavy and echoed in his ears as everything around him seemed to be in slow motion, yet he knew he was moving as fast as he could. He kept his eyes fixed on the door at the end of the hallway, screams echoing in the distance as he pushed his way past people dressed in white. Every other step, a loud BEEP punctuated the air, almost ear-piercing. His heart pounded as he tried to push through the crowd and stumbled over the unfortunate people in his way.

He looked down and saw that his hand was covered in blood, but he couldn't figure out why he was bleeding. Quickly surveying his body, he saw that the injury was just below his left breast near his armpit and put his hand on the wound to apply pressure to slow the bleeding. "BEEP… BEEP… BEEP" kept ringing in his ears. "Almost there, I'm almost there," he said to himself, everything still feeling as though he was trying to run through mud.

He heard a familiar voice yelling in the distance, but he couldn't make out who it was or what they were saying. He strained to see who it was, but to no avail. His eyes, again, locked onto the door facing him, he was close. BEEP… BEEP… BEEP, the sound getting louder the closer he got to the doors. "I can make it," he said to himself, taking deep breaths as his feet carried him towards his intended target. With one final push through two more people in his way, they went flying off, their screams of rage piercing his ears.

A bright light began to fill the cracks of the doors as he felt pressure on his shoulders, and Thomas yelled "Let me go!" He grabbed the door handles, but the force on his shoulders dragged

him backwards just as he pulled down on the handles, pulling the doors open. A bright light filled the opening, so bright that Thomas was unable to keep his eyes open. BEEP... BEEP... BEEP!

The sound of the blaring alarm clock cuts through the quiet darkness of the room, jolting him from his slumber. With a groan, he slams his hand on the snooze button to silence the damned BEEP. Rubbing the sleep from his eyes, he sits up and stretches his arms above his head, feeling his muscles protest the early hour. Glancing over at the nightstand, he reaches for the water bottle he had placed there the night before and takes a few sips. Next to the water bottle, his pack of cigarettes lies waiting for him. He hesitates for a moment before grabbing one and lighting it up, inhaling deeply as he tries to shake off the remnants of his dream.

He felt a sense of unease and confusion wash over him as he struggled to remember the details of the dream he had just woken up from, but the memory of running down a hallway filled with white-coated people and an incessant beeping sound still lingered. As he sat up and rubbed his eyes, he tried to shake off the feeling of dread that had settled in his chest. He couldn't help but wonder, and not for the first time, if the dream held any significance or if it was simply his mind's way of processing the ongoing stress of his life.

He spent a few minutes in silence, thinking, before mashing his cigarette out in the marble ashtray his father had given him years ago. Although he didn't normally keep sentimental objects, he did hang onto a few items for emotional practice in hopes of creating a connection to them. Despite these efforts, he found himself detached from things that often held meaning for others.

Now fully awake, Thomas turned on some music and opened the blinds, allowing the sunlight to flood the room. Mornings were his favorite part of the day, filled with a sense of hope and endless possibilities. He often felt like a robot by the end of the day, just going through the motions. If only he could maintain that feeling of being truly alive all day long, he thought to himself. He gazed out the window at the landscape, lost in thought as he waited for the water to heat up. As he checked his phone for his schedule, a text from an associate at *Turner Research* confirmed Thomas' attendance at a seminar later that day.

After a refreshing shower was accomplished, Thomas gulped down a couple of cups of coffee and proceeded to select his attire for the day. After giving it some thought, he settled on a sleek black suit with a light blue shirt and matching tie. As he dressed himself, he couldn't help but recall his father getting ready for work when he was a child. Once he had put on his favorite watch, he scrutinized himself in the mirror and applied a cologne that best complemented his outfit. He meticulously tended to every detail, taking his time to ensure perfection, as this gave him the motivation he needed to tackle the day. It wasn't that he was a perfectionist, but he found that striving for perfection made him feel content.

Since he had received a text message while he was in the shower, Thomas typed out a quick response, confirming his attendance with a simple "YES." However, he couldn't help but feel a sense of dread in the pit of his stomach. He had agreed to attend the seminar about a month ago, out of guilt from a colleague/ex-girlfriend who had brought up a previous situation he was involved in about a year ago. Thomas knew that his attendance would help to resolve the past and satisfy history, but he still wasn't looking forward to it. This individual was somewhat close to him, but the memories still weighed heavily on his mind about the on again-off again romance.

Once he finished his morning routine, Thomas settled at the kitchen table and turned on some Mozart. The music filled the air and helped set the tone for the day ahead. As he peeled a banana, he found himself humming along to the melody, lost in his own thoughts. Suddenly, a loud pounding on the front door interrupted his peaceful morning.

Chapter 2

The Hump Day Begins

Thomas stared challengingly at the door as if testing to see if the uninvited person would cease knocking and just leave. No such luck! He stood up reluctantly and proceeded to the door. "Hello?" he asked cautiously, pausing with his hand on the doorknob.

"It's Darius," came the reply. "C'mon, Thomas, open the door, man, I *hate* standing at doors!"

Thomas Rene chuckled as he opened the door. "Sorry, Dee, I didn't know who it was. Thought you might be the next-door neighbor!" he said as he let his good friend Darius in. Darius James is tall and confident black man, his well-built frame giving him an air of strength and power. His smooth, dark skin is a contrast against his bright white smile, and his piercing gaze exudes a sense of intensity. His clothing may be a bit thuggish, but his sharp sense of style and the way he carries himself suggest a man who is not to be trifled with. Despite his tough exterior, Darius had a heart of gold and a loyalty that ran deep, making him a valuable friend and ally to those few who had earned his trust. Thomas was one such.

The two greeted each other with handshakes and a chuckle. "So, what's up with the neighbor situation?" Darius inquired, referring to Thomas' latest love interest and smirking.

"I actually went on a date with her," Thomas replied, grinning self-consciously.

"No way! The one with the big, red truck?" Darius asked, eyes wide.

"That's the one," Thomas confirmed.

"I've seen her. She's a babe! Not the truck, the girl, I mean. How did the date go?" Darius probed, trying to look innocent while holding back his amusement.

"It went well," Thomas answered shortly, steering the conversation firmly back to anything else besides his love life. "Do you have it with you?" he asked.

Darius replied with a straight face, "I have it tucked up my ass for safety." Thomas was momentarily horrified before realizing Darius was joking. "Nah man, I ain't putting anything up my ass," Darius clarified with a chuckle.

"That's why they didn't like you in prison, I take it," Thomas joked back at him, openly laughing.

Darius then took a small bag of cocaine out of his jacket pocket, an 8-ball, and handed it over to Thomas. "No charge on this. I got you, bro," he said with a smile. Thomas thanked him, appreciative of both their long history together and Darius's innate generosity.

After appreciatively snorting a small amount of cocaine, Thomas started making breakfast for himself and Darius. "Want to stick around for some bacon and eggs?" he asked with a grin. He knew the answer before Darius even responded with a grunt of excitement as he headed to make a cup of coffee and grab a seat at the kitchen table. The aroma of sizzling bacon soon filled the room, a comforting scent that reminded Thomas of his childhood. Memories of his mother making bacon in the early morning hours flooded his mind - the low light as the sun came up, the smell of coffee brewing. These memories helped him remember what life *should* be like, even during his gray, mundane routine.

The two sat at the kitchen table, relishing breakfast and reminiscing about the past. Darius always brought up moments with the old crew he used to run with, as they always triggered either laughter or provoked deep reflections on life. It was true; Thomas felt that Darius's stories had that effect on him. He could listen to Darius for hours, as his drug-loving friend was not only a great storyteller but had many intriguing tales to share. He also

5

did not come across as someone who exaggerated, which only added to the enjoyment.

Thomas realized he didn't care much for people, generally speaking; in fact, he often found himself faking his way through relationships with others just to make life easier and less dramatic. Darius, on the surface, might not seem like someone he would normally befriend, but that was just because of the difference in what Thomas perceived as superficial societal status between them. Truthfully, Darius either made him laugh or contemplate, things few others could evoke from him. He admitted to himself that he simply found most people phony and self-centered when push came to shove.

After they finished cleaning up from breakfast, Darius used the small notepad on the counter and jotted down a few numbers. "These are my new digits, hit me up if you need anything." Thomas thanked him before seeing him out the door.

Chapter 3

If You Could

Thomas arrived at the headquarters *of Turner Research* early and parked his car, a sleek black Mercedes. He sat in the driver's seat, hesitant to go inside yet so, instead, spent his time scrolling through his phone, playing games and reading online gossip. He stumbled upon a captivating post about a famous social media influencer who had been arrested for killing a neighbor during a dispute over noise complaints. The influencer had been filming the encounter to gain more views, but the situation had quickly escalated and turned violent. The neighbor had angrily knocked the phone out of the influencer's hand and, during the ensuing struggle, was pushed into the path of an oncoming delivery truck hurrying to deliver its next package. Later, the influencer attempted to defend herself by claiming that the neighbor had *fallen* backwards into the delivery truck, but the live stream footage on her own phone showed otherwise. The phone had amazingly landed in the perfect position to capture the entire incident, leaving little for the police to further investigate as the damning footage had already gone viral on social media.

He sat in his car, a bit stunned by the weird story he had just read. As he sipped his coffee, he couldn't help but shake his head at the craziness of the situation. A noise complaint leading to death? It was hard to fathom. What puzzled him even more were the people who defended the influencer who had started the whole incident. Some of them seemed to base their support solely on her physical appearance. He could not deny her beauty, but, in his opinion, it was such a trivial factor compared to the grand scheme of things. "What a waste," he muttered under his breath. It was alarming how much of an impact social media was having on society. It seemed that people were turning to these apps for guidance on what is right and wrong, regardless of their upbringing or education.

There were moments when Thomas pondered the idea of having a child, but ultimately felt grateful that he never did. He struggled to understand the current direction of culture and found that teenagers were, from his observations, often overly indulged and pampered. The recent tragedy he had just read about only reinforced his belief that he might have been fortunate to have been spared the responsibility and trials of parenthood. However, despite his current reservations, he couldn't help but envision what it would be like to have a son. His thoughts consumed him as he wondered what the boy would look like, whether he would take after him or his mother, and whether he would have a strong bond with him.

Thomas had never had any real interest in having a daughter. It wasn't that having one was bad, but he couldn't bear the thought of the emotional responsibility that would come with raising a girl. The thought of some hormonal teenage boy showing up at his doorstep and professing his love for Thomas Rene's own beautiful daughter made him feel angry. He remembered all too well from his own teen years that boys hardly ever think about the consequences of their actions and usually only care about satisfying their own immediate desires. It is not that they intentionally meant to harm others, but they could get carried away by their passions of the moment all too easily.

As he adjusted the rearview mirror, Thomas caught a glimpse of his own slightly bloodshot eyes, the result of staying up late the previous night. He rubbed his eyes in a vain attempt to reduce the puffiness and quickly gathered his belongings, not wanting to be late for the seminar.

Chapter 4

Please Pay Attention

"Hallelujah, amen!" Thomas thought to himself. Arriving just in time for the seminar, Thomas found it more challenging than expected to locate the woman who had invited him since the lights were already dimming for the presentation. He treaded warily down the aisle, scanning the darkened rows carefully, hoping she would spot him and call out. Everyone's attention seemed to be fixed on the speaker, a man whom Thomas knew little about except that he was one of the founders of *Turner Research*. The gentleman was well-dressed with thin black hair slicked back, thin build and black dress slacks paired with a white polo shirt and an Omega watch as the finishing touch. Thomas appreciated the man's attention to detail, which was not overstated but rather classy. "Good afternoon, everyone" the man said. "My name is Dr. Stephen Crane, and I am the Senior Scientific Researcher for *Turner Research*. I am grateful for everyone taking the time to attend and hope that today's seminar will further your understanding of our Stem Cell Research and Development program," he greeted the audience.

Thomas was about to resign himself to sitting just about anywhere when he finally heard a familiar voice calling out to him. "Tom, over here... over here," Evelyn said, with a grin on her face. She clearly found it amusing that he appeared so lost. As he attempted to make his way to the seat beside her, he was faced with a decision familiar to all movie-goers, whether to show his backside or his groin to the people who were already seated as he sidled across the row. Personally, he found the situation amusing, as neither option seemed pleasant for the onlookers. With a smirk towards Evelyn, he decided to present his backside to the attendees in his path, even popping it out a little bit extra for humor's sake. This made Evelyn chuckle, and she couldn't help

9

but smile when one of the people in his path grimaced and had to lean their head backwards to avoid getting too close to the invading posterior.

As Thomas settled into his seat next to Evelyn, he leaned in close to whisper, "Thanks for the invitation." She smelled incredible, as usual. "I'm glad you came; I wasn't sure you would," she replied with a playful nudge of her shoulder. Evelyn Perdita was stunningly beautiful and had impeccable style. Her long black hair was pulled back in a ponytail, accentuating her dark eyes. She wore a lovely sun dress that highlighted her figure, and her lips were painted with a bright shade of lipstick that made her smile even more radiant in the dimly lit room.

"Hey, do you have an extra pen?" she whispered to Thomas.

He searched through his bag and whispered back, "Sorry, I don't have an extra one, but you can use mine."

She thanked him and they both settled back into their seats.

"What's this seminar about again?" Thomas asked, trying to catch up.

"Stem cell research and the advancements that they have been making. Stephen Crane is leading the project, and he has been making a lot of progress."

Thomas nodded, "I've heard of him before, but don't know much about him because he was in that hush-hush department."

"Well, maybe we should listen to the presentation and learn more," Evelyn urged with a small, secretive grin.

"Sounds like a plan," Thomas said, smiling.

As the speaker, Crane, continued his presentation, Thomas struggled to keep up with the complex information being shared. He looked through the presentation slides, filled with graphs and data, trying to make sense of it all. "The future of science lies in stem cell research," Crane proclaimed confidently. "We are on the brink of being able to control our own destinies. Even the most basic applications of stem cells have the potential to cure burns, strokes, cancer, spinal cord injuries, diabetes, Alzheimer's,

Parkinson's, amyotrophic lateral sclerosis, heart disease, and osteoarthritis." The speaker gestured towards the graphs on the screen behind him, pausing with dramatic effect to emphasize his point by taking a sip of water. The audience took advantage of the pause and murmured between themselves while diligently taking notes concerning the information presented so far.

Meanwhile, Thomas couldn't help but feel a bit overwhelmed by the advancements being made in the field of stem cell research. It was hard to imagine a world where so many debilitating diseases could be cured. He wondered what impact these developments would have on society and what challenges might arise as a result. For that matter, there were always *some* crazies out there who could find fault with anything, and often used God as an excuse.

The speaker proceeded on to the next slide, this time displaying a picture of Leonardo's famous "Vitruvian Man", which was a drawing of a man of perfect proportions with arms and legs outstretched within a circle and a square superimposed, a perfect representation of art and science intermingled. "Imagine the possibilities", said Crane, "of using this technology for even greater purposes, to make life more artistic and to create something extraordinary for us." He paused again, cocking his head as he peered through the bright lights at his audience. "Many believe that there are *limitations* to these benefits to humanity due to the adult stem cells not being as versatile or as durable as embryonic stem cells. It is further said that adult stem cells may *not* be able to be manipulated to produce all cell types, which limits their potential use to treat diseases." At this point, the speaker snorted to himself in apparent disgust at the stupidity of humanity. "Moreover, they are more prone to contain abnormalities due to environmental hazards." He paused, an indulgent smile on his thin lips. "However, here at Turner Research, we are proud to dispute this benighted point of view. Instead, based on our continuing research, we believe that we are indeed on the verge of creating a solution that will change the very fabric of humanity, itself!" He raised his arms outwards, purposely copying the Vitruvian Man to include the audience in his gesture. "Instead, *we* will become the artists of the human

11

body, providing solutions to the problems that have plagued us all for all time!" The crowd erupted into a standing ovation, and Crane beamed with appreciation for the show of passionate support.

Evelyn nudged Thomas as the presentation continued and whispered, "Impressive, isn't it?" Thomas, still intently focused on the screen display, responded, "Absolutely. I had no idea they had made this much progress in stem cell research!"

Chapter 5

Matthew 4:23-24

[23] Jesus went throughout Galilee, teaching in their synagogues, proclaiming the good news of the kingdom, and healing every disease and sickness among the people. [24] News about him spread all over Syria, and people brought to him all who were ill with various diseases, those suffering severe pain, the demon-possessed, those having seizures, and the paralyzed; and he healed them.

The seminar continued for another hour with even more technical data, theoretical concepts, and a Q&A session being offered. The audience continued to show great interest in the seminar and seemed to generally support the research that had been done so far. However, Thomas noticed a man in the line for questions who stood out from the others due to his rigid posture and frustrated expression. As the up-tight man approached the microphone, his Bible clutched firmly in his hands, he self-consciously cleared his throat and asked, "Dr. Crane, have you considered the *spiritual* implications of your company's actions?"

Dr. Crane's initial surprise quickly transformed into visible disdain as he responded to the man's question about spiritual implications. "I don't believe religion has *any* bearing on scientific discoveries," he snapped. However, the worried parishioner persisted with his concerns about the potential for genetic manipulation and the danger of unintended consequences. Crane listened impatiently and then responded in a dismissive tone, "Yes, yes, yes, there are risks involved in *any* scientific advancement, but we *must* continue to push forward and overcome our limitations. Science is constantly improving our understanding of the world and ourselves, and we must use this

13

knowledge to benefit humanity. You might even say that Science is the *new* God!" he smugly concluded.

Crane continued to argue further that science had brought tremendous benefits to society, from medical treatments to new technologies that significantly improved people's everyday lives. He stressed that the research they were conducting had the potential to help millions of people suffering from various diseases and conditions. He noted that the use of stem cells in medical research was already yielding promising results in treating cancer, diabetes, spinal cord injuries, and other conditions.

The religious man persisted, accusing Crane of "playing God" by altering what God had already created. The lecturer paused for a moment, taking off his glasses and making a show of forbearance as he diligently wiped the lenses, all the while thinking hard about the best way to deflect this potentially explosive assertion. Finally done with wiping his lenses, he looked up and said, "I understand the concern, but science does not seek to replace or challenge faith or religion. Our research aims to help people and alleviate suffering. I believe that science and faith *can* coexist, and that we can use our knowledge to improve the world and benefit humanity."

Crane forged ahead, explaining that, like any other scientific research, the work they were doing was subject to rigorous protocols, testing, and review. He emphasized that the research had checks and balances in place to ensure that the work was ethical and responsible. At this, the religious man snorted indignantly, leaning over to say something to the next person in the row. Crane chose to ignore it and closed with saying that the scientific community was truly committed to transparency, and that the results of their research were subject to peer review and scrutiny, all the while glaring balefully at the objector and his cohort in the audience.

As the Q&A session was winding down, Thomas had a sudden realization come over him and blurted out as he leaped to his feet, "Matthew 4: 23-24!". He had felt something on the tip of his tongue for the last ten minutes. Now, he knew what it was. The passage he miraculously remembered from the Bible spoke about Jesus healing the sick and afflicted, and how his fame for these selfless acts spread throughout the land. Thomas' mother had dunned it into his head often enough, that was for sure! Crane, of course, was able to flawlessly quote the passage on the spot over the microphone.

"Does that about sum it up, Mr. Rene? Yes, I recognize you. You still work for our Research Department, don't you?" responded Crane.

While Thomas was impressed with the accuracy of Crane's recall, he had a point to make of his own. "Yes, yes I do, thank you. Doesn't that imply that Jesus wished that *everyone* be healed? I mean, why would he have bothered to do all of that if he didn't care about *all* people, not just the ones he could personally help?" Of course, this sparked an immediate debate between Thomas and the religious zealot, who was still standing and seemed ready to engage anyone just to be contrary, if nothing else. However, before their side conversation could go any further, the audience microphone was disconnected by the organizers, and one of them approached the red-faced zealot to ask him to please sit down and to stop interrupting.

Thomas turned and apologized to Evelyn for getting involved, but she seemed more amused than disturbed and expressed a desire to hear more from the speaker, Dr. Crane. By this time, it was clear to everyone present that the topic of religion versus science was still a contentious issue, and one that was unlikely to be resolved anytime soon.

At this point, Crane, having successfully regained his control over both the mike and the situation, wrapped up the Q&A section, thanking everyone for their questions and support. "I am grateful for all of you being here today and for your interest in our research," he said with a self-congratulatory smile. "We are certainly excited about the possibilities that our stem cell research holds for the future of medicine, and we are fully committed to continuing our work to help those in need. Thank you again for joining us." With those final words, Dr. Stephen Crane stepped down from the stage and began shaking hands with the nearest members of the audience like a shady politician seeking votes while kissing babies.

Evelyn turned towards Thomas with an appraising glint in her eye, "So…, your place or mine?"

Chapter 6

I'm So Sorry

The next morning, Thomas sat on the edge of his bed, cigarette in hand, and listened to the peaceful sound of birds chirping outside his window and the small snores of the sleeping Evelyn. It was 7:00am, and he was still feeling groggy from staying up so late the night before. As he sat there in his boxers, he couldn't help but think that today was his father's birthday. They hadn't spoken in years, and the last time they did was uncomfortable. "Should I call him?" he asked himself, considering it for a moment, then decided not to, trying to think instead about what he had to do on the day still in front of him.

Thomas's childhood memories were marred by the huge shadow of his father's absence. When Thomas was just 4 years old, his father had left the family and was barely present throughout Thomas' childhood due to living far away. When he did make an appearance, it was often underwhelming and left an unsatisfied Thomas longing for still more since he loved his father dearly. One particularly painful early memory stood out - a trip to the supermarket with his mother and sisters. They had had a great time shopping together at the store, but when they returned home, everything suddenly seemed different. The house was empty, and it felt like they had been robbed. It wasn't until his mother found a note from his father that they realized what had happened. The note was short and seemed to Thomas years later to be a feeble attempt at justification for his father's actions in leaving. Thomas felt completely lost at the time and couldn't understand why his father would abandon him.

As he took another drag, Thomas realized he was down to the butt of the cigarette, the burning filter leaving a harsh taste in his mouth. Crushing it out, he savored the pain, still lost in the memory of his troubled childhood. In his mind's eye, he saw himself as a young boy, eagerly waiting by the window for his father's promised weekend visit. A seven-year-old Thomas, dressed in checkered pants and a polo shirt, had clutched a 70s-style suitcase filled with clothes and stuffed bears. The thought of a whole weekend with his father had filled him with joy and anticipation, and he bounced back and forth between the windows, hoping to catch a glimpse of his dad's car. Visions of fun and adventure filled his head, and he couldn't wait to spend time with his dad.

At 8:30pm, the phone interrupted Thomas's vigil by the window. His mother delivered the news that shattered his hopes and dreams - his father wouldn't be coming to spend the weekend with him. No explanation was offered by his mother, just a quick statement of fact. The weight of disappointment crushed the young Thomas as he tried to gather the strength to lug his suddenly much heavier suitcase back upstairs. All night long, he wept uncontrollably, the tears that poured from his eyes mirrored the pain in his heart. The sorrow he felt was deeper even than what he had felt when his father left the family years before. This time, the rejection felt personal and directed solely at him. In his mind's eye, Thomas watched his younger self and wished he could travel back in time to offer comfort and solace.

As Thomas's thoughts drifted to his father, the no-longer-comatose Evelyn rolled her head onto his lap and stretched, revealing her enticing stomach as her shirt rode up. Thomas instinctively reached over to touch her stomach, eliciting a giggle and a small sigh of enjoyment from the beautiful young woman. She noticed his distant gaze and asked, "What are you thinking about? You seem zoned out."

"Just thinking about my father, it's his birthday," Thomas replies, his eyes slightly misting up.

"Are you going to call him?" she asked with a sidelong glance.

"No," the despondent young man responded. "It's complicated, and I don't care to discuss it, if that's okay with you," he continued awkwardly, unwilling to be quite so vulnerable with her. Things had never worked out with him and Evelyn in the past for anything more than sex. He guessed he just didn't feel *that* way about her, but damn, she did look good.

"Sure, I get it. Fathers can be complicated," Evelyn said flippantly, gripping his hair and pulling him down for a kiss. "But I know how to take your mind off of absolutely everything," she suggests, pulling up her gray shirt slowly and giving him a knowing look.

"Well, that's one way, I guess," Thomas responds with a somewhat forced smile, giving in to the inevitable and accepting the invitation. After all, the sex was really the only thing he had missed about Evelyn. Truth was he just couldn't trust her. She tended to look out for number 1, and that certainly wasn't him.

Chapter 7

It's Just Dinner

The sound of sizzling bacon filled the kitchen, and the aroma of freshly brewed coffee wafted through the air. After indulging in a line of the cocaine Darius had gifted him, Thomas felt like he was off to a good start for the day. Evelyn emerged from the bedroom, still drying her hair. "I take it that's the breakfast of champions," she quipped with a smile.

"I assume you don't want any?" Thomas responded dryly.

"Bacon and coffee? Absolutely," she exclaimed, deliberately misinterpreting what he had said while grabbing a brush from the waistband of her pants.

When they sat down to eat, Evelyn wanted to reminisce and laugh about old times. Problem was that Thomas didn't think those times were that funny, especially since they always seemed to leave him "holding the bag", so to speak. Time seemed to fly by as they downed cup after cup of coffee and discussed their plans for the day. After finishing her third cup, Evelyn asked with a certain tone to her voice, "Hey, what did you think of that seminar we went to last week? Did you find it interesting?"

"It was alright, I guess," Thomas said absentmindedly, scrolling through his missed messages on his phone.

"Would you be interested in helping with that division of the company?" she asked Thomas directly.

Thomas looked up from his phone, "Stem-cell research is not typically my area of expertise, you know?"

Evelyn laughed dismissively and said, "You don't really *have* a specific area, Thomas."

Thomas replied, "I may not have a *specific* area, but I *am* good at helping other people solve their problems." He thought about it for a moment. "I suppose I'm good at facilitating communication between individuals who need help talking to each other, too. I usually let the experts handle the science and number crunching."

Evelyn doggedly continued, "But that's exactly what Crane needs! I happen to know that he was impressed with how you handled that heckler at the seminar. In fact, he asked me to inquire if you'd be interested in helping them out. He has a lot of influence, and I wouldn't worry about your current contract, if that's your concern. This company is loaded!"

Thomas' well-honed instincts all clicked into place. He had been here before with her. He had learned the hard way with her that he'd best make sure before committing to anything involving Evelyn Perdita!

Thomas sighed, "And just how do *you* know this?"

"Well," she said, dragging it out, "it just so happens that my new job I told you about is working for Dr. Crane and I suggested *you* as the answer to all his problems."

Thomas cocked an eyebrow at this revelation, realizing that, once again, Evelyn had sucked him into her world. The question was *why* and how much it would hurt, he supposed.

"What kind of problems does he need help with?" Thomas asked somewhat reluctantly, already not wanting to get involved.

"Convincing people to help with various things. Make a few things happen that some might not want. Of course, this is the kind of stuff you are great at, Thomas! You're so persuasive!" she argued. "Besides, you could make a lot of money from this. I'm just looking out for you is all." She pouted and rolled her eyes as she assured him, although he couldn't see that because he had walked over to the window.

She sidled up to him from behind, wrapping her arms around him and saying, "Think about it, and let me know. I promise you won't regret it!".

Thomas groaned inwardly. He freed himself from her arms and responded carefully, "I'll give it some thought, but, first, I need to finish cleaning up the dishes." Privately, he was starting to wish he'd never gone to the damned seminar in the first place. Figures that she had a motive for inviting him!

"In fact, why don't we make a dinner date to talk it over with him?" Evelyn leaned in towards Thomas, her breath tickling his earlobe. "It'll be just an informal dinner meeting to discuss the project, nothing more," she reassured him. "And if you're not interested, you can always walk away. But trust me, this could be a great opportunity for you. Plus, think of all the extra time we could spend together, including traveling." She emphasized her point by running her long nails down his chest while inhaling deeply and pointing her attention-grabbing breasts at his face. Certainly, they got his attention!

Thomas couldn't help but chuckle and squirm a little under her touch. "Just dinner, huh? Sounds harmless," he replied with a hint of sarcasm. "Will anyone else be there?"

"Just you, me, and Dr. Crane," Evelyn replied, her lips tantalizingly close to Thomas's ear. "Maybe one other person, but I'm not sure yet." She continued to tease him with promises of what she would wear, before turning him around and kissing him softly on the lips, then working her way down his chest heading for the Promised Land.

As she opened his belt buckle, Evelyn looked up from her knees, determined to make eye contact with Thomas. "So, is that a 'yes'?" she whispered coyly, unzipping him with agonizing slowness.

Thomas's heartfelt response was a simple, "Yes, for God's sake!" Life is good, he thought to himself as her lips finally completed their mission of lust.

Chapter 8

Just Another Day

Thomas and Darius were sitting at a bar they occasionally visited in the local area, enjoying a couple of cold beers. Darius, as friends will often do, couldn't help but to comment on Evelyn Perdita, the beautiful woman that Thomas had been seeing off and on. "She's stunning, man." Darius said while taking a swig of his beer. "How did you manage to pull a catch like that?!"

Thomas shrugged, "Not entirely sure, but I guess I have more game than I thought." They both clink their glasses and take another sip.

"What about that next door neighbor-girl you've been telling me about?" Darius asks, his curiosity piqued. He signals the waitress for two more beers.

"You're in the mood for some juicy gossip, huh?" Thomas teases him with a raised eyebrow.

Darius bursts into laughter. "Come on, man! She's your *neighbor*. It's not like you can hide Evelyn from your newest catch. New gal's gonna be shocked when she sees Evelyn. This is gonna to get awkward... fast!"

Thomas hadn't given much thought to this possibility before, but now that Darius had mentioned it, he realized it could truly be a problem. He laughed at the same time as taking a sip of beer, causing it to come out of his nose. He grabbed a napkin, composing himself and mopping the foam off his face. "Looks like I might have a problem, you're right. This is going to be awkward as hell!"

Darius continued to snicker for a bit, his infectious laughter causing the waitress to start chuckling as well. "It's not like you guys are serious or anything, just a couple of dates," he said, trying to be reassuring.

"Yeah, nothing too crazy, but we did sleep together on the second date," Thomas admitted, feeling a little embarrassed.

Darius raised an eyebrow. "So, why'd you ghost her?". He seemed genuinely curious.

"I didn't mean to ghost her. It just seemed like she was way too casual about the whole thing. Maybe I should have called her?" Thomas shrugged, feeling a little unsure of the correct etiquette for modern dating.

"Or maybe you just sucked in bed," Darius joked, causing Thomas to roll his eyes.

"I don't think it was *that*. Maybe she just wasn't into me, or I messed up by not calling her. Either way, it is what it is," Thomas said with a shrug, trying to brush off the whole confusing situation of his love life, such as it was. Unsurprisingly, he found himself far more interested in watching the boxing match on the bar's TV screen. In a moment of humorous insight, he wondered why more married couples didn't pursue boxing as a means of settling their arguments. "Ha!", he snickered to himself, imagining his stepfather and his mom duking it out. Thomas shook his head ruefully, privately betting on his mom any day and twice on Sundays! She might look beautiful and slight of build, but she was a gamer, for sure.

"Hey, Dee!", as Thomas would sometimes call Darius, "What do you think about boxing for couples? It might be great therapy, don't you think?".

Darius looked at him like he just grew a third eye in the middle of his forehead. "Huh?! What do you mean?"

"Well, it just struck me that some women are feisty these days when it comes to fighting with their beaus, and some guys are way too quick to throw their weight around when they're being stupid. What if people had to fight in the ring with gloves on and rules to even it up? Heck, I bet people would pay just to watch that!". Thomas was cracking up.

Darius responded, "Hell, yeah! I'd be up for that myself. Remember that girl, Emily, I was seeing last year? I'd have loved to take a shot at her, dumb bitch."

Thomas burst out laughing, "She was a big girl, man! I bet she'd pack a mean right!"

"I know, I know, but making up after was the bomb, man!" Darius sighed, thinking wistfully of the large woman who got away. "They just don't make 'em like that anymore".

Thomas practically choked on his drink, "You better pray to God they don't, Bud!", remembering the marks often left behind on his friend's face and arms from the impassioned woman. Personally, Thomas just couldn't comprehend the attraction for make-up sex after a fight, but he guessed it took all kinds!

After a few moments Thomas decided to share more. "All I'm asking is why don't couples that desire to duke it out and are always getting physical with each other just rent a ring? They pay $50 and then *legally* deal with their anger issues if they have them. The guy can agree to use just his left hand while the woman can use both. I had a girlfriend once who was a serious drinker, and she would constantly try and fight me when she was drunk. She would shove me, even slapped me a couple of times. When I told her to stop, she would antagonize me, saying I was just a wimp, all because I wouldn't lay her out the way she deserved. She acted like she could take me, but I didn't want to engage her. She was much smaller than me, a woman, and *that* was the reason I wouldn't engage her physically. I offered to take her to the ring and do it legally, and she declined. It shut her up quick, though." Thomas chuckled as he took a big swig of his drink.

As the night wore on, the bar slowly emptied out with patrons calling it a night and heading home. Suddenly, Thomas felt like he was being observed. He'd learned to trust those instincts over his years of field work, so he surreptitiously glanced around the bar, seeking the source of his internal alarm. Sure enough, he spotted a man in the corner of the bar who was staring at him. "That guy is staring at me," he mentioned to Darius as he finished the last of his beer.

"Maybe he thinks you're cute," Darius replied jokingly.

"I doubt that's it, although I *do* consider myself a good-looking guy," Thomas said archly, while carefully avoiding making direct eye contact with the man in question. "He's still staring at me."

Darius snorted, "Who cares? Let's get going. *Some* of us have to work in the morning." He stood up and grabbed his jacket. "Fuck that guy. I mean, fuck that guy in the way of ignoring him, not actually *fucking* him. I just want to be very clear about that and not have that kind of recommendation haunting me all night!"

"Cute," Thomas replied sarcastically as they made their way out of the bar.

The older man's gaze still followed Thomas. Thomas decided to acknowledge him with a slight nod in his direction before leaving. To his surprise, the man nodded back. In fact, as they pulled away, Thomas noticed that the man was *still* watching him through the bar-window. "This is getting weird," Thomas muttered. The strange man was dressed in a tan suit with a black t-shirt, and Thomas shared this information with Darius as they got into a ride-share. Darius simply peered through the window at the man and quickly flipped him off.

Abruptly changing the subject with characteristic aplomb, Darius turned and said, "Hey, when's that "woo-you" dinner you were talking about, man?"

"Friday at 6pm," replied Thomas.

"Is it at a nice place, at least? I mean, if these stem cell folks are trying to charm you, they better bring their A-game." Darius cleared his throat from all the menthol cigarettes he had smoked that evening despite his frequent statements that he was going to quit.

As luck would have it, later in their drive home, they went by the address of the restaurant discussed earlier. Thomas was pleasantly surprised to find that the restaurant was one of the most elegant places in the area, owned by the renowned Chef Pepperstone. Thomas found it amusing that the chef had named the restaurant after himself and couldn't help but feel a little excitement and even a hint of bragging as he mentioned the name to Darius.

His friend seemed equally impressed. "That's the place? Wow, man, they really *do* want to make an impression on you" he said, his eyes lighting up. He turned and looked directly at Thomas in a beseeching way. "If you get the chance, you should try and sneak me a steak. I mean, it's not like they're going to miss one, right?", he whined, sounding just like a hungry mutt.

Thomas rolled his eyes. "Yeah, because leaving a fancy restaurant with a to-go box won't make me look ridiculous at all." The driver then pulled up to his apartment building, so Thomas said his goodbyes and exited the vehicle. "Have fun at work tomorrow!" he said as the car door closed with a thump.

"It's just another day, man." Darius breezily shot back out the window as the car began to accelerate away, heading into the starry Arizona night. Thomas shook his head, laughing as he turned and headed for the front door of his house while fumbling for his keys.

Chapter 9

To Friendship

When Thomas stepped into the restaurant, he felt his stomach grumble in anticipation of the steak he had been dreaming of all day. The maître d' quickly approached him and asked for his name, cutting him off mid-sentence. "I have a reservation under Turner…" Thomas had started to say before the maître d' interrupted him, "Ah, yes, Sir. Right this way, the other guests are waiting for you."

Thomas followed the maître d' through the restaurant, taking in the intricate details that adorned the walls and tables. The hand-carved trimmings with gold accents were stunning, and the small flames dancing in the center of each table added a cozy ambiance. The warm amber lighting filled the room and even extended to the bar top, which glowed from within. Thomas couldn't help but admire the impressive Formica-covered walls. "This place is amazing," Thomas muttered under his breath, admiring the ambience.

As Thomas settled into his chair, the maître d' swooped in to assist him with a flourish, pulling out his chair and pushing it in for him to sit. "Here you are, Sir," he announced, offering to fetch Thomas a cocktail as he acquainted himself with his dining companions. Thomas opted for a classic gin and tonic, and the maître d' promised to have it delivered shortly. "Very well, Sir, I will have it brought to you momentarily. My name is Sebastian, should you need me. Please enjoy your dinner, and welcome to *Pepperstone*," he said with a slight bow before taking his leave.

As Thomas turned his attention to his tablemates, he recognized Dr. Stephen Crane, but the other man was a stranger. He appeared to be in his mid-thirties, balding, and dressed in a rather awkward fashion that screamed "no sense of style." Crane treated Thomas to a toothy smile and asked if he had found the restaurant without difficulty. Thomas assured him it had not been a problem, commenting on how easy it had been to find with the help of Google Maps. Just before he was going to request an introduction to the mystery guest, Crane interjected, "Ahh, yes, please forgive me, Mr. Rene, I took the liberty of inviting a colleague of mine to our dinner. I hope this is acceptable. I feel his input on the matter at hand would be invaluable. This is Samuel Nouvel. He assists me with my research, and I do find him to be quite indispensable. Samuel, this is Mr. Thomas Rene."

"Good evening, and may I call you Thomas? It's a pleasure to finally meet you in person." Nouvel says as he stands up, offering his limp-looking hand for a handshake Thomas was sure he would regret. And he did, shuddering internally as he kept the handshake as brief as possible. Thomas privately despised a limp handshake even more than the occasional "macho man" who got overly enthusiastic about it as a means of dominating others---which emphatically didn't work with Thomas, who had an exceptional grip of his own. Firm and short was the ticket!

Thomas reciprocates, "Of course, as long as I may do the same!", surprised by the man's formality.

Nouvel continues, "I've been looking forward to this dinner and learning more about you".

Thomas smiles, a bit surprised by the man's obvious interest. "Thank you, I'm glad to be here, too. I was actually wondering if Evelyn was going to join us."

Crane jumps back in with alacrity, happy to regain control of the conversation, "Yes, she'll be here shortly. I told her I wanted to speak with you and Samuel first so that we might get to know each other a bit before she arrived. Man to man, you know."

Thomas nods, understanding the somewhat dated sentiment, and his attention is caught by Samuel's intense gaze. "Yes, I can see you value Samuel's input," Thomas says wryly.

Just then, the waitress arrives with Thomas' gin and tonic, setting it down on an impressive cocktail napkin. The attention to detail is not lost on Thomas as he takes a sip, savoring the flavors.

After another 20 minutes of conversation, the men had covered a wide range of topics but avoided business talk. It was clear that they were all trying to get a read on each other. Just as the waitress brought fresh cocktails, Evelyn Perdita arrived with the same maître d' that had led Thomas to his table. After Sebastian, the maître d', took Evelyn's cocktail order, he gave a slight bow and left them to their own conversational devices.

"Hello, everyone, I hope you all are enjoying yourselves!" Evelyn greeted them with a cool smile that seemed directed more at her boss, Crane, than anyone else. They all exchanged polite pleasantries and welcomed her in turn. Thomas couldn't help but be taken aback by her stunning beauty and the dress she wore that hugged her hips and breasts like a second skin. He tried to keep his eyes up, away from those points of obvious male interest, knowing they still had a professional dinner to get through before anything else. Besides, he wasn't sure how much she had told her boss, Dr. Crane, about her relationship with Thomas Rene. He thought it was probably best to keep that on the down-low, at least for now.

They continued chatting and sipping their drinks for another 15 minutes or so. Just as Thomas was starting to wonder about dinner ever actually happening, the waitress mercifully arrived to take their orders. She went through the standard restaurant introduction, including the owner's history and the type of cuisine they offered. She provided recommendations and mentioned the special of the night, roast duck with raspberry demi-glaze. Crane led off by ordering the duck, but Thomas noticed that both Evelyn and the assistant did the same. Thomas, just to be contrary, ordered a 26-day aged T-bone steak, medium rare, with caramelized onions and sautéed mushrooms. He couldn't wait to dig in. And it amused him to once again be the odd man out, even if it was only with the ordering.

As they waited for their food to arrive, Crane suggested it was time to discuss business, if everyone was agreeable.

"I think that's a good idea," Thomas replied, taking a sip from his drink, feeling relaxed, but also anticipatory. "Now, it begins", he thought to himself.

"You're a man of great interest to us, Thomas. You have quite a reputation!" Crane continued.

At this point, Evelyn interjected with a giggle and a smile, "He's a lubricator!"

Thomas looked at her with a mixture of shock and amusement at her choice of words. "Yes, I guess she's right. I lubricate things when they need to keep moving."

"Exactly what we need," Crane said. "We've hit a few snags with our project and we're looking for someone to help move it along." He sat up even straighter, looking directly at Thomas. "Can you tell us how you might be able to help us even without hearing any details about the project?"

Evelyn was taken aback by the directness of the question. Frankly, she had never heard Thomas speak much about his actual jobs in much detail, as he was usually very close-lipped about his work. However, she had found out a bit by asking around from her shadier associates. Of course, she had never admitted this to Thomas.

She needn't have worried about the dinners' guest of honor. Thomas sprang into action, his words flowing effortlessly. He was a pro at navigating the business world. "I offer a range of services to help move things forward when you need it most," he stated confidently. "For example, if you require additional funding, I can seek out potential investors. If you're facing obstacles from other companies or organizations, I can handle negotiations and ensure they work in your favor. I can even monitor your team members to ensure they remain loyal and motivated. And if you ever find yourself in a sticky situation, let's just say I can help with that, too."

Thomas paused briefly, then continued, directing his gaze at Samuel. "I believe you *already* know exactly what I do for a living, Mr. Nouvel. And I'm confident that you wouldn't have asked me here tonight if you didn't need my specific expertise."

Evelyn's eyes locked onto Thomas, her desire for him palpable. She had always been intrigued by his enigmatic nature, but now she was even more curious about what he could offer. Thomas caught her seductive gaze as she chewed on her cocktail straw, and he knew that he would be rewarded for his expertise by the end of the night.

"Indeed, Mr. Rene, you are quite correct. We *need* someone with your skillset," Nouvel said, smirking slightly. "I must say, I am impressed with what I've seen from you tonight. Perhaps we can not only make a lot of money together, but also become good friends?" With a clink of their glasses, everyone toasted to the possibility of a fruitful partnership.

As soon as the plates were set down by the server, Thomas waited on the chance that someone would want to pray first, but Crane dove in without hesitation. Mentally shrugging and saying grace in his mind, Thomas followed suit and eagerly dug into his steak, savoring every bite as the flavor exploded in his mouth like a fireworks display. The meat was so tender, it practically melted on his tongue. He looked around the table as he chewed, taking his time. He noticed that the scientists both ate with almost clinical precision, while Evelyn attacked her duck with abandon, totally focused on the food. He was almost surprised she didn't grunt like a greedy piglet, so absorbed was she. "She must *really* like that duck!", he thought to himself with a mental chuckle, but realized this was how Evelyn approached life in general. She consumed with enthusiasm. It didn't matter if it was roast duck or macaroni and cheese, having sex or skydiving. That was just how she was. Thomas just wished she could demonstrate a little more restraint, though. In his mind, he thought that a more measured approach to life was certainly more attractive. Maybe that was why he was more drawn to his new neighbor with the big, red truck? She was certainly a lady, despite being a bit of a hippy-type. He frowned to himself, reminding himself that this was no time for thinking about the neighbor. He still had a business dinner to get through!

As the 'get to know ya' evening ground to a close, Crane predictably made a big deal out of paying the tab, his plastic credit card magically appearing in his left hand. Thomas expressed his gratitude for the meal to him, and he replied, "I'm so happy you were able to attend" as though it was hard for him to express such sentiments. Nouvel, the colleague who gave off real "lackey" vibes to Thomas, chimed in, "Indeed, we'll be sending you a standard Non-Disclosure and Confidentiality agreement to review so we can move forward with sharing more information with you." Thomas nodded in agreement and shook their hands. Everyone proceeded to the sidewalk outside the restaurant. The scientists turned, almost in unison, and got into the waiting car. Nouvel awkwardly waved goodbye as they drove off. Crane never looked back. Thomas thought to himself, *"Elvis has left the building!"* and internally snickered at the pomposity of Crane.

Thomas turned to see the maître d' coming out of the restaurant with a bag in his hand. "Here's your T-Bone steak, Sir, the one you ordered to go." Sebastian handed him the bag, and Thomas gave him a small fold of cash as a tip. "Thank you, Sebastian," Thomas said, having remembered the maître d's name. Thomas had learned long ago to always ask and remember wait-staff's names. The service was much better when staff knew that *you* knew who they were. "My pleasure, sir. Have a lovely evening," Sebastian replied, giving a slight bow to Thomas before returning into the restaurant.

As Thomas turned back around, he saw Evelyn looking pleased with herself and heard her ask him with a purr in her voice, "Now, are you finally ready for a special dessert?", as she twirled her hair around an outstretched finger.

Chapter 10

How Much

Thomas was in the middle of enjoying his morning cup of coffee when he heard a knock at the door. Glancing at the clock, he realized it was already 9 am. He wondered who could be bothering him at this time but decided to answer the door anyway. Looking through the peephole, he saw a delivery man holding a small package.

Opening the door, Thomas took the package and signed for it. As he closed the door, he couldn't help but feel curious about the contents.

Upon opening the package, Thomas was pleasantly surprised to find an offer agreement and a check for $25,000 as an initial signing bonus. He couldn't believe someone was willing to pay such a generous amount just for his signature, although he did realize that wasn't strictly true. He had a feeling he'd be earning his pay after all. As he examined the offer, a sticky note attached to the check caught his attention, "This is just the beginning! As you can see, we are eager to hire your services. We can discuss the details later." The note left him feeling uneasy as it was too vague and cryptic for his liking.

Sitting down at the kitchen table, Thomas weighed the pros and cons of accepting the offer. He was, by nature, a cautious person and always thought things through before deciding. Despite his reservations, though, the opportunity for a new challenge and financial gain excited him. However, he couldn't shake off the feeling of uncertainty and wondered what this offer could mean for his career and reputation. He had to admit that the $25,000 was a nice way to get his attention!

Thomas weighed his options and decided to take the risk by signing the document. After all, he knew Evelyn would be disappointed if he didn't at least try it out. He then mailed his acceptance back and deposited the check via his mobile banking app. The confirmation message on his phone brought a sense of excitement and anticipation. This opportunity could be the one he had been waiting for, and he was determined to make the most of it. Thomas headed out to his car with renewed energy, ready to tackle whatever lay ahead.

Thomas faced heavy traffic on his drive to the airport in Phoenix, Arizona, causing him to consider switching to ride-sharing services. The bumper-to-bumper traffic made the 15-minute drive take 45 minutes. To break the monotony, he turned on the radio and listened to a prank show as his car inched along following the long line of others in front of him. The male host of the show had excellent delivery and skillfully pushed the recipients to the brink of a breakdown, making for great entertainment, in Thomas' opinion. However, the host always displayed a degree of compassion and would stop if the person was seriously losing their mind. Thomas appreciated this as it made him feel like his own sudden laughter was not being particularly cruel to the plight of the folks on the show. Although he didn't care much about seeming insensitive to others, he tried to be a good person overall by following a set of rules and joked that it was better to be on the safe side of things just in case there truly *was* a God.

Thomas finally arrived at his destination, his mother's house, swearing to himself that that drive had seemed like an eternity. Retrieving the flowers he had carefully strapped in the passenger seat, he closed the car door and was immediately greeted by his mother at the front door. She was beaming with a giant smile and ready for a hug. "Hey, hey, hey!" she exclaimed as she enveloped him in a warm embrace. After they released from the hug, she asked, "How are you, and what have you done with my son?" with mock concern in her voice.

"I brought you some flowers, Mom. I'm sorry I haven't been able to visit you this last month," Thomas explained as he handed her a mixed bouquet. She smiled, brought the flowers to her nose, and took a deep breath. "They're beautiful. Let me find a vase for them. Why don't we go inside?" Thomas nodded and followed her into the house.

Thomas had always admired his mother's eclectic taste in interior decoration. Each room in her house was a unique blend of different cultures and themes, yet everything flowed seamlessly. From modern decor to vintage pieces and even Egyptian art, she somehow managed to make it all work.

As they walked to the kitchen, the delicious aroma of his mother's marvelous stew hit Thomas's nose, making his stomach grumble. He had always loved her stew, and he immediately craved a bowl. His mother knew him all too well and offered to get him some, which he happily accepted. She even served it with fresh French bread slathered with a special butter she claimed was made from cows that were massaged daily. He didn't care if it was true or not; it tasted amazing with a sprinkle of salt.

Thomas suspected his mother had prepared the stew just for him in honor of his visit. He had texted her the night before, letting her know he would be stopping by in the early afternoon, and she always went out of her way to spoil him in her own special way.

As they chatted over second helpings, Thomas couldn't help but feel the weight of the job offer on his mind. He eventually decided to bring it up to his mother, seeking her opinion. "I got a job offer the other day, and I wanted to get your thoughts on it," he said as he swirled his drink in his hand.

Curious, his mother asked, "What's the subject matter?"

Thomas hesitated for a moment, knowing he shouldn't be discussing his work, but he trusted his mother completely. "Basically, they're trying to clone adult organs," he whispered. "Or at least that's the goal."

As he watched his mother's expression shift from confusion to concern, Thomas realized that he may have made a mistake in bringing up the topic. "I know it's a bit outside of my usual scope, but it's a good opportunity and the pay is great," he tried to explain. "But I also know it's a touchy subject, especially with our Catholic beliefs."

His mother nodded slowly, still processing the information. "Well, I don't think I need to tell you that human cloning is not something our faith would condone," she said softly. "But I also know that you're an adult and capable of making your own decisions. Just make sure you're doing what's right for you, and not just following the money."

"It's just a strange feeling, you know?" Thomas replied, looking down at his glass. "I mean, the idea of cloning human organs for transplant purposes is a noble cause, but it's also a delicate ethical issue. It's not something I ever imagined myself getting involved in."

His mother nodded in agreement. "I understand your concerns, Thomas. It's important to follow your own moral compass and make decisions that align with your values."

Thomas sighed and leaned back in his chair. "I know, but it's also a big opportunity. I don't want to pass it up without fully considering it."

His mother put a comforting hand on his shoulder. "Just take your time to weigh the pros and cons. Ultimately, the decision is yours to make. I trust you to make the right one."

Thomas smiled gratefully at his mother. "Thanks, Mom. You always know just what to say."

"How much did they offer in compensation?" his mother asked, eyeing him with concern.

"Triple," Thomas replied, raising his eyes to connect with hers.

"Triple? Triple your normal pay?!" she exclaimed with a shocked tone.

Thomas walked over to the stove and picked up the spoon resting on the napkin near the pot of stew. He scooped up one more mouthful of stew and, after swallowing, he explained, "That's what gave me the strange feeling, that's the something that made me wonder how far it could go. I get that I am good at what I do, but triple seems a bit much, doesn't it? They knew my normal pay rate, and they made a carefully considered choice when making that offer. The tasks seemed normal compared to previous ones I have handled in the past for their organization."

"You will figure it out. You always do. Are you going to accept their offer?" his mother asked curiously.

"The money might cause me to be cautious, but it was too good to pass up. I accepted this morning," Thomas replied with a sigh.

Chapter 11

You're a Good Friend

The man was wearing nothing but blue briefs and his glasses, lying on the bed with excitement coursing through him. He quickly sent a text on his phone before placing it on the nightstand and readjusting his glasses. His heart was racing, beads of sweat forming on his forehead, and no amount of wiping his forearm across it could stop the nervous perspiration. He tried to make himself seem sexier by readjusting himself multiple times, but it only made him feel more anxious and self-conscious. After taking a few puffs of marijuana from the bowl next to his phone, he felt a little calmer. Finally, a noise came from the bathroom. He could see the light around the rim of the closed door before it disappeared. It was almost time. This was it, he thought to himself as he fruitlessly wiped at the sweat one more time.

The door opened slowly, and the woman for whom he had been waiting stepped out from the darkness. She was dressed in a leather corset, leather skirt, and high heels. Her pink panties were pulled up high to showcase she had them on. In her right hand was a whip, and in her left hand, a greasy lubricant called *Love Slick*.

Affecting a fake Russian accent, Mistress Violet said, "I am going to hurt you; you understand this, correct? You know that you are going to serve *me* tonight, not the other way around." She continued in a firm but sensual voice, adding, "You are merely my toy, and I play with my toys *rough*." To build the dramatic effect, she then separated her legs slowly while he watched and then reached under her skirt to expose a pink strap-on dildo of prodigious size.

His eyes widened. All he could muster, after swallowing nervously, was "Yes, Mistress."

"Stand up and bend over, do it now!" she barked at him while slapping her whip against the door of the bathroom. It made a *SWAAAT* noise that was undeniably intended to cause fear and anticipation at the same time. It worked. He obeyed swiftly, leaping up to please her, exclaiming "Yes, Mistress!", while bending over and placing his hands on the edge of the bed for support. She walked slowly back and forth behind him, surveying her intended victim with his flabby butt up in the air. After a painful crack of the whip against his right ass cheek, she commanded him to lower his briefs. He complied as fast as he could, his hands shaking with excitement and a big grin on his face of anticipation for what was to come next.

Just as the dildo sank into his depths, a sudden white flash went off, and then another, and then yet another! The first two flashes had partly blinded him. It wasn't until the third blinding flash that the man with his butt up in the air was able to locate where the flashes were coming from. As his eyes adjusted, he saw the silhouette of a man standing there in a dark suit, with a smirk on his face and a camera in his hand. The man told the dominatrix, who was still penetrating her victim with sinister intent, "Thank you, Violet. That will be all for now."

"Sorry he interrupted us." Violet said to the decidedly less excited client on the bed as she slapped his ass, feeling this was equivalent to a handshake considering the awkwardness of the moment. After removing the foreign object from the now painfully stretched rectum to the accompaniment of a sudden yelp, she went into the bathroom to change into her civilian clothes.

The well-dressed stranger standing in the low light then proceeded to sit down and light a cigarette. He leaned over to grab the client's water glass that was half empty, sitting on the nightstand, and places it carefully on the small table near his seat to use as an impromptu ashtray.

As the flabbergasted man stands up slowly, frustrated from not having had his eagerly anticipated time with the dominatrix, he confronts the stranger with a mix of confusion and anger. "Who *are* you, and what the hell are you doing in my room?" he demands petulantly.

The intruder puts a finger to his lips and gestures towards the bathroom where the woman was still changing. "Let's wait until we have some privacy. I don't want to embarrass you even further, if we can avoid it" he says ironically, arching an eyebrow and taking a drag of his cigarette and exhaling slowly a perfect circle of smoke which slowly disappeared into the darkness.

After a few more moments, Mistress Violet emerges from the bathroom, dressed much more normally and clearly quite ready to leave. The well-dressed man signals for her to come over, and he whispers something into her ear before handing her a wad of cash. She chuckles briefly before exiting the hotel room with a "Thanks, Tom." As the door closes, Thomas turns on the lamp, contemplating what had just happened.

"That looked like it hurt. Did it?" Thomas asks innocently as he flicks the ashes into the water glass.

The sulking man refuses to answer Thomas' question, instead asking, "What do you want?" in an annoyed tone and crossing his arms across his chest as he stood there staring accusingly at Thomas. Unfortunately, all he accomplished was to look ridiculous.

"You look like you might need to sit, so please feel free. If you wouldn't mind, would you be so kind as to pull up your underwear?" Thomas gestures towards the edge of the bed with his hand holding the cigarette.

The man hesitates, then bends over and pulls up his briefs. He sits on the edge of the bed, grimacing from the earlier violation. "Can you *please* tell me what you want?" he whined.

"Marty, I have someone who needs a favor. I think you are the perfect fit to help with this, considering I can help *you* as well." Thomas says pleasantly.

"*Please* don't call me 'Marty'. Call me 'Martin", if you must call me anything at all." he grumbled. "What do you mean, *help* me?!"

Thomas looks the agitated man straight in the eyes and says, with a dead pan look, "I know how to fix the flux capacitor."

"What the hell?! What are you talking about?" Martin Blake grunts as he shifts to a different angle on the bed to relieve the pressure on his tender bottom.

Thomas raised his eyebrows and shook his head in mock disappointment. "You know, I thought I was being pretty witty with that reference to the movie, *Back to the Future*," he joked, but Martin didn't seem amused. "Anyhow, let's get down to business. I know what I saw here tonight, and I can keep it a secret, but I need a favor in return." He pulled out his phone and showed Martin the pictures he had taken. "Your reputation is safe with me, but I don't think your family would be too happy to hear about this! Do you? You see, I need your expertise on a certain matter. And, trust me, you don't want to say no to a friend who knows your dirty little secret."

"Friend, huh?! This doesn't seem like a great way to start a friendship. What do you want, *pal*?" Blake says sarcastically, finally showing some backbone and glaring at Thomas.

"Well, it just so happens that I need some sensitive information on several people. They are not friends like us, of course, but maybe with a little sharing, they *could* be. I really like having friends, don't you? I could use a few more, no doubt. Can you help me, friend Marty?" Thomas puts out his cigarette by dropping it into the water glass that was now murky from the ashes.

Martin says sourly, "You know they are going to bill me for the smell of smoke in my room. It's like a $250 penalty." as he points to the glass.

Thomas takes out a money clip from the inside of his suit jacket near his chest and pulls out three $100 bills and places them on the small table beside him. He then lights up another cigarette, "Let's not worry about *that* anymore. So," he says, drawing it out, "Will you help me?"

"Do what, exactly?" Martin asks in a defeated way.

Thomas stands up, puts out the freshly lit cigarette in the water glass, and hands Martin a folder piece of paper. "Here is a list of names, and what I need from each of them. Look it over, and I will be back in touch with you soon to discuss it further." Thomas does a quick once-over in the mirror and brushes some grey ash from his pants.

"Do you want my cell number?" Martin asks, as if he already knows the answer.

"No, I have it." says Thomas. "You have a wonderful evening. I do apologize for the intrusion and for ruining all your fun. In fact, if it is alright with you, I would like to make it up to you as I leave. As I implied before, friends should help each other." Thomas walks towards the door and opens it.

"And just how do you plan to do that?" the sweaty man mumbles in an exhausted tone, clearly nonplussed and getting up to begin dressing.

Violet enters the room, having been waiting outside the door all this time because of Thomas' earlier whispered instructions. Martin stands there, frozen, torn between embarrassment and hope, totally unsure of what to do next. But Violet is far from done with him. "Did I tell you to get dressed, slave? I am not finished with you yet," she barks at him, brandishing her whip and the still impressive strap-on. Martin looks like a deer caught in headlights, frozen in excitement and terror at what is about to happen. "I am going to make you bleed, slave!" she declares, striding towards her willing victim.

Thomas winces at her last words, inwardly cringing at what is about to happen. As he exits the room, though, Martin yells out to him, "You *are* a good friend!"

The door clicks shut behind a rapidly exiting Thomas as he hears the crack of the whip and Martin's first yelp of pleasure mixed with pain. *"Takes all kinds"* he muses to himself a bit wonderingly and shakes his head as he walks even faster.

Chapter 12

How Can You Say That

Thomas sat on the hood of his car, enjoying the breeze of a notably less hot day on an August morning. September was fast approaching, so it was helping to take the edge off the oppressive Arizona heat. He had just grabbed an energy drink from the gas station to boost himself up a little. He had always preferred the warmer weather, but there was something about the briskness of winter that he couldn't resist. He chugged down the first energy drink and then grabbed the second one sitting next to him and cracked it open while lighting a cigarette he felt he had earned. The sun was barely visible behind the thick clouds, but the daylight still provided some comfort. He felt a sense of calmness in the quietness of the winter day.

The convenience store door creaked open, and a disheveled couple emerged. They looked worse for wear, dressed in ragged clothing, and shuffling awkwardly. Their skin was weather-beaten, with wrinkles in all the wrong places, and they carried the stench of too much sun exposure. The man, wearing a stretched-out muscle shirt, carried a case of cheap beer, while the woman held an open bag of potato chips. Thomas observed their stumbling gait for a moment before the man set down the case of beer and turned towards him, asking, "Do you happen to have a spare cigarette?"

Thomas picked up his pack of cigarettes from the car hood and extended it to the man, letting his actions speak for him. "Here you go," he said when the man eagerly grabbed two. The woman also reached out for one of the two, and the man reluctantly handed her one. "Gimme the lighter," he demanded, growing increasingly impatient as she dug through her worn-out purse. He barked at her to hurry it up.

Thomas observed the man's tension over the lighter for a few seconds before deciding to flip open his well-used Zippo with one hand and smoothly lighting his own cigarette.

"That's a nice lighter," the man remarked as he casually leaned back against Thomas' car. "I couldn't trade you a couple of beers for it, could I?" Thomas declined, shaking his head. However, he handed the Zippo over for the man to use without a word, his expression unchanged as he returned to enjoying the warmth of the sun on his face.

"You rule, man, you rock!" the man exclaimed gratefully, assuming that Thomas was letting him keep the lighter.

Thomas couldn't quite put his finger on why he gave the man his lighter. Maybe it was out of sympathy, or maybe it was just a small act of kindness. He couldn't help but feel disgusted and shocked as he watched the couple lean against the car, the woman digging through her beat-up purse and the man chugging his cheap beer. Thomas found himself questioning how society could let individuals become so lost and disconnected from basic human dignity. How could these two have ended up in such a shabby state?

The more he thought about it, the more his disgust grew. It wasn't just about the couple in front of him, but about the system and society that failed them. It reflected the broader problem of how society tends to discard people who are struggling, who have fallen through the cracks of an unequal system.

Instead of just enjoying the feel of the winter sun on his face, he thought about how the couple must have faced countless obstacles and challenges to end up where they were now. Perhaps they had been born into poverty, with little access to quality education or job opportunities. Perhaps they faced systemic discrimination or had mental health issues that had gone untreated. Regardless of the specific circumstances, it was clear that something had gone wrong along the way.

Thomas felt both sadness and frustration as he realized that society often blames the individual for their circumstances

46

without considering the broader factors at play. The reality was that many people are born into situations that are difficult to escape, and it's not always a matter of personal responsibility or a lack of effort.

As he finished his second energy drink and flicked his cigarette butt at the wall, Thomas couldn't help but feel a deep sense of disappointment in society's failure to support and uplift those who are struggling. It was a sobering reminder of the harsh realities that so many people face every day.

The man approached Thomas again with a sheepish look and a half-smoked cigarette between his lips. "Hey man," he mumbled, "ya got another smoke I can bum off ya?"

Thomas nodded and reached into his pack, but before handing over the cigarette, he posed the man a question. "How about this," he said, "I'll give you each $20 to answer one question for me."

Thomas didn't have any intention of helping the couple improve their lives by giving them money. He simply saw it as a worthwhile investment to learn more about their story. When the man had asked for even more cigarettes, Thomas saw it as an opportunity to pose a question and learn more about their pasts. He reached into his left inside chest pocket and pulled out his money clip, not because he truly wanted to give them money, but because he saw it as an enticement to get them to answer honestly. The couple stood there in disbelief, looking at each other, unsure of what to make of the proposition. Their greed won out, but to Thomas, this was just another transaction, an exchange of money for information.

The man's eyes widened in surprise, and he looked skeptically at Thomas. "What kind of question?" he asked suspiciously.

"If you could blame one person, one person only for how you ended up like this, who would it be?" Thomas asked.

The man and his companion looked at each other, clearly taken aback by the unexpected question. They took a moment to consider their answers, and then the man spoke up. "My old man," he said bitterly. "He was a real piece of work."

Thomas nodded, urging him to continue. "Why is that?" he asked.

As the man answered his question, he watched him carefully, trying to read his expressions and body language.

The man took a deep drag on his cigarette, then exhaled a cloud of smoke. "He was always drunk, always angry. Used to beat the shit out of me and my brothers for no reason. I guess I just grew up thinking that's how things were supposed to be."

Thomas handed the woman a cigarette and posed the same question he asked the man earlier. "If you could blame one person and one person only for how you became who you are now. Who would it be?"

The woman looked down for a moment, thinking, took a drag from the cigarette and then responded, "My mother. She was always too busy drinking and getting high to really take care of me. She didn't care about me at all."

Thomas turned away from her, handed the man $20 and gave him half of the cigarettes from the pack, then turned to walk away from them both.

"Wait, what about *my* money?" The woman asked, annoyed, while turning her head back and forth at the two men as though she might start throwing a tantrum.

"*You* weren't honest." Thomas said, not even bothering to look back at her as he walks towards his car and unlocks it with his key fob.

"What do you mean, I wasn't honest?" She asked, following him to the car.

"Your answer was too similar to your friend, and it sounded convenient," Thomas said as he got in the driver's seat and started the car.

"I told you the truth!" She said, her voice raising.

"Really? Because it sounds like you're just saying whatever you think I want to hear so you can get some quick cash." Thomas retorted as he lit another cigarette and rolled down the window.

"I'm *not* lying, why would I?" The woman said, now standing by the window of the car.

"I don't know, maybe because you're desperate for money and think you can just say anything to get it," Thomas said, his tone harsh, but his words had been fair.

"I'm not desperate! And I'm not a liar!" The woman swore, her voice shaking with anger.

"Sure, keep telling yourself that," Thomas said as he started to pull away, the woman still standing there fuming.

She quickly spoke up, "Wait, I have another reason."

Thomas braked and turned around, intrigued. "Another reason?" he asked, eyebrows raised in surprise.

The woman nodded eagerly, "Yes, about my mother. She never cared about me, never supported me about anything. She just wanted me gone."

Thomas still didn't buy it. He looked at her skeptically and said, "That's not true, is it?"

The woman hesitated for a moment before admitting, "No, it's not."

Thomas shook his head in disappointment. "I thought so. You're not being honest with me, and I can't reward that behavior."

The woman looked offended and crossed her arms in defiance. "So, you're just going to give *him* the money and not me?" She complained.

"Yes, because he was *honest* with me," Thomas replied firmly. "You are just making things on the spot."

"How the *fuck* can you say that to me? You don't even know me, man. You don't know nothin' 'bout me or what I've been through." The woman tapped her foot angrily on the pavement.

"I don't need to know your whole life story to know you lied," Thomas responded calmly.

"Whatever, man, I need the money." She pleaded with him, her voice getting more desperate. A cunning look passed over her face. "Maybe there's something else I can do for you?" she wheedled, cocking one hip out in a pathetic attempt to entice him.

"No," Thomas firmly replied. "I gave the money to the one who was honest with me, and I'm definitely not interested in anything else!"

Thomas took his foot off the brake and accelerated away, catching a glimpse in the rear-view mirror of the woman standing there, yelling, and gesturing angrily. He shook his head, feeling a mix of disappointment and disgust. He turned on the radio to his favorite jazz station, letting the smooth sounds of the saxophone soothe his mind as he drove away.

Chapter 13

I Apologize

The bright sun on this Saturday afternoon filled Thomas with a sense of joy. Open skies always made him feel alive. Through the years, he had lived in many different places, but Seattle had been the worst due to the endless rain. It was dreary six out of seven days of the week, leaving a gloomy grey film over everything. The people who lived there always boasted about how beautiful the summers were, but he felt it was 'Stockholm Syndrome' at work. The citizens of Washington State were so accustomed to being abused by the constant rain that, when the sun *did* shine, it was perceived as magical. It was like having to eat nothing but plain, dry bread for five years, and then, suddenly, a gas station cheeseburger that had been sitting under the warmer for four hours would taste like a gourmet meal!

Thomas adjusted his grip on the grocery bags and made his way up the stairwell. As he ascended, he could hear music growing steadily louder. The source of the noise was the partly open door of Gabrielle Amadeo, his new next-door neighbor in the apartment complex. As he approached his own door, the singing became even louder, and he paused to listen. He recognized the song, "Life is a Highway" by Tom Cochrane, although the voice he primarily heard was the neighbor. The lyrics echoed down the hall as he walked towards his door. He had to admit, she had a good voice.

Curiosity getting the best of him, he slowed down as he passed her doorway, hoping to catch a glimpse of her. He was rewarded with a view of her passionately belting out the lyrics to the song while cleaning, wearing rubber gloves, a bandanna, and holding a duster as though it was a microphone. *"Through all these cities and all these towns, it's in my blood, and it's all around, I love you now like I loved you then, this is the road, and these are the hands".*

Thomas continued to his own door, smiling to himself as he listened. Gabrielle's voice echoed down the hall. He could still hear her singing as he fumbled with his keys, trying not to drop any of the grocery bags in his arms. He finally managed to unlock the door and toss his keys in the bowl, but as he started to put away the groceries, he found himself getting lost in the melody of the song she was singing. He had left the door slightly open so he could keep listening as he swung the bread around like a guitar, juggled the apples, and used a wooden spoon as a microphone to sing a few verses of the song. "*Life is a highway, I wanna ride it all night long!*" he belted out, unable to resist the urge to sing along.

As he twirled around, lost in his own imaginary concert, he suddenly became aware of a pair of eyes fixed on him. Turning, he caught his beautiful neighbor now watching *him* with a huge grin on her face. Embarrassed, he scrambled to put down the spoon and awkwardly stood there, hands on his hips, trying to play off his singing as cool as he could while the music faded into the background.

Gabrielle raised the duster up and half-seriously said, "I feel the duster gives me the best results with my voice."

"I'm new to the industry, I haven't learned all the best gear yet," Thomas replied, playing along.

"Have you found a manager yet? If not, I would be willing to represent you, for a fee of course," Gabrielle offered, rubbing her fingers together in the universal sign for money.

"We should talk. Leave me your number and I'll call you if I am interested," Thomas said with a lecherous grin.

After their brief exchange, there is an awkward pause as they stand there staring at each other, unsure of what to say next. Finally, Gabrielle broke the silence.

"How have you been? Haven't seen you in a bit," Gabrielle asked as she took off her bandanna and let her long, dirty blonde hair flow freely. "Sorry I haven't called you; I was caught up with personal matters."

Thomas shook his head to minimize the lack of recent communication. "It's no problem. I've been slammed as of late, myself. I ended up taking on a new project and I've been traveling more than normal. You want a beer or anything? Can I get you something?" Thomas realized he had been rude not inviting her to stay or at least offering her something to make her feel welcome.

"It's just past noon, it's a little too early for a beer, though I'll take you up on some of that pineapple juice, if you still have some." She walked over to his kitchen-island and grabbed a seat.

With a smile, Thomas reached into the fridge and retrieved two cans of pineapple juice. He poured the juice into two glasses filled with ice, placed them on cocktail napkins, and handed one to Gabrielle. She adjusted the glass, looking nervous, as if something was on her mind. "So neat and tidy," she said as she looked around, taking a sip of the pineapple juice, enjoying the refreshing taste.

Thomas sensed her nervousness and asked, "Is everything okay?"

Gabrielle replied, "With me? Yes, everything is fine. I just feel a bit overloaded with some personal stuff. Nothing too crazy, just some things I need to deal with eventually." She took another sip of the pineapple juice and wiped her lips before leaning in towards him and saying, "I hope I didn't upset you by not calling or stopping by for so long."

Thomas had never experienced being ghosted by a woman before; he was usually the one doing the disappearing act. "No worries," he responded in a low tone, avoiding eye contact unintentionally. He was usually good at maintaining a strong gaze with people when he was talking to them, but for some reason, he couldn't do it this time. "To be honest, I was a little worried things might get awkward after that night, given that we live next to each other."

"It wasn't weird, and I wasn't uncomfortable with that at all," Gabrielle responded in an equally soft voice, shyly struggling to hold eye contact herself. "I had a nice time, even though I don't usually behave that way so soon. Getting intimate, I mean. I was just enjoying myself, and maybe the stars aligned that night."

Now that that subject had been addressed, like the pink elephant in the room, they chatted effortlessly for a while, sharing laughs, and discussing music choices that got them in the cleaning mood. Thomas found himself engrossed in the conversation, her smile lighting him up and her laughter lifting him even higher. Her laugh was so genuine, coming straight from her soul. It all reminded him forcefully of why he had been drawn to her in the first place. Suddenly, she looked at the clock and realized it was later than she thought.

"I'm sorry, but I have to go. I have dinner plans," she said, slowly standing up and grabbing her duster and bandanna.

"Hot date, huh?" Thomas half-joked but wanted to know the answer.

"No, it's with my mother," she shot back with a grin, her hand on the doorknob.

"Thank God!" Thomas thought to himself.

As she opened the door to leave, she paused and said, "Do you want to come to lunch with me tomorrow? My friends are doing their monthly get-together, and I always feel like the odd one out because I'm there by myself." She looked at him expectantly.

Thomas hesitated, then decided to trust his instincts and be up front with her. "Gabrielle, I should tell you I've been seeing someone since we last time we hung out."

Gabrielle laughed, seeing the look on his face that accompanied his confession. "I know! I saw her coming out of your apartment one morning a few weeks ago," she replied dismissively.

Thomas looked at her in fascination, his eyes locked on hers. He found himself starting to mumble and sternly forced himself to speak up. "Really? I'm embarrassed, and I apologize."

She smiled. "You can make it up to me by joining me for lunch tomorrow. That is, if you want to."

Thomas smiled back. "Alright. Deal. That sounds great!"

She perked up, her tone changing as if she knew how he would respond. "Terrific! I'll pick you up at 1:00 pm. Look nice for me." she warned. "You're my arm candy tomorrow." She winked at him and exited with a regal wave of her hand, her long legs swiftly taking her down the hall, away from him.

He realized his apartment suddenly felt emptier than it had before. Shaking his head, he returned to putting away the groceries while snapshots of her ran through his mind.

Chapter 14

I Have Faith In You

Thomas once again found himself in a familiar dream where he was a child peering through the crib bars, begging his father to release him from his nighttime prison. "Daddy," he called out, his voice small and trembling. "I get out."

His father continued folding clothes and watching the television, apparently ignoring Thomas' heartfelt pleas. "Daddy," Thomas called out again, desperation in his voice. "I get out!"

But his father remained where he was, responding, "No, it's time for you to be in bed."

Thomas's frustration grew, and he tried to climb the crib bars, his little hands gripping the rails as he attempted to pull himself up and over. His father, realizing that the young boy was in distress, quickly got up and lifted him out of the crib, holding him close to his chest as he gently soothed him.

In that moment, Thomas felt an overwhelming love for his father. He cherished the feeling of safety and comfort he found in his father's embrace, and the sound of his father's humming was like a lullaby that eased his fears and worries.

"Daddy," Thomas said, sniffling as he tried to hold back tears. "I don't want to go to bed. I want stay with you."

His father smiled and replied, "I know, Thomas. But you need to sleep. You'll feel better in the morning."

Thomas nodded, trusting in his father's words. As his father laid him down, he gently rubbed Thomas's head and hummed a song that he had always sung to him, a song that filled him with a sense of warmth and love.

The dream faded away, and when he awoke, Thomas was left with mixed emotions. He longed to feel the same safety and comfort that he had felt as a child with his father. Strangely, he had never had that same trust and closeness with his mother. Although he had developed a close relationship with his mother since he had become an adult, he wondered where that had been when he was a boy. Weren't boys usually closer to their mothers? He shrugged to himself, consigning that subject to the depths of things which we will never know.

Thomas lay in his bed, staring at the ceiling and his mind drifting. As he thought about it, tears welled up in his eyes, and he felt a deep sense of pain and longing. He couldn't help but feel envious of the father-son bond he sees everywhere in the media, movies and TV, something he believed he had never experienced with his own father. He wished he could have felt the warmth of his father's embrace more often, heard his laughter, and had had the opportunity to listen to his words of wisdom. But all he had were distant memories of a man he barely knew. It was a painful reminder of what Thomas had lost and what he would probably never have. He fussed at himself for being so maudlin, and resolved to get going, instead. No use crying over spilt milk, he admonished himself as he swung his feet over the edge of the bed.

After a refreshing stretch and taking a sip of water, he turned on some Beethoven and stepped into the shower. When he got out, he stood in front of his closet, debating as to what to wear. Should he go with a suit or something more casual like dress slacks and a polo shirt, or even jeans and flip-flops? After some contemplation, he settled on dress slacks and the polo as the safer choice.

Choosing his watch was easy, but when it came to selecting cologne, he found himself pondering over which scent would be best for the lunch he had planned. After spending altogether too much time on the decision, he finally chose his most versatile scent, realizing he had been obsessing over the entire process. He grabbed the cologne and sprayed it on, hoping it would be the right choice. He hummed cheerfully to himself, miles away from where he'd been when he first woke up.

He contemplated what lunch they might be having and opted to have a light breakfast just in case. Sometimes people look at you oddly if you don't eat with them. They think you're either on a health kick or not relaxed enough. As he wrapped up his breakfast, such as it was, his phone rang, and he reached for it. He assumed it was Gabrielle calling to say she would be running late. But to his surprise, it was Nouvel. "Hello, Samuel." Thomas loved calling scientists by their first names rather than their titles just because it took them down a peg. "What can I do for you?" he asked in a professional tone.

"Thomas, we need you to leave tomorrow for Italy. There is someone we need you to meet with. We need his help on a particularly important project, and he's proving difficult. We need you to convince him to cooperate."

"No problem. Italy? Where in Italy?" Thomas asked, grabbing a notepad and pen from his pocket.

"Turin."

"What is the man's name?" he asked while taking notes. He titled the page "Italy" in large letters.

"His name is Francesco Ajello." Nouvel pronounced the name with a tinge of Italian accent, which amused Thomas.

Thomas inquired, "Will Ajello be expecting me? Or not?"

"He's aware that someone will be delivering a package to him, but that's all he knows" Nouvel responded. "I must stress that this man is *critical* to the success of our project. We must have his support to accomplish our goals."

Curiosity getting the best of him, Thomas inquired, "What's in the package?" However, his thoughts were interrupted by his buzzing phone, signaling a text message from Gabrielle. She was indeed running late and wouldn't be able to make it to his apartment by 1:00 pm sharp. Thomas quickly replied, assuring her that he was in no rush and to take her time.

Nouvel hesitated before saying, "What's in the package is not your concern. We just need you to ensure the package's integrity and delivery to Ajello."

"Understood. I'll make sure it's secure," Thomas replied, jotting down the word "CONFIDENTIAL" in his notes, under the bolded title of "VITAL". "Do you have anything for me?"

"Yes, when you stop by headquarters on your way to the airport, my assistant, Rebecca, will provide you with a folder containing private information on Ajello, an envelope with $50,000 in US dollars to give to him, a list of his frequented addresses, and the details of the scheduled meeting. And, of course, your first-class flight arrangements."

"Will the $50,000 be given to him as well as the package?" Thomas asked, wanting to make double-sure while making a note next to the word envelope.

"Consider it a cherry-on-top," Nouvel replied with a chuckle.

"Then consider it done, Sammy," Thomas said with some humor of his own.

"Just take care of it." Nouvel said with a peeved voice. "Good day, Thomas," Nouvel said before ending the call.

Later that day, having returned to his digs, Thomas methodically packed his carry-on luggage, carefully choosing which items to bring on his upcoming trip. He opted for two suits with matching ties and shirts, a toiletry bag, cologne, laptop, and a particular book on Buddha that he believed would help him with one of the people he was supposed to contact on this trip. After double-checking everything, he heard a knock on the door. He looked at the clock and saw that it was 1:17pm. *"It must be Gabrielle,"* he thought to himself.

He quickly zipped up the last carry-on and made his way to answer the door. He peered through the spy hole to the lovely sight of Gabrielle standing outside, wearing a beautiful, blue sun dress with white flowers and her hair pulled back in a bow. His heart skipped a beat as he took a deep breath and opened the door with a smile.

As he opened the door, Gabrielle gave him a warm smile and stepped inside. The faint smell of her perfume only added to her natural presence. Thomas thought she looked stunning.

"Hey there," Thomas welcomed her, returning her smile, then closing the door behind her. "It's great to see you!"

Gabrielle leaned in and gave him a promising kiss on the cheek. "It's great to see you, too," she replied.

Thomas led her to the kitchen, asking, "Would you like something to drink? Whiskey, gin, tequila shots with the worm?"

She laughed at his hopeful look. "Water would be great, thanks," she said, taking a seat at the table.

As Thomas filled a glass with water that claimed to be from a glacier and had been frozen for 10,000 years, Gabrielle noticed the luggage in the corner of the kitchen. "Are you going on a trip?" she asked curiously.

Thomas reluctantly admitted, "Actually, yeah. I just found out this morning that I have to leave for Italy tomorrow."

Gabrielle was surprised. "Italy? That's so sudden! Are you sure you have time to go to lunch today?"

Thomas smiled warmly at her, pleased at her instant consideration. "Of course! I've been looking forward to it, and I wouldn't want to miss spending some overdue time with you."

Gabrielle nodded, still looking a bit concerned about the shortness of time until his leaving. "Ok, as long as you want to. I can't believe a trip to Italy could be such a last-minute thing."

Thomas laughed at that. "Yeah, I guess I'm pretty important, huh?"

Gabrielle smiled and rolled her eyes. "Oh, you're something, that's for sure."

They both laughed, then Thomas had to grab his wallet before they headed out for lunch. After he found it in the last place he looked, off they went, happy just to share a moment together under the blue skies of the Arizona day.

Chapter 15

In Science We Trust

Thomas and Gabrielle walked into *Toppin*, a bustling restaurant known for their delicious lunches. Gabrielle scanned the room, searching for her friends who were supposed to be already there and seated. A group of people waved at her, and she began to make her way over with Thomas following closely behind.

As they approached, one of the guests spotted Gabrielle and called out, "Gabrielle! Come sit here!"

As they arrived at the table, the rest of the group greeted them with a chorus of hellos and introductions. Thomas smiled and shook hands with each of them, making a mental note of their names and faces.

At the table, Thomas and Gabrielle were welcomed by six well-dressed individuals, three men and three women, who were sitting in an alternating pattern. He could see why Gabrielle had wanted him to come, since they were all couples. Thomas scanned the menu, but nothing really caught his eye. He finally settled on a turkey club with extra bacon and cheddar cheese on white bread. Gabrielle followed suit with a simple, "I'll have the same." The waiter took their orders and began pouring white wine into the glasses, but Gabrielle politely declined and requested mineral water instead. Two of the other ladies also declined the wine. As the waiter walked away, the group engaged in small talk and Thomas couldn't help but feel a bit out of place among the well-heeled crowd.

As the group chatted about light topics, Thomas felt a certain air about them that hinted at their religious beliefs. Sure enough, the conversation turned towards religion as they discussed different sermons they had heard recently. Thomas found himself putting on a smile and feigning interest, despite not being overly religious himself.

It wasn't long before one of the men, Jason, asked Thomas about his own faith. "I am Catholic," Thomas replied.

"We are Catholic as well. Do you practice?" Jason asked with a smile, happy to have found some common ground with Thomas.

Thomas took a sip of his wine before answering. "Not really. I attend services occasionally with my family, but I wouldn't say I'm an active follower. But I do believe there's something more in the world than just us."

Jason seemed to accept Thomas's answer and raised his glass in a toast. "God is a part of us all, even if you don't constantly practice. He loves us all."

The woman in the red sundress looked at Thomas and Gabrielle and asked, "How do you both know each other?"

Gabrielle answered simply, "We live next to each other."

Thomas chimed in, "Yes, my irresistible charm won her over as I strolled by her door while she was unpacking from the move."

Gabrielle laughed and teased him, "Oh yes, the charm. I almost forgot about that! I thought it was because you were a big, strong man who offered to carry up my boxes" She playfully grabbed a strawberry from Thomas's plate while everyone snickered.

The group continued to discuss the mysteries of God and the universe with stories and anecdotes being shared around the table. Thomas tried to stay engaged in the conversation but found himself struggling to keep up. He took sips of his wine and tried not to let his impatience show. Suddenly, the topic of the immaculate conception came up, referring to Jesus, and Thomas couldn't resist correcting their misunderstanding.

"Actually, "immaculate conception" refers to *Mary* being born without sin, not the conception of Jesus," Thomas interjected, his tone light but matter of fact.

The group initially laughed, assuming Thomas was making a joke, but when they realized he was serious, they became intrigued.

"Really? I had no idea," one of the men said, pulling out his phone to verify the information.

As they all looked up the correct definition, Thomas felt a sense of satisfaction. He may not have enjoyed the conversations up to this point, but at least he was able to contribute and correct a common misconception.

"Thomas, you mentioned earlier you believe that something is there, with regards to God. May I ask what you believe in with a little more detail?", one of the men asked as he leaned in closer to hear Thomas' response.

"David, is it?" asked Thomas. David nodded. Thomas said, "I believe in science. Just plain science, really."

"Oh, that *is* a curious response!" said David, looking at Thomas with renewed interest. "So, I take it from your answer that you are more interested in *how* things work rather than what they're *for*?"

This unexpected question from David frankly stumped Thomas for a moment. He had never boiled it down to that degree before, but he felt it was both a sincere and valid question. What *did* he think? He had a flash of insight that knowing just how something works is *not* the same as understanding *why* it's there and what it is *for*. Perhaps the line between science/knowledge and God was not so big after all? In fact, he wondered if this was all part of God's plan, that humankind needed to go through this phase of growth in our understanding of the universe and our place in it. After all, in the Bible we were told that we humans were to be the "stewards" of everything around, including our own bodies, one would think. Could it be that the stem cell research really wasn't out of line with God's plan after all? Suddenly, Thomas was glad that he had accepted Gabrielle's invitation for another reason than just the pleasure of her company. He enjoyed solving problems that others might run from, and this one subject seemed interesting.

"That's a great question, David, and I admit that I've never thought of it quite that way before." He swiveled in his seat and looked directly at the man. "But I would have to say the evidence that surrounds us begs to be understood, quantified, and categorized for us to use it effectively. Wouldn't you agree?"

David and the others who were listening nodded affirmatively, curious where he was going.

Thomas continued, "Then it makes sense to me that there is no problem in continuing our attempts to understand every bit as much as we can. In fact, I would say that the stage mankind is in right now is the 'figure out how things work' and pray we don't blow ourselves up on the way!"

In the meantime, one wiseacre sitting with David piped up and said, "So, I noticed you mentioned praying that we don't blow ourselves up on the way to understanding. Does that mean science can prove that God exists? Consider, before you answer, that *most* people these days would say that science would probably prove that He does *not* exist."

Thomas answered his new heckler confidently, "Science proves there is *something* out there that is real, no matter which version of religion you follow." Thomas was quickly interrupted, "Real?!" one of the women who hadn't spoken much before blurted out.

Those at the table looked slightly shell-shocked at Thomas' assertion but were drawn to his more modern take on the relationship between religion and science. Of course, they hadn't had time yet to process the implications of a different view on the age-old dividing line between the old subjects. But Thomas was thinking fast, already starting to imagine what this could mean to a world-society still mired in the old separatist thinking. Was it possible that the Church had created this mess themselves when they persecuted Galileo? They claimed it was because Galileo was trying to alter the 'natural order,' but it was really their own ignorance and prejudice being revealed by their actions. "How curious...," Thomas mused to himself, his mind afire with possibilities, both past and present.

"I didn't mean to give offense. It is part of your faith, Catholicism, that you believe in Jesus, God and the Virgin Mary, but I think science proves that something important does exist." Thomas said, now using a gentler tone. "I have studied the Bible a little and tried to practice the faith. I even went so far as to try and disprove on my own that God even exists. However, I wound up proving to myself that there *is* something or someone there. I am just not sure I believe in all the details involved."

David raised an eyebrow, looking intrigued. "So, what *is* this something or someone?"

Thomas took a sip of his wine before replying. "Energy, most importantly. The universe and everything in it are made of energy. We are all made of energy. Energy is the force that binds everything together, and it's something we don't fully understand yet. Call it God, call it the universe, call it whatever you want, but it's there."

The group fell silent for a moment, mulling over Thomas's words. "That's an interesting perspective," David finally said. "I've never thought of it that way before. So, the real question is whether God just *uses* energy to accomplish His goals, or is God the actual energy, itself."

Gabrielle leaned in closer, intrigued by the direction the conversation was taking. She had always been curious about the intersection between religion and science, and Thomas seemed to have a fresh perspective on the subject. She also thought that he was *so* cute when he got serious, giggling to herself as she listened more intently.

Thomas took a deep breath, "Let's consider the concept of dimensions. We live in a world of three physical dimensions which we can directly experience, but what if there are other dimensions that we can only experience *in*directly? Einstein theorized that there are nine dimensions, and while it's now believed there may be even more, let's work with nine for the sake of this discussion."

The wiseacre friend of David's apparently decided that this was his opportunity to feel important and burst out with, "No way there are 9 dimensions!"

Thomas ignored him like one would the class idiot and continued, "It has been proven already that one-dimensional beings could not possibly perceive two-dimensional objects or above, and the same is true for two-dimensional beings not being able to perceive the third dimension and so forth. However, if we live in the first 3 dimensions and *can* see the first and second, it's mathematically unlikely that there is something existing in those dimensions that we cannot see. But, if something *does* exist in another dimension, it could conceivably alter or affect other dimensions causally despite our own inability to perceive it directly. In other words, we can only see the *results* rather than the *action*." Thomas paused to increase the dramatic effect on his rapt audience. "And don't we see results in the world around us all the time? But we don't always know *why*. These other dimensions *could* be where God is doing his work, so maybe Einstein was not so far off after all, hmmm? After all, He has to do His work *some*where, doesn't He?," looking directly at the heckler and raising one eyebrow like the character, Spock, in the tv-series, *Star Trek*. The heckler looked suitably chastened and completely absent a smart reply.

The group had listened intently the entire time Thomas had spoken. One of the party members asked, "But what about an entity above that one, in an even higher dimension? Wouldn't *that* be the higher power?"

Thomas nodded but hastened to point out that the use of terms like "higher" and "lower" could be misleading. He preferred more straight-forward language. He continued, wincing internally as he changed his word-choices to adapt to his audience. "Yes, you would keep going to the highest level, and the being with the most influence and perception would be, by definition, God the Almighty. The entity that perceives the most would control everything, making them the ultimate effective power."

Gabrielle pondered Thomas' explanation. She had never thought about the existence of God in such a way, and it provided a new perspective that resonated with her. It also sparked a lively discussion at the table as they explored the concept further.

"Is there anything else you have figured out that would support your theory?" David spoke up and asked.

Thomas took a deep breath, thinking on the quick, "Sure, there are many things. Take the food chain, for example. Many species go extinct every day, but they are quickly replaced by new ones. It's too mathematically harmonious to be a coincidence, in my opinion. And further, if you look at the codependency between different species, it argues for design rather than random occurrence. If we came from amoebas alone, without there being a grand designer, why did some of those amoebas evolve into trees that provide oxygen while needing carbon dioxide, while others turned into something needing oxygen but *providing* carbon dioxide? The fact is, we started out as amoebas, and we have been developing from that point ever since. Sure seems likely to me that someone or something has a plan in mind!"

The group continued their discussion, with some members passionately sharing their experiences and beliefs. Of course, most of them were just repeating themselves, having covered much of this before at prior get-togethers. However, one of the women at the table who had been quiet for most of the time, suddenly spoke up, a complaining sound in her voice. "If God is real, then why doesn't he just speak to us or tell us what to do? It would make everything sooo much easier." Now that she had advised God of her opinion, she sat back down triumphantly.

Several people at the table attempted to answer her question by claiming that God wants us to make our own choices and learn from our own mistakes, but the woman wasn't swayed. "That just seems like a cop-out answer to me. If God is all-powerful and all-knowing, then why doesn't He just make everything clear and keep it simple?" She was clearly proud of herself.

Thomas, who had been listening carefully to the discussion, interjected at this point. "What?! You want to just skip all the pain and suffering that goes with learning? Pain and suffering produce change, and change is necessary for survival. The others at the table looked at Thomas expectantly, waiting for him to elaborate. "Think about it," he said. "Have you ever had a feeling that something was right or wrong? That's your conscience, and some people would say that it's God speaking to you. Or, maybe you've had a dream that gave you clarity on a situation. Some people would claim that's a message from God." Thomas could see the interest in their faces and the curiosity in their eyes. He took a deep breath, gathering his thoughts before he spoke again. "Our conscience is the fork in the road between right and wrong. I am not sure if that is scientific enough for you. As humans, we desire to be better than we are. Throughout history, we have proven that we are willing to sacrifice our lives to protect those in need. Our conscience speaks to us, pushes us, and makes us do better. Is it divine? It's anybody's guess."

The wiseacre launched back into heckling without hesitation. "Everything we need to know is in the Bible, 'Sigmund Freud'. Everybody knows that!" he announced triumphantly, standing up and taking a mock bow to his self-imagined adoring masses.

Thomas paused, wishing fervently that he had just 5 minutes alone with the irritating heckler to administer some true country justice, before continuing. "Throughout the history of mankind, we have either been oppressed ourselves or, at the minimum, witnessed oppression to others. True? At great cost, some of us have sacrificed ourselves to stop it. We collectively strive to be better; we attempt to right wrongs against others. Something or someone is surely driving us, speaking to us or, at the least, created a compassion for others in us." He grimaced, "Sure, there are a few sick individuals who don't, but the majority of us have good intentions most of the time."

"In God, we trust," Gabrielle added with a smile, thoroughly pleased with Thomas, her date/arm-candy.

"Or, just as true, in *science* we trust," Thomas replied with a laugh. It was true, there was something within humans that pushed them to be better, to strive for more, and he believed that it reflected a greater power than our own.

As the conversation slowed, the waitress approached the table with the bill. Thomas quickly grabbed it and pulled out his credit card to pay. *"In for a penny, in for a pound!"* he thought to himself, aware that this would raise Gabrielle's standing with the group. "Thank you all for allowing me join in on the discussion today," he said, looking around the table. To his great surprise, they looked at each other and gave him an impromptu round of applause, even the self-appointed heckler, although he did have a "sour grapes" look on his face.

David smiled and extended his hand towards Thomas for a shake. "It was a pleasure to have you with us today. And if you're picking up the tab, you're more than welcome to come back anytime," he joked, earning a few chuckles from the group. They all stood up to go, chattering amongst themselves as they left the restaurant.

Gabrielle beamed proudly at Thomas as she took his arm to leave and, suddenly, he knew that paying for everyone's lunch was *exactly* the right thing to have done. *"I guess this calls for a 'Hallelujah, amen'!"* He humorously thought to himself as they left, tempted to do a little jig. But he didn't.

Chapter 16

The Flight

Thomas settled into his first-class seat on the flight to Turin, Italy, thankful for the extra legroom and the relative quiet after the chaos of the airport. As he stowed his carry-on luggage in the overhead compartment, he glanced around at the other passengers settling into their seats.

To his left, a middle-aged couple was bickering over who had forgotten to pack the sunscreen. To his right, a man was staring blankly at his laptop, ignoring the woman next to him who was trying without success to engage him in conversation. Thomas couldn't help but observe the diverse types of people on the plane, each with their own story and their own individual struggles.

After the plane took off and leveled off at cruising altitude, Thomas opened the book on Buddha he had brought with him, hoping to find some peace and clarity amidst the chaos around him. He read through a few pages, trying to absorb the teachings of the great philosopher, but his thoughts kept drifting back to the people around him.

He couldn't help but wonder about the purpose of Life and why people seemed so lost and disconnected from one another. Why did they argue with their loved ones more than with strangers? For that matter, why did they seek escape in their electronic devices and, paradoxically, why did they seem so distant and alone when they were in a crowded airplane?

Thomas closed his eyes and took a deep breath, trying to center himself and find his *own* sense of purpose and meaning. He pondered that perhaps the answers were not found in a book or in the external world, but already within himself, just waiting to be discovered.

He opened his eyes and glanced around the cabin, feeling a rush of compassion for the people around him. They were all on their own journey, struggling to find their way, just like him. And, perhaps, in that shared struggle, there was some sense of connection and hope.

Thomas went back to reading his book with a newfound appreciation for the people around him and the journey of Life they were all on.

After a few more hours into the flight, Thomas felt the urge to take a small nap. He closed his eyes and tried to relax, but the sound of the engines and the occasional turbulence made it difficult for him to fall asleep. Later, just as he was finally starting to doze off, he was abruptly wakened by the woman sitting next to him. She looked nervous and was fidgeting with her seatbelt.

"Excuse me," she said softly, "I'm sorry to bother you, but I couldn't help but notice your accent. Are you an American? Are you traveling to Turin for business or pleasure?"

Thomas, still groggy from his nap, struggled to keep a polite smile on his face. He was annoyed that his rest had been interrupted for small talk, but he didn't want to be rude to the woman.

"Yes, I am American, and I'm actually going there for business," he replied, hoping his brief answer would be enough to discourage further conversation. He closed his eyes again and semi-turned away from her as far as the seat would allow him.

Unfortunately, the woman took his verbal response as an invitation to chat. "My name is Emily Dunwitty." and proceeded to tell him all about her family and their travels, not noticing that Thomas was groggily barely listening and just nodding along politely as best he could.

As she continued the riveting tale of the entire Dunwitty clan over the last 200 years, Thomas realized he was frustrated with the way people often mask their true feelings and intentions. He wished that people could be more honest and direct about what they wanted instead of feeling the need to resort to small talk. Of course, to be fair, he was much more bothered by this with people other than Mrs. Dunwitty. She was just trying to connect with someone to take her mind off the trip and the possibility of disaster over the sea in an airplane. He couldn't fault her for that, although he still wished she'd let him sink into a delicious coma for the rest of the journey. He ironically suspected that Mrs. Dunwitty might be an agent of Satan, chuckling to himself, though he was willing to be polite and listen to her rambling, if only to help calm her nerves.

Eventually, the woman, having exhausted her favorite topic of conversation, the Dunwitty clan, fell mercifully silent. Thomas, being smarter than Gabrielle said he looked, quickly took the opportunity to put on his headphones and dive back into his book again, pondering over the question of life's purpose and the meaning behind all the strange interactions people have with one another. *"Bo-ring!"* he thought to himself. Small wonder he had been falling asleep!

Later, as the plane began its descent into Turin, Thomas felt a slight jolt as the landing gear extended. He looked out the window to see the beautiful Italian landscape passing beneath him. Mrs. Dunwitty, cycling between being unnerved and exhilarated relief, grabbed his arm tightly, and Thomas couldn't help but smirk at her sudden show of strength. He tried to focus on the landing, but her iron grip was a bit distracting.

Finally, the plane touched down, and there was a collective sigh of relief from the passengers. The woman next to Thomas released her grip and let out an apologetic laugh. Thomas couldn't help but chuckle to himself at the absurdity of it all. As the passengers began to disembark, chaos ensued. Everyone seemed to be in a rush to get off the plane, pushing and shoving their way past each other to be the first to grab their bags. Thomas observed the scene with a mixture of frustration and amusement. It was a perfect illustration of the self-serving nature of people, he thought to himself.

After finally retrieving his own bag, Thomas swiftly made his way through the terminal seeking a rental car. He couldn't wait to be out of the airport and into the beautiful Italian city of Turin. He wondered if it would live up to the travel brochure's claims.

Chapter 17

Turin, Italy

He was relieved to have finally landed in Turin, but the frustration of attempting to rent a car quickly mounted. He approached the rental car desk in the airport and began to speak in English to the Italian attendant, but the attendant responded in the broken English of a typical high school student who had graduated to the real world some years earlier, and he was clearly struggling to both remember his old classes and simultaneously understand Thomas's reservation details.

As the awkward conversation dragged on, Thomas felt himself getting more and more annoyed. He wondered if he should just give up and find another way to get around but, just as he was about to throw in the towel, the woman who had been seated next to him on the flight approached the desk and offered to help translate.

Thomas was surprised and grateful for Mrs. Dunwitty's timely assistance. With her surprisingly fluent Italian and English, she quickly resolved the communication issues and enabled Thomas to secure the rental of a car. Thomas realized that this wouldn't have happened if he had not been nice to her on the plane. *"Ah, the value of small talk!"* He thought to himself wryly, shaking his head. As they walked away from the desk, Thomas earnestly thanked her for her help.

"No problem!" She assured him, playfully taking his free arm in her own as they walked. Thomas was touched by her kindness and felt a correspondingly greater faith in people, much to his internal surprise.

After he and Mrs. Dunwitty parted ways, Thomas reflected on his frustration at the rental car desk and how it would have been so much easier if the attendant had been more proficient in English. He mused about the importance of being able to communicate effectively in this global world and made a mental note to improve his own foreign language skills.

As he drove the car through the bustling streets of Turin, he took in the sights and sounds of the city, marveling at its rich history and culture. The architecture was stunning, with ornate buildings and cathedrals lining the streets. Chatter and laughter filled the air from the crowded piazzas as Thomas attempted to navigate the narrow streets.

He noticed that the city was filled with history, evident in the numerous statues and monuments that dotted the landscape. He felt a sense of awe as he drove past the Palazzo Madama, a Baroque palace that once housed the royal family of Savoy. The Mole Antonelliana, a towering landmark and the symbol of the city, was visible from almost every angle.

As he continued his drive, he felt admiration for the city's culture. The Italian language filled the air, and the aroma of fresh espresso and baked goods drifted to his nose from the local cafes. He saw people enjoying their meals outdoors, soaking in the sun and the vibrant atmosphere.

But, amidst all the beauty and culture, Thomas also saw some of the city's internal struggles. There was graffiti and rundown buildings in certain areas as well as the presence of homeless individuals on some of the street corners. He felt a pang of sadness at the contrast between the opulence of some parts of the city and the struggles of others.

Thomas decided to stop for a light snack at a café he saw as he turned north bound. After finding a rare parking space, he made his way to a table and chair on the sidewalk in front of the café. *"Life is good!"* he thought to himself as he sank gratefully into the chair. An attractive waitress took his order after he glanced at the menu, conveniently in both English and Italian. Apparently, they had quite a few foreign visitors. Right after he placed his order, he received a text from Nouvel asking if he had landed. Thomas quickly typed out a response, "Yes, I have landed and am on way to the meeting. I will arrive at the scheduled time." and hit "Send" on the phone, feeling relief that he had taken care of the matter.

As he finished his biscotti and coffee, he felt anticipation for the upcoming meeting with Francesco. He wondered what kind of person the client would be and how he would react to Thomas' proposal. Thomas felt confident in his ability to persuade other people over to his way of thinking, but he also knew that there were no guarantees.

After finishing up his snack, Thomas paid for his order and left the café. As he made his way back to the car, he continued to absorb the sights and sounds of the bustling city. The people, the architecture, and the energy of the place all combined to create a unique and vibrant atmosphere. Despite the beauty of the city, Thomas couldn't shake his internal feeling of being a bit on edge. The stakes were high, and the success of the project depended on his own ability to convince Ajello to lend his support. Thomas took a deep breath to calm himself, focusing on the task at hand.

As he drove to the meeting location, Thomas thought about the recent text from Nouvel. *"Why is he micro-managing me?"* he thought to himself. Was there something Thomas needed to know? He had found, over the years, that it was wise to consider people's reasons for the things they do. What was Nouvel's motivation? Thomas grimaced. It didn't matter. He had a job to do, and he couldn't afford to get distracted.

He was supposed to meet the client at a different café not too far from the last one he had just visited. Arriving at the cafe, Thomas parked the car and took a deep breath, slowly exhaling before getting out. He walked confidently into the café while taking note of his surroundings. He scanned the crowd, seeking his target, Francesco Ajello. It didn't take long. He saw a man who fit the description sitting in the corner, sipping espresso, and staring nervously out the window. Thomas stopped in front of him and introduced himself. "Hello, I'm Thomas Rene. Would you be Francesco?", starting the conversation that would determine the success or failure of the mysterious project.

Chapter 18

What If I Say No?

"It's great to meet you." Thomas said to the man with a smile and an outreached hand as he took a seat in front of him.

"Yes, it's nice to meet you, too, Mr. Rene. Although I must admit, I'm a bit nervous about meeting with *you*."

Thomas noticed that the man was avoiding eye contact with him while fidgeting a bit. His nervousness was palpable, and it was clear that something was wrong. Thomas thought back to his earlier mental conversation with himself about Nouvel's micromanagement and Thomas' concern about what he didn't know. *"Damn it!"* he thought, irritated because his instincts were telling him that Francesco was going to try to get out of it before Thomas even knew what *it* was!

Thomas said, "I can understand why you'd be leery of meeting with me," although he had no idea, "but let me assure you that we're all on the same side here." Thomas continued smoothly, mentally crossing his fingers for the fib. "We have a common goal, and I believe we can achieve it together."

"And what exactly *is* that goal?" An extremely doubtful Ajello asked, one eyebrow arching high on his forehead. The effect was mitigated by the fact that Francesco was a uni-brow man; just one brow that desperately needing pruning reached from one side of his forehead to the other.

Thomas had no idea what the goal was either and very little about anything else, really. However, this was the sort of skullduggery where Thomas truly shined and why companies held his ability in high esteem. Thomas could bullshit his way through anything given half a chance. Companies seemed to like that: it limited their risk. Thomas, of course, didn't mind being in the dark if it was unavoidable.

Thomas answered as if he knew more than he was willing to say out loud in a public place. "Let's just say it's something big, something that could change everything. But we need your help to make it happen. That's why we're both here today."

"I'm not sure I understand exactly what you're asking of me." Francesco said as he fiddled with his expresso cup.

"I know this may sound vague, but trust me, we do have a plan. And, with your expertise and influence, we can make it a reality. By the way, I have something for you." Thomas pulled out the envelope of money.

"What is this?" Francesco asks Thomas as he hands it to him.

"Consider it a token of our appreciation for your time and effort." Thomas was continuing to think on his feet and added, "But also, it's a reminder that there's no turning back now. We're in this together, and there's a lot at stake."

Francesco's eyes widened underneath his truly eye-catching unibrow as he picked up the envelope, feeling the thickness of the cash inside. "This is a lot of money," he murmured hesitantly, looking up Thomas with concern in his eyes. "But I still don't know if I can help you."

"Our company has faith in your ability based on what we have heard." Thomas said, bluffing, even though he personally had no such information about the other man whatsoever.

Francesco seemed to visibly relax as he obviously was making mental connections based on what Thomas had just implied, and his nervous ticks and fidgeting began to lessen. Thomas decided that it was time to back off Francesco a bit, so he switched to innocuous small talk, all while maintaining an authoritative but pleasant tone to his voice.

The small-talk tactic seemed to be working, but Francesco returned to the subject on his own soon enough. "I must know---

what about the package?" he asked while looking Thomas up and down to see if he had the package with him.

"That's something I can't talk about here. Let's just say it's vital to our cause, and we need to ensure its integrity. So, please do not open it in my presence. Preferably, open it in a more secure environment, like at home." Thomas then reached into his suit jacket pocket and pulled out a small rectangular object wrapped in a brown cloth. He placed it on the table and slides it into the middle.

Francesco just looked at the package, making no move to pick it up, and said, "I don't know if I want to get involved in something that could put me at risk."

"Francesco, meeting with me today *already* puts you at risk." Thomas answered in a wry tone, "But the truth is, we're *all* at risk, and the only way to minimize that risk is to support each other. Think about what's at stake here. Think about what we can accomplish together. We believe you can help us to make a difference."

Francesco just leaned forward, his expression taut. "I need you to understand that this request you're making is not a simple matter, Mr. Rene," he said in a low voice. "What you're asking for, it's not easy to obtain. It's heavily watched, and there is the matter of great risk for *me*, particularly!"

Thomas shifted in his seat, suddenly feeling a bit uneasy with the direction the conversation was taking. He had no earthly idea what Ajello was talking about, but he knew enough to keep up his authoritative demeanor. "I understand that this is a difficult task, Francesco. That's why we need *your* help. You're the only one who can get us what we need. Besides which, what do you think the money is *for*? It's not just to make you feel better, Francesco!" Thomas looked him directly in the eyes, projecting certainty and assurance.

Francesco sighed heavily. "The security is incredibly tight." He thought for a moment, considering. "I'll need more information about what you're planning to do with it."

Thomas hesitated, then decided to take a chance. "I'm sorry, Francesco, but I'm not at liberty to discuss any further details of our plans," he said firmly. "What I *can* tell you is that we need this item for an important project, and that it's absolutely vital that we obtain it."

Ajello looked skeptical, but Thomas could see the wheels turning in his head. "I'll need some time to think about it," he equivocated. "I can't make any promises right now."

Thomas smiled like a tiger about to eat his dinner. "Actually, that money I gave you *is* your promise! But, of course, take your time and do it right. We do need your help sooner rather than later, though. I'll be in touch." With that, Thomas got up to leave, figuring that he had accomplished as much as he could for the time being.

On seeing Thomas make the move to leave, Francesco spoke up, sounding a bit alarmed. "Wait! One more thing---What happens if I say 'no'?"

Thomas paused, then showed his 'big stick' like President Teddy Roosevelt would have done. "Let's just say that it's better for everyone involved if you say 'yes', especially for *you*." Thomas then exited the café, and deliberately didn't look back.

Later, reflecting on the meeting in the rental car, Thomas felt that his initial assessment of Francesco's body language and demeanor had been spot on. By adjusting his own approach to suit the situation, he had been able to establish a rapport with the man and ultimately achieve what appeared to be a positive outcome. He felt confident the man would do as he had been asked.

Thomas took his phone out and sent Nouvel an update via text:

"The meeting with the contact went well. He's cautious and concerned about risks. He said the item Is heavily watched and won't be easy to access. Pushed him hard. Will keep you posted on progress. - Thomas"

His phone beeped. Nouvel had texted back, "Excellent work, Thomas. Keep pushing him and keep me updated on any developments. Be careful, the item is very valuable, and we can't afford any mistakes. Keep me informed."

Nouvel certainly had responded quickly! Thomas wondered if Nouvel had been holding the phone in his hand and staring at it in anticipation of his text. Once again, Thomas Rene had that funny feeling there was something he didn't know.

Chapter 19

I Can't Wait Until You Get Back

Thomas woke up early that next morning, and he was eager to start his planned day of sightseeing in Turin. After a quick continental breakfast at the hotel, he checked his phone for any updates from Nouvel or Francesco, but there were none. He decided to take it as a good sign that there was no reason for him to cancel his sightseeing. After all, how often was he in Italy?!

He thought carefully about it and decided to spend his free day exploring the city's famous landmarks and attractions. After looking up the most popular destinations in the area on his cellphone, he made a short list of the ones he really wanted to see. Top of the list was the Mole Antonelliana, a towering landmark that offered stunning panoramic views of the city. He took the elevator to the top, marveling at the stunning sights below him.

Next up on the list was the Palazzo Madama, an impressive Baroque palace that now housed a museum of ancient art. Thomas spent several hours walking around admiring the intricate sculptures and paintings. By this time, he felt that he had done enough to deserve a nice lunch and decided that micro-managing Nouvel could pay for it.

For his free lunch, he tried some of the local cuisine at a small trattoria, indulging himself in a plate of handmade pasta and a glass of their more expensive red wine. He was relaxed and content, enjoying the peacefulness of the moment even more knowing that little prick, Nouvel, was paying for it. *"Nothing better than an expense account!"* he thought to himself, smirking. He considered dessert for just that reason, but reluctantly told himself 'no' due to waistline concerns. He didn't want to get back to Gabrielle carrying a belly roll!

After lunch, he visited an Egyptian Museum which was touted to be one of the largest collections of ancient Egyptian artifacts outside of Cairo. He was fascinated by the history and symbolism of the artifacts, spending several hours immersed in the exhibits. Thomas wasn't the only one, as many people seemed gob smacked by the mummies and exhibits of gold.

As the sun finally began to set, he made his way on foot to the Piazza Castello, the central square of Turin. Sitting on an available open bench, he watched all the people passing by as they went about their day enjoying the lively atmosphere.

Checking his phone, he saw that there were no messages or calls from either Ajello or Nouvel. He wondered when the follow-up meeting would take place, but he pushed the thought out of his mind and decided to enjoy the rest of his rapidly darkening day. Thomas had the sudden desire to throw a few drinks back at a local bar, so he headed off in a random direction and quickly located one that met his requirements.

While Thomas indulged himself and had a few drinks at the bar, he struck up a conversation with some locals about the best places to eat in the city. They recommended a small family-owned restaurant that served authentic Italian cuisine, and Thomas decided to try it for dinner.

The restaurant was tucked away in a small alley, but it was bustling with activity. The smells of garlic, tomatoes, and freshly baked bread filled the air caused Thomas' mouth to water in anticipation. He ordered veal with a side of pasta coated in a rich garlic and parmesan tomato sauce. A glass of red wine accompanied the order. After a short while, the food was delivered to the smiling Thomas, carried by a beautiful native girl of Turin. He tried not to look at her, thinking of Gabrielle and feeling a bit guilty that he wasn't more immune to the server's charms. After the woman swayed gracefully away, Thomas savored every bite until he could handle no more.

After dinner, once again skipping dessert, Thomas walked around the city taking in the sights and sounds of the evening. He practically stumbled upon a street musician playing a beautiful piece of music on his guitar, and he stopped to listen for a while, fascinated with watching the guitarist's hands as they moved lovingly over the instrument. As it grew dark, Thomas made his way back to his hotel room where he sat on the balcony and simply enjoyed the view of the city lights, feeling contentedly tired from his sight-seeing and at peace with himself. He reflected on the day he had just had, grateful for the opportunity to experience the locals, even the beautiful ones, he thought to himself ironically.

As he got ready for bed, Thomas realized that he had better follow-up with Francesco the next morning when he wakened. He made a mental note to check his schedule in the morning. With that thought in mind, he started to drift off to sleep, but then he heard the familiar sound of his phone buzzing with a text message. He picked it up and saw a message from Evelyn Perdita. *"Odd!"* he thought to himself, *"What does she want?"*

Thomas felt a little guilty as he read her text message. "Hi, Thomas! Haven't heard from you in forever! How's Turin? I miss you!" He replied cautiously, unsure of how much she knew about his assignment.

As they continued to exchange messages, Thomas became increasingly curious about how much Evelyn knew concerning his trip to Turin. He tried to find out subtly, but she didn't seem to want to give him a straight answer. Eventually, Thomas decided to let it go and just enjoy the conversation. Thomas found himself feeling more and more attracted to Evelyn despite knowing it was a *bad* idea. "Evelyn," he texted, "I've got to get some sleep, got a lot to do tomorrow."

All she had to say in response was, "Ok. I understand, but I can't wait until you get back. I am going to fuck you unconscious!" This, in true Evelyn fashion, was followed by a picture of her naked and making bedroom eyes at him.

Thomas sighed. "Why is being good so *hard*?!" he mused, adjusting himself under the bedclothes and signing off with her, refusing to respond to either the picture or her last statement of intent.

Later, as he lay there in the bed, Thomas couldn't help but wonder how he was going to navigate this situation with Evelyn. On the one hand she was sexy, and he had to admit he enjoyed the attention given to him. He knew it was risky and could potentially jeopardize his involvement with Gabrielle, not to mention *Turner Research*, his current employer for whom Evelyn worked as well! He adjusted himself once again and tried to think *good* thoughts, but his mind was not cooperating very well as he drifted off to sleep.

Chapter 20

Great Job, Thomas

Thomas woke up early the next day feeling refreshed and energized after a good night's sleep. He had ordered breakfast to be delivered to his hotel room and enjoyed it on the balcony, sipping on his coffee and taking in more of the stunning views of Turin. As he finished his meal, he received a text from Francesco Ajello requesting an in-person meeting. Thomas quickly replied in the affirmative and asked for the location and time of their meeting.

A few hours later, Thomas arrived at the designated meeting place---a quiet cafe tucked away in the northwest corner of the city. Ajello was already there, seated at a small table in the corner, once again looking nervous and fidgety. The introductions between the two were polite, but there was a coldness to them that was hard to ignore. Something was wrong, and Thomas quickly adjusted his demeanor, adopting an authoritative but pleasant tone. "What's up, Francesco? You done it already?"

Ajello began to speak in a hushed voice, leaning closer to Thomas as if he didn't want anyone else to hear what he had to say. "Look, Mr. Rene, I've been thinking it over and I just can't take the chance, my family could be hurt by this if it goes bad. I'm sure you can understand that."

Thomas listened a bit impatiently, aware where this was going. Time for the brass knuckles to come out, he decided. "Francesco, there's no stopping this now. It's gone too far, and I couldn't stop it even if I wanted to!"

The man looked shocked. This wasn't going the way he had thought it would. Francesco had gravely underestimated the depth of his own involvement with this heist. "What do you mean, 'gone too far'?! Here, take your money back. I just want out!" and he slid the brown package of money across the table, a desperate look in his eyes.

Thomas took out his phone and showed the screen to Francesco. "Is this your family?" he asks casually, knowing full well that it was. Ajello looked at the pictures and nodded slowly. "Yes, it is," he responded, his voice panicked and questioning.

Thomas just leaned back in his chair and folded his hands. "I understand your concerns, Francesco, but we expect you to do this job for us. And we have *already* paid you handsomely for it. Do you get where I'm going with this? There's more than one way for your family to get hurt." Of course, Thomas was bluffing, but he sure didn't want Francesco to know that he would never hurt women or children.

Fortunately, Francesco finally got the implication, and his face blanched. "What the hell?!" he gasped. "You wouldn't dare!"

Thomas just looked at the visibly distraught man, not saying anything more, just letting it sink in. He liked watching people convince themselves to do what he wanted.

Thomas leaned forward, a serious expression on his face. "Francesco, you *know* that time is of the essence here. I hate to tell you, but not only do *we* need this done right away, *you* do, too!" Thomas paused, deliberately seeming reluctant to share anything further about Francesco's family. "I think you know why, don't you?" and Thomas gave his best impression of being remorseful, adding "Don't shoot the messenger!" while pointing to himself with his thumb.

Francesco looked genuinely rattled at this, and he quickly blurted out, "I can do it! I can do it! Just leave my family out of it!"

Thomas relaxed at this, realizing things with Francesco were back on track. *"Good!"* he thought to himself. He firmly pushed the brown paper package of money back across the table in front of the defeated man.

Francesco took the money and replaced it in his jacket pocket. He let out a deep sigh. "If there *is* a God, we are all damned," he muttered.

Thomas furrowed his brow, confused. "What do you mean?" he asked.

Francesco shook his head, clearly dismissing the errant thought. "Never mind, forget I said anything. Just rambling, I suppose," he replied, avoiding eye contact with Thomas.

Thomas sensed that Francesco was holding something back, but he didn't push it any further. Instead, he simply shrugged and said, "Well, let's focus on the task at hand, then. *You* have a job to do, and you need to do it quickly". Francesco nodded, but he looked like all he wanted was for all of this to just be over.

After the conversation concluded, Thomas left the cafe feeling a mix of relief and residual anxiety, a normal thing after conflict for him. He realized better now that the stakes were even higher than he had initially believed. When he got into his rental, he sent Nouvel another text update.

"Dear Sammy," he started off sarcastically, knowing Nouvel would hate the overly familiar greeting, "Ajello tried to get out of it, but is back on track now. Shouldn't be much longer." Amused by his inspired use of 'Sammy' in the text, Thomas chuckled to himself as he put the phone back in its holder and drove away.

Chapter 21

The Uncomfortable Gift

After a long flight back from Italy, Thomas was just glad to return with his mission accomplished. He glanced around his apartment and was relieved to be in his own space once again. He set down his bags and moved towards his couch when he noticed something on the coffee table that certainly wasn't there before he had left on his journey to Italy. It was a box of Cuban cigars and a note from Nouvel thanking him for traveling on such short notice and having completed the task successfully. Thomas felt a mix of emotions - on one hand, he was pleased that Nouvel seemed to appreciate his work but, on the other hand, he was uneasy about the fact that someone had entered his apartment while he was gone without his permission.

As he sat down on the couch, he couldn't help but feel like he was being watched. He knew that he needed to be cautious and on guard. Now, he wondered if he should check for listening devices and cameras, then immediately began to do so. He realized there was no time like the present! The note from Nouvel, while seemingly friendly, also made him wonder if there were a hidden message or warning behind it. He took a deep breath and tried to push these thoughts out of his mind, reminding himself that he had done his job well and there was nothing to be worried about. But, as he walked around his apartment, he noticed that some things were slightly out of place. It was nothing major, just small things, like a picture frame that had been shifted an inch or a drawer that had been left slightly ajar. Thomas started to feel even more uneasy and became increasingly convinced that someone had gone through his things. He decided to check his computer and phone to see if there had been any suspicious activity or messages, but everything seemed to be in order. He started searching his apartment to see if anything was missing. Everything *looked* fine, but he still knew that something was off.

After the very thorough search, he concluded that the gift box of cigars was the only thing that was different in his apartment. He took a closer look at the note from Nouvel, trying to decipher if there was any hidden message or threat contained within it, but the note appeared to be nothing more than it was---which still didn't excuse the break-in as far as Thomas was concerned!

Despite his attempts to stay calm, Thomas couldn't shake the feeling of unease that lingered in the pit of his stomach. He knew that he needed to be extra cautious and vigilant from this point on, but he couldn't help but feel like he was trapped in a dangerous game with no clear end in sight.

He decided to act on his gut feelings and reached out to a friend in the Federal Bureau of Investigations, Peter Barlowe, to see if he could help him learn more about Nouvel and the stem cell company.

He dialed the number in his contacts list. "Hey, Peter, it's Thomas," he said when Peter picked up. "Long time no talk."

"Thomas, my man! How's it going?" Peter responded.

Thomas, not one to beat around the bush, decided to dive right in. "I need your help with something sensitive. I'm working with a guy named Samuel Nouvel and I need to know more about him and the company he works for. Could you investigate this for me?" Thomas asks hopefully.

"Sure thing, Thomas. What's the deal? Is this something you're working on for your agency?" Peter asks.

"No, a side project. I just need to know who I'm dealing *with*," Thomas says, a hint of concern in his voice which Peter immediately picked up on.

"No problem, partner. Glad to do it. I'll see what I can find. Can you give me any more details about this guy or the company?" Peter asks.

Thomas told him what he knew, and Peter promised to get on it right away.

"Thanks, Peter. I really appreciate it. Let me know what you find," Thomas said.

"No problem, man. Always happy to help a friend. Just be careful, okay? If you're asking *me* to investigate this guy, you must have some serious questions," Peter comments with an unspoken but real concern in his voice.

Thomas nodded, even though Barlowe couldn't see him over the phone. "Yeah, I do. I don't know what I'm getting into with this guy, but I have a feeling it could be trouble."

Peter laughed. "Well, let's hope it's nothing too serious. In the meantime, I'll start digging and let you know. Talk to you soon, Thomas," Peter said before hanging up and going back to his work.

Thomas put down the phone, feeling a sense of relief knowing that Barlowe would be looking into Nouvel and *Turner Research* very closely. He hoped that whatever Peter found would ease his concerns or, at least, shed some light on who he was really dealing with. Thomas took a deep breath, looked around his apartment, and decided to take a walk around the block to help clear his head.

He couldn't help but think about everything that had happened over the past few days. He felt uneasiness over the mysterious job he had taken on. He wondered if he was in over his head this time, but he also recognized it was the thrill of the challenge that kept him going.

As he walked, he noticed the city of Phoenix around him, the people going about their lives. He took a few deep breaths, grateful for the tranquil moment of peace.

Eventually, he returned to his apartment and decided to relax for the rest of the night. He poured himself a glass of red wine he had found after his recent trip to Turin and picked up a book he'd been meaning to read. As he read, and started to relax, his mind began to wander, and he began to ponder what kind of person Nouvel would turn out to be after Peter worked his magic. Mildly frustrated at this point, he tried to push those thoughts out of his mind, but the sense of unease continued to linger.

Despite his concerns, Thomas knew he couldn't back out now without a damned good reason. Taking another sip of wine, he reminded himself that he was a professional at his job. He was determined to see this job through to the end, no matter what it took.

Chapter 22

Ducks and Deep Thought

Thomas had been waiting for a few days now, hoping to hear from anyone at *Turner Research* for his next assignment. He had been spending his time idly, not really knowing what to do with himself. He had already caught up on all his favorite TV shows, read a few books, and even managed to work out at the gym a few times.

Eventually, he decided to go for a walk around the city to entertain himself at the same time as getting some exercise. He didn't have a specific destination in mind. He just wanted to enjoy the day. As he walked, he came upon a quiet park with a pond in the center. Taking a seat on a bench, he watched as the ducks swam by making characteristic duck sounds and splashing each other which, as everyone knows, is the highest form of duck humor. Thomas cackled a bit at that thought.

While sitting there, he started to ponder the meaning of life and the purpose of existence. Was there a grand design behind everything, or was Life just a series of random events with no inherent meaning? Thomas thought about the different cultures and religions throughout the world, each with their own beliefs and peculiar explanations for Life's mysteries. Could any of them really provide the answers he sought? Or were they just different interpretations of the same fundamental questions?

As he contemplated these deep existential questions, he couldn't help but feel a familiar sense of unease. Was he wasting his life chasing after the elusive next assignment, never really understanding what it all meant? Or was this his true purpose, his inevitable destiny? Thomas knew that he might never find *all* the answers he sought, but that didn't stop him from questioning and searching. In the end, perhaps the journey itself was the true purpose, and the destination was secondary.

After a while, he grew restless with just walking around aimlessly and decided to explore the surrounding area. Conveniently, he stumbled upon a small coffee shop that promised all the answers to pointless human existence through the magical intervention of the coffee bean. This encouraged him to immediately order a latte and a croissant, of course, and he took a seat inside the shop at a small table next to a window. From there, he was able to watch as people passed by on the street and enjoyed the warm sunshine that poured in.

As he sipped his coffee, he took out his notebook and started jotting down some thoughts. He didn't really have a plan, but just wrote down whatever came to mind. He wrote about his travels, and even about the strange item that Nouvel had asked him to obtain. He wondered what it was about that particular object that made it so important and why Nouvel had asked him to retrieve it. Thomas wondered anew if he was being watched or followed and found himself looking around with a more suspicious eye for the unusual.

He shook his head, finished his coffee, put his notebook away and left the coffee shop to walk aimlessly around the city again.

As the sun began to set, Thomas realized he had been walking for quite a while. He was tired, but also felt clarity. He felt like he had been able to clear his mind and focus on the present. He made his way back to his apartment, feeling content with his day even though he had accomplished nothing of significance. Thomas suspected that sometimes it was better to just relax and wait for what comes next.

When Thomas arrived at the hallway of his apartment, he saw ahead of him a shadowy figure waiting by his door. As he came closer, the figure revealed itself to be Evelyn Perdita, her captivating eyes shimmering in the dim light. Thomas couldn't help but feel a guilty surge of lust as he took in her obvious beauty.

She wasted no time in greeting him with a kiss, her lips soft and inviting. The scent of her perfume filled his senses, intoxicating him, but Thomas immediately thought of his neighbor, Gabrielle, and this thought ruined a perfectly good kiss for him. After they made their way into his apartment, she assumed the role of hostess and poured them each a glass of Thomas' new red wine, the rich aroma filling the air.

Thomas mentally assured himself that there was nothing wrong with friends visiting, so they spent the evening lounging on the couch, sipping wine and chatting about everything from their work to their personal lives. She was easy to talk to when she was like this. They discussed their hopes and dreams, fears and regrets, and everything in between. Evelyn had a way of focusing on her target which made them feel important and willing to share.

As the night wore on and the wine flowed, Evelyn grew bolder in her flirtations. She leaned in closer to Thomas, touching his arm and laughing at his jokes. Thomas found himself getting lost, unable to resist her charms.

Before he knew it, Evelyn was straddling him on the couch, their lips locked in a passionate embrace. Their bodies pressed against each other, the heat of the moment overwhelming them both. The physical attraction between them was undeniable, and they explored each other's bodies with growing excitement. Thomas' guilt was simply blown away in the turbulence of the passion, but his rational mind suspected he would regret this.

As the night ended, Evelyn slipped out of Thomas's apartment with a sly smile on her face, leaving him feeling both sated and a little bit uneasy.

As he lay in his bed, his mind wandered back over his evening with Evelyn. He couldn't deny that he had enjoyed her sensuality, but something about her made him uneasy. Maybe it was the way she seemed to know things she shouldn't or her uncanny ability to manipulate him with her body. Or maybe it was the fact that she was connected to the same company that currently controlled his life and his every move.

As he drifted off to sleep, Thomas couldn't help but think that getting involved with Evelyn was a mistake. Could she be a dangerous distraction? Was she just a woman looking for a good time? He reluctantly realized he needed to be careful around her, but at the same time, he admittedly had trouble resisting the allure of her beauty and the thrill of the danger that came with getting involved with her.

Chapter 23

They're Just Actors

Thomas groaned as he rolled over in his bed, the buzzing of his phone pulling him out of his slumber. He fumbled around on his nightstand for the device, blinking away the remnants of sleep. He squinted at the screen and saw a text from Crane requesting a meeting. "Hey Thomas, can you stop by my office later? I want to follow up on things. Shall we say 7:00 am?"

"It's 6:03am, does this guy ever sleep?" Thomas muttered under his breath as he rubbed his eyes. Thomas responded with a simple 'yes'.

He let out a heavy sigh as he tossed the phone back onto the nightstand. He couldn't believe Nouvel wanted to meet so early in the morning! It was much earlier than he usually woke up, and he was feeling a bit groggy post-Evelyn. He lay there for a moment, staring up at the ceiling and trying to motivate himself to get up and get ready. After a few minutes, the still sleepy man grudgingly got out of bed, his bare feet hitting the cold hardwood floor. He shuffled to the bathroom and splashed some water on his face. After looking at himself in the mirror, he realized he was in no condition to go to a meeting. His hair was sticking up in all directions, and his eyes were still droopy with sleep.

Thomas took a deep breath, stretching his arms above his head and yawning before making his way over to his closet. He ran his fingers over his suits, feeling the fabric and selecting a dark navy one with pinstripes. As he pulled it out, he inspected it carefully, checking for any wrinkles or imperfections. Satisfied with its condition, he laid it out on his bed and went to his drawer to pick out a crisp white shirt and a matching navy tie. As he dressed, he paid meticulous attention to every detail - making sure the knot was tied perfectly, the collar was pressed, and the cuffs were straight. He took a step back, admiring his reflection in the mirror and gave himself a small nod of approval.

It wasn't just about looking good, though. It was about projecting an image of professionalism and competence. Thomas knew that, in his line of work, appearance mattered. He wanted to show Dr. Stephen Crane and anyone else he might bump into at *Turner Research* that he was serious, organized, and detail oriented.

After a few more adjustments and a quick once-over, Thomas grabbed his briefcase and a cup of coffee on his way out the door. He checked his phone again and saw that it was now 6:40am. *"Good grief,"* he thought to himself, *"I'm barely awake, and this guy is already making moves."* As he headed to his car, Thomas couldn't help but chuckle at the absurdity of the situation. *"Who schedules a meeting this early?"* he thought to himself. *"Fucking scientists!"*

As he took his seat in the car, he took a deep breath, inhaling the familiar scents of leather and old cologne. He turned on the engine and the car obediently hummed to life, the dashboard lighting up in a warm orange glow. He adjusted the mirrors, then settled back into the driver's seat.

The radio was already tuned to his favorite sports station, and he listened as the announcers discussed the latest news in the world of football. One fan called in, complaining about the lack of offense on their favorite team, and the announcer passionately responded, defending the team's strategy.

Thomas chuckled, finding it amusing how worked up people could get over a game. As he continued listening to the radio show, he shook his head in disbelief. The callers were so *passionate* about a game that, in the grand scheme of things, didn't really matter at all. They talked about players as if they were gods, and yet these players weren't doing anything truly meaningful or important for society, other than to entertain. Thomas thought about the many doctors, nurses, and other healthcare professionals who worked tirelessly to save lives every day, yet received a fraction of the recognition and praise that these athletes did for simply playing a game. He couldn't understand why society placed so much value on something so trivial.

Furthermore, Thomas knew that many athletes were paid exorbitant amounts of money for their talent, much more than people who worked in essential jobs such as teachers, police officers, and firefighters. He couldn't reconcile this imbalance of priorities and resources. He shook his head in disbelief. It wasn't just the obsession with sports that baffled him, but also the worship of movie stars. "I mean, come on," he muttered to himself, "they're just actors. They're not *really* tough or cool, they're just playing a part." He thought about all the times he had seen interviews with famous actors, only to find out that they were quite awkward and introverted in real life. Real-life heroes were of more interest to him; people who put their lives on the line every day to protect or improve their communities. He admired their dedication to a higher cause and the passion they exuded. Thomas wondered why society placed so much value on the wrong things. Instead of idolizing people who simply entertain us, why not focus on those who truly make a difference in the world? The problem was that we have been teaching children to desire emulating the wrong type of person. It was a question he had pondered many times before, and one that he knew he would never find a satisfying answer to. But, at the same time, he knew he was in the minority, and most people seemed to find a sense of identity and community through sports and movies. Much as he knew this, he found himself unable to listen to the nonsensical conversation any longer, so he changed the station to some smooth jazz.

As he drove through the city, the sky gradually lightened, the first rays of sunlight casting a warm glow over the buildings. The streets were quiet at this early hour, with only a few other cars on the road. Thomas sipped on his hot drink, relishing the slightly bitter taste of under-sweetened coffee, and took in the view of the city around him. He enjoyed these quiet moments of solitude, just him and the road ahead and the opportunity to gather his thoughts before tackling the busy day.

Finally, he arrived at his destination – *Turner Research* headquarters. He parked his car in the lot and, as he stepped out of his car, he stretched, feeling his muscles unwind after the drive. As he glanced around the parking lot, he noticed the sleek lines of the modern building in front of him. The architecture was striking, a blend of glass and steel that seemed to shimmer in the morning sun.

Thomas surveyed the lot. It was still early, and there were only a few other cars parked nearby. He couldn't see any people around, but he knew that scientists often kept unconventional schedules. He chuckled to himself, *"Typical scientists, always working strange hours."*

Chapter 24

Consider It Done

As Thomas walked through the sterile, white hallways of the lab on the way to his appointment with Crane, he was awestruck. The cutting-edge technology and advanced machinery that filled the facility were a testament to the brilliance of the scientists who worked there. It was a world far removed from his own, but one that he found fascinating, nonetheless. Thomas reflected on his recent experiences with the company. He had been working for the new department at *Turner Research* for a few months now, though he had actually been working for the company about 6 months. While he had initially been skeptical of the corporate culture, he had grown to appreciate the money he was making combined with the freedom of movement.

As he made his way to Crane's office, Thomas thought about that last dinner he had shared with Dr. Crane, Nouvel and Evelyn Perdita. The discussion had been fascinating, but it had also left him. He wondered what *kind* of groundbreaking research Dr. Crane was working on now, and how it might further blur the lines between what was considered moral or immoral.

When he arrived at Crane's door, Thomas rapped lightly with his knuckles before stepping inside. Crane was sitting at his desk, typing away at his computer, but he looked up and smiled primly when he saw Thomas.

"Thomas, good to see you again," he said formally, standing up to shake Thomas' hand.

"Likewise, Stephen," Thomas replied, taking a seat across from him.

They both sat down, and when Crane got comfortable, he had a perfunctory smile on his face. "Thomas, I wanted to take a moment to thank you for the work you've done for us over the past few months. Your assignments have all been completed successfully, and I personally appreciate your dedication to getting things done."

Thomas nodded, "Thank you, Stephen. I am enjoying my time with your company."

"I'm glad to hear that." Crane replied. "And I wanted to take this opportunity to get to know you a bit better. What drew you to this line of work?"

Thomas thought for a moment before responding. "Well, I suppose it's the challenge of it. Finding solutions to problems that others can't and doing it quickly and discreetly. It's satisfying to be able to help companies which are in need."

"I understand," Crane said, nodding. "And what do you see for yourself in the future? Do you plan on continuing in this line of work?"

Thomas shrugged, "I haven't really given it much thought. I suppose it depends on the opportunities that come my way. But for now, I'm happy where I am." Crane leaned back in his chair and steepled his fingers. "Well, I hope that you'll consider staying with our company for the long term. We could use someone with your expertise and dedication."

Thomas smiled, "I appreciate that, Stephen. I'm definitely open to the idea of staying on."

"Good to hear," Crane said, placing his hands flatly on his desk. "And now, onto the #1 reason I called you here today. We have a new assignment for you. It's a bit more complex than your previous ones, but I do believe you're up for the challenge."

Thomas raised an eyebrow, curious. "How can I help?"

"We need you to handle a situation with a former employee who is threatening to leak confidential information about our research and development projects. This individual has already been terminated for violating our company policies, but we believe he still has access to sensitive information that we are not ready to release yet."

Thomas asked, "What is his name?", being practical about it.

Crane leaned back in his chair and rubbed his chin thoughtfully. "The ex-employee in question is a man named David Kim. He was a researcher in our nanotechnology division."

Thomas leaned forward, fully engaged now. "And what *kind* of information did he have access to?"

Crane sighed. "All kinds of confidential data related to our latest projects. We're talking about nanobots that could revolutionize medical treatment, advanced materials with unparalleled strength and durability, and much more."

Thomas raised both eyebrows. "Sounds like some pretty cutting-edge stuff."

Crane leaned forward, his voice dropping to a low, confidential tone. "We're talking about highly advanced genetic modifications, Thomas. The kind of technology that can fundamentally alter the genetic makeup of a living organism at a molecular level."

Thomas was taken aback. "That's...that's some heavy stuff, Stephen. What kind of applications does this technology have?"

Crane leaned back in his chair. "The applications are endless, Thomas. We're talking about the ability to cure genetic diseases, create personalized medicine tailored to an individual's specific genetic makeup, and even extend the human lifespan by repairing damaged DNA. It's the kind of technology that can change the world as we know it."

Thomas sat back, a look of disbelief on his face. "It sounds like science fiction!"

Crane chuckled. "It may sound like it, but it's very much science *fact*. And that's why we need you to handle this situation with Kim carefully. We can't afford to have this technology fall into the wrong hands."

Thomas was fascinated by the possibilities. "How do these nanobots work exactly?"

"Well, they're programmed to recognize certain sequences of DNA and RNA, and can then manipulate them on a molecular level," Crane explained enthusiastically. "They can insert or remove specific genes or gene sequences, alter the expression of certain genes, and even repair or replace damaged DNA."

Thomas nodded slowly, trying to wrap his head around the complexity of the process. "And what kind of modifications can be made using this technology?"

"It really depends on the specific application," Crane replied. "We've had success using it to correct genetic disorders such as cystic fibrosis and sickle cell anemia, but it can also be used to enhance physical traits such as muscle strength, endurance or even cognitive abilities like memory retention or problem-solving skills."

Thomas was in awe of the potential of this technology. "But what about the ethical implications of modifying human genes? Is there any danger of creating a new class of genetically enhanced individuals?"

Crane nodded solemnly. "Yes, that is definitely a concern. We need to tread carefully and ensure that any modifications we make are for the greater good and not just for the benefit of a privileged few. That's why we have strict ethical guidelines in place and work closely with regulatory bodies to ensure that our research is conducted in a responsible and ethical manner." Crane cleared his throat, wanting to bring the conversation back to the present situation. "But let's not lose sight of the task at hand. We need to retrieve any information this ex-employee may have and prevent it from being leaked to the wrong hands."

Thomas nodded. "Understood. Do we have any leads on where this person might be?"

"We *believe* he has gone into hiding, but we have reason to suspect he may still be in the area," Crane said hopefully. "Here is all the information we have, and we trust you to handle this discreetly." Stephen sighed while handing over a small folder, his expression turning serious. "This is a delicate matter, Thomas. We don't want to cause any harm, but we cannot risk our company's future over a disgruntled former employee."

"So, why was he disgruntled?"

Crane hesitated, then responded angrily. "He violated our confidentiality agreement by talking with an outside researcher about our projects! Fortunately, one of our people overheard him and turned him in."

Thomas nodded his head, "When you let him go, did he make any demands?"

"He hasn't made any *specific* demands yet," Crane admitted. "But we suspect he's looking for some kind of financial compensation."

Thomas nodded, yawning. "Alright, then why not just buy him off? Might be cheaper in the long run."

Crane leaned forward again, a steely glint in his eye. "Because we will *not* be blackmailed! To avoid that, we need you to use your expertise to locate Kim and remove any proof he may have. We don't want to get the authorities involved at this time, so we need you to be discreet. Can you handle that?" He challenged.

Thomas grinned, a flash of excitement in his eyes. "No problem! Consider it done. Is there anything else?"

"No." Crane shook his head, indicating that the meeting was over.

Thomas rose from his seat, thanked the man for his time, then made his way out of the office. As he walked down the hallway, he pulled out his cellphone and sent a text to Peter Barlowe, requesting all information on the present whereabouts of one David Kim.

Once back inside his car, he opened his laptop and began searching for any information he could find on Kim. He searched through public records, social media profiles, and news articles, but found nothing that could help him.

Frustrated, Thomas closed his laptop and leaned back in his seat, hoping that his buddy, Peter, would have more luck. He knew that it would be wise to start several things in motion at once to ensure that he would be able to track David Kim down in a reasonable amount of time. Suddenly, an idea struck him. He remembered a private investigator, Kelly Brown, he had worked with on a previous job. That investigator was very skilled at finding people and had access to a few more local resources than Thomas did. He quickly called the P.I. and explained the situation. Fortunately, the freelancer agreed to take on the job and promised to have information for Thomas within a few days.

As Thomas drove away from the office building, he turned on some Frank Sinatra and rolled down the windows to light a cigarette, letting the warm spring air flow through the car. *"Glad that's over!"* he thought to himself, covering yet another yawn with his hand.

Chapter 25

I Didn't Think It Would Be Fun

Thomas scheduled the long-awaited second meeting with Martin Blake in the lobby of a nearby hotel in Tucson, Arizona. He arrived early, as was normal for him, scouting out a discreet corner booth where they could talk without being overheard. He was going to find it interesting to see Martin again after the hotel incident with the dominatrix. Considering the incident, he was going to have to make a real effort to hold back from laughing. That had been a unique moment in both their lives, Thomas snickered to himself.

After a few minutes of Thomas' waiting, Martin arrived, looking decidedly unenthusiastic about it. Thomas stood up to greet him, offering a handshake and a knowing little smile. "Hello, it is good to see you walking again without looking like it hurts!" Thomas said. He just couldn't resist. Blake's cheeks blushed, but he didn't say anything, obviously preferring to let it slide.

They took their seats and Thomas leaned back while stretching his arms comfortably across the booth sides. He got straight to the matter at hand. "So, what do you have for me?" he asked in a low voice. Martin shifted uncomfortably in his seat, clearly unhappy about being there. Blake just looked at him but didn't offer anything but a sullen expression on his chubby face.

Not liking how this was starting, Thomas leaned forward, his tone hardening. "You *agreed* to this, Marty! I need information on these people, and you're the one who is supposed to give it to me. Though I *do* remember someone giving it to *you* rather passionately at the hotel where I first I met you." Thomas let that little memory percolate for a moment, then said, his voice low and dangerous. "Just remember, if anyone finds out about *that* little incident, it could be *very* embarrassing for you and for your family."

Martin's face went pale, and he looked as if he might be sick.

"So, let's hear it." Thomas said sternly, tired of having to remind this shithead who the boss was.

Martin sighed heavily, apologizing and reluctantly began to speak, giving Thomas the juicy details about each person on the list Thomas had originally given to him - their personal lives, their habits, the people they associate with. Thomas listened intently, taking notes, and mentally filing away the useful bits of information for later use.

However, as they talked further and Blake loosened up, Thomas began to see him in a different light. He realized that Martin wasn't just some sleazy informant - he was also a person in his own right with hopes, dreams, and fears, just like everyone else. His reluctance to 'rat' on the listed folks was actually because of his Christian principle of "Do unto others...". Once he realized this, Thomas started to relax a little, asking the hard questions in a less threatening way.

Martin then surprised Thomas by offering to buy him a drink. At first, Thomas was hesitant - he had never socialized with a 'mark' before. But something in Martin's demeanor made him feel like it might be a good idea, and so he changed the subject.

"So, Martin, what do you do for fun? Of course, I mean besides the bedroom stuff!" Thomas asked, almost choking on his drink as he laughed.

Martin looked surprised and wary at the unexpected question but answered anyway. "Uh, I don't have much free time, but I like to go fishing when I can."

Thomas stopped snickering, genuinely interested. "That sounds like fun. I haven't been fishing in ages. Maybe we should go sometime if you're interested?"

Martin looked at Thomas skeptically, but a small smile played at the corners of his mouth. "You *fish*, Thomas?! I can't picture it."

Thomas chuckled, thinking back through his memories. "Believe it or not, I used to go all the time with my dad when I was a kid." He made a face. "It's been a while, but I think I still remember how to do it."

Martin seemed to relax a little at that, and they continued small talking more amiably now. Thomas couldn't help but feel a little bit guilty for using Martin the way he had been for information but, at the same time, he was starting to see Blake as potentially more than just a means to an end.

Thomas found himself telling Martin about some of his own interests outside of work. In that moment, it felt like they were just two guys having a friendly chat, rather than a gruff detective and his reluctant source. Thomas leaned forward and asked, "What else do you like to do in your free time?"

Martin hesitated for a moment before answering. "Honestly, not much. I usually just go home and watch TV or read a book. I'm not really the outgoing type."

Thomas nodded understandingly. "I get it. Sometimes it's nice to just relax and unwind. What's your favorite book?"

Blake's face lit up, and Thomas could see a spark of genuine enthusiasm in his eyes. "Oh, I love sci-fi and fantasy. My favorite book is *The Lord of the Rings*. I've read it so many times, I've lost count."

Thomas smiled, knowing from his own experience what Martin meant. "That's a classic! I'm more of a crime thriller kind of guy myself, but I can appreciate a good fantasy novel. Have you ever read the *Harry Potter* series?"

Martin nodded eagerly, clearly enjoying the direction of the conversation now. "Yes, I love those books, too! They're so well-written and engaging. I feel like I'm in another world when I read them."

For the next few minutes, Thomas and Martin chatted about their favorite books and movies, laughing and joking now like old friends. Truthfully, it was a side of Thomas that few people ever saw - relaxed, friendly, and genuinely interested in getting to know someone better.

Blake took a deep breath, looking down at his hands. "I always wanted to be a musician, you know," he said quietly. "But my parents were never supportive of it. They just wanted me to go to college, get a degree, and have a stable job. I guess I just didn't have the courage to go against their wishes. They sacrificed a lot for me."

Thomas nodded sympathetically. "I understand. Sometimes it's hard to go after what we really want, especially if it means going against our parents."

Martin grinned and looked up at that, "Thanks for understanding, Thomas. You know, you're not really like other people I've met. You seem...*different* somehow."

Thomas chuckled. "I'll take that as a compliment, then! But really, I'm just doing my job, like anyone else. It's not always glamorous, but it pays the bills."

They chatted for another hour, discussing their shared love of jazz music and their favorite musicians. Martin was surprised by how easy it was to talk to Thomas when they weren't discussing business matters. Thomas settled back in his seat, taking a sip of his drink. "So, Martin, what the hell made you decide to get into *accounting*, of all things?!"

Blake shrugged. "It was the practical choice, I guess. I was good with numbers, and I figured it was a stable career path. Plus, it pays well."

Thomas nodded thoughtfully. "For my part, I always wanted to be a detective when I was younger, but I ended up taking a different path."

Martin raised an eyebrow. "Detective, huh? You seem to have a knack for it from what I've seen."

Thomas chuckled. "It's just a job, Martin. But thanks! It must have been the influence of all those Mickey Spillane novels I read growing up."

As the evening wore on, Thomas realized that he was genuinely enjoying Martin's company. It was a strange feeling, considering that they had met under such odd circumstances, but there was something about Martin's quiet, unassuming demeanor that Thomas found refreshing. Even Martin's earnest, chubby face had grown on him.

As they prepared to leave, Thomas shook Martin's hand. "Thanks for the chat, Martin. It was good to get to know you a little better."

Martin looked up at him, surprised. "Really? I mean, I guess I didn't think this would be...fun, you know?"

Thomas chuckled and tossed over his shoulder on the way out, "Yeah, me either, but sometimes it's nice to just talk, isn't it?" and headed for the car, whistling.

Chapter 26

Me, Too

Thomas sat in his car, beads of sweat trickling down his forehead as the scorching sun beat down on him. The heat seemed to penetrate his skin, making him feel sticky and uncomfortable. He took a long drag on his cigarette, inhaling the bitter smoke deep into his lungs. The car radio blared out the haunting melody of a blues song, the soulful voice of the singer filled with pain and longing. Thomas found himself lost in the music and equally lost in thought as he pondered the frustrating complexities of life. Some cars honked impatiently in the long line moving at a snail's pace, but Thomas barely noticed. His mind was focused on the pain and suffering that came with growing old. It seemed unfair to him that people had to endure so much physical and emotional anguish as they aged.

He took another drag on his cigarette, the smoke curling around his face like a veil. He thought about his *own* mortality, and the fact that he was certainly not getting any younger himself. He wondered if he would end up like the people he had seen in nursing homes, their bodies frail and their minds deteriorating. *"Depressing thought!"* he commented internally. The singer's voice reached a crescendo, and Thomas felt a parallel upswelling of emotion. He crushed out the cigarette and tried to resist the tug of the strong emotions in him but was only partially successful.

As the traffic slowly inched forward, Thomas lit another cigarette and exhaled a cloud of smoke out the window. The blues music on the radio spoke to him in a way he couldn't quite explain. The lyrics were filled with pain and longing, and Thomas felt a sense of empathy for the singer's woes. He looked around at the other cars on the road, feeling a sense of disconnection from the world. Everyone seemed to be in such a rush, going about their business without a second thought for anyone else. It was a lonely feeling being stuck in traffic with so many people around, yet still feeling like an outsider looking in.

The heat was oppressive, the sun beating down on the car relentlessly. Thomas wiped sweat from his brow, feeling exhaustion creeping over him. He wondered just how many more years he could keep this up; i.e., the long hours, the stress, the constant pressure to perform. It all seemed so pointless in the grand scheme of things. He took a drag from his cigarette and closed his eyes to let the blues wash over him, getting lost in the raw emotion of the singer's voice.

As if on cue, the traffic finally began to move again, and Thomas snapped back to reality. He flicked the cigarette out the window and put the car into gear, ready to face whatever lay ahead in the day to come.

Just then, his phone rang. It was his lovely neighbor, Gabrielle, asking if she could see him when he had a moment. Thomas replied that he was running some errands, but he could swing by her apartment later that evening when he got home.

Gabrielle seemed hesitant on the phone and Thomas could tell she was holding something back. "What's up, Gabby? Is something wrong?" he asked.

"No, no, nothing's wrong, just thinking." she answered in the time-honored fashion of women everywhere in that her answer just begged more questions from the hapless male in her sights--- which happened to be Thomas, of course!

He gently prodded her to explain, but she insisted that it wasn't the right time or place to discuss it. Instead, she suggested as though she had just now thought of it that they relax and watch a movie together on her couch later that night. Thomas was naturally curious about what was on Gabrielle's mind, but he didn't want to push too hard. He agreed to the movie like any male of sane mind. As the traffic began to clear and Thomas resumed his journey, he felt anticipation building inside him.

114

After completing his errands, Thomas parked his car outside their apartment building and made his way to Gabrielle's door. She answered quickly, after only one knock, wearing a comfortable-looking sweater and jeans.

"Hey, good-looking!" she said, smiling at him. "Thanks for coming over."

"No problem, I appreciate the invitation," Thomas replied. "So, what's going on? You gave me the impression you wanted to talk about something." He added this a bit warily, although he knew that Gabby was different from Evelyn Perdita.

Gabrielle's apartment was a cozy haven that reflected her personality. Neat and organized, everything in its place, from the patterned throw pillows on the plush couch to the intricately arranged family photos on the walls. The living room was brightly decorated, with cheerful colors like sunny yellow and soft pink. There was a small bookshelf in the corner, filled with religious tracts and various devotional materials. The dining room had a homey feel to it with a small, wooden table and mismatched chairs. A vase of fresh flowers sat in the center, bringing a burst of color into the space. The kitchen was compact, but well-equipped, with gleaming stainless-steel appliances and plenty of counter space. A faint scent of vanilla lingered in the air, most likely from the freshly baked cookies Gabrielle loved to make. She was a burgeoning health-nut, so she made them more for the smell and to give away than to eat them herself.

As she led him into the living room, he noticed her bedroom door was open and snuck a peek inside. He had never been in there before and was curious. The one time they were intimate, it was at Thomas' place. Her bedroom was simple and serene, with a fluffy, white comforter on the bed and a cross hanging on the wall above the headboard. Thomas was just glad that the cross wasn't mounted by a full-form statue of Jesus bleeding with a crown of thorns adorning his head. That would be a bit daunting for a lovelorn suitor on his first visit to her bedroom! Soft sunlight filtered through the gauzy, white curtains and created a warm and peaceful ambiance. The bathroom was immaculately tidy with gleaming white tiles and neatly arranged toiletries. Overall, Gabrielle's apartment felt like a tranquil oasis, a place of comfort and calm in a weather-tossed world.

Once they had settled on the couch, Thomas noticed that she had already set up a movie on the TV and it was ready to go. "What are we watching?" he asked with a smile, sliding closer to her.

"An old favorite of mine," she said, tilting her head and looking up at him with her big, beautiful blue eyes. "It's a classic noir film." Gabrielle's expression then changed to contemplation. "You know, I was watching one of those talent shows earlier," she began, her voice tinged with perplexity. "It strikes me as odd how often the singers come out on top. They're up against performers who've devoted their lives to honing rare and risky skills, yet all it takes is a well-delivered cover of a popular song for a singer to win."

Thomas, keen on Gabrielle's sharp insight, leaned in, encouraging her to continue.

"There's something fundamentally wrong about it," she pressed on, her hands gesturing expressively. "They're just borrowing someone else's art," she continued, her words flowing more freely now. "Most of these songs are timeless hits, familiar to everyone. It lacks a certain... creative spirit. And isn't singing one of the most common talents?"

Thomas nodded, his eyes reflecting agreement. "That's a great observation," he remarked.

Gabrielle leaned in, her blue eyes bright with fervor. "There should be a rule for singers in these competitions. They should write their own songs. That would level the playing field. Otherwise, it's unfair to non-singers. They're not crafting anything new, just echoing someone else's creation."

A grin emerged on Thomas' face, mirroring Gabrielle's passion for the subject. "You've said it perfectly," he expressed, his tone rich with enthusiasm. "It's a reflection of the superficial idolization we see so often today. We're missing out on the true essence of talent."

116

Gabrielle's expression grew more intense, her passion for the subject evident. "Talent shows ought to be about celebrating innovation, genuine creativity, not just about who can best mimic an existing song."

"Absolutely," Thomas replied, his voice echoing her sentiment. "It's high time we redefined our perceptions of talent."

After a few chuckles, Gabrielle started the movie. As the movie began, Thomas found himself relaxing in the comfortable surroundings. Gabrielle seemed at ease, so he decided whatever it was she wanted to talk about couldn't be that important. Thinking logically, he figured they'd get to whatever it was after the movie. Logical, but also absolutely wrong.

Gabrielle spoke shyly, "Thomas, there's something I need to tell you."

Thomas, having been caught completely off guard, felt his heart rate increase. He braced himself for the worst, expecting her to reveal some terrible secret or dark truth.

However, when Gabrielle spoke next, her words bushwhacked him. "I'm starting to have strong feelings for you, Thomas," she said, her eyes looking down at her lap with her hands interlocked across her tummy.

Thomas was flat-out stunned. He felt a rush of conflicting emotions - surprise, confusion, fear, and a small spark of hope. He had always felt a strong and very natural connection with Gabrielle from the first moment they met, but he hadn't allowed himself to fully acknowledge his feelings for her.

As he struggled to find the right words to say, she said firmly, "I know it's a lot to take in, and I don't *expect* you to feel the same way. I just needed to tell you."

Thomas reached out and took one of her hands. "Gabby, I don't know how to say how I feel," he admitted, his voice quiet and thoughtful. Gabrielle squeezed his hand gently. "You don't have to say anything," she said softly, and repeated, "I just wanted you to know." She rested her head on his shoulder.

They sat this way in companionable silence for a while, each lost in his or her own thoughts. Finally, Thomas spoke up. "Gabrielle, I *do* care about you," he said, his voice filled with pent-up emotion. "But I need some time to figure things out. Can we just...take things slow for now?" He admitted to himself in his mind that he felt a little odd saying these words. They were usually uttered by the woman, ironically enough!

Gabrielle nodded, a small, satisfied smile on her soft, sweet lips. "Of course," she said. "I'm just glad we're talking about it." After saying this, she leaned in to kiss him, and they both took their time.

Thomas felt relief wash over him as their lips parted from each other---not because he was glad the kiss was over, but because what she had wanted to talk about was actually a *good* thing. Like all males who wish to survive in a relationship, he knew that he had a lot to think about, but, for now, he was content just to sit with her and enjoy the moment.

As the movie played on, Gabrielle snuggled up next to Thomas on the couch, resting her head on his shoulder. Thomas realized he didn't have the slightest idea what the movie was about.

"You know, this is kind of nice," he offered into the comfortable silence. "Just relaxing and watching a movie with you."

Gabrielle smiled at him with a twinkle in her eyes. "I know, right? It's almost like we're a normal couple or something."

Thomas chuckled back at her. "Yeah, I guess so! Except for the fact that I'm an insensitive asshole while you seem to be sweet and caring."

Gabrielle snorted at his descriptions. "Well, nobody's perfect."

As they sat on the couch, still snuggled up together, Thomas and Gabrielle watched the movie. The room was dark, except for the flickering light of the television. Gabrielle shifted slightly, turning to look at him, her eyes warmly affectionate. "You know," she admitted softly, almost as if she were talking to herself, "I really *like* spending time with you like this."

Thomas smiled, feeling a frisson of warmth spread through his chest. "Me, too," he replied, his voice low and husky. He reached out and took her hand in his, interlacing their fingers. She leaned in closer, and he wrapped his arm around her, pulling her even closer until they were practically wrapped around each other.

They watched the movie like that, completely lost in each other's presence. Thomas could feel Gabrielle's body pressed against his, the heat of her warming him through his clothes. He leaned in to kiss her, softly at first, then more passionately as they gave into their twin desires at last.

Chapter 27

I Don't Think I Can Stop

That next morning, Thomas once again went to meet Gabrielle at the restaurant where she was to have lunch with her Catholic church friends. Once inside, he approached her table and recognized a few familiar faces from the previous lunch discussion.

"Hey, Thomas! Welcome back!" said a few of them. "Lunch is on Thomas!" shouted another, rather hopefully, it seemed to Thomas.

Thomas just grinned at the enthusiastic welcome, but privately hoped they weren't serious about lunch being "on Thomas" again! For her part, Gabrielle just seemed glad to see that he had made it, but she snickered along with the others when Thomas blanched at paying for everyone's lunch again.

Since the food had already been ordered earlier for the whole table, they were served quickly. As they began their meal, they started discussing the existence or not of God as though this was perfectly normal lunch conversation. One of them, a small, older woman who was dressed in a habit, named Sister Anne, argued that the complexity of the world and the intricate design of the human body were ample evidence of an intelligent Creator. Another much larger woman, Linda, countered that the theory of evolution and the process of natural selection were just as valid explanations for the diversity of life on earth.

Thomas, who had always been fascinated by the gap between Faith and Science, listened intently to their conversation. He offered some of his own thoughts, pointing out that there were scientists who believed that the "Big Bang" theory was the beginning of the universe and that the concept of God could still fit into that framework.

Sister Anne nodded in agreement, surprisingly, while the other woman, Linda, looked both skeptical and still hungry. They continued to discuss different interpretations of the Bible with Thomas bringing up the rear with the story of Adam and Eve, the apple, and the snake. He argued that, while the story might not be literally true, it still had value as a metaphor for the human experience and the consequences of our actions.

Gabrielle watched Thomas with admiration in her eyes as he spoke, impressed by his depth of knowledge and thoughtful insights. Of course, she had reason to see him differently than the others because she had a major crush on him.

As the conversation wound down around the table and the attention to food went up, they all agreed to disagree. However, their fellowship certainly enjoyed an upsurge of conviviality at the arrival of dessert---pecan pie made the southern way, warm from the oven and topped with authentic whipped cream made right there on the premises.

As the diminutive Sister Anne and the larger Linda continued their little holy war discussing their differing beliefs, Thomas became completely engrossed in their conversation. He found it fascinating to hear their different viewpoints.

"I'm telling you," said Sister Anne like a pro baseball pitcher winding up for a fast ball, "God thinks about *everything* well ahead of time, believe you, me!"

Her opponent, Linda, countered quickly with, "Uh huh...then why didn't He stop that big asteroid from hitting us and starting the next ice age? How do you explain *that*?!"

The nun, shrugged and folded her arms across her chest, attempting to look down her nose at the larger woman. "I *told* you---God thinks ahead! Who do you think sent the asteroid in the first place?!"

Linda looked confused, but she wasn't the only one. Thomas wasn't so sure about how to respond to that himself, so he asked the little nun to explain.

Sister Anne seemed more agreeable since it was Thomas asking rather than her feisty opponent. "Well, if God hadn't sent that hunk of space junk to us, *we* wouldn't exist! That event is what caused the changes in our atmosphere and oceans that eventually allowed us to live at all. Do you see? God is *truly* omniscient. Thanks be to God!" And she made the sign of the cross, looking just a bit too pleased with herself, but feeling a little guilty about her own smugness at the same time. Thomas loved her answer *and* her attitude, and he realized there was plenty of scientific evidence to back up Sister Anne's assertions. He had just never thought of it that way before.

He listened carefully as the good Sister continued to speak about the intricacies of the world, pointing out how it was impossible for everything to exist *without* the guiding hand of the Creator. Linda stubbornly countered with the theory of evolution, stating that it categorically provided a more scientific explanation for the diversity of life.

This time, Thomas dove into the fray. "Linda, I don't mean to interrupt, but science is just a way of explaining things so that we can understand whatever it is or how it works in causal terms and then be able to replicate it, assuming we have all the ingredients, so to speak. That is *very* different from understanding *why* something happened in the first place. I'm a big fan of science, but don't make the mistake of thinking that *describing* something is the same as *creating* 'something', you know?", which temporarily shut up the heavy woman arguing the cause of science as she stopped to consider what he had said. To her credit, she *did* listen to the arguments of others. Of course, it didn't hurt that the pauses where someone else got the chance to speak had more to do with her tackling yet another piece of that wonderfully warm and gooey pecan pie!

As they finished their meals, the conversation drifted to other topics, such as the upcoming church fundraiser and plans for an upcoming mission trip. Gabrielle's friends asked Thomas about his own affiliation with a church, and he admitted that he didn't subscribe to any religion even though he had been raised Catholic, but rather he saw spirituality as a personal journey.

Sister Anne nodded knowingly. "I believe that God reveals himself to each of us at different times and in different ways," she said. "Whether it's through scripture or nature or even our interactions with others; there are many paths to understanding."

Thomas paused for a moment to gather his thoughts. "I think that, if there is a God, there must be a way He is revealed. It's in the beauty of the world. When we see a sunset or a rainbow, when we listen to music or admire a painting, there's something within us that stirs. It's a feeling of awe and wonder, a sense that there's something greater than ourselves at work. To me, that's evidence of a Divine Creator who imbued the world with beauty and purpose."

Gabrielle nodded in excited agreement. "I know what you mean! Sometimes, when I'm one with nature, I feel a connection to something larger than myself. It's hard to put into words, but it's a profound experience."

Jason, a regular attendee of the group who had been silent during most of the conversation, looked thoughtful. "I can see where you're coming from, but couldn't it just be a byproduct of evolution? Our brains have evolved to be stimulated by certain things, like the color, green, for example, because it helped our ancestors survive. Maybe our sense of beauty is just a result of that."

Thomas shook his head. "I don't think so. I mean, sure, evolution certainly played a role in how we perceive the world, but it doesn't explain the feeling of transcendence we get from beauty. It's something more than *just* a survival mechanism."

On this note, the group finished their meals and parted ways, with many hugs and promises to see each other soon. Even Linda embraced Sister Anne warmly. As they walked out of the restaurant, Gabrielle slipped her arm through Thomas's and leaned into him. "I'm so glad you came with me today," she said. "I always feel better after spending time with my church family."

Thomas smiled and squeezed her hand. "I'm glad I came, too," he said. "It's always good to have these kinds of conversations, to challenge our beliefs and learn from each other."

They continued walking, enjoying the warmth of the sun on their faces and the comfortable silence between them. Gabrielle suddenly stopped and turned to face Thomas, her eyes sparkling with a mischievous glint.

"You know," she said, "there's something I've been wanting to do for a while now."

Thomas raised an eyebrow, intrigued. "And what's that?"

Gabrielle kissed him on the lips, a gentle and tender gesture that spoke volumes. Thomas was momentarily stunned, but quickly responded in kind, deepening the kiss, and pulling her closer to him.

As they broke apart, Gabrielle grinned at him. "I've been wanting to do that since we got to the restaurant," she said. "And now that I have, I don't think I want to stop."

Thomas chuckled at her heartfelt confession, feeling a corresponding warmth spreading through his heart and chest. "I don't think I want you to stop, either" he admitted, pulling her in for another kiss. The rest of the world just faded away as far as the couple was concerned.

Chapter 28

Cheers To That

Thomas sniffed the air, savoring the aroma of the steak being grilled in the restaurant. The dim light of the flickering candles on each table contributed to the rich ambiance of the dining room. The female singer and piano player set up in the corner only added to the already luxurious atmosphere.

The sultry singer crooned into the microphone, singing the arrangement of "Summertime" by Ella Fitzgerald, with a smoky voice that filled the dimly lit restaurant. Her honey-brown hair cascaded down her shoulders, framing a seductive face that exuded confidence. Her curvaceous figure swayed to the rhythm of the piano player who matched her sultry tones with his fingers on the smooth keys of his instrument. Dressed in a form-fitting black dress that hugged every curve, the singer was the epitome of glamour and elegance. Her eyes seemed to twinkle with mischief as she sang, holding the attention of every patron, male *or* female, with her effortless charm.

Thomas cut into his Wagyu steak, marveling at its tenderness and flavor. Each bite was a revelation, and he savored the experience, taking his time to appreciate the meal more fully. The attentive waitstaff ensured that his wine glass was never empty, and the sommelier had recommended the perfect bottle of wine to complement the dish. Frankly, Thomas felt both pampered and indulged, luxuries he appreciated immensely.

A waiter approached Thomas's table, a polite smile on his face. "How was the steak, sir?"

Thomas took a moment to savor the last bite before responding. "Absolutely fantastic, one of the best I've had in a long time."

The waiter beamed at his praise. "I'm so glad to hear that, sir! Our chef takes great pride in his work. May I get you anything else?"

Thomas shook his head. "No, I'm good, for now. Just want to enjoy the music and the atmosphere some more."

The waiter nodded his understanding. "Ah, yes, of course, Sir. Miss Delaney is one of our regular performers. She is quite popular with our patrons."

Thomas raised an eyebrow curiously. "Miss Delaney? Is that her name?"

The waiter nodded. "Yes, sir. She's quite talented, isn't she?"

Thomas smiled appreciatively and teased the waiter. "Yes, she certainly is. I just might have to come back, if only to hear her sing again!"

The waiter chuckled. "I don't blame you, sir. Is there anything else I can do for you?" Thomas shook his head. "No, I think I'm good for now." The waiter nodded and left, and Thomas returned his attention to the restaurant around him. He was contented, full and at peace.

As he sipped his wine, he couldn't help but overhear fragments of the conversations of the other patrons. A couple at a nearby table were talking about their recent trip to Europe, mentioning the museums and historical sites they had visited. A group of businessmen were discussing their latest deals, throwing around industry jargon and impressive dollar-figures. At the bar, a pair of women were giggling and gossiping about their friends and latest dating experiences. The music and chatter blended into a comforting hum, and all these things were a reminder that Life goes on beyond the walls of Thomas' own private world.

Thomas checked his watch, noting the time. He knew that Peter would be arriving soon with the information he had requested. In the meantime, the sultry singer on the stage continued to sing, her voice like honey and bourbon, filling the room with emotion. The piano player accompanied her with expert precision, his fingers dancing over the keys. At that moment, he saw Peter Barlowe entering the restaurant, scanning the room before making his way over to Thomas' table. Barlowe had a limp, a remnant of his time with the police which had forced his early retirement.

As Barlowe approached the table, he was greeted with a smile and a firm handshake from Thomas. The man says, "Thomas, it's good to see you again!" Thomas returned the mercifully firm handshake and nods in greeting. "Likewise, Peter. Have a seat."

"I see you couldn't resist the allure of a good meal and some live music." Peter says with a smirk.

Thomas grinned back, happy to see Peter. "I figured I'd get here early and indulge a bit before we got down to business. Plus, I couldn't resist the sound of that beautiful voice."

"Can't say I blame you. She's got quite the set of pipes on her." Barlowe says with a nod of approval.

They both sat down, the waiter approaching to take the new guest's drink order. "I'll take a whiskey, neat," Peter said, glancing at Thomas. "And you?"

"I'll have another glass of red wine, please," Thomas replied. The waiter repeated their choices back to them, then left to retrieve the drinks.

As they waited, Peter leaned back in his chair and glanced around the restaurant. "You know, I've always been a fan of live music. Jazz, in particular."

Thomas nodded, taking a sip of his wine. "Me, too. There's just something about it that can't be replicated by recorded music."

"I couldn't agree more," Peter replied. "There's a certain energy that comes from live performances, a connection between the musician and the audience that's unique."

Thomas smiled. "I couldn't have said it better myself. Who's your favorite jazz artist?"

Peter leaned forward, an infectious smile spreading across his face. "You're asking me to pick just *one*?! That's impossible, but if

I had to pick, I'd say John Coltrane. His work on 'A Love Supreme' is nothing short of genius."

Thomas nodded, thinking that was a good choice. "Coltrane is definitely a legend, but I'm more of a Miles Davis fan myself, though."

By this time, the waiter had returned with their drinks, setting them down on the table with a self-satisfied smile of achievement having overcome a great challenge at personal risk. "Here you are, gentlemen. Can I get you anything else?"

Peter glanced at Thomas, who shook his head. "No, I think we're good for now. Thank you."

The waiter nodded and walked away, leaving the two men alone once again. Peter took a sip of his whiskey, savoring the burn as it slid down his throat. "God, I needed that. It's been a while since I have had a *good* whiskey."

Thomas took a sip of his red wine before shifting the conversation to the task at hand. "So, what have you learned about Samuel Nouvel?" he asked, hoping for some progress on the elusive investor.

Peter leaned back in his chair and sighed. "I wish I had more to report, but the guy is a complete enigma. He's got a web of holding companies and shell corporations that makes it nearly impossible to trace his investments or track his movements. The only thing I've been able to confirm is his heavy investment in the pharmaceutical industry and that he has significant connections in the Middle East."

Thomas frowned, disappointed. It wasn't much to go on, but it was a start. "What did you learn about those political connections?"

Peter leaned forward and lowered his voice, as if sharing a secret. "Let's just say that Nouvel has some pretty powerful friends in high places. He's got connections in some of the most influential political circles in America and overseas. From what I've been able to gather, he's been able to use those connections to his advantage in the business world."

Thomas listened closely, intrigued. "Do you think he's using his political power to gain advantage in the pharmaceutical industry in some illegal way?"

Peter shrugged. "It's hard to say for sure, but, given his investments and connections, it's certainly a possibility. The guy is a master at "playing the game", and he's got all the right pieces in place to come out on top."

After taking another sip of whiskey, he studied Thomas carefully for a moment. "So, are you *in*volved in anything with Nouvel?" he asked curiously. "Or is this purely professional curiosity?"
Thomas raised an eyebrow. "No, I'm not involved in anything with him, personally. It's just that I'm currently working with *Turner Research*, which happens to have gotten some heavy investments from him."

Peter nodded, understanding the connection. "Ah, I see. So, what exactly are you doing for *Turner Research*?" Thomas hesitated for a moment, not sure how much he wanted to reveal, even to Peter. "Just some investigative work," he said vaguely. "Trying to dig up some information on one of their former employees."

With a raised eyebrow, Barlowe was not entirely convinced by Thomas' explanation. "I *know* you, Thomas. Investigating a company that Nouvel is heavily invested in seems a bit too tame for you."

Thomas grinned, raising his hands in mock surrender. "Alright, alright, you got me. But you know the deal, Peter. I can't divulge too much about my clients or my work."

Barlowe chuckled, nodding in understanding. "Fair enough. I won't push it any further, but I will say this - if there's anyone who can get to the bottom of Nouvel's operations, it's you."

Thomas smiled, grateful for Peter's confidence. "Thanks, Peter. I appreciate that."

The waiter returned with another round of drinks, interrupting their conversation. After he left, they each took a sip of their respective drinks before Peter spoke again. "So, what's the next step? Where do we go from here?"

Thomas took a deep breath, feeling the weight of the task that lay ahead. "I think we need to focus on breaking through that wall of holding companies and shell corporations. I think it's our best shot at figuring out who Nouvel is and what he is all about."

Peter nodded thoughtfully, sipping on his whiskey. "Sounds like a plan. I'll keep digging to see what else I can find, but keep me posted, ok?"

Thomas grinned, feeling an alcohol-fueled sense of camaraderie with Peter. "Will do. But for now, how about we enjoy the rest of our drinks and this beautiful music?"

Peter raised his glass in agreement, clinking it against Thomas'. "Cheers to that!"

Chapter 29

Father And Son

Thomas woke up to the sound of his favorite symphony, the opening notes of Beethoven's Fifth filling the room. He groaned and stretched his arms and legs before getting out of bed, relishing the feeling of the cool hardwood floor under his feet. He walked over to the window and opened the blinds, letting in the warm sunlight which illuminated the room.

He walked over to his closet and took a moment to select his outfit for the day, carefully choosing a navy-blue suit that he paired with a crisp, white shirt, and a bold red tie. He spent extra time making sure his tie was perfectly centered and his collar was neatly pressed. Thomas was thorough in his preparations for everything. Clothes were just the first challenge of the day.

Next, he made his way to the bathroom, turning on the shower and adjusting the water temperature to his liking. He took his time washing his face and hair, enjoying the feel of the hot water against his skin.

After getting out of the shower, he dried off and meticulously groomed his hair, making sure every strand was perfectly in place. He walked back into his bedroom and took a moment to apply a squirt of his favorite cologne. Thomas paused for a moment, taking a sniff of the cologne he had just applied. The scent brought back memories of his youth, when he would sneak into his father's bathroom to try on his colognes.

He remembered one afternoon, when he was around 10 years old, trying out a scent that was new to him when his father unexpectedly walked in. Thomas froze, certain he was going to be scolded for going through his father's things. But, to his surprise, his father just chuckled and sat down next to him on the edge of the bathtub.

"What do you think?" his father asked, nodding toward the cologne bottle in Thomas' hand.

Thomas hesitated for a moment before admitting, "I like it. It smells fancy."

His father smiled. "Yes, it does. And you know what, son? You're fancy, too. You can be anything you want to be in this world, and you'll always be the fanciest one in the room."

It was a small moment, but one that had stuck with Thomas throughout his life. He felt a pang of sadness as he realized he hadn't spoken to his father in years, but the memory still brought a small smile to his face as he finished getting ready for the day. Thomas realized that memories like this were precious, to be remembered many times over through one's life.

As he stood in front of the mirror for one more double-check, he noticed the necklace with the cross hanging from it. It was the symbol of a father sacrificing his son for the redemption of humanity. It was a powerful image, one that resonated deep within him. The relationship between a father and son was a theme that had always fascinated him, both in literature and in his personal life.

He thought back to the story of Abraham and Isaac wherein a father was willing to sacrifice his own son to obey God's will. It was the ultimate test of faith and obedience. It was also a difficult story to comprehend, but it certainly was one that spoke to the complex nature of the father-son relationship.

It was hard for him to reconcile the idea of a loving father with the memories of his own absent father, but he couldn't deny the comfort he found in the symbol of the cross as a reminder of extreme sacrifice and total forgiveness.

As he continued to get ready, his mind drifted to his own relationship with his father. He was a man he barely knew, who had abandoned him and his mother when he was just a child. It was a wound that had never fully healed, a void that seemed as though it could never be filled. The truth was that, in the absence of his father, he had found solace in his mother who had been

132

both mother *and* father to him. He wondered what his life would have been like if his father had stayed. Would Thomas have had a stronger sense of identity and purpose? Would he have been a different person altogether? These thoughts of his father and their fractured relationship flooded his mind. A lump formed in his throat, and he felt the sting of tears welling up in his eyes.

This was a familiar feeling, one that still seemed to surface at the most unexpected times. Even the simplest of things could set this off, like watching a father and son bonding on the TV screen or seeing a father and young son walking hand-in-hand on the street could set off this strong emotional reaction. He didn't know why it happened, and this frustrated him.

Thomas took a deep breath and fought back the tears. He knew he couldn't let himself be consumed by these feelings, especially not today. He had work that needed doing and a job to focus on, but the emotional tug-of-war inside him continued to simmer beneath the surface.

As Thomas started to prepare breakfast, the aroma of sizzling bacon and brewing coffee filled the air. He cracked a few eggs into a bowl and scrambled them, his mind still wandering as he continued to think about his cruelly absent father.

Once breakfast was completely ready, he settled down at the kitchen table and turned on the news. The screen flickered to life, showing images of war and reports of political strife, reminding him of the darker side of humanity.

Thomas' eyes flicked towards the television screen as the national news-anchor reported yet another gruesome crime. A woman in Mississippi had pushed her car off a bridge, deliberately leaving her children inside. He shook his head, his disgust for humanity was growing more profound with each passing day. How could anyone be capable of such horrors? How could humans be so unutterably cruel and heartless? He took a bite of his eggs, but they were suddenly tasteless. He switched to drinking more of his coffee, hoping to push away the bad feelings that were creeping in.

It seemed like every news story was worse than the last. Wars, famine, political corruption, and senseless violence filled the headlines. Cumulatively, it was hard to stomach, and he could not help but wonder if there was any hope left for the future of humanity. He decided that he was officially horrified. Didn't take long for that to happen when he watched the news!

He took another sip of his coffee, the warmth of the brew spreading through his stomach. As he continued to watch the news, his thoughts drifted to the people *behind* the stories. Both the victims and the perpetrators were making choices that affected the world around them.

He got up from the table and put his dishes in the sink. While passing by his bedroom door, he glanced once again at the cross hanging on the mirror. Despite his doubts about God, it served as a reminder to Thomas that there was potentially something greater in the world. While he didn't consider himself a particularly religious person, he did admire the emphasis that many religions placed upon compassion, kindness, and forgiveness. "Maybe," he thought to himself, "it isn't about following a specific doctrine or belief system, but about embodying these attitudes in our daily lives?".

Chapter 30

It Works Both Ways

Thomas stood in the man's dingy living room, breathing heavily from his recent exertions. The room was sparsely furnished with only a few pieces of mismatched furniture scattered about. There was a large window occupying one wall and the curtains were drawn tightly shut, letting only a sliver of light filter through. A bookshelf sat in the corner, filled with dusty old books, and a few family photos hung crookedly on the wall. A faded rug covered the center of the floor, and it provided little cushion for the man, Jacob Cummings, as his head bounced off the floor. Thomas was trying hard not to hurt him *too* much, but the sound of Cummings' head whacking the floor pleased him greatly at this moment. The man had refused to cooperate at the beginning of their meeting, so Thomas had been forced to adopt more forceful measures to ensure compliance. Unfortunately for Cummings, he was still stubbornly putting up a fight. His long, sandy blonde hair was a mess after the repeated bouncing of his head off the floor. His plain white t-shirt and faded blue jeans were now stained with dirt and sweat from the struggle. Despite the beating he had taken, the man remained annoyingly defiant.

"What the *HELL* is your problem?!" Thomas frustratedly demanded of the still struggling man. "Give it up already!" He held the man face-down on the thin rug with his right hand holding a handful of his dirty blonde hair while putting his right knee into the small of the man's back.

Cummings howled into the floor, "Owwwww!", then coughed at the dust coming off the dirty rug.

"Listen to me, dumb bunny! I already told you *before* to keep your mouth shut about *Turner Research*," Thomas yelled, "and now I find that you have been a *very* bad boy. Didn't you ever

135

hear that 'loose lips sink ships? I've been patient with you, but no more, do you hear me, Jakey?" He ground his knee in to emphasize his complete seriousness, but the sudden escalation in pain inspired Cummings to desperately roll out from underneath Thomas' hurtful knee. The man sneered and lunged at Thomas, grabbing a nearby vase, and swinging it at his head. Thomas ducked just in time and knocked the vase out of the Cummings' hand. It shattered noisily on the floor. "You know, you're just making a mess, and it's not going to help you any."

"You think you can scare me?" the man spat, having grabbed a lamp this time. He brandished it like a spear, jabbing it at Thomas threateningly, but only managing to look comical. "I'm not afraid of you!"

Thomas shook his head, thinking that this idiot was slow to learn, and stepped forward, dodging the man's clumsy stabs with the lamp and delivered a swift kick to the back of the man's knee. "You *should* be," Thomas said in response, and quickly grabbed the man in a headlock from behind and cut off Cummings' air supply with his forearm. "You're going to pass out, if you don't stop struggling," Thomas warned, tightening his grip. "And after you wake up, we're going to do this all over again. Fun, huh?" Thomas deliberately laughed as though this last statement of his was the very height of humor. "I've got time, believe me!"

The man gurgled and thrashed, trying to break free, but eventually, he went limp in Thomas' grip. Thomas reduced his pressure on the man's throat then stepped back, watching as the man gasped for breath.

"I'm sorry it had to come to this," Thomas said, straightening his tie. "But you left me no choice. You're going to keep your mouth shut on your own, or it will be shut *permanently*. Understand what I'm saying to you, Jakey?"

Cummings' face was red and swollen. His eyes finally filled with fear as he realized his danger. Thomas could see a real change of heart going on right before his eyes.

"You're going to stay silent about *Turner Research* and anyone who works there," Thomas said firmly. "I don't care what kind of shit you *think* you know." He mentally chuckled to himself and added, "'You know nothing, my little bunny!' You're going to keep your mouth shut. Understand?"

The man nodded frantically, still gasping for air and looked up at Thomas, confused and panicky. What he saw in Thomas' face did little to reassure him, and he gasped out, "Y-yes, I understand. I won't say anything. I swear!"

Thomas studied the man for a moment, making sure he was sincere. Satisfied with his assessment, he stepped back, leaving room for the sobbing man to get up off the floor. He looked down at Cummings with a mixture of frustration and disappointment. "I can't believe it had to come to this," he said, shaking his head.

The man coughed, his eyes wide with fear. "You have no idea what you're involved in," he sputtered out.

Thomas scoffed. "I've heard *that* before, but you know what really gets me?" He adjusted his suit jacket, composing himself. "I hate it when I can't just talk my way through a situation. But, no, you just *had* to be difficult." He leaned in close to the man's face. "Now, are we clear? You're not going to say a word to anyone. Got it?"

The man nodded weakly, his eyes still wide with fear. Thomas stood up straight, dusting off his pants as best he could from the dirty floor. "Good. Then I suggest you buy yourself something nice." He said, while throwing an envelope of cash at the man. "See?" he said. "It works both ways. There might be more where that came from if you're good. You already know what happens if you're not!"

Thomas then walked over and stood in front of the mirror brushing off his suit jacket. As he straightened up, he noticed that a button had popped off his dress shirt, leaving a small gap at the top of his chest.

"Great," he thought to himself, *"now I look like I'm auditioning for the role of an Italian mobster."*

He tried to smooth out the shirt as best he could, but the gap remained. With a sigh, he grabbed his jacket and made his way out of the house, trying his best to avoid any extra scrutiny from the neighbors.

As he got in his car, he reached for the list he had provided Martin Blake, his new sort-of friend with the odd sexual interests. He glanced at it before taking out a pen and crossing out one of the names, Jacob Cummings. It was a small victory, but still a victory, nonetheless. Thomas still had more names on the list to visit, but not today.

He drove away from Cummings' house, the adrenaline of the scuffle still coursing through his veins. He took a deep breath to relax. As he exhaled, he reached for a pack of cigarettes and lit one, watching the smoke swirl around the car and out the open window.

When he heard the opening riff of Muddy Waters' "Mannish Boy" coming from the radio, a smile spread across his face. He so enjoyed the bluesy guitar sound as it filled the car. This was his kind of music. He turned up the volume and let the song wash over him. The driving rhythm and gritty lyrics were a perfect match for his mood. He felt alive and in control, even more so because of the violence he had just experienced.

Thomas tapped his fingers on the steering wheel while muttering some of the lyrics, nodding his head along to the beat. The cigarette dangled from his lips, almost forgotten as he sang along with the final chorus. He felt a strong sense of satisfaction wash over him at a job well done, but he also felt a curious remorse. This was not normal for him, but he dismissed the thought and crushed the butt of the cigarette out in the ashtray as he drove off into the distance.

Chapter 31

Don't Be Shy, Baby

Thomas and Darius were shooting pool and having a few drinks at their favorite bar. They were both relaxed, enjoying the evening, and catching up on each other's lives. Darius spoke about his job as a bouncer at *The Night Stick*, a strip club in the city of Phoenix. Thomas kept mentioning Gabrielle, though not to Darius' surprise, considering she was Thomas' new love-interest.

The bar was dimly lit, with soft lighting casting a warm glow over the space. The walls were paneled in a dark wood of some kind, and the floors were covered in well-worn hardwood. The bar itself stretched the length of the room, with a polished brass rail running along the edge. The bar stools were plush and well-worn, with dark leather. Behind the bar, shelves were stocked with an impressive array of bottles, all of them lit from underneath their shelves. A large pool table dominated one corner of the room, with smaller tables scattered throughout the space. The walls were adorned with vintage beer signs, and a jukebox played old rock and blues tunes softly in the background.

Thomas laughed and shook his head. "Man, I can't believe you still work at that place! How do you put up with all those crazy guys and naked women all the time?"

Darius grinned. "It's not all bad, man. I get to meet some interesting people, and the pay is decent. Plus, I get to be my own boss in a way, you know?"

Darius took a sip of his drink before launching into a story with a grin on his face. "Bro, you won't believe what happened the other night at the club. This drunk guy stumbled in and started throwing cash around like he was made of money. I mean, he was practically bathing in it."

"Go on." Thomas said.

"Well, he kept ordering lap dances from all the girls, but he was so wasted he couldn't even sit up straight. At one point, he fell off the chair and hit his head on the stage. The DJ had to cut the music and turn on the lights to get everyone to stop and see if he was okay. Then, the guy gets back up in his seat, only to toss more money at the dancers while proceeding to throw up all over the place!" Darius chuckles as he shakes his head in disbelief. "Bro, you would not believe the amount of vomit this dude spewed all over the VIP section. It was like he had been saving it up for weeks just for that one special moment! I mean, I've seen some strange shit in my time, but that was just disgusting." He paused for a moment, a sly grin creeping onto his face. "But the best part was when he tried to stand up and slipped in his own puke. He went down *hard*, man. The look on his face was priceless!"

Thomas broke out laughing at the mental image, shaking his head in amusement. "That sounds fucking nasty!"

Darius nodded in agreement. "Yeah, it was definitely one for the books. But hey, at least he left a lot of cash for the girls to split. They were happy about *that*, even if I was the one who had to clean up the mess!"

The friends decided to shoot some pool and just gabbed about whatever. However, as Thomas leaned over the table to take a shot, he was surprised when he caught sight of the man they had seen once before in the same bar, and the stranger was watching him again, just like the last time he and Darius had been there. The man's gaze was riveted on Thomas, not Darius, and it made him uneasy. The man was wearing a well-tailored dress shirt and dress slacks, and he had salt and pepper hair that gave him a distinguished air, even though he acted like a stalker.

Despite his unease, Thomas took his shot and kept playing pool with Darius, trying to ignore the man, but he couldn't shake his awareness of the man watching him. It made his skin crawl and his shots wild. Suddenly, he realized that there was something naggingly familiar about this guy. Hadn't he seen him before?

Darius noticed Thomas's distraction and followed his gaze to the man in question. "Yo, you good, bro?" he asked his friend, sensing something was off. Thomas shook his head, grunting in the negative, he was still trying to place where he had seen the man before.

"*That's* the guy from last time," Thomas said, sounding disturbed.

Darius furrowed his brow and looked over at the man. "*That* guy?"

"Yeah, he is the same one who was watching us as we left the last time we were here," Thomas reminds him.

Darius squinted his eyes and looked at the man again more carefully. "Oh yeah, I remember him now. What do you think he is doing here again?"

"I have no idea," Thomas replied, taking a sip of his drink. "But I'm considering confronting him about it."

Darius shook his head. "Bar fight! Nah, man, just ignore the guy. He probably just thinks you're sooo good looking or something," referring to an episode of *Seinfeld* on TV. Then, the beginning-to-be-wasted Darius made girly eyes at Thomas and broke up laughing at himself as he spilled his drink.

Thomas chuckled. "Thanks for the compliment, but I don't think that's it. Are you going to clean that up?" He pointed at the spilled drink.

Darius shrugged his shoulders. "The waitress will get it. Well, whatever it is, it's probably nothing. Let's just play pool and forget about it."

Darius took a sip of his beer and looked Thomas up and down. "Bro, speaking of being eye candy for the men, what's up with that unbuttoned shirt? You're starting to look like some kind of Guido or something," he says with a laugh.

Thomas chuckled and rolled his eyes. "Hey, I was just trying to look good for you, man," he joked.

Darius smirked and shook his head. "Don't flatter yourself, bro. Even if I was back in prison, I wouldn't touch you," he quipped, taking another sip of his beer.

Thomas laughed. "You know you wouldn't pass *this* butt up." he said sarcastically, grabbing his cue stick and lining up for his next shot. "I popped a button while I was out today and didn't have time to go change."

Darius put the thin end of his cue stick between his legs with the thicker, larger part, exposed. "Bro, you wouldn't want that sweet boy ass of yours to pop like that button. So be glad we ain't in prison, man, and the fact you are my boy!"

Turning around, Thomas noticed that the man who had been watching him was gone, so he started to relax. He turned to Darius and started joking around, both laughing as they finished their last of their drinks. As they headed out, Thomas thanked Darius for the fun night and the two of them headed to their cars.

As Thomas walked towards his car, he felt someone's eyes on his back. He quickly scanned the area and saw nothing out of the ordinary. Nevertheless, he couldn't shake off the feeling of being watched. He lit a cigarette, took a long drag, and exhaled a plume of smoke into the night sky, wondering if it was his imagination kicking into overdrive.

He drove off, but he kept checking his rearview mirror just the same. *"Can't be too careful after the day I've had!"* He thought to himself, but the streets were empty. He felt sure it was the same man who had been watching him earlier. He shook his head, dismissing the thought.

Before too long, Thomas arrived at his apartment and parked his car. He sat in the driver's seat for a moment, lost in thought. He knew he had to let go of his paranoia, so he took another drag from his cigarette and finally got out of the car, ready to put it all behind him.

He walked up to his front door, fumbling with his keys, and his phone buzzed in his pocket. Pulling it out to look at the screen, he saw Evelyn Perdita's name pop up and sighed, suspecting what she wanted. He hesitated before answering, knowing it would be better if he didn't hear her sultry voice, but he realized he couldn't ignore her forever.

"Hey," he answered, trying to keep his voice neutral.

"Hey, yourself," Evelyn purred. "What are you up to tonight?"

Thomas hesitated before replying. "Just got home. Why?"

"I was hoping to see you," she said coyly. "Maybe I could come over and have a drink with you?"

Thomas felt a twinge of guilt as he immediately thought of his next-door neighbor, Gabrielle, but he couldn't deny the pull of Evelyn's seductive intentions. "I don't know if that's a good idea," he said weakly.

"Come on, Thomas," she coaxed. "Don't be like that. You *know* you want to see me."

Thomas sighed, shamefully giving in. "Fine, you can come over for a little while, but just for a drink."

Evelyn's voice turned playful. "Oh, I'm sure we can find something else to do besides just drinking." And she hung up, victorious.

Thomas felt his face flush as the call disconnected. He knew he was playing with fire, but he couldn't seem to resist Evelyn's manipulations, even when he *knew* she was doing it! He decided it would be wiser to go to her place instead, not wanting to risk Gabrielle seeing Evelyn arrive at his home, especially at that time of night. He called Evelyn back and said he was coming over there. She agreed but sounded amused. As he walked to his car, he couldn't shake the feeling that he was making a huge mistake.

Thomas had the whole drive over to Evelyn's place to develop a frothy mix of equal parts guilt and anticipation. He hesitated only a moment after Evelyn opened the door wearing only a silk robe, revealing her lacy lingerie underneath. He knew he shouldn't be there, but his resolve to leave after a single, friendly drink had suddenly vanished. She reached out and pulled him in the doorway, but all he could do was reach for her hungrily.

She leaned in close, her breath warm on his ear, as she whispered seductively, "Don't be shy, baby. I've been waiting for you fuck me senseless."

He tried to resist, but her touch was electric, and he found himself powerless to resist her charms. As she led him further into her apartment, she slowly removed her robe, revealing more of her toned body.

At that moment, the last of Thomas' willpower to resist vanished like water drops on a hot skillet and he knew he was in deep trouble. He followed her into the bedroom and lost himself in pleasure, but somehow, the guilt stubbornly refused to completely go away.

Chapter 32

Run, Thomas, Run

Thomas woke up to the sound of his phone ringing. He groggily reached over to the nightstand to answer it. As he fumbled for the phone, his eyes landed on Evelyn lying next to him, the blanket only partially covering her naked body. He had spent most of the night with her in an intimate way, and it was clear that she was still fast asleep. Her nude body was distracting him from the phone call, but he eventually managed to answer.

"Hello?" Thomas muttered into the phone, trying to shake the sleep from his voice.

"Thomas, it's Kelly Brown. Just wanted you to know I found David Kim," the investigator announced triumphantly on the other end.

Thomas struggled to focus on what Kelly was saying. He was still lost in the sight of Evelyn's naked body. But he managed to reply, "What?! That's awesome! Where is he?"

"He's at his aunt's house in Mesa," Kelly replied. "I'll text you the address."

"Got it and thank you!" Thomas responded, quickly ending the call. He let out a deep breath, still feeling half-awake. He knew he had to get up and start moving, but the sight of Evelyn's nakedness made it much more difficult for him to leave the bed.

He successfully managed to exit without waking Evelyn. As he got dressed, she stirred and opened her eyes, giving him a sleepy smile. "You're not leaving here *yet*! I still have plans for you." She said seductively, lifting the blanket to entice him to get back into bed with her.

While her charms had been effective the night before when she caught Thomas off-guard, such was not the case in the morning. He still reacted with the normal morning erection at the sight of a beautiful naked woman begging for attention, but he was much more in charge of his libido this morning. He smiled politely and turned away from the invitation to continue getting dressed in last night's clothes. He was determined not to make this mistake again.

Evelyn pouted. This was not going the way she had planned.

For his part, Thomas just kept going. *"Run, Thomas, run!"* he thought to himself, but he forced himself to walk, just for appearance's sake.

Chapter 33

Nothing Is More Important Than Family

Thomas pulled up to the address of the house that the investigator, Kelly Brown, had provided him earlier on the phone. It was now early afternoon, and he had arrived later than he wanted because he had to go home to shower and change clothes. As he drove slowly down the street, he surveyed the neighborhood, making sure to keep an eye on any people coming and going just in case the mark he was ultimately searching for made an appearance.

The house itself was a modest single-story residence with a well-kept front yard and a few potted plants lining the walkway. It was painted a pale-yellow color with white trim and had a small porch with a rocking chair and a small table. The windows were covered with simple white curtains, but Thomas thought he could see some movement inside as he approached. Someone had been at the window and peeking out the curtains.

He parked his car on the street and got out, taking a moment to adjust himself. He walked up the walkway and knocked on the door, waiting patiently for someone to answer.

The door suddenly swung open revealing a plump, kindly-looking woman in her early sixties. She stood there wearing nothing but a big smile, her gray hair neatly combed and pinned up. "I've been waiting for you!" she said cheerfully.

Thomas must have jumped a foot in the air, he was so shocked. He had to fight the urge to make the sign of the cross at the appearance of the crazy, naked woman who was clearly glad to see him! "Excuse me!" he said quickly. "I must have the wrong house." With that, Thomas turned and started to run away from the second naked woman of his day. If he had still been sleepy, he wasn't anymore!

She looked confused at his reaction. She called out to his retreating back, "Aren't you the masseur I requested?"

Thomas slowed down his escape, turning back around only to be startled by the sight of her enormous snatch of long, gray pubic hair. He shuddered, flashing back to the similar viewing he had had that morning with Evelyn Perdita, although that one had been smooth-shaven. *"What a day* this *is turning into!"* he thought to himself, thoroughly rattled.

By this time, the poor woman had obviously realized that Thomas was definitively *not* the masseur for whom she had been waiting in such a state of excitement. She shrieked and ran back into the house searching for her clothes, her elderly flab wobbling inelegantly around her frame.

Thomas didn't know what to do but wait at the open door, praying for guidance and clothes, but not necessarily in that order! He heard frantic movement inside the house. Moments later, the poor woman reappeared, mercifully wearing clothes this time in the form of a simple floral dress that was a little too big for her but looked comfortable and well-worn.

Her blushing rosy cheeks gave her a motherly appearance, and she addressed Thomas apologetically this time "I'm so sorry about that! I had you confused with someone else, I'm afraid. I'm Lillian Kim. How can I help you, dear?"

Thomas smiled warmly at the woman. "No problem, Ma'am!," and introduced himself as a local community member running for City council. He explained that he was looking to better understand the needs and concerns of the residents in the area, and asked if she would be willing to chat with him for a few minutes. The woman nodded, a still embarrassed smile on her face and invited him inside. Thomas thanked her and stepped into the house, his eyes scanning the living room as he tried to spot any signs of his target, David Kim.

"Please sit on the couch there," she said, pointing, having regained her composure. The still unused massage table set up in the middle of the living room proved she hadn't lied.

Although she had been exceedingly embarrassed, she seemed very gracious to Thomas considering the circumstances. Thomas engaged her in conversation, asking about her family and how long she had lived in the neighborhood. Thomas' innate charm seemed to be working its magic. She even offered him coffee, which he happily accepted.

After voicing his admiration for the décor of the house, he convinced her to show him around the place. She obliged, taking him on a tour, pointing out various features and telling him stories about her family history in the area. Thomas guessed that she would probably talk about *anything* else at this point just to forget the earlier scene. He was still curious what had prompted that disaster of a first meeting!

Thomas was careful to keep up his facade of being a potential city council member, but his mind was focused on finding any sign of David Kim. As he followed the old woman through her house, he kept his eyes peeled for any clues that might bring him closer to the real target.

"Mrs. Kim," he began to say, but she interrupted him, explaining, "I know it's unusual these days, but I never married. Kim is my family name. Please, just call me Lillian." she requested.

"Happy to do so, Lillian! Please call me Thomas if you would be so kind" Thomas responded in turn. As he made his way down the hallway, he noticed a door that was slightly ajar. He peered inside and saw several bags on the bed. "Sorry, Lillian! I didn't mean to be nosy, but I thought I heard something in there. Is there someone else here who I should introduce myself to?" He assumed that someone must have recently arrived and was staying in the guest room. This thought brought him some confidence, as he realized that he might be getting closer to finding the elusive David Kim.

"Oh, that's just my nephew's stuff. He just got here a couple of days ago. I'm so glad to see him!" She offered all of this without tripping a single mental alarm for Thomas, so he figured she was, once again, just telling the unvarnished truth. She added, "I think family is so important to keep in touch with, don't you?"

Thomas could only agree, bemused at this little old lady, now that she was *clothed*, of course! Truthfully, he was starting to like the old gal. "I couldn't agree more, Lillian. Nothing is more important than family." he assured her earnestly, meaning every word of it.

Lillian gave him a measuring glance, then nodded in satisfaction, causing Thomas to feel like he had just passed a test he didn't even know he was taking. She stopped and took his arm as they stood in the hallway once more. "I think you should have a talk with my nephew, David. He has always been terrible at staying in touch! Maybe you could get him to understand how I feel when he doesn't talk to me for such a long time!" She looked up at him hopefully.

"Ah, I see. I suppose I could if you want me to. It's nice of you to take him in, anyway. How old is he?" he asks, trying to keep the conversation going.

She explained that David was 32 and had, unfortunately, lost his job, so he truly needed the support of family, and she was the only family he had nearby since everyone else to whom he was related lived in Florida. Thomas nodded sympathetically and remarked that it was tough out there these days. The aunt agreed but added that she was happy to have David around and would be glad to help him out until he was back on his feet. Thomas smiled and said, "You're a good woman to help him in his time of need."

Lilian appreciated the recognition of her support and replied with a warm smile.

Thomas took a mental tally of the information he had gathered thus far from Lillian and realized that she probably had no idea about David's activities with *Turner Research*. He felt relieved, knowing that he wouldn't have to confront her about David. It would have been difficult for him to do so, as he understandably found it hard to be ruthless with people who are innocent. He continues to chat with the aunt, but his mind is already moving onto the next steps in his investigation.

"Well, Lillian, I thank you for your hospitality, but it's time I get to my next appointment. I meant to hopefully have a bit more conversation about the community and what I can do to help. However, this will need to be on another day." Lilian understood and walked him to the front door, saddened by the end of such a pleasant conversation. As he exited the house, he paused, and asked her one more question. "I hope you don't mind me asking, but do you *usually* answer the door in the nude?"

"Heavens, no!" she responded vehemently, shaking her head. "That was the first and the last time! My friend, Helen, told me that is how people greet their masseur in France, and the masseur just recently moved here from France. I will *never* let that old biddy in my house again after that debacle!" And she and Thomas shared a good laugh as he left, waving goodbye over his shoulder.

As Thomas drove away from the aunt's house, he took out his phone and used the talk-to-text feature to send a message to Peter Barlowe alerting him to the fact he could cease looking for David Kim, and that Thomas had already located the target. However, since Thomas had interacted with the aunt so closely, he decided it was wiser not to risk being seen waiting for David to return, especially by Lillian. To be safe, he asked Kelly to handle the stake-out and to alert him when David returned.

After a few minutes, Kelly responded, letting Thomas know that he could not be there until the next morning. Thomas accepted this and sent a payment through his payment app.

Thomas then quickly spoke another message to Dr. Crane, informing him, "I've located David Kim. He is staying at his aunt's house in Mesa. More news to follow within 24-48 hours." He hit 'send' and drove on, satisfied with the day's work.

Chapter 34

December 25th

Thomas entered his apartment and flicked on the light switch to reveal a soft, ambient glow. The gentle light of the lamp on the side table cast shadows on the wall, giving the room a cozy feel. He headed over to the kitchen, uncorked a bottle of wine, and poured himself a glass. He heated up some leftover pasta and sat down at the table, took a sip of wine and enjoyed the rich, complex flavors. In the background, a show played softly on the TV, providing a soothing background noise. It was a welcome break from the chaos over the past few days, and Thomas found himself able to finally relax and unwind. Just then, a text notification interrupted the peacefulness of the evening, causing him to pause and check his phone. He saw a text from Gabrielle, "Hi, handsome! What are you up to tonight?" and another from Evelyn coyly suggesting that they should repeat their last get-together. He paused for a moment, considering his options, but ultimately decided to ignore both texts and enjoy his peaceful night at home by himself, but he was truly avoiding the conflicted feelings he had over his love-life.

He could not shake the guilt that he felt about having anything to do with Evelyn Perdita outside of work. He knew she was only a convenient fling who happened to be extremely sexy...and available. The male side of him liked that. On the other hand, he thought he might be falling in love with Gabrielle, and he didn't feel ready for that yet. He sipped his wine and pondered what he truly wanted out of Life and what he needed to do to achieve it, but he didn't like the results. *"Guilt sucks!"* he thought to himself, and not for the first time.

Thomas received another text, this one from Francesco Ajello. He had initially assumed it was one of the women again, but quickly realized it wasn't. He looked at his phone's clock and saw that it was 8:15pm, which meant that it was currently 4:15am in Turin, Italy, where Francesco was. Thomas was surprised that he was awake so early. Francesco's text said, "Got it figured out. Will take care of picking up the package on December 25th when people are gone for the holiday. Can I meet you the next day here in Turin to hand it off to you?"

Thomas did not hesitate, replying quickly, "Good news! Can do. Will meet you at same place as before at 12:00 noon your time."

Thomas finished his dinner, then picked up his phone to text Nouvel, updating him on the completion date of December 25th in the US but December 26th in Italy and that he would have to fly there for pick-up of the item. He hit 'send' and put his phone down, feeling like a weight had been lifted off his shoulders. He leaned back in his chair and let out a small sigh of relief.

Thomas plopped down on the couch and grabbed the remote to turn on the TV. He browsed through the channels, pausing for a moment on a cooking show before moving on. The news caught his attention, but the first few stories were about the usual stuff; traffic accidents, local politics, and the weather. But then, a breaking news report caught his attention.

"Religious protesters have gathered in front of *Turner Research,* the same stem-cell company that recently made the news for some groundbreaking breakthroughs. The protesters are voicing their opposition to human cloning!" the news anchor reported, as footage of the picketers filled the TV screen.

Thomas watched as people of all ages and backgrounds held up signs with slogans like "Cloning is playing God!" and "Life is sacred!" The camera zoomed in on one man leading a prayer circle while the rest of them marched around waving their signs and chanting, "Stop playing God! Stop playing God!", their faces grim with determination.

The reporter on the scene interviewed one of the protesters, a middle-aged woman with tears in her eyes. "I just can't stand the thought of scientists playing with human life like it's some kind of

153

toy," she said. "God created us in His own image, and we shouldn't be trying to change that."

As Thomas watched, he couldn't help but feel conflicted. On the one hand, he believed in scientific progress and the potential benefits of cloning technology. But, on the other hand, he could understand the protesters' concerns about scientists playing God and the ethical implications of such research.

The news anchor shifted the topic to the Senior Scientist at *Turner Research*, Dr. Stephen Crane, who was at the center of the human cloning controversy. The news anchor provided a brief background on Crane, highlighting his expertise in the field and the numerous awards and accolades he had received for his work over the recent years.

The news clip then cut to a previously recorded interview with Crane wherein he passionately argued for the benefits of human cloning. "Imagine a world where we can clone organs and tissues to save lives. We can also help couples who can't have children by using their own cells to create embryos," Crane said in the news clip.

However, the anchor went on to report that not *everyone* was in favor of such research. Religious groups who believed that cloning was interfering with God's work had been picketing outside *Turner Research* for days. The camera panned to a live shot of even more protesters carrying signs. Their numbers seemed to be growing in Thomas' opinion. The anchor noted that tensions were high and that there had been so far unsubstantiated reports of altercations between the protesters and the supporters of the ongoing research.

Thomas let out a heartfelt sigh and reached for the remote, turning off the television. He placed the remote on the coffee table and picked up his phone to turn it off. It was high time for Thomas to escape reality, even if just for a little while. He yawned and walked to his bedroom, crawled into bed, and pulled the covers up to his chin. The darkness of the room was comforting, and he closed his eyes gratefully, letting out a deep breath.

For a moment, he just lay there in silence, feeling the weight of the day lift off his shoulders. He cleared his mind of all the chaos and confusion, focusing instead on the rhythm of his own breathing. Slowly but surely, he drifted off, too tired to even think about protests or *Turner Research*. Sleep took him at last, and the sound of his breath became one with the sounds of the night.

Chapter 35

Ruth Weber

As Thomas was savoring the last of his breakfast, the phone rang, banishing the tranquility of his morning routine. He checked the caller ID and saw it was his mother. He answered and greeted her warmly. "Good morning, Mom. How are you doing?"

"Good morning, Thomas! I'm doing well, thank you for asking. Do you have a minute?" she asked. Thomas replied in the affirmative, and she continued. "I just wanted to give you an update on the Airbnb property I'm remodeling. I went to an auction house yesterday to look for some furniture to fill the apartments, and I found some amazing pieces. They're old western-style pieces, really unique and charming. I think they'll give the place a cozy, rustic feel."

Thomas listened intently, picturing in his mind the kind of furniture his mother was describing. "That sounds really interesting, Mom. Did you get everything you needed?"

"Well, almost. There were a couple of pieces that I couldn't get my hands on, but I'll keep looking. I want to make sure everything is perfect for my guests."

Thomas smiled at his mother's determination to make her Airbnb a success. "I'm sure you'll find what you need. It's great that you're putting so much effort into this. I'm sure your guests will love it."

"I hope so, honey. I just want to create a warm and welcoming space for people to enjoy. Anyway, I won't keep you. I just wanted to share my excitement with you. Have a wonderful day."

"You too, Mom. Talk to you soon." Thomas ended the call and sat there for a moment, feeling grateful for his mother's positivity and enthusiasm. He had to admit to himself that he was a little curious about the furniture she had described. He made a mental note to visit the property soon to see it for himself.

After cleaning up from breakfast, he decided to check his emails, expecting them to be mostly spam or otherwise unimportant messages. However, one email caught his eye. It was from Ruth Weber, a name he recognized from his time at *Turner Research*. Ruth had worked closely with Dr. Crane, and she was well-respected in the fields of biology and medicine, with numerous published papers to her name. She had resigned from *Turner Research* a year ago, but now she had requested a meeting with Thomas Rene, surprisingly enough. The email was cryptic, with no mention of the purpose or topic of the meeting.

. . . .

Dear Mr. Rene,

I hope this email finds you well. I am writing to request a meeting with you as soon as possible. While we have not directly worked together, I am familiar with your reputation through several circles we share. I assume the same is true for you in reverse. There is a matter of considerable importance that I would like to discuss with you in person rather than through normal channels.

Please let me know if you are amenable to this so that we can arrange a time that works for both of us. Thank you for your time and I look forward to hearing from you.

Sincerely,

Dr. Ruth Weber

. . . .

Thomas sat there, pondering Ruth Weber's cryptic message. He had never really interacted with her during his time at *Turner Research*, but he had heard her name mentioned before by people who had great respect for her work.

As he sipped his coffee, he glanced at the clock on his computer screen. It was already mid-morning, and he had a busy day ahead of him. He took a quick shower, got dressed, and headed out the door. As he walked to his car, his mind kept going back to the enigmatic message from Ruth Weber. He couldn't help but feel intrigued. Why had she chosen to reach out to *him*, specifically? And what could she possibly want to discuss that was so important she needed to meet with him in person?

Thomas was almost to his car when something struck him, his sixth sense was jangling an internal mental alarm. He stopped and looked back at his apartment building contemplating going back to respond to Weber's email immediately. *"Best not to wait!"* he thought to himself, reversing his course so he could type his response to her e-mail. For that matter, he needed her phone number now that she didn't work at *Turner Research!*

. . . .

Dear Dr. Weber,

Thank you for contacting me. I am currently available to meet with you on Friday to discuss the matter you referenced. Please let me know the time and location that works best for you, and please include your phone number.

Best regards,

Thomas Rene

. . . .

Chapter 36

Let All Pay The Price

Thomas drove up to the headquarters of *Turner Research*, taking in the chaotic scene as he parked the car. Protesters were yelling and moving their signs around as they tried to catch his attention. Thomas found the whole situation amusing, but he maintained his professional demeanor as he made his way towards the door.

As he walked through the crowd of protesters, one of the security team members he knew approached him and joked. "Hi, Mr. Rene! This is *some* kind of mess, huh?!"

Thomas chuckled and shook his head in wry agreement and proceeded to enter the building.

The security team welcomed him and opened the doors. Upon entrance, the noise outside slowly faded away. Thomas walked down the hallway, hearing an occasional shout through the windows. Despite the seriousness of the situation, he found the whole thing somewhat amusing.

As he walked towards the door leading to the main hallway of the labs, he saw the familiar checkpoint situated between the staff breakroom and the security office. The guard on duty looked up as he approached and asked for his credentials. Thomas chuckled and made a joking complaint about the guards checking their badges every time they used the bathroom. The guard did not seem amused.

Thomas did as he was asked and showed his security clearance. The guard humorlessly inspected it, returning it to him with a cursory nod and motioning him to get the hell through the doors.

Thomas walked down the hallway, glancing at the glass walls and doors of the many offices on either side of him. People in lab coats bustled around, all of them focused on their work. As he walked, he couldn't shake the nagging feeling that he had been in this hallway before, but he couldn't place when or how. This was the first time he had authorization to enter this section of the building.

The sound of his footsteps echoed down the hall and drew his attention to the double doors at the end. They were not made of glass, so he couldn't see through them, unlike the other doors he had passed along the way.

The long walk was a little mesmerizing for Thomas. He tended to lose himself in his thoughts. Amused at himself, he snapped back to reality and remembered that he was supposed to be looking for Zack Pawloski, a technician who had worked closely with Ruth Weber for several years.

The feeling of unease continued to grow as Thomas approached the double doors. He wondered what might be wrong.

Thomas soon reached his goal, the lab where Zack worked. Zack spotted him and greeted him warmly while shaking his hand.

Zack was a tall man with a lean build, standing around 6'3". He had a sharp jawline and piercing blue eyes that seemed to sparkle with intelligence. His dark hair was cut short and neatly styled, and he had a well-groomed beard that added a touch of ruggedness to his appearance. Pawloski wore a white lab coat over button-down shirt and slacks, and his ID badge hung from a lanyard around his neck. Overall, he gave off an air of competence that was fitting for someone working in such an important and complex field.

A few other technicians were around, so Thomas exchanged some friendly banter with them before turning to Zack and asking if they could talk privately. Zack nodded his agreement and suggested they head to the atrium. As they walked, Thomas noticed the intricate architecture and lush greenery in the space. The waterfall in the center of the atrium filled the air with a soothing background noise.

Once they reached a quiet corner, Zack turned to Thomas and asked, "Is everything okay?"

Thomas hesitated for a moment, not wanting to sound paranoid, but he had decided to be honest with Zack on his trip there. "Look, Zack, I recently got a request for a private meeting with a Dr. Ruth Weber who used to work here. Do you know who I am talking about?"

Zack raised an eyebrow in surprise, "I haven't heard that name in a while! What do you want to know?"

"I'm looking for a reason that she would want to talk to *me*, of all people?! Did she ever say anything to you about why she quit *Turner Research*?"

Thomas listened intently as Zack recounted the conversation he had shared with Weber after her resignation. "She told me that she didn't agree with the direction of the research anymore," Zack said. "She said that she just couldn't support it anymore. When I asked what she meant by that, she just clammed up and told me that she didn't want to talk about it and that I wouldn't want to know."

Thomas furrowed his brow, "That's odd. Do you have any idea what she could have meant?"

Zack shook his head, "No, I don't, but there was one thing she said that stuck with me. At the end of the conversation, she said something in Latin. It was '*Sit pretium omnes stipendium.*'"

Thomas's eyes widened, "That's a strange thing to say. Do you have any idea what it means?"

Zack shrugged, "I looked it up, and it roughly translates to 'Let all pay the price.' I have no idea what she meant by that."

Thomas rubbed his chin, lost in thought. "I'm not sure what that meant, either. It sounds like she had strong convictions about something, or she wouldn't have quit."

Zack rubbed his head, thinking about it. "It's true. She wasn't one to shy away from voicing her opinions, but she was very respectful and professional about it. She never caused a scene or anything like that."

Thomas nodded, taking it all in. "What about her work? Was she a good scientist?"

Zack's face lit up. "Oh, absolutely. Dr. Weber was one of the best we had. She was meticulous in her work, and always went the extra mile to make sure everything was done correctly. I mean, I guess that's why it was so surprising to me when she quit like that. It just didn't seem like her."

Thomas furrowed his brow again. "What do you mean? Did she give any indication that something was bothering her?"

Zack shook his head. "No, not really. She just seemed...I don't know, a little more distant than usual, maybe. But nothing that would make me think she was planning on leaving."

Zack chuckled. "Maybe she wants to see you for help to figure out why she didn't get her 401K benefits matched when she quit," he joked.

Thomas smiled at the silly remark, but his mind was still racing. He wondered what Weber could want from him, and why she chose to contact him after a whole year had gone by. "Well, I'll find out soon enough," he said, patting Zack on the shoulder. "Thanks for the chat, Zack. Good to see you again!"

Zack nodded. "Likewise, Thomas. Let me know if you need anything else."

Having made their goodbyes, Thomas turned and made his way out of the atrium, still mulling over the possibilities of what Dr. Weber could want from him that she couldn't get from someone else.

He walked towards the entrance of the building, and he noticed that the protesters outside had multiplied. Their chants had grown even louder, and now there was an angry undertone to the voices crowding the air.

When he stepped outside, he was immediately bombarded by people yelling and shoving each other. Thomas privately marveled at all the fuss going on. He managed to walk without incident to his car, unlocked it, got in, and turned on some Muddy Waters to drown out the noise.

Driving away, he lit a cigarette and tried to shake off the strange feeling that had been following him all morning. The protesters grew smaller in his rearview mirror, but the thought of Dr. Weber and her cryptic email lingered in his mind.

Chapter 37

The Very Same Book

Thomas sat in his car, the smooth bluesy sound of Muddy Waters filling the space around him. He closed his eyes for a moment, hoping to find a moment of peace before the long day began. Unfortunately, the list lying on the passenger seat kept calling his attention back to reality. He picked it up and ran his finger down the names, his eyes eventually settling on only one. Thomas made a mental note on the information Martin had provided and tucked it in his pocket. There were so many things happening, so many people to meet and talk with. It would be overwhelming for most people, but this was his chosen profession.

After turning off his car, he stepped out into the bustle of the city and walked into the large bookstore that occupied the streetcorner. Thomas walked at a casual pace, his eyes scanning the seemingly endless rows of shelves filled with books of every genre. He made his way to the 'Self-help' section, his fingers trailing along the spines of the books as he searched for a particular title. Finally, his eyes landed on Silent Night, The Peace Within in Us All, an obscure book by an author he had never heard of.

He pulled the book out and flipped through the pages, pausing every now and then to read a passage. Once satisfied that he had found what he was looking for, Thomas tucked the book under his arm. He made his way to the little cafe located inside the bookstore. After ordering a double espresso and a bacon, egg, and cheese breakfast sandwich, he found a seat to enjoy his meal and read the book.

Thomas read for a while, sipped his espresso, and enjoyed the quiet atmosphere of the cafe. Eventually, he became aware that the woman seated at the small table next to him was glancing at him surreptitiously. Thomas realized that she wanted to say something and lifted his head to turn and look at her more directly.

She lifted her book slightly to reveal that she was reading the very same book as Thomas. He smiled at the apparent coincidence and raised one thumb up to her. She returned the gesture, prompting him to lean in her direction and whisper to her.

"What do you think of the book so far?" he asked with a pleasant, non-stalkerish smile.

She looked at him, pleased at his interest. She was a dumpy little woman in her forties, so it wasn't often that handsome men like Thomas paid her much attention. "It's fascinating, actually! I've been reading a lot on this topic lately, and this book provides a unique perspective."

Thomas nodded in agreement, and they continued talking about the book and discovered other mutual interests. She found him to be both witty and charming, which prompted her to move over to his table.

"By the way," he said, "I'm Thomas."

"I'm Jessica," she replied with a smile.

Thomas and the woman start chatting about everything from favorite foods to travel destinations. When the topic of work came up, Thomas went first and said that he worked in pharmaceutical sales. She seemed mildly interested in his work and asked if he enjoyed it. He responded in the positive, saying that he found it fulfilling, but didn't offer why. He quickly turned the conversation back to her and asked whether she enjoyed what she did for a living.

She responded that she had loved her most recent job but had to resign due to family complications. Thomas noticed her tone and expression changed when she mentioned 'family complications' and sensed that there was more to the story.

"Look," he said, "I swear I'm not trying to pry, but what kind of 'complications' are you talking about?"

She hesitated for a moment, but then opened up, explaining that her husband had recently received a job offer in Seattle that they felt that they simply couldn't afford to pass up. She added, "The move is only a month away and I was finding it difficult to balance the demands of my job with also preparing for such a big change. So, even though I do love the job, I had to resign."

Thomas leaned forward, intrigued. "What kind of job did your husband get that was so important you'd be willing to uproot your life and resign from a job you say you love?"

She smiled wryly. "He's an aerospace engineer, and he was offered a position at a big company in Seattle. It's a great opportunity for him, but it means a lot of changes for me, too. No way around it."

Thomas nodded in understanding. "That does sound like a big move. Do you have any plans for once you get to Seattle?"

She hesitated, as if she were thinking it through on the spot. "I'm not sure yet. I've been thinking of taking some time off to travel and maybe figure some things out. I'm hoping I'll find a job I like there in Seattle eventually."

Thomas smiled encouragingly at her. "Sounds like a plan. Seattle is a great city, lots to explore. Who knows, maybe you'll find your next great adventure there!"

She grinned back at him. "That's the hope!" Then she neatly turned the tables on him. "What great adventures do *you* have planned?"

Thomas shrugged nonchalantly. "Just work. It tends to keep me pretty busy, but it's not very exciting, I must admit."

Not much later, Thomas finished the conversation, saying, "It was great talking to you, Jessica. I wish you both all the best with your move to Seattle."

Jessica smiled and responded, "Thank you, it was really nice meeting you, too, Thomas."

As Thomas walked out of the bookstore, he tossed the book onto a nearby table and made his way to his car. *"Don't need that anymore!"* he thought to himself, pleased that his little ruse had gone so well. As he got in his car, he pulled out his phone and sent a text to Nouvel with the update on Jessica Jenkins. He typed in, "Jessica Jenkins is clean, resigned due to her husband's new job. Do you want me to 'scrub' the husband's new job as well?" Nouvel replied promptly once again, "No, that's unnecessary. Go to the next one on the list."

Thomas pulled out the list from his pocket and scanned it one more time. He found the name, 'Jessica Jenkins,' and crossed it off with a pen. As he did, he felt a small sense of relief knowing that he wouldn't have to apply any pressure to the quite trusting Jessica. He folded the paper and put it back into his pocket. He was just glad that Jessica's former co-worker had been correct about what Jessica was currently reading!

Chapter 38

Why Wouldn't I?

Thomas had gone to the store to pick up some arabica coffee, medium roast. Now, he just sat in his car, thinking. Frankly, he was a little depressed. His thoughts were confused. On the one hand, he knew that he could go get laid by Evelyn Perdita, and the physical connection would feel good---for all of about 5 minutes, just about long enough to get dressed and hit the road. He and Evelyn never had much to say afterwards. On the other hand, although he didn't have that casual physical relationship with Gabrielle, his next-door neighbor, he suddenly realized that he truly enjoyed every moment he spent with her. It didn't *have* to be physical at all to enjoy their time together. That thought, oddly, bothered him. He didn't like to feel that he needed anybody, but he had enough self-awareness to admit that he was moping around because he was starting to want more than just getting laid. At times, he felt like a traitor to his entire gender since most males don't really think much past the chase.

He reached for his phone, selecting "Life by the Drop" by Stevie Ray Vaughan. As the music played, he felt himself getting lost in the melody, but the words seemed to resonate with him today in a way they never had before. Suddenly, he felt a bit overwhelmed and had a strong urge to see Gabrielle.

Without a second thought, Thomas put his phone back in the holder and turned his keys in the ignition, started the engine and drove towards Gabrielle's studio where she worked. He knew that she was busy with her art, but he felt compelled to see her.

When he arrived, he parked the car and made his way to the door, taking a deep breath before knocking. Gabrielle answered with a warm smile, and Thomas felt his heart skip a beat at the sight of her. He thought that she was breathtakingly perfect in that moment, and he was glad he was there.

"Hey there," she said, pushing strands of her hair back from her face. "What brings you by?"

Gabrielle had her hair pulled back into a ponytail, but a few strands dangled in front of her face. Her bright, blue eyes were sparkling with interest at the surprise visit. Small dots of paint had done a polka on her forehead. She wore a white t-shirt and a pair of beat-up jeans that were liberally stained with various colors of paint. Around her neck, she had tied a colorful bandanna which added a pop of color to her outfit. Thomas could tell that she had been working hard on her art, and he admired the passion that she put into it.

He hesitated, unsure of what to say for a moment before answering her, "I don't know. I was listening to some music and suddenly felt the urge to see you. I hope I'm not interrupting anything important."

Gabrielle's eyes sparkled with humor as she grinned at the hapless male in front of her, "No, not at all. Come on in."

As Thomas stepped into Gabrielle's studio, he took a moment to look around. The space was larger than he had expected, with high ceilings and natural light streaming in from the skylight. The walls were lined with various artworks, some in progress and some finished. He saw an assortment of paints, brushes, canvases, and other art supplies scattered about the place.

In one corner, there was a large canvas where thick brushstrokes of vibrant colors had been used, creating an abstract composition that caught his eye. In another corner, he saw a sculpture made of twisted metal standing proudly on a pedestal. A small table was covered in sketches and drawings, with pencils and charcoal sticks scattered about.

As he took it all in, he thought he could feel the creative energy pulsing through the space. Gabrielle's passion and dedication to her craft were evident in every corner of the room. He couldn't help but smile as he imagined her in the midst of creating all these works, totally lost in the moment.

As Thomas looked around the studio, his eyes caught sight of a few pieces of religious art depicting various moments in Jesus' life. He paused, "Hey, what about them?" pointing at the pieces.

Gabrielle smiled and said, "I'm making them as a gift for Sister Anne, the woman we had lunch with last time. Remember her? She's been asking for some new pieces for the chapel at her church, so I thought I'd surprise her with these."

Thomas nodded, impressed by Gabrielle's talent and thoughtfulness. "They're really beautiful! Sister Anne is going to love them." he said, admiring the intricate details of the paintings.

Gabrielle curtsied like a noble woman in the royal court. "Why, thank you, kind Sir!"

Thomas thought she was adorable, paint on her face or not. He cleared his throat before speaking, feeling a bit nervous. "So, I was wondering if you wanted to do something tonight?" he asked, stumbling over his words slightly.

Gabrielle smiled at his nervousness. "You're so cute," she said. "Of course, I'd like to see you tonight! Why wouldn't I?" She asked innocently, deliberately batting her long eyelashes at him coquettishly while she twirled a long strand of escaped hair around her finger.

Thomas went from delight that she said 'yes' to belatedly realizing she had asked him a question that he wasn't sure how to answer. As he floundered, she broke out laughing. He breathed a sigh of relief and smiled. "You got me good, that time! I could imagine a thousand reasons why you *wouldn't* want to see me, but all I cared about was that you said you *would* see me tonight." he admitted sheepishly.

Gabrielle reached out and gently took his hand. "I feel the same way," she said softly, "I was just teasing you, and I thought your answer was perfect!"

170

Thomas's phone rang suddenly like an intruder into the comfortable silence. He looked down, irritated, only to see that it was Kelly Brown calling. "I'm so sorry, Gabby. I need to take this call. It's important," he said in a regretful tone.

She smiled and nodded understandingly, then leaned in and kissed him on the cheek. "I'm looking forward to tonight," she breathed into his ear. "Let's do something fun." Then, she went right back to her waiting work, completely ignoring him.

Thomas looked at her retreating back in astonishment. *"What a gal! Evelyn wouldn't have stopped asking who was on the phone."* he thought to himself as he brought the phone up to his ear.

Chapter 39

The Black Sedan

As Thomas walked out of Gabrielle's studio, he finally answered the phone. "Hey, Kelly, sorry to keep you waiting. What's up?"

"I just wanted to update you on David Kim," Kelly replied. "I got to the stake-out a bit earlier than I had originally planned, and I saw Kim arrive at his aunt's house. The interesting thing is that he exited the house *twice* to meet with someone in front of the house who was driving a black sedan. The two meetings were about one hour apart."

Thomas listened intently, his mind busily figuring out the possibilities for the meetings. "Did you get a license plate number?" he asked.

"No, I couldn't get any closer without being seen," Kelly grumpily replied. "When the car took off, I stayed behind because I didn't want to risk losing Kim. By the way, it's a Mercedes-Benz black sedan."

Thomas instructed Kelly to keep him informed on any further developments and urged him to stay close to David Kim, but not to put himself at risk. He emphasized the importance of Brown remaining out of sight, and to stay on task regardless of the cost.

Thomas sat in his car and took a drag from his cigarette. He leaned his head back against the headrest and stared out the window, lost in thought. He thought about the new information Kelly had just given him. *"Why would someone be visiting David Kim?"* he wondered. *"Could it be the same reason that Kim is on the list Nouvel gave me?"*

He ran his hand through his hair, trying to clear his head. *"Dear God,"* he thought to himself. *"Where's the coffee when I need it?!"* Something was off about that black Mercedes, he mused to himself. *"Why would David be meeting someone in front of his aunt's house? And why at two different times?"* Thomas can feel a knot of suspicion forming in his stomach as he contemplates the possibilities.

One thing he knew for sure: David was definitely on the run. But from whom, and why?

He took another drag from his cigarette and the smoke swirled around him as he contemplated his next move. Sighing to himself, he started the car. It was time for him to go.

While he drove, he called Dr. Stephen Crane, over at *Turner Research*. Crane seemed surprised by Thomas' call, but he was quite willing to help. Thomas asked if Crane had any more information he could share about David Kim. He wanted to know what type of person Kim was.

Crane thought for a moment, then replied, "David is a very nervous guy, always seeming to be looking over his shoulder, never really interacting with anyone outside his few friends." Crane asked Thomas, "Does that help any?"

"No, not much! What else can you share with me?" Thomas asked.

"Kim kept to himself most of the time and didn't seem willing to share much about his personal life with anyone, at least, as far as I'm aware." Crane paused as a thought occurred to him. "I do think David became more and more paranoid over the time he worked here" he added.

"Any idea why he was getting like that?" asked Thomas, but Crane didn't know, so Thomas thanked him and hung up. *"Hmmm"* he thought. He was beginning to think that David Kim might be a lot more dangerous than he had initially thought.

Chapter 40

I Can't Do This Right Now, Evelyn

Thomas and Gabrielle arrived at the fancy restaurant and were politely greeted by the maître d' who took them to their reserved table. The restaurant was dimly lit, and there was soft, romantic music playing in the background. The tables were elegantly set with white linens and candles, and the waitstaff were impeccably dressed.

As they sat down, Thomas pulled out Gabrielle's chair for her and they both smiled at each other. They ordered their drinks, and as they waited, they perused the menu. They finally settled on a few dishes to share between them, including a delicious looking charcuterie board and a grilled seafood platter. As they ate, they chatted about a variety of things, from their favorite music to childhood memories. Gabrielle told Thomas about some of her recent art projects, and Thomas was genuinely interested in hearing about them.

After they were done with dinner and back in the car, Gabrielle shared a story about forgiving a friend who had betrayed her in the past. Thomas listened intently as she spoke, impressed by her capacity for forgiveness after hearing the story.

"I don't know if I could ever do that," he admitted when she finished.

"Do what?" she asked curiously.

"I suppose I just feel like, once someone has wronged me, that's it. I can't let it go."

Gabrielle looked surprised "Forgiveness isn't about the other person, it's about *you*. It's important to free yourself from the burden of anger and resentment. When you can forgive someone, you're not excusing their behavior. You're simply choosing to let it go and move on with your own life."

Thomas mulled over her words for a moment. "I guess I never thought of it that way."

"It's not easy, believe me!" Gabrielle continued. "But I've found that when I choose to forgive someone, it's like a weight has been lifted off my shoulders. It's a selfless act but, in the end, it benefits you just as much as the other person."

Thomas was silent, thinking for a moment before responding. "You know, I think you might be right. I guess I will need to work on that, but it won't be easy for me, you know?"

"Of *course*, it isn't easy, Thomas! But it *is* important." she offered with simple understanding in her voice.

Thomas asked her how she developed such a capacity for forgiveness. Was it something that her parents instilled in her, or did it come naturally? Gabrielle, who had never been asked such a question before, replied that it was probably a combination of factors, to include her upbringing, her faith, and her own personal experiences.

Thomas admitted that he often struggled with expressing his own emotions in an acceptable way and often kept his distance from people to avoid such problems. She nodded understandingly but encouraged him to try to open up and truly connect with others on a deeper level.

When they arrived at their apartments, Thomas invited her to join him at his place. Gabrielle seemed very pleased that he had done so, and he held the door open for her to enter ahead of him. His eyes were gratefully fastened on her hips as she seemed to almost float to the couch.

While he took a seat next to Gabrielle a sudden 'buzz' filled the air as Thomas' phone signaled a text message. Without thinking, he took out his phone from his pocket and glanced down at the screen, only to see that it was from Evelyn Perdita. She was predictably asking for yet another nightcap and referred to him as

"Lover." Gabrielle's eyes were reflexively drawn to the lite screen of the phone. She couldn't help but notice the name of the sender, but she didn't say anything.

Thomas, who had just suffered a truly massive stroke of guilty conscience was utterly at a loss! He knew Gabrielle had seen the name, but she was clearly not going to ask him who it was. In fact, he noticed with equal parts admiration and relief that she deliberately looked away to preserve the fiction of privacy for him. He was so impressed with this act of simple decency that something finally broke inside him. He realized that, come hell or high water, he was going to tell her---now.

If there was one thing Thomas was not, it was a coward. He figuratively dove into the deep end of the pool, hoping he'd survive.

"Gabrielle, there's something we need to talk about. Truthfully, I didn't realize that we needed to talk until just now."

Gabby, looking a bit shell-shocked by the suddenness of all this, turned towards him on the couch and gave him her full attention. She folded her hands in her lap and said, "You're breaking up with me, aren't you." But it was a statement, not a question, delivered in a flat monotone.

"Dear God, no!" expostulated Thomas, shaking his head. "That's the *last* thing I want, Gabby!"

She looked confused, but Thomas also saw some hope burgeoning in her eyes as she looked up at him. "I don't understand. When I saw that woman's name pop up and she called you "Lover," I thought..." and her voice trailed off as her eyes glimmered with unshed tears.

Thomas felt even worse now. He had gone from being momentarily in the grip of stunned realization and horror at seeing Evelyn's name on the call screen to now feeling responsible for ruining everything to do with the lovely woman beside him. He realized that Evelyn had to go. She just wasn't worth the cost, regardless of whether he and Gabby survived this impromptu confession.

He tried again. This time, he reached out and lifted her chin so that he could look into those beautiful blue eyes. "Her name is Evelyn Perdita, and I sort of work with her at *Turner Research*. We went out a few times in the past, but there has never been anything *serious* between us. I'm sorry that I haven't talked about it with you, but I just didn't think it was that important."

She repeated his words, "Not important?" but she listened calmly enough that Thomas believed he might actually survive, so he went for it and leaned in, hoping for a kiss to get this evening back on track. Instead, he found himself kissing air. He opened his eyes in shock, only to see her back as she marched determinedly for the door.

"Gabby!" he burst out, jumping to his feet. "Where are you going?!" but the only answer he got was the slam of the door as she exited. He was completely at a loss in that moment for what to do, just like every other male in the history of the world. *"I can't win for losing!"* he thought to himself.

The apartment felt strangely empty with Gabby gone. This was not how the evening was supposed to go, he thought, and he knew he had only himself to blame, much as he was very irritated by the unexpected text message from Evelyn. Grudgingly, he admitted to himself that Evelyn hadn't known that it was terrible timing. No, this was squarely on him.

Thomas walked around his apartment on autopilot, picking up and cleaning here and there. He came to the realization that he had to do *something*, anything to fix this. Taking a deep breath and downing half a glass of his favorite red wine for courage, he girded his loins, whatever that meant, and crossed the hall to stand in front of her door. Now that he had gotten this far, he realized he didn't know what to do next, so he just stood there, listening.

Gabrielle was apparently investing in some late-night deep cleaning of her place, in Thomas' opinion. The volume of crashes and curses was a bit deafening. His knuckles rapped on the door, but he didn't remember deciding to do it. There was a sudden silence, and he considered briefly making a run for it back to his place. However, he never got the chance.

The door opened and Gabrielle, breathing heavily, said, "Yes?" and waited impatiently, looking for all the world like she had been doing exercises in an evening dress and heels.

"Uh..." started Thomas, realizing at that very second that he had no desire whatsoever to engage in a conversation with an angry woman, especially *this* one and not when he was at fault. Instead, he caved - totally and completely. "I'm sorry!" he said, then he stopped because a miracle happened.

She forgave him. Not all at once, and not for forever, but he did catch that she was open to hearing him beg for mercy and that was a miracle by his way of thinking. He happily did so, artistically and with fervor that did his gender proud. Thomas figured he had learned something of Life-importance this night with Gabby. It wasn't who was right that mattered in a relationship. It was showing that you care.

After he left her cleaning up the mess she had made earlier, Thomas got back to his place feeling much better than when he had left. He decided he'd better contact Evelyn to let her know he wouldn't be coming over. He felt virtuous about his decision, thoughts of Gabby filling his head as he called Evelyn's number. As it rang, he caught himself humming a little tune he'd picked up from Gabrielle "Life is a Highway". Evelyn responded, asking him when he would get there. When he thanked her for the invitation and said that he was just going to go to bed after he finished up some work, she argued.

"Oh, come on, Thomas! You're *always* working. You sure you can't spare a little bit of time for *me*?" She wheedled.

Thomas coughed and said, "I'm sorry, Evelyn. I really *can't* tonight."

Evelyn then tried to persuade him by being more seductive, saying in a husky, knowing voice, "You *know* you want to see me. You miss me, don't you?" She didn't wait for a response before adding in a leading way, "I can make it worth your while."

Thomas resisted her charms and answered, "I can't do this right now, Evelyn. I have things I need to attend to."

Evelyn sighed and said, "Fine, Thomas." while sounding like it was anything *but* fine. "Do what you must do. Just know that I'm here when you finish your 'work', naked and covered in your favorite perfume." With that, she severed the call.

Thomas couldn't shake off the guilt that was eating away at him again. He had been so certain that he could handle Evelyn Perdita. He knew that he had made the right decision by turning down Evelyn's invitation, but a part of him still longed for the sexual tornado that was Evelyn. This was new for him, a battle between what he only *desired* and what he truly *wanted*.

This internal struggle was not getting any easier, either. He decided that he wanted to see Gabrielle. Not later, but *now*. He needed to be with her and to forget about everything else.

He knocked on her door again, his heart racing. He listened but didn't hear any breaking of crockery and no cursing in different languages. *"Things are looking up in the world!"* he thought more calmly. When she opened the door and smiled at him, he felt relief wash over him. It was as if she had known he would be back, and he felt grateful for her understanding.

She took his hand gently and led him inside. He felt a sense of peace wash over him. Somehow, he knew that he had made the right decision, and he was glad he had. As they embraced, he felt a passion and love that he had never felt before. For the first time in his life, he knew that he was exactly where he was meant to be.

Chapter 41

What Do You Do For A Living Again?

Thomas slowly opened his eyes, taking in the soft morning light filtering through the curtains. He realized he wasn't in his own bed and that he wasn't alone. He shifted slightly and became aware of Gabrielle's body entwined with his, her head resting gently on his chest. He could feel the rise and fall of her breath against his skin, and the warmth of her body pressed close to his. It was a feeling he wanted to never end.

He breathed in deeply, taking in the sweet fragrance of her hair, which reminded him of fresh strawberries. The scent filled his senses and made him feel even more alive. He gazed at her face, taking in her delicate features and the soft curve of her lips as she slept. He felt a sense of tenderness for her that he had never felt before for anyone else.

As he lay there, he realized that, for the first time in his life, he felt completely at peace. All his worries and troubles seemed to have vanished. He felt content, happy, and fulfilled.

He gently stroked her hair as he watched her sleep, feeling gratitude for this moment in time. It was a special moment that he knew he would cherish. He felt hope for the future and a sense that things could be different, that *he* could be different.

As the morning light grew stronger, he felt a longing to stay in this moment, but he knew that wasn't realistic because he had responsibilities to attend to. He quickly reached for his phone when he heard it ring and saw it was Kelly Brown again. He hoped not to disturb Gabrielle who was still asleep beside him. *"He's got to stop calling me so early!"* Thomas thought grumpily.

"Hey, Kelly, what's up?" Thomas asked, trying to mask his irritation.

"Hey, Thomas, just wanted to let you know that David Kim is on the move. He's using an Uber, but I'm following him," Kelly replied.

Thomas sighed resignedly. "Alright, keep me posted with any updates. Did you manage to get any sleep last night on stake-out?"

Brown chuckled. "Yeah, I got *some* shuteye, but it's part of the job to lose some sleep, you know."

Thomas sleepily agreed, saying "Yeah, I know. Listen, I'll send over another $2,000 for your services. You're doing great work."

Kelly sounded grateful. "Thanks, Thomas. I appreciate it."

"Sure thing. I'll send it over as soon as we hang up," Thomas said, before ending the call.

He carefully reached over the sleeping form beside him to grab his phone and sent the payment to Brown. When he turned back to Gabrielle, he smiled, glad that she was still sleeping peacefully beside him.

As Thomas lay in the bed with Gabrielle still asleep on his chest, she mumbled softly, not opening her eyes, "What do you do for a living again?" Thomas chuckled softly and stroked her hair some more, listening to her satisfied moan of pleasure as she completely forgot her question. He leaned down and gently kissed the top of her head, savoring this time of bliss they shared in this stolen moment together.

Chapter 42

Took Her Long Enough!

Thomas slowly slipped out of Gabrielle's arms, careful not to wake her as he got up from the bed. He quietly dressed himself and exited her apartment, feeling energized and alive. As he made his way back to his own apartment, he felt a sense of excitement and anticipation building inside of him.

Once inside and the door was safely closed, Thomas set his music to play at a louder volume than usual, feeling the beats of the music pulse through him. He moved with a newfound confidence and energy as he got ready for the day. Every little task seemed to fill him with a sense of accomplishment, and he couldn't help but hum along to the music as he went about his morning chores.

As he finished getting ready, Thomas took one last look in the mirror, making sure he felt confident and ready to take on the day. He picked up his phone and sent a quick text to Gabrielle to tell her how much he had enjoyed waking up next to her and how much he looked forward to seeing her again. With a smile on his face, he set out into the world.

He walked out of the building towards his car, feeling the sun shining down on him. He got into the driver's seat, put the key in the ignition, and turned on the radio. As "Back in Black" by AC/DC started playing, he turned up the volume and rolled down the windows. He enjoyed feeling the wind on his face while he drove.

When he pulled out of the parking lot, Thomas felt an energy within him that he hadn't experienced in years. He felt alive, as if he had just woken up from a long sleep. He sang along to the lyrics of the song, not caring if anyone saw him doing it. The wind blew through his hair as he drove down the road, and he enjoyed every moment of it.

Even the sunshine looked different to him now, almost like it was illuminating the world in a new light. The colors seemed more vibrant, the smells more intense, and the sounds more alive.

As he sat at a red light, he checked his phone and noticed a new email from Dr. Ruth Weber confirming their meeting for the coming Friday at 12:00 pm. He had been so distracted by thoughts of Gabrielle that he had forgotten to check his emails. Glancing at the time on his phone, he realized it was already 11:37 am. His heart started racing as he quickly typed the address into his Google maps and revved his engine, eager to make up for lost time.

Thomas' heart was pounding as he raced towards Gilroy Avenue, the address of the meeting with Weber. He couldn't believe he had almost missed this important meeting. As he sped down the streets, he cursed himself for being so irresponsible. He had heard Dr. Weber was not the type of woman to tolerate tardiness, and he did not want to complicate his chance of making a good impression on her.

As he approached the office building, he noticed that it was 12:15pm. "Fifteen minutes late, damn it!" he spoke to himself, irritated at his tardiness. He parked his car haphazardly on the side of the road, not bothering to check if he was in a legal spot and ran towards his destination. He was out of breath by the time he reached the entrance to the office building and attempted to compose himself as best he could as he entered the lobby where Weber's office was located. He was immediately struck by the elegant décor of the hallway. The polished tile under his feet amplified the sound of his rapid footsteps.

He approached the door to Weber's office, took a deep breath, and knocked. A moment later, the door opened, and he was greeted by the good doctor herself. She stood tall and confident in a crisp white blouse along with black slacks. Her salt-and-pepper hair was styled in a sleek bob, and her dark eyes sparkled as she welcomed him inside. Apparently, he had worried too much about being late. She didn't *seem* upset at him, but he figured he'd find out soon enough anyway!

183

The office was just as impressive as the hallway, with large windows offering a stunning view of the city skyline. A mahogany desk dominated the room, adorned with a few tasteful art pieces and a vase of fresh flowers. The walls were lined with bookshelves filled with law books and legal tomes. A comfortable armchair sat across from the desk, and Thomas took a seat as Dr. Weber sat behind the desk.

Her eyes were appraising as she took in Thomas' somewhat disheveled appearance. "Mr. Rene," she said, her tone cool and measured. "Thank you for coming."

Thomas nodded affirmatively, his gaze locking onto Weber's. He could sense that she knew something, and he was eager to find out what it was. "Of course. You wanted to see me?"

She leaned forward, her gaze intent. "I understand that you work for *Turner Research*," she said, her voice low and measured. "I'm curious as to why someone of your stature would choose to work for a company like that?"

Thomas felt a flicker of annoyance at Weber's tone. "I believe in the work they're doing," he said, his voice firm. "And as for why someone like me would choose to work there, I'm not sure what you mean by that."

Dr. Weber smiled slightly, as if she were enjoying the challenge of sparring with Thomas. "I'm curious as to what specifically you do for the company?"

Thomas hesitated, not wanting to reveal too much about his work. He dodged the question. "I'm involved in a number of projects related to scientific research and development," he said.

Weber's expression remained guarded as she leaned back in her chair. "So, why did you choose to accept my invitation to meet with me today?" She asked.

Thomas felt a surge of confidence as he met Weber's gaze. "Because I'm aware of the possibility that you might have some information that could be valuable to me. Otherwise, why else would you contact me?"

She studied him for a few moments before speaking again. "Very well," she said, her tone cautious. "If you have specific questions, I'll do my best to answer them, but I must warn you, Mr. Rene, that I have my own interests to protect. I'm sure you can understand."

"How do you know who I am?" Thomas asked. He didn't enjoy cat-and-mouse games when he was on the receiving end of it, and he truly wanted to know how she had managed to find out about him. After all, he now worked directly for Crane and Nouvel who both wanted to keep Thomas in the shadows. Thomas could be more effective that way.

The woman hesitated for a moment, focusing on her interlaced hands resting on her desk. "A man by the name of David Kim contacted me recently," she said finally, her voice measured. "He was concerned about a person he saw on his aunt's security doorbell camera. He believed this person to be associated with *Turner Research*."

Thomas felt a knot form in his stomach as Weber mentioned in passing that there was a security doorbell camera. He couldn't believe that he had missed such an important detail during his recent visit to David Kim's aunt's house. He mentally berated himself for not having been more thorough, knowing that, in his line of work, even the smallest oversight could have major consequences. "I see," he said, his tone equally measured. "And did you find out who this person was?"

The doctor met Thomas' gaze squarely, her expression guarded. "Yes," she said simply. "It was you."

Thomas felt frustration mixed with some relief. "I see," he said again, keeping his voice neutral. "And what else did Mr. Kim discuss with you?"

She answered quickly. "Several things," she said carefully. "But he seemed convinced that you were involved in something...unethical, shall we say?"

Thomas couldn't help but chuckle at the word "unethical." "I assure you, Dr. Weber, that everything we do at *Turner Research* is for the betterment of the human race," he said, quoting the party line. "Our work is well grounded in scientific principles and adheres to rigorous ethical standards." He chuckled internally at his verbal evasions, *"Put that in your pipe and smoke it!"*

The scientist studied him for a few moments before speaking again. "I understand," she said, her tone sounding doubtful, "And I appreciate your commitment to your work. But I must ask - is there any truth of which you are aware to Mr. Kim's claims?"

Thomas shook his head. "I don't think so, but I'm sorry, Dr. Weber, I cannot discuss the details of my work with anyone outside of *Turner Research*," he said firmly. " I *can* assure you that everything we do is in the best interest of the wider scientific community."

Weber nodded, her expression thoughtful. "I understand," she said. "And I don't mean to imply that I doubt your own integrity or the value of your work, whatever it is that you do. But I think it's important for us to have a frank conversation about Mr. Kim's concerns and how we can address them."

He sat back in his chair, studying Weber carefully. He knew that she had left *Turner Research* the year before, but he couldn't shake the feeling that she still had an interest in the company. "What do you suggest we do, Dr. Weber? I am going to need to speak directly with Kim myself, there is no getting around that fact." His tone was direct and confident.

She hesitated for a moment before answering. "I can arrange a meeting between you and Mr. Kim, if that's what you wish," she said. "But, before I do, I need to know why you want to meet with him."

It was at this point that his phone suddenly buzzed with a new text message which he decided to ignore. He didn't want to appear rude by checking his phone. Instead, he focused on what Weber was saying. He pushed the thought of the text message temporarily aside, though he wondered who was trying to reach him at such an inconvenient time.

He shifted in his seat, suddenly feeling uncomfortable. "I'm sorry, Dr. Weber, but the nature of my meeting with Kim must remain confidential," he said firmly. "All I can say is that it's important."

His opponent studied him for a few moments before graciously changing the subject. "You might ask yourself why I have such an interest in *Turner Research*," she said, her tone thoughtful. "I resigned from the company a year ago for reasons of my own, but that doesn't mean I'm not still interested in the work going on over there."

Thomas raised an eyebrow. "'Interested' how?"

She looked at him, her expression enigmatic. "Let's just say that my departure from *Turner Research* wasn't exactly amicable," she said cryptically. "There were...differences of opinion about the use of the science."

Thomas felt a surge of curiosity at her words, but he knew better than to press the matter too hard. "I'm sorry to hear that" he said carefully. He couldn't help but wonder what kind of "differences of opinion" could have caused such a respected scientist to leave her job. Unable to contain his curiosity any longer, he took advantage of a momentary lapse in the conversation.

"Dr. Weber, forgive me for asking, but when you say, 'differences of opinion,' what do you mean exactly?" he asked somewhat warily, unsure of what she might say and whether he would want to know.

She leaned forward, her expression serious. "The scientific community works together to provide accurate explanations of how the natural world works," she said somewhat pedantically. "But *sometimes*...not everyone agrees on what's best for the greater good."

Thomas felt a chill run down his spine at her words. He knew that the kind of research conducted at *Turner Research* was cutting-edge stuff and could potentially have far-reaching implications. And he also knew that there were people out there who might not share the same values as his company when it came to using the science.

Despite his curiosity being piqued, Thomas realized that it wasn't his place to pry any further. So, he simply nodded and said, "I see. Thank you for explaining, Dr. Weber."

Weber nodded in response, but Thomas was sure that there was more to the story than what she had revealed. So, he pushed his curiosity aside for the moment and focused on the next matter at hand: meeting with David Kim.

"I'll make the arrangements for you to meet with Kim." Weber volunteered, then reached for her phone. "Excuse me for a moment. I need to ask someone to join us who *is* on time."

Thomas cringed inwardly as he caught the veiled criticism. *"Took her long enough!"* he thought to himself.

A moment later, there was a knock on the door. Weber called out for the person to please come in, and Thomas turned, quite curious to see who it was.

Chapter 43

Too Little, Too Late!

To Thomas' surprise, David Kim entered Dr. Weber's office, his eyes darting nervously around the room before riveting on Thomas. Kim was a short Asian man in his early thirties with dark hair that was neatly combed to the side. He wore a white dress shirt and black slacks, and his hands trembled slightly as he took a seat next to Thomas in front of the doctor's desk.

Thomas couldn't help but feel a little put off by Kim's unexpected appearance. He had thought of meeting with him privately, *not* in front of Weber. Despite this, Thomas kept himself composed and tried not to show any signs of discomfort.

Dr. Weber greeted Kim reassuringly and introduced him to Thomas. "I know you've seen him on your door camera already, but this is Thomas Rene, the person you've been wanting to meet," she said to Kim.

Kim nodded his understanding, but his eyes remained fixed on Thomas. "Yes, I've been wanting to speak with you," he affirmed, his voice shaking slightly.

Thomas leaned forward in his chair, studying Kim carefully. He could tell that the man was nervous, but wondered what Kim wanted to discuss with him. Kim had apparently gone to great lengths to track Thomas down and set up a safe meeting.

Weber remained quiet, watching the two men as they sized each other up. She knew that this meeting could have significant implications for both *Turner Research* and David's personal interests, and she was interested to see how it would play out.

Kim turned to face Thomas more fully, his eyes narrowing. "Why did you go to my aunt's house?" he asked, his voice hardening.

Thomas felt annoyance flare up inside him. He had been hoping to control the tempo of the meeting, but it seemed like he was going to need to flow with it. He took a deep breath before answering. "I wanted to speak with you about whatever materials or information you might still have in your possession from your employment with *Turner Research*," he said, watching David's body language closely.

Kim's face took on a furtive look, "Believe me, I am well aware I can't discuss anything about my employment with that company," he said in a shaky voice. "I haven't forgotten the confidentiality agreement I signed!" he added with a note of defiance in his voice.

Thomas wasn't convinced. He could tell that Kim was holding something back. He wondered what it was that Kim was so afraid of.

The doctor remained quiet for the moment and watched the two men with interest.

Thomas raised an eyebrow and his tone turned more serious. "Why did you feel the need to take refuge at your aunt's house in the first place?" he asked pointedly.

Kim shifted in his seat, clearly uncomfortable with the direction this conversation was taking. "I'm not stupid, Mr. Rene! I hear stuff, and I've heard of things happening to previous employees," he answered, his voice tremulous. "And considering the danger of the project that Dr. Crane is working on..." His voice trailed off as Weber coughed warningly, her eyes pointedly flicking to Thomas before settling back on David.

Kim immediately stopped talking about that and cleared his throat. "I don't want any trouble from *Turner Research*," he said, his voice sounding a bit desperate. He assured Thomas, "They have nothing to worry about from me at all."

Thomas looked over at the doctor, annoyed at her involvement in this conversation. He wondered why she had coughed at that moment. What was it that she wasn't telling him? For now, he decided to focus on Kim and getting the answers he needed.

190

Thomas leaned forward, his eyes boring into Kim's. "What *exactly* do you have that would be considered sensitive?" he demanded.

Kim hesitated, looking woebegone. "I...I just have some documents and research data," he said, his voice shook slightly and his eyes implored Thomas for understanding. "But I haven't shared them with anyone, I swear!"

Before Thomas could say anything, Dr. Weber stepped in. "Thomas, if I may," she said, looking directly at him. She reached into her briefcase and pulled out a small zip drive, sliding it across the desk towards him. "This should resolve any concerns that Dr. Crane may have. This is all that David had in his possession."

Thomas picked up the zip drive and examined it carefully. He couldn't help but wonder why Weber was the one who had it in her possession in the first place, but he decided not to press the matter for now. Instead, he turned his attention back to Kim and asked directly, "Is this everything?"

Kim nodded vigorously and said yes.

Dr. Weber spoke up again. "Thomas, I would also like to add that, should anything happen to David in any manner, I would be very displeased with *Turner Research*," she said, her voice hard. "And I would be forced at that point to become more involved, and you wouldn't like that at all, I assure you! Would you please relay that to your superiors personally?"

Thomas wanted to ask Weber what she meant by "becoming more involved", but he decided not to ask. He simply nodded his assent and stood up. Without saying anything else, he took the zip drive and made his way out of the office, his mind racing with questions and doubts.

Once he was safely out of the doctor's office and her door firmly closed behind him, Thomas checked his phone and saw that there was a brief message from Kelly Brown. Kelly reported that he had followed David Kim to an office building. What had struck Kelly as odd was that he had seen Thomas' car in the parking lot of that same office building!

191

After reading Kelly's text, Thomas sarcastically thought, *"Too little, too late!"* and replied, "Thanks for letting me know. You can stop following Kim now. I'll be in touch later." He was relieved that Kelly no longer had to tail David Kim, but his unease about the rest of the situation remained, and such feelings demanded resolution in Thomas' experience.

Chapter 44

We Will See...

Thomas sat in his dimly lit apartment, staring at the zip drive on his desk, feeling the weight of the decision he had to make. He took a sip of his whiskey, savoring the smoky flavor, and considered his options. On one hand, his curiosity was piqued, and he couldn't help but wonder what secrets the drive might hold. On the other hand, he had a strict code of ethics and knew that betraying the trust of his client and examining the contents of the drive would be a breach of that code. But who would know?

He lit a cigar, taking a puff and making smoke rings with his mouth, trying to clear his mind. He considered whether even the temptation to plug the drive into his laptop was a violation of his professional standards. He had been hired to protect the interests of *Turner Research,* and he refused to let his personal curiosity compromise that responsibility.

With heavy heart, he made his decision. He picked up the drive and dropped it into his desk drawer, locking it away. He took another sip of his whiskey, trying not to think about it anymore. It had been a difficult decision, but he couldn't let himself be swayed by his own innate curiosity. He was a professional, and he was paid well to prioritize his clients' interests over his own.

Just as he thwarted the temptation, the phone rang. He glanced at the caller ID and saw that it was Samuel Nouvel. *"Damn it, what does he want now?!"* Thomas thought.

"Hello, Samuel," Thomas answered, and rebelliously took another sip of his smoky whiskey.

"Thomas, how are you?" Samuel's reedy voice came through the line. "I assume you've been enjoying your downtime?"

"What *downtime?!"* Thomas thought to himself sulkily, then answered out loud, "I have been, thank you. So, what can I do for you?" Thomas asked a bit warily.

"I have travel plans for you. We need you to fly to Oviedo, Spain, on Monday. First class, of course," Nouvel added.

Thomas quickly grabbed his notebook to jot down the details. "Who will I be meeting with?" he asked.

"Archbishop Hugo Rodriguez. It's a sensitive matter, Thomas, so we need you to be on your best behavior," Nouvel cautioned.

Thomas grunted affirmatively, his mind already racing with possibilities. "Of course, Samuel. No problem."

"Excellent. I'll send you the details shortly. Enjoy the rest of your evening," Nouvel said curtly before he hung up.

Thomas sat back in his chair, taking another puff from his cigar. He was a bit excited at the new assignment. The opportunity to meet with an archbishop only heightened his curiosity, but at the same time, he couldn't shake the feeling of unease that came with *every* new assignment. He wondered what he would find in Oviedo, and whether it would be something he could live with. *"We will see...,"* he thought while reaching defiantly for the whiskey.

Chapter 45

It's Okay Not To Have *All* the Answers

Thomas peered through the peephole of the door and saw Gabrielle standing on the other side holding a large, rectangular package. He smiled to himself and quickly opened the door, greeting her with a warm embrace. "Hey there, gorgeous! What have you got there?" he asks, nodding towards the package.

Gabrielle grinned, "It's a gift for Sister Anne. It's the painting I made of Jesus being crucified. I hope she likes it."

Thomas assured her, "I'm sure she will."

As they drove to the restaurant, *Toppin*, where they were to meet once again with members of Gabrielle's church, Thomas mentioned that he would be leaving on Monday for a business trip and would be gone for several days. Gabrielle asked where he was going, and Thomas kept it vague, saying it was for work.

"So, where exactly are you headed on your trip?" Gabrielle asked.

Thomas replied dismissively, "Just a business trip, nothing too exciting."

She turned towards him and frowned, "You're always so *secretive* about your work. Is it *really* that top secret?"

"I suppose you could say that, but trust me, it's not as glamorous as it sounds." He forced a chuckle.

Gabrielle sighed, "Well, just promise me you'll stay safe, okay?"

Thomas smiled reassuringly at her, happy that the interrogation was over, "Always do."

They rode in a comfortable silence until they arrived at the restaurant. As they got out of the car, Gabrielle grabbed the large painting and muttered to herself, "I hope she will like it." Thomas just smiled at her.

When they arrived at the restaurant, they were greeted by the entire group of seven people sitting at a large table. Thomas recognized several faces from the previous meals with Gabrielle's church group.

After a few minutes of small talk, the conversation shifted to the upcoming Easter holiday. One of the attendees brought up the topic of the resurrection of Jesus, and soon everyone was chiming in with their thoughts and opinions.

As they talked, Gabrielle placed the large, rectangular package she had brought with her onto the empty table next to them and announced that it was a gift for Sister Anne. Sister Anne, surprised and touched, burst out with "Gabrielle, you shouldn't have!" and eagerly unwrapped the package to reveal the beautiful painting inside of Jesus. The table of people erupted into applause, and Sister Anne thanked Gabrielle effusively for the thoughtful gift. Sister Anne gazed at the painting with a mixture of awe and reverence. "It's so beautifully done," she said softly, but just loud enough for Thomas and Gabrielle to hear the sincerity in her voice.

Gabrielle smiled, pleased with Sister Anne's reaction. "I'm so glad you like it! I just wanted to do something to help, you know?"

Sister Anne nodded, her gaze still fixed on the painting. "It reminds me of the return of Christ," she said, her voice tinged with excitement. " I see the hope and promise of His return, when He will judge the living and the dead."

The rest of the group nodded in agreement as Sister Anne showcased the art by holding it up in their direction, some adding their own thoughts on the subject. Thomas listened intently, silently observing the group. While he respected their communal faith and convictions, he couldn't help but feel a sense of detachment from it all.

He took a sip of his water, feeling a sudden inexplicable urge to check his phone. As he reached for his pocket where he kept it,

Gabrielle shot him a disapproving look of warning. He quickly withdrew his hand and apologized with his eyes to Gabby.

As their lunch arrived, one of the new members by the name of John asked Sister Anne, "Sister, can you explain why so many people believe that Jesus' return will happen soon?"

Sister Anne took a sip of her tea before responding. "Well, it's written in the Bible that no one knows the exact day or hour of His return, but there are signs mentioned in the Bible that are supposed to happen before His return. For example, there will be wars and natural disasters like earthquakes and famines. These things have been happening more frequently in recent times which is why some people may believe that His return is near."

Thomas listened to Sister Anne's explanation. Personally, he was fascinated by the topic. He had never been a particularly religious person, but he could not help but be intrigued by the concept of Jesus' return. He wondered if it was all just a metaphorical way of speaking about the end-of-times or if it was something that would truly happen one day, be it near or far.

As the conversation continued, Gabrielle leaned over and whispered to Thomas, "You know, I've been thinking about what you said earlier about your work. Is everything okay?"

Thomas looked at her and nodded, "Yes, everything is *fine*. It's just a routine business trip."

Outwardly, she seemed to accept his answer, but Thomas was surprised that she had brought it up again so soon after their conversation in the car. He wasn't sure he would bet against it coming up again.

As the group enjoyed their meals, Jason brought up the topic of Armageddon. He cleared his throat and began to speak, his voice larded with conviction.

"Armageddon," he said, "is the pivotal moment in the Bible when the final battle between Good and Evil takes place. It is the ultimate showdown between the forces of Light and the forces of Darkness. The Book of Revelation tells us that the armies of the

Antichrist will gather in the valley of Megiddo, and that's where the great battle will be fought."

He paused for a moment, looking around the table to make sure everyone was following along. "But make no mistake," he continued, "this is not a battle that we humans can win on our own. We *need* the strength and guidance of our Lord to prevail in the final battle. That's why it's *so* important that we stay faithful to Him, no matter what trials and tribulations are given to us along the way."

The room fell silent as Jason's words sank in. Eventually, someone broke the silence with a quiet "Amen, Brother!" Then, the conversation moved on to other topics, but the weight of Jason's words lingered on.

Thomas leaned back in his chair, composing his thoughts. After a brief pause, he spoke up, "The idea of Jesus returning has always been a source of confusion for me. It just doesn't add up."

"What do you mean, Thomas?" Gabrielle asked, cocking her head inquisitively at him.

"Let's say, for argument's sake, that Jesus was a real person." He noticed a few members of the group raised their eyebrows in surprise at his use of the term 'real', so he quickly adjusted his wording, "What I mean is, Jesus died on the cross in order for us to be forgiven our sins. Despite this, it is also believed that Jesus will return and bring Armageddon with him. Isn't that... strange? I mean, imagine this scenario: I love you and I forgive you, but I am also going to come back some random day way in the future and rain hellfire on your descendants. *That* just doesn't make sense to me because it seems contradictory."

Sister Anne took the time to adjust her habit before responding, "Brother Thomas, I understand your confusion. We Catholics believe that Jesus is patiently waiting to return *because* He loves us and wants to give humanity as much time as possible to choose voluntarily to follow Him. It's not about vengeance and raining hellfire down on descendants, but rather about fulfilling His promises and bringing about a new heaven on earth where there will *be* no more pain or suffering. We also believe that *every* day is a fresh, new opportunity to accept Him as our Lord and Savior."

Thomas leaned back in his chair; his brow furrowed as he listened to Sister Anne's explanation. "I can understand that perspective," he said slowly, "But if God is truly all-powerful, couldn't He choose a different way to bring about a new heaven-on-earth without causing so much horror and suffering along the way? I mean, He could figuratively just snap His fingers and make it happen, right?" He took a sip of water before continuing. "I'm not saying that *I* have all the answers, but it just seems like there's a disconnect there. I apologize, though, if what I say offends anyone. I've been told that I'm too pragmatic for my own good, sometimes." He snuck a glance at Gabrielle as the one who had told him that before.

Sister Anne nodded her head. "Please, Thomas, do continue. I want to hear more of your thoughts on the matter." The others at the table showed their agreement with murmurs of assent.

Thomas hesitated for a moment, but decided to continue, saying "Ok, If God is truly all-powerful, why does He need to allow Armageddon at all? Just to fulfill His promises? Or is it a threat? It seems to me more like God is *angry* about something that *we* did and is using this as a way to punish us rather than simply bringing about a new heaven on earth."

Gabrielle turned to Thomas and asked curiously, "Are you referring to divine retribution?"

Thomas leaned forward, a considering tone in his voice, "Yes. If you look at the moments in history where God punished humanity, it was usually in response to specific actions on our parts. The great flood was a response to the wickedness and corruption of humanity. Next thing you know, Noah is frantically gathering the animal kingdom for a forced all-expenses-paid trip on his gigantic Ark! Sodom and Gomorrah were also destroyed because of their people's sins of pride, gluttony, and sexual immorality. The plagues in Egypt were punishments for the Pharaoh's repeated refusals to let the Israelites leave." He paused, taking a sip of water. "But the idea Jesus Christ suddenly returning without cause just doesn't seem consistent with the nature of God as I understand it. God, in the bible, has always reacted when we do something bad. If there were a plan or structure to it, then perhaps it would make more sense. It just comes across as punishment to me, and not just a great random return."

Thomas had hoped to hear more thoughts on the subject he had brought up, but no one seemed at all anxious to go down that rabbit-hole at that moment. He sighed to himself.

When the meal came to an end, everyone stopped their chatting and started paying their bills, getting ready to leave. They all said their goodbyes, and Sister Anne thanked Gabrielle again for the beautiful painting of Jesus. As Thomas and Gabrielle left the restaurant, Gabrielle casually asked what he had thought of the lunch conversation. Thomas admitted that he was not quite sure what to think, but that he *had* found the discussion interesting, as usual. The two walked hand in hand to the car, and Thomas even walked around the car to open the door for Gabrielle before getting in himself. As he started the car, Gabrielle turned to him and said, "You know, Thomas, sometimes it's okay not to have *all* the answers." Thomas nodded that he understood and the two drove home in silence again while both mulled over the lunch conversations on their own.

Chapter 46

I Take Confidentiality Seriously

When Thomas got out of bed, he shuffled over to the window and drew back the curtains to see the bright blue sky outside. It was a bright November day, and he felt a sense of relief and calm wash over him as he took in the beauty of the wide-open blue.

His phone vibrated, and he saw a text from his mother reminding him that Thanksgiving was only nine days away. A smile spread across his face as he remembered how much he loved that holiday. His mother always went all out, cooking up a feast for the family that would last for days. He quickly typed out a reply, his fingers tapping on the screen as he expressed his excitement and promised not to miss it for anything.

He took a quick shower, shaved, and got dressed in a black suit and tie, then grabbed his leather travel bag and began packing. He checked the time and realized he needed to hurry. Thomas quickly ate some toast and eggs, drank his coffee, and then placed a note on Gabrielle's door which read: "Off to my flight, missing you already."

As he stepped out of the building, he looked at his watch and realized he was running a little late. Thomas walked briskly to his black Mercedes and threw his bag into the trunk. He got into the driver's seat, lit a cigarette, and started the engine. He glanced at the clock on his car's dashboard and began driving towards *Turner Research* to drop off the zip drive before heading to the airport.

Thomas maneuvered his car through the sea of picketing religious groups and pulled up to the building. He stepped out of his car and moved through the crowd, doing his best to ignore their fervent protests. He made it into the building and headed straight to Dr. Stephen Crane's office.

As he approached the open door, Thomas could see Crane sitting on the couch, surrounded by stacks of technical documents and data reports. Crane looked up and greeted him. "Good morning, Thomas," he said, motioning for him to come in. Thomas stepped inside the office and took a seat in one of the chairs across from Crane. He noticed that Dr. Crane looked a bit stressed, with dark circles under his eyes and a slightly disheveled appearance. Despite his appearance, Crane got straight to business. "Do you have the zip-drive with you?" he asked.

Thomas carefully placed the drive on top of the documents that were spread out on the coffee table. He told Crane that the David Kim problem had been successfully resolved. He explained that David was quite frightened, so Thomas didn't anticipate any future problems from him, but if anything else came up, Thomas would handle it. Dr. Crane thanked Thomas for his efficiency and the timely resolution of the matter.

Thomas took a deep breath and said, "Before I go, Dr. Weber wanted me to convey a message to you directly. She said that she hopes everything stays settled and that David Kim remains safe and unaffected now that he has given up the remaining documents from *Turner Research*. However, she also mentioned that if anything happened to David in the future, she would be very displeased with you and would be *forced* to become 'more involved'. Her words, not mine. Don't shoot the messenger!"

Crane's face contorts with a flash of anger when he heard what Ruth said. He sat back on the couch, his fingers steepled together in front of his mouth, thinking for a moment. He dismissed Thomas' request not 'to shoot the messenger' comment with a wave of his hand, saying gruffly, "Don't worry about it, Thomas. Ruth can be a bit... overprotective at times. I appreciate you bringing it to my attention, though. As Thomas stood up to leave, Crane hesitated, then asked, "Have you looked at the contents of the zip-drive?"

Thomas looked at him sharply, offended by the question even though he had wrestled with his own conscience over that very thing. "Dr. Crane, I'm a professional. Maintaining confidentiality is part of my job. I take that seriously." Crane nodded a bit reluctantly, recognizing that he would just have to take Thomas' word for it. "Of course, I know that, Thomas. I just had to ask. Have a safe trip to see the Archbishop."

Thomas thanked him for his time and left, still miffed at being asked if he had examined the contents of the drive.

Thomas quickly exited the building, picking up his pace as he made his way to his car. His mind was already on the upcoming flight and the meeting with Archbishop Hugo Rodriguez. When he reached his car, he fumbled with his keys before finally unlocking the door and sliding into the driver's seat. He took a moment to collect himself before starting the car and pulling out of the parking lot. Traffic was light, but he didn't want to take any chances with the time. He navigated the streets with practiced ease, his mind already turned to the next task at hand.

As he approached the airport, Thomas felt that familiar sense of excitement mixed with apprehension. Traveling always felt like a new adventure, but he knew that the meetings ahead would be serious and would require his full attention. He pulled into the parking lot at the airport, parked his car, and headed into the terminal, ready for whatever came his way.

Chapter 47

What Are *You* Doing Here?!

Thomas boarded his flight from Phoenix Sky Harbor International Airport in Arizona to London Heathrow Airport with a layover of four hours before his connecting flight to Asturias Airport in Spain. During his layover, he explored the airport and ate a quick meal at one of the many restaurants available inside the terminal. He then boarded his next flight to Asturias Airport, a smaller airport with few amenities. The flight was relatively short, only two hours, but Thomas was still able to get some rest.

Thomas finally landed around 7am, local time. After grabbing his luggage, he headed over to a rental car center and picked up his reserved vehicle. From there, he made his way to Oviedo, a beautiful city in northern Spain.

As he approached the city center, Thomas was taken aback by the stunning architecture of the old town. He followed the signs to his hotel, a 5-star luxury property with a grand entrance and a beautifully landscaped courtyard. The hotel lobby was just as impressive with lofty ceilings, ornate chandeliers, and an elegant marble staircase.

Thomas checked in and was shown to his room, which was spacious and beautifully decorated in neutral tones with high-end furnishings. The room came with a luxurious bathroom stocked with expensive toiletries and a thick white robe that felt incredibly soft to the touch.

After a refreshing shower, he reviewed the notes provided by Crane about his upcoming meeting with Archbishop Hugo Rodriguez. Thomas took his time going through the details to ensure that he would be fully prepared. With everything in order, he decided to take a nap, knowing that the meeting wasn't scheduled until 4pm, so he had time.

He lay down on the plush bed, surrounded by soft pillows and high-quality linens. The room was quiet and serene, and he quickly fell asleep, enjoying the comfort of the accommodations.

Thomas woke up to the sound of his phone alarm, feeling refreshed and ready for the meeting ahead. He picked up his phone and saw a text from Gabrielle which brought a smile to his face. He got out of bed and stretched before heading to the bathroom to freshen up.

After a quick shower, Thomas put on a dark navy suit, crisp white dress shirt, and black leather shoes. He took his time adjusting his tie and made sure everything was perfectly in place. He looked at himself in the mirror and felt ready to tackle the meeting ahead of him.

As he mentally prepared, Thomas put in his earpieces and started playing AC/DC's "Back in Black" and "Highway to Hell". The music pumped him up and got him into a focused state of mind. His ears were filled with the sound of the electrifying guitar riffs and heavy drums. He took a deep breath, closed his eyes, and visualized a successful outcome of the meeting. With a final adjustment to his tie, Thomas headed out of his room and into the lobby of the hotel.

Thomas walked out of the elevator, his eyes quickly scanned the room, looking for any signs of the Archbishop's representatives. And then, he saw the last person he had expected to see. Seated in the corner of the lobby, with a cup of coffee in her hand, was Evelyn Perdita. For a moment, Thomas was frozen in shock. It took him a few seconds to realize that it was her sitting there. Memories of their past sexual liaisons came flooding back to him. "Evelyn?" Thomas finally managed to say. "What are *you* doing here?"

Perdita looked up, and a smile spread across her face. "Hello, Thomas," she said cheerily. "I was sent to accompany you to see the Archbishop."

Thomas was taken aback. He did not know what to say. He had been expecting to meet with Rodriguez by himself, but he had had no clue that Evelyn Perdita would be there, too.

"I didn't know you were joining me," Thomas said, thinking frantically.

Evelyn gave him a seductive smile that seemed a touch too smug to Thomas' taste. "Consider me a gift from Dr. Crane," she said with a wink.

Thomas could feel his face turning red. He was not sure what to make of Evelyn's comment or her presence. He spoke up, trying not to whine, "I don't understand why you're *here*, Evelyn. I typically work alone. Don't want a partner, either!"

Evelyn responded with a wry smile and flicked imaginary dust off her sleeve, "Well, *Stephen* thought it would be a good idea for me to accompany you. Think of me as an extra set of eyes and ears."

Thomas looks at her skeptically. "So, you're calling Dr. Crane by his first name now? What does that even *mean*?!'""

Evelyn raised an eyebrow, completely dismissing Thomas' poor reaction to her presence. "It means that I know enough to help you. And I *don't* see why you're being so resistant. We used to work well together, remember?" Of course, she was referring to their activities in the bedroom, not the work-world.

Thomas let out a deep sigh. "Evelyn, things have changed for me."

Perdita leaned in closer to him, her impressive breasts just brushing his arm. "Have they really?"

Thomas just shook his head. "This isn't about entertaining ourselves with sex, Evelyn. This is about the job at hand and getting it done well." Thomas said. "But this is *my* job, and I work best alone. Plus, I don't know how much you know about the situation, and I don't want to risk anything going wrong."

Evelyn replied, "I understand your concerns, Thomas, but I assure you, I have been briefed quite enough on the situation here and I am to assist you in any way I can. Stephen wouldn't have sent me here, otherwise."

Thomas sighed, realizing that Evelyn wouldn't back down and that he would have to accept it, regardless of his misgivings. "Fine, but you need to follow my lead and not jeopardize the assignment."

Perdita agreed to his stipulations, but Thomas had a *bad* feeling about this!

Chapter 48

Surprise!

Thomas and Evelyn both stood up as the two representatives of the Archbishop approached. The man and woman introduced themselves, rather formally, to the reluctant pair. The woman, Carmen, had a warm and friendly demeanor, while the man, Jorge, seemed more reserved.

Carmen spoke with a Spanish accent as she introduced herself and Jorge. "We have a vehicle waiting outside for you," Carmen said, gesturing towards the exit. "Please, allow us to take you to your meeting."

Thomas and Evelyn followed them outside and were greeted by the sight of a black SUV with tinted windows. The four of them climbed into the waiting vehicle and were driven through the winding streets of Oviedo towards their destination, the Cathedral of San Salvador.

Carmen seemed to be very knowledgeable about the local area, pointing out landmarks and providing interesting tidbits about the city. Jorge, on the other hand, remained quiet and focused on the road ahead.

Carmen, their self-appointed tour guide, gestured out the window of the car as they got out. "The Cathedral of San Salvador still stands tall, a magnificent feat of architecture that commands the attention of all who behold it. Its walls, made of ancient stone, stretch high into the sky, pointing towards the heavens themselves. You see? Its spires, adorned with intricate carvings and sculptures, seem to reach for the sun, as if in worship of its radiant light."

As Thomas and Evelyn got closer to the famous cathedral, they could see the sun's rays dancing off the colorful stained-glass windows, casting a kaleidoscope of colors onto the polished marble floor. The air was heavy with the scent of incense and the sound of hushed whispers, as if the very walls of the cathedral held sacred secrets.

The interior of the cathedral was equally breathtaking with its towering arches, intricate frescoes, and ornate altars. Everywhere you looked, there was something to marvel at, to appreciate, and to wonder about. It was truly a place of beauty, of reverence and awe, a testament to Man's capability.

The representatives brought them to a small antechamber just outside the Archbishop's office. The silence of the chamber was only punctuated by the echoes of their footsteps on the ancient stone floors. They were ushered into a private room, and once the representatives left them, they waited in the silence for their appointment surrounded by the history of the centuries-old building. The stillness and serenity of the cathedral exerted a calming effect on both Thomas and Evelyn as they waited for their meeting.

The room was lavishly decorated with ornate furnishings and exquisite tapestries that adorned the walls. The ceiling was high and domed, with intricate designs painted in gold leaf. The floor was covered in a plush carpet that had seemed to almost swallow their footsteps when they walked in. A large wooden desk sat in one corner with various books and papers scattered about. The room was dimly lit with several wall sconces that cast a warm, flickering light that gave the space a cozy, yet elegant, ambiance. There was also a subtle scent of incense which further added to the tranquil atmosphere of the room. Overall, the space exuded a sense of grandeur and importance, well befitting the Archbishop's position in the Church.

As they waited, Evelyn suddenly broke the silence and said, "You know, Thomas, I was thinking about our partnership on this trip. Maybe we should have a code name for it, like Batman and Robin."

Thomas chuckled wryly, "I'm not sure I'm ready to be Robin just yet, Evelyn."

She smirked, "Well, I was thinking more along the lines of Wonder Woman and her sidekick."

Thomas laughed outright, then hastened to quiet down, "I don't think I have the legs for *that* costume."

Evelyn shook her head, "No, no, no. You can be Steve Trevor, the dashing pilot who always gets into trouble and needs Wonder Woman to rescue him."

Thomas smiled at this, "I don't mind the sound of that, but let's hope we don't need any rescuing *today*."

Evelyn nodded, "Agreed. We can just stick to being the dynamic duo."

They both chuckled at that. Evelyn took a deep breath and then spoke up, "Thomas, I have to say I'm glad to see you loosen up a little bit. I know it was a surprise for me to show up. I should have given you a heads-up." She paused, glancing at Thomas from under her long eyelashes for his reaction. "I just thought it might be fun for you to see me here. Surprise! I guess I was wrong." She finished, looking down at her hands with well-rehearsed shyness.

Thomas just looked at her, trying to figure a way out of this mess. This was exactly the conversation he had not wanted to have at this moment. Of course, he belatedly realized, that was precisely why she had done it. Her female cunning was on full display, and there was no way he was going to discuss this right now, just before meeting the Archbishop, and he told her so.

Evelyn's face fell slightly, her gambit having failed, but she tried to hide her disappointment from him.

Thomas just sighed.

Chapter 49

God Help Me!

It was a good thing that Thomas had refused to be suckered in by Evelyn's manipulations because the door to the office opened just then.

Archbishop Rodriguez greeted them warmly, "Hello! Please come in. I'm sorry to have kept you waiting!". His presence was commanding, despite not being large of stature, physically. Thomas felt a sense of awe as he stepped into the room of one of the most powerful men in the entire Church. The office was spacious, with high ceilings and ornate furnishings that spoke to the enormous power and prestige of the Catholic Church.

He shut the door behind them and gestured to the comfortable chairs near the fireplace. "Please, make yourselves comfortable," he said with a welcoming smile. "I'm so glad you could join me today." There was a feeling in the room that was a combination of love and coldness, an odd sensation that Thomas noticed.

Thomas thanked the Archbishop for granting them an audience, addressing him with the proper reverence for his position in the church. "Thank you, Your Excellency! We appreciate your time." However, Thomas noticed the solemn expression on the Archbishop's face, as if he were experiencing a deep inner struggle of some kind. He wondered what could be troubling this powerful member of the Church enough to show in his demeanor.

Thomas used his intuition and people-reading skills to navigate the conversation. He observed the archbishop's tone and body-language, listening carefully to every word. However, Thomas couldn't shake the feeling that something momentous was at stake in this meeting, something that would have a profound impact on both his own future and the fate of *Turner Research*, but he couldn't put his finger on what it was.

The Archbishop sat in his chair, his eyes fixed on the flickering flames of the fireplace. After a few moments of introspective silence, he turned to Thomas and asked him, "Are you a religious man?"

Thomas felt a lump form in his throat as he struggled with an answer. He suspected that Rodriguez was looking for something more than a simple 'yes' or 'no' response. After a moment, Thomas wisely decided honesty was the best policy.

"I was raised as a Catholic, Your Excellency," Thomas replied, "but I have to admit that I haven't truly been a practicing Catholic since I was a teenager."

Rodriguez nodded thoughtfully at Thomas' answer. "Faith is a complex thing," he said slowly. "It's not just about beliefs or traditions. It's about relationships; your relationship with God, with others, with oneself. It's about finding meaning and purpose in life and holding onto hope even in the face of adversity."

Thomas listened intently, feeling the Archbishop's words were important beyond the obvious. "How does anyone hold onto Faith when they're suffering?" Thomas asked, his voice filled with a genuine curiosity for the churchman's answer.

The Archbishop leaned forward slightly in his chair, his brow furrowed. "Suffering can be a *test* of faith, certainly," he said. "But it is also an essential component of growth. As the weak mortals we are, we tend not to value suffering very much!" He chuckled at this, and so did Thomas and Evelyn once they realized the humor of it.

The Archbishop's eyes were fixated on the flickering flames, and he was lost in his thoughts. Suddenly, he reached into his pocket and produced a small, brass box, an inch wide and tall. With a delicate touch, he rubbed his thumb over it for a few moments, as if the act of touching it gave him strength. After a brief pause, Rodriguez finally spoke. "I should probably give you what you have come for," he said, still staring into the fire, "But I would prefer to talk a bit more with you, first, if you don't mind."

Thomas and Evelyn both responded in the affirmative.

"My son and daughter," he begins, "I believe that God is not absent from our world. Quite the opposite, in fact! He is always present, in every moment and in every place. It is only our limited human perspective that can cloud our ability to see His hand in action."

Rodriguez's voice took on a more solemn tone. "But the true test of faith, my children, is not in our collective suffering or even the hopeful triumph of Good over Evil. It is in holding to the steadfast belief that God is with us *always*, even in the darkest of times. I contend that the greatest test of our faith lies in maintaining our unwavering conviction that He is working *through* us and *with* us to bring about a greater good for us all." He paused, "So, I declare to you, my children, do *not* lose faith. For, even amid darkness and chaos, God is still present, still working in ways we may not yet comprehend. We must simply trust in His plan and continue to strive towards the Light." The Archbishop turned his gaze towards Thomas and asked simply, "What is *your* opinion on Fate, Thomas? Do you think there is such a thing?"

Thomas took a moment to order his thoughts before answering. "I believe that Fate is what we make of it," he said. "We are not simply pawns in some predetermined game, but quite the opposite. We have the power to shape our own success or failure through the choices we make."

The Archbishop considered Thomas' words for a moment, before nodding enthusiastically. "Yes, I also believe that to be true," he said. "We may not be able to control every outcome, but we certainly do have control over our own choices along the way."

He leaned back in his chair, steepling his fingers together in thought. "And yet, there are times when what we call Fate seems to play a role in our lives, forcing us in directions we do not fully comprehend," he continued.

Thomas listened intently to the Archbishop's words and took a measure of comfort in the idea that there might truly be something beyond Thomas' own personal control at work in the world. He looked over at Evelyn, but her hooded eyes avoided his.

Rodriguez just sat there looking at them as though trying to weigh the value of their souls while fiddling with the small box in his hands. After a few moments, he muttered "Deus me adiuvet" to himself and proffered the box to them, whatever it was. Evelyn, surprisingly, was the one who moved first to take it. She extended her hand, and the bishop carefully placed the box onto her outstretched palm. Evelyn seemed quite pleased with herself, while Thomas wasn't sure what to think of any of this.

Thomas had overheard Rodriguez use the Latin phrase and did know its meaning. He translated it into English for the benefit of Evelyn, "God help me!", and she looked relieved to know for herself.

Archbishop Rodriguez glanced over at Thomas with a pained expression and added, "May He help us *all*, my son. Go in peace, and take care of *that*.", pointedly meaning the little box which had already disappeared into some hidden pocket of Evelyn's.

Thomas and Evelyn assured him they would do so and respectfully bid the Archbishop farewell, leaving the office behind them as they headed for the car.

Chapter 50

Just For A Little While

As they rode in the car carrying their precious cargo towards their hotel, Evelyn looked over at Thomas with a sly grin. "You know, I'm starving," she said, "and I could use a drink."

Thomas chuckled, pleased to also feel a sense of accomplishment after the successful meeting. "I could go for a drink, too," he replied.

The archbishop's driver, Carmen, who was on loan to them, spoke up. "The hotel you're staying at has a wonderful restaurant. I've eaten there before, and the food is fantastic."

Evelyn looked intrigued. "Really? What kind of food do they serve?"

"They have a mix of traditional Spanish dishes and some international cuisine. It's definitely worth a visit." Carmen replied.

Thomas nodded in agreement. "Sounds perfect. Can't do any harm. I'm hungry, too."

Once they arrived, they made their goodbyes to Carmen and immediately entered the restaurant. The decor was modern and chic, with warm lighting and sleek furnishings. As promised, the menu featured a mix of tapas, seafood dishes, and grilled meats, all with a unique twist on traditional Spanish flavors.

Thomas and Evelyn perused the menu and ordered a variety of tapas to start with, including croquetas de jamón, tortilla española, and gambas al ajillo. For their main course, Thomas ordered arroz con pollo while Evelyn opted for the more adventurous pulpo a la gallega. They both thoroughly enjoyed their meals, savoring each bite and commenting to each other about the unique flavors and textures of the Spanish cuisine.

Throughout the meal, they shared several pitchers of sangria and continued to chat and laugh, enjoying the moment together. The atmosphere of the restaurant was lively and festive, with Spanish music being performed in the background while the chatter of other diners filled the air.

Once they finished their meal, Evelyn invited Thomas to dance with her. Thomas hesitated for a moment, feeling a bit self-conscious about his dancing skills and a bit guilty about being there with Evelyn at all, but after a couple more drinks, he agreed to dance with her. After all, he rationalized to himself, it wasn't as if he had *chosen* for Evelyn to be there. It was a *business* trip, period.

They made their way to the small dance floor, where a few couples were already dancing. The band was playing a traditional Spanish song with a lively rhythm. Evelyn took Thomas' hand and pulled him closer to her, swaying gently to the music.

As they danced, Thomas felt greatly conflicted. He had to admit that dancing with Evelyn Perdita was...stimulating. *"God knows she is sexy as hell!"* he thought to himself, a cascade of sensations suddenly feeling quite important. His body was betraying him, but it felt so good through the haze left by the Sangria. He told himself that it was fine, just dancing with a business associate, but his conscience was sending up alarms that the rest of him completely ignored.

While dancing, a waitress walked by with a tray of tequila shots. Evelyn squealed and quickly grabbed two for herself and two for Thomas. Thomas briefly demurred, but with the whooping encouragement of Evelyn and the warm feeling in his belly from the Sangria, he gave in and slammed them down back-to-back. The smooth tequila burned down his throat and ignited a lingering heat in his chest. They both laughed and Evelyn took Thomas by the hand and pulled him back onto the dance floor. Strangely, this time, Thomas didn't feel so reluctant, and that still, small voice inside him seemed much harder to hear.

Evelyn's body moved in perfect rhythm with the music, and she swayed closer to him, her eyes sparkling with mischief.

"I know we've had our ups and downs, Thomas," she said, her voice low and sultry. "But I can't help feeling this chemistry between us. Just for tonight," she looked up at him, "Can't we let go of everything and just enjoy ourselves?"

Thomas was caught off guard by her sudden change in tone, but his brain, which was about the size of a pea by this time, had no intelligent response. The music and the drinks made him feel free and alive, and he found himself pulling her closer, their bodies swaying together as if they were the only two people in the world. And that finally scared him through the warm fog of tequila shots.

"I don't know, Evelyn," he says, his voice hesitant. "I am sort of in a relationship now, and I don't want to do anything that would hurt her."

Evelyn presses her body closer to his. "Gabrielle can have you any other night," she whispers in his ear. "But, for tonight, let me have you all to myself. Just for a little while?" She wheedled, knowing that his willpower was on the wane.

Thomas felt a shiver run down his spine as Evelyn's hands slid down his back, pulling him in even closer. For tonight, he groggily decided, he would just live in the moment with this sexy woman who was in his arms, across the wide ocean and far from Gabrielle. *"What could it hurt?"* he thought to himself, but he never heard the answer. The still, small voice was gone.

Chapter 51

Sure, You Didn't...

Thomas slowly opened his eyes, wincing at the bright light shining through the hotel window. He turned his head to the side and was dismayed to see Evelyn Perdita sleeping peacefully next to him. Memories of the night before flooded back to him as he groaned and put his hand to his aching forehead. He had never been one to drink to excess, but the combination of delicious food, tequila, and Evelyn had clearly gotten the best of him. He had let his guard down with all the drinking, and now he would have to pay for it, he thought grimly. Heading for the bathroom as quietly as he could, he wanted nothing more than to use the facilities and feel better---immediately, if not sooner!

Guilt started to creep over him as he slowly realized the enormity of what he had done the night before.

When he finished his ablutions, he stood in the doorway of the bathroom and stared at Evelyn who was framed by the morning sunlight. Her skin had a slight sheen that glistened softly in the too bright light. Her dark hair was tousled and fell loosely over her bare shoulder, framing her face and adding to her already mesmeric beauty. Despite the tidal wave of guilt he felt, he still appreciated the sight of the alluring woman lying there in the nude, apparently unaware of his scrutiny. Something about her supposedly unconscious presentation made him wonder if she were actually awake.

At that moment, Evelyn woke up and stretched, the bed sheet limply pooling at her waist. The nipples of her breasts were hard, and Thomas felt a familiar rise in his shorts. Noticing his growing condition, she sleepily crawled towards him on all fours on the bed looking for all the world like a sleepy lioness with definite intentions. Thomas didn't know if he should run or go for it one more time. Ruefully, he realized his brain was *still* the size of a pea!

Thomas wisely chose to run. He headed to the bathroom again, this time turning on the shower. Evelyn, disappointed at his decision, climbed out of the bed and followed him into the bathroom. She giggled and said, "I had *such* a good time with you last night!" But Thomas didn't know how to respond to that, so he settled for grunting "Mmmhmmm" as he put his head under the needle spray of the blessedly hot shower.

Evelyn leaned against the sink, still gloriously naked, and looked at him consideringly through the glass of the shower stall. After crossing her arms under her breasts, which had the effect of pointing those gun barrel nipples straight at him, she spoke up. "Are you feeling guilty about last night?" she asks, her voice edged.

Thomas didn't respond at first, the water from the shower pouring over his head. Eventually, he nodded. "Yeah," he said, his voice barely audible over the sound of the shower. "I am."

Evelyn sighed and walked closer. "It's not like you're *married* to her, Thomas," she said, "You're allowed to have a *little* fun."

Thomas looked at her, the water from the shower streaming down his face. "That's your idea of 'a little fun'?" he said, his voice rising. "I think we had *too* much fun."

Without another word, Evelyn stepped into the shower. She squeezed some shampoo into her hands and started massaging his scalp, letting her fingers run through his hair. Thomas closed his eyes and enjoyed it, but his mind was in overdrive trying to think a way out of this fine mess he'd gotten himself into.

Evelyn continued her attentions, taking the soap and scrubbing his back. But this only served to ratchet up Thomas' uneasiness even further. He cringed internally, realizing that this was entirely too much intimacy. Sex under the influence of copious quantities of alcohol was one thing. *Intimacy* was entirely different, he realized, and he felt extremely uncomfortable that Evelyn had invaded his shower.

They stood there for what seemed like an eternity to Thomas, each lost in their own thoughts, the sound of the shower the only thing that broke the silence.

Thomas rinsed the soap and shampoo off him and fled the shower, wishing to God that he had not been such an idiot the night before. Wrapping a towel around his waist, he walked over to the sink to brush his teeth. As he started, he heard his phone ringing back on the nightstand next to the rumpled bed. He quickly spit the toothpaste into the sink and left the bathroom to answer it. Truthfully, he was relieved to have an excuse to get out of the bathroom since Evelyn was in there. Unfortunately, the caller was Gabrielle. He groaned inside himself, desperately not wanting to answer. *"Of all times to call me!"* he thought to himself, feeling trapped between the Devil and the deep blue sea.

Evelyn cheerfully called out from the running shower, "Who is it?!"

Thomas cringed at the sound of Evelyn's voice and ran back to close the bathroom door. He managed to answer the phone just before it went to voicemail. "Hey, Gabrielle," he said, trying to sound glad to hear from her. "How are you doing?"

"I'm fine, Thomas, how about you?" Gabrielle replied, the excitement in her voice evident. "How's your trip going?"

"It's going great," Thomas replied, intending to keep the conversation light and brief as possible. "But I can't talk right now. Is everything okay?"

"Everything is good here, Thomas. I was just missing you and wanted to know you were alright. I hope you don't mind me calling!" said Gabby, her voice starting to sound a bit unsure of herself.

Thomas could feel his stress rising rapidly. He knew that Evelyn was still in the shower and that the walls of the hotel were thin. Just as he was about to end the conversation, Evelyn chose to yell out from the bathroom one more time. "Hey, can you order us room service, Thomas?" she called out. "I'm craving an omelet. How about you?"

Thomas froze, his heart pounding in his chest as he tried to decide what to do. What could he say? He could hear Gabrielle's breathing on the other end of the line, and he was certain that she had heard the request for an omelet by an obviously female voice.

"Thomas, is someone else there?" Gabrielle asked, unsure of what was going on.

Gabrielle's voice *seemed* calm but there was an underlying question in it which Thomas could sense from a country mile away. His stomach knotted up as he realized there was no avoiding it. He was screwed. A difficult conversation was about to take place, and it was all his fault. Thomas paused for a moment, realizing that he couldn't lie to Gabby. She was too important to him. *"Oh, dear God!"* he thought to himself. He took a deep breath and braced himself for the unavoidable. The worst part was realizing that he would be hurting the one person he had absolutely no desire to hurt in any way. "Yes," he replied, his voice barely audible. "That's Evelyn Perdita. Crane sent her, too. I didn't realize she would be on this trip, but we're almost done. One more meeting to go. "Thomas was not normally a praying man, but he came very close to it at this moment. He hoped fervently that Gabby would let it go for now, and silently swore to fix this when he got back to Phoenix.

There was a pregnant silence on the other end of the phone. Gabrielle's voice trembled slightly as she spoke, her hurt and disappointment evident. "Thomas, you told me that was over."

"Well, it *was* over! I mean, it *is* over." Thomas floundered. "Look, we went drinking last night to celebrate and my head is killing me. Can we *please* talk about this when I get back?"

"What is there to talk about, Thomas?" she coolly replied, obviously suspecting more than she was saying.

"Never mind, I can't do this right now. I think I might throw up." He really wasn't handling this well, and his normal confidence in handling situations had vanished.

She just said, "I'm sorry to bother you. Have a good flight." She was masking her hurt behind a veneer of civility, but Thomas could still feel the weight of her disappointment. He wanted to reach through the phone and hold her, to make everything right again, but he realized that he had to give her space and time to come to terms with what her woman's intuition told her.

She hung up.

Thomas sighed, even though she couldn't hear him anymore. "Of course," he said to the silent phone, feeling a lump in his throat. "I understand. I'm so sorry, Gabby."

Thomas stood there, feeling a scalding mix of guilt, regret, and heartbreak. His mistake weighed heavy on his shoulders as he wondered how he could have been so foolish. He wished that he could turn back time and make different choices, but he knew it was too late for that. The only thing he could do now was to hope that she would forgive him.

Evelyn emerged from the bathroom, now wearing the thick fluffy white robe, her hair still damp from the shower.

"Did you hear me before about the omelets?" she asks, holding the end of a towel to her head as she dried her hair.

Thomas turned towards her, his face devoid of expression. "Yes, you were loud and clear. *Both* Gabrielle and I heard you." he said.

Evelyn's eyes widened in pretended shock, and she clapped a hand over her mouth while releasing a nervous laugh. "Oh, my God," she says. "I had no idea you were on the phone with her. I'm sorry."

"Sure, you didn't..." Thomas thought to himself. He knew better.

Chapter 52

Enjoy Your Flight, Sir

Thomas walked through the airport, his mind preoccupied by the mess he had gotten into with Gabrielle. He completed the check-in process in a daze, hardly registering the flight attendant's smile as she handed him his boarding pass.

Once he settled into his first-class seat, he reached inside his suit pocket and pulled out the small box the Archbishop had given to Evelyn Perdita. It was simple in design, but there was a mystery about it that intrigued him. He'd had some difficulty retrieving the item from Evelyn after they left Archbishop Rodriguez. She had wanted to keep it with her, but Thomas had insisted that she give it to him for safekeeping. After all, he had said to her, it was his job and his responsibility to be sure it made it back to Dr. Crane at *Turner Research*. Privately, he knew that he was the better choice if physical conflict became an issue. Pouting, she had relinquished possession of the item to him.

Thomas examined the small box, his mind still aching with guilt and regret over his recent mistaken revelry with Evelyn. He was so deep in thought that he didn't notice the flight attendant standing next to him until she spoke up.

"Excuse me, Sir, would you like a drink of some kind?" she asked, interrupting his thoughts.

Thomas looked up at her, momentarily startled. He then realized he could use a stiff drink to calm his nerves. "Yes, please," he replied, his voice sincere. "Whisky, double, on the rocks."

The flight attendant acknowledged his order and walked back down the aisle, her hips moving that extra bit when a woman thinks someone is watching. Thomas hadn't even looked. Instead, he stared down at the box in his hand, feeling a strong temptation

223

to open it and see what was inside. He knew that he shouldn't, but his curiosity was overwhelming. Just as he was about to give in to the temptation, the flight attendant returned with his drink. Thomas hastily placed the box back into his pocket and took the glass from her like he had been dying of thirst in the desert.

"Enjoy your flight, Sir," she said with a smile before moving on to attend to the other passengers in First class.

Thomas took a deep sniff and sip of his whisky, feeling the burn of the alcohol as it went down his throat. He closed his eyes and leaned back in his seat, trying to clear his mind. It had been a long day since the morning's excitement with Evelyn and Gabrielle.

The soothing hum of the airplane's engines filled his ears, and Thomas felt himself begin to relax. The cabin lights dimmed and most of the passengers around him were settling in for the long flight. The gentle vibrations of the plane and the soft music playing over the speakers created a peaceful atmosphere.

Thomas took another sip of his whiskey and felt his eyelids growing heavy. He adjusted his seat to a more comfortable position and closed his eyes. The gentle sounds around him lulled him into a peaceful sleep, his mind temporarily freed from the turmoil of the past day.

As he drifted off, Thomas couldn't help but wonder what would happen when he returned home. Would Gabby be willing to listen to him? Would their relationship survive? And would Evelyn make trouble, or could she accept that Thomas was lost to her? As the plane continued its journey across the Atlantic, these questions swirled around in his mind but, for the moment, the calming sound of the plane's engines offered him a welcome respite from his worries.

Chapter 53

No Problem

Thomas sat at his desk in his apartment, his laptop open and a pile of emails on it to respond to. His eyes kept wandering back to the little brass box that sat on his desk, its small size seeming to taunt him with its mystery. He had barely resisted the temptation to open it since leaving Spain, the curiosity of it still lingered in the back of his mind.

He hadn't seen Gabrielle since returning home a few days ago, but he still believed she just needed her space to figure things out. He hoped that she would call so that they could talk and work things out. For the moment, he tried to focus only on his work.

The phone rang, and Thomas saw that it was Nouvel calling for their scheduled phone meeting. He picked up and greeted Nouvel, who immediately started speaking about the project.

"I just wanted to let you know that the Archbishop was very impressed with you. "Nouvel said. "He felt much more comfortable after meeting with you. You played your part perfectly, Thomas, and I want to show my appreciation."

Thomas was pleasantly taken aback when Nouvel told him that he had wired $25,000 to his checking account as a bonus. "Thank you, Samuel, I'll take it!" he exclaimed.

"That's not all," Samuel continued. "If you keep up the good work, there will be even more rewards in store for you. I can't say too much, but let's just say that there will be a nice Christmas bonus waiting for you after the next item is obtained." Thomas couldn't help but feel a thrill of excitement at the prospect of even more rewards for his work. Nouvel's voice boomed through the phone, "Thomas, Dr. Crane is expecting the item by 2:00 PM today. Can you make that happen?"

"Yes, of course. No problem." Thomas replied confidently.

Nouvel finished up the conversation by thanking Thomas again for his hard work and reminding him to keep everything confidential. Thomas assured him that he understood. After he hung up, Thomas sat back in his chair and sighed. He glanced down again at the little brass box on his desk and wondered what secrets it might hold. But, for the moment, he simply returned to dealing with his emails in the effort to keep his mind from wandering again.

Chapter 54

Chemistry?

Thomas wove his way through the protesters outside Turner Research, their chants becoming a dull background noise as he entered the building. He stopped at the front desk to sign in before continuing his way to Dr. Crane's office.

Crane looked the worse for wear since the last time Thomas had seen him. He looked tired and disheveled, the bags under his eyes speaking of long days and even longer nights. His eyes lit up at the sight of the package in Thomas's hand.

"Thank you, Thomas!" Stephen said, his voice tiredly exuberant. "I can't tell you how much this means to me."

Thomas offered a small smile. "Glad to be of service," he said. "By the way, are you getting any sleep these days?"

Crane grunted wryly. "Sleep? What's *that*? People in my position never get any quality sleep.

Thomas took a deep breath before asking Crane if he could speak with him about something a bit more personal. Crane agreed, shutting the door behind him, and invited Thomas to take a seat. Thomas sat down and looked the doctor in the eyes. "I just wanted to ask you about Evelyn Perdita," he said, "Why did you send her, too? Especially without telling me?"

Dr. Crane sighed and rubbed his temples. "That wasn't totally my decision," he said, "It was a request from Samuel. He said that he didn't want to take any chances, and that Evelyn would be an ideal choice to send with you, considering that you have chemistry together."

Thomas raised an eyebrow in surprise. "Chemistry?" he repeated.

Crane grinned in a just-us-men-here sort of way. "Yes, apparently Samuel thinks that the two of you work well together," he said, "I'm sorry if this wasn't acceptable, Thomas."

Thomas shook his head. "No, it was fine," he said, "I was just curious."

Crane leaned back in his chair and folded his arms across his chest. "Thomas, I need to be frank with you," he said. "The project we're working on right now is the most important one I've ever been a part of. We're dealing with highly sensitive information that needs to be kept confidential. There may be moments when things have to change on the fly, so to speak, and I need to be certain that you will handle those changes without any problems."

Thomas understood the gravity of the situation. "No problem, Dr. Crane. I appreciate your candor." he said. "Rest assured that I will do everything in my power to make sure this project will be a success."

Crane looked at Thomas for a moment before inclining his head. "I trust you, Thomas," he said. "But know that the stakes are high, and we can't afford any missteps." With that, Crane ended the meeting in his usual abrupt manner, indicating that Thomas could leave with a perfunctory wave of his hand.

Thomas made his way out of the office. As he walked down the hallway, he noticed that the protesters outside had grown even louder. As he exited the building, he saw Zack Pawloski, one of the researchers at *Turner Research*, who called out to him. "Hey, Thomas! Want to come grab a quick coffee with me in the staff breakroom?"

Thomas remembered that he didn't have any pressing matters to attend to at the moment and he could use a short break. "Sure, why not?" he replied with a smile.

Zack led Thomas into the breakroom and quickly began making coffee for the two of them. He also grabbed a couple of cheese Danishes from the breakroom fridge and set them on the table. As they sat down, Zack leaned in and asked Thomas in a hushed tone, "Hey man, did you ever end up meeting with Ruth Weber?"

Thomas sighed, "I can't really discuss that, Zack. You know, confidentiality reasons."

Zack raised his eyebrows, "Confidentiality reasons? What does that mean?"

Thomas took a sip of his coffee, "Let's just say, I'm not at liberty to discuss my meetings with *any*one."

Zack nodded his understanding and sat up straight in his chair while taking an enormous bite of his cheese danish. "Okay, I get it. But I did see Dr. Weber here at the office the other day and that was ironic timing since I haven't seen her in this building in about a year. She seemed agitated; I heard from one of the security guards that she was meeting with Dr. Crane."

Thomas raised an eyebrow, "Really? That's interesting."

Zack shrugged, "That's what I said! Yeah, I don't know what it was about, but I figured I'd ask you, since you've been working with Dr. Crane."

Thomas thought for a moment before responding, "I really can't say much about that, Zack. Sorry."

Zack nodded, "No worries, man. Just thought I'd give it a try."

Thomas finished his rapidly cooling coffee and said goodbye to Zack before heading out. He wondered what Weber could have been meeting with Crane about.

Chapter 55

I Feel Like I'm Losing Control

Thomas and Darius walked into their favorite bar, a dimly lit dive with a pool table in the back. They found an open table and started to rack up the balls for a game of pool.

"So, how's work been treating you, man?" Darius asked as he took a sip of his beer.

Thomas leaned against his cue stick and shrugged. "It's been alright. Same old, same old. How about you?"

Darius chuckled. "You know me, always hustlin'. But hey, that's how I keep the bills paid."

They both laughed and began the game of pool, taking sips of their drinks in between turns. As they played, they caught up on each other's lives, talking about a variety of subjects.

After a few games and a couple of rounds of drinks, Darius leaned in close to Thomas. "Hey, man, can I ask you something?"

"Sure, ask away." Thomas replied.

Darius hesitated for a moment before speaking. "I know we don't really talk about this kind of stuff much, but how are you doing with Gabrielle?"

Thomas let out a heavy sigh and took a long swig of his beer. "Honestly, not good. We haven't talked since I got back. I'm not even sure where she *is* right now, 'cause she sure isn't home!

Darius nodded sympathetically. "I'm sorry to hear that, man. I know she means a lot to you."

Thomas nodded, feeling a cold knot forming in his stomach even while talking about it with his friend. "Yeah. I told myself she just needed some space, but she is *gone*. I've kept my eye out for her when I got back from my trip, but no luck."

Darius patted Thomas on the back. "Wow, that's cold, dude! Something must have come up and she didn't have time to tell you. She'll be back. Just remember, bro, I'm always here for you if you need anything."

Thomas smiled ruefully at his friend. "Thanks, man. I appreciate it. I really blew it with Gabrielle when I fooled around with Evelyn on that trip." Thomas paused, having a thought. "I think I'll check with her church friends at their next lunch-meeting tomorrow. Maybe one of them will know something?"

Darius just grunted 'Maybe...' as he took his shot and missed, cursing under his breath.

Thomas decided to change the subject. He took a gulp of his drink and looked at Darius. "You know, Darius, I've been thinking a lot lately about how we define success. It seems like such a subjective thing, you know? I mean, is it all about money and power, or is there more to it than that?"

Darius had reclaimed his chair while waiting for Thomas to take his next shot at the pool table. He took a swig of his beer. "Interesting question, my friend. I think success is different for everyone. For some folks, it's all about the money and the status. For other dudes it's about making a difference in the world. What do *you* think, oh great sage?"

Thomas furrowed his brow. "I don't know. I feel like I've been so focused on my career for so long, and I'm not sure if that's what success really means to me anymore. At the same time, I feel like I can't really talk about it with anyone, you know? There are certain things I can't discuss because of my work's confidentiality clause."

Darius nodded knowingly. "I hear you, man, but you don't have to figure it all out right *now*. Sometimes, it takes a while to understand what success means to you as a person. When you *do* figure it out, you'll know what steps to take."

Thomas said thoughtfully, "Yeah, you're probably right. I just wish there was an easier way."

"I hear you, man," Darius continued, "But sometimes the harder path is the right one. And, if you can stay true to yourself and your beliefs, you'll come out right where you're supposed to be."

Thomas took a swig of his beer and sighed. "Man, I just don't know what to do about Evelyn," he said to Darius, leaning against the pool table. "I can't seem to resist her when she puts the moves on me, no matter how hard I try."

Darius chuckled at Thomas' admission and raised an eyebrow. "Is this why you're being all deep and shit tonight?" he asked.

Thomas shook his head, "Nah, man, it's just been on my mind lately. I don't know why I have so much trouble just saying 'No,' dammit!"

Darius leaned back in his chair, rocking precipitously on two legs of his chair, "Well, what's the problem then?"

Thomas let out a frustrated sigh, "It's like I can't physically control myself around her. She has some sort of mystical spell over me or something."

Darius laughed disbelievingly, "Man, that kinda sounds to me like a *good* problem to have, bro! Why you stressing about it?"

Thomas frowned, "It's just not *like* me. I feel like I'm out of control, and I don't like it!"

Darius leaned forward and looked Thomas in the eye, "Look, Thomas, you're a grown-ass man! You control your own destiny. Don't let some girl mess with your head. You gotta be strong and resist those temptations. Ain't no woman alive got that kind of power over you unless you give it to her, first."

Thomas thought about that. He knew he needed to regain control over his love-life, but it was easier said than done. He opted to take a long gulp of his drink, like so many other men who had been in his shoes before him. *"Keep it simple, Stupid!"* he thought to himself, realizing as he swallowed that he did tend to overthink such things. He wondered if Gabby was okay but feared in his heart-of-hearts that she was not. He resolved to remember the acronym, K-I-S-S, then he chugged the last of his beer to 'seal the deal' with himself. He was *going* to that lunch meeting no matter what!

Chapter 56

Destined To Be Alone

The sun was high in the sky as Thomas hurried towards the small bistro, the popular spot for the monthly luncheons of Gabrielle's church group. His heart raced with a mix of hope and anxiety. It had been a while since he had last heard from Gabrielle, and her silence was both uncharacteristic and worrying.

As he entered the bistro, he scanned the room, hoping to catch a glimpse of Gabrielle. Instead, he saw the familiar faces of her church friends, gathered around a large table, fully engaged in light conversation and laughter. Gabrielle, however, was nowhere to be seen.

Approaching the table with a forced calmness, Thomas greeted them. "Hello, everybody. I'm looking for Gabrielle. Is she here?" His demeanor was calm, but his voice betrayed his urgency.

The group exchanged puzzled glances. Sister Anne, the older woman he remembered from the last luncheon, spoke up gently, "No, Thomas, we haven't seen her today. Is everything alright?"

Thomas experienced a wave of frustration laced with fear. "I've been trying to reach her. She's not answering her phone, and no one seems to know where she is." His voice was tense with worry.

They collectively expressed their concern, but they all said basically the same thing – they had no information about Gabrielle's whereabouts. Linda, the woman who had debated evolution at their last meeting, added, "We're just as worried now as you are, Thomas. But none of us know where she is, unfortunately."

Refusing to accept that there was no more to learn, Thomas' worry suddenly morphed into more aggressive tactics. "You *must* know something! She wouldn't just disappear without telling anyone." His voice had grown louder, attracting the attention of other patrons of the popular bistro.

Sister Anne, with a calming presence developed over years of dealing with parishioners, tried to soothe him. "Thomas, we understand that you're worried, but we truly don't know anything. Gabrielle has always valued her privacy. Perhaps she needed some time alone?"

Thomas realized his outburst was drawing unwanted attention from the strangers around them and took a deep breath, trying to regain his composure. "I'm sorry," he apologized, his voice quieter but still laced with desperation. "I just... I need to find her. I'm *worried* about her."

The group tried to help in any way they could, suggesting places Gabrielle might visit or people she might contact. Thomas thanked them for their efforts while fruitlessly combing through the assorted verbal bric-a-brac they offered, his mind racing with possibilities. Despite their best efforts, nothing emerged as a real clue.

When he left the bistro, Thomas fought a sinking feeling of helplessness. Gabrielle's absence was an unsolved mystery, and her total silence was an agonizing void in his life.

As he stepped outside, the bright sunlight seemed to contrast sharply with the turmoil brewing within him. He walked aimlessly through the semi-crowded streets, his mind a whirlwind of thoughts and emotions. People brushed past him in their busy lives, but he felt invisible, a solitary figure amidst the hustle. With every step he took, his frustration grew, morphing into a palpable anger that he struggled to contain. He bumped into a passerby and muttered a half-hearted apology, his thoughts elsewhere. The physical jolt momentarily brought him back to reality, but it did little to ease the turmoil inside.

Thomas's mind drifted back to his childhood, to a time when he had felt a similar sense of abandonment. The memory of how felt when he realized his father was gone echoed in his mind. It was a wound that had never fully healed, a scar that had resurfaced in this moment. The feeling of being left behind, of not being worthy enough for his father to stay gnawed at him.

He chanced upon a quiet park, and he took a seat on an available bench, staring blankly at the ground in front of him. Even the laughter of children playing nearby seemed to mock his loneliness and frustration. He couldn't shake the feeling that somehow he was destined to be alone, and that every time he let someone into his heart, they would inevitably lose interest and leave. It was a pattern he had observed before in his life, a cycle of closeness followed by abandonment.

As he continued to sit there, a couple walked past him, laughing and holding hands. Something about their easy affection and the way they seemed so certain of each other's love triggered a sharp pang in his chest. It was a stark reminder of what he had lost, or perhaps of what he had thrown away. He didn't know!

The moment came flooding back to him unbidden – that night when he had betrayed Gabrielle. The memory was vivid, uncomfortably so. He remembered the rush of excitement as he had taken Evelyn mixed with a gnawing sense of wrongness, the way his heart raced for all the wrong reasons. The guilt of that night had since settled deep in his bones, a constant, aching presence that he truly regretted.

He closed his eyes, finally letting the weight of his own actions truly sink in. For the first time, he allowed himself to fully admit to himself the magnitude of his betrayal. He had hurt Gabrielle, the one person for whom he had finally felt something special. In his thoughtless pursuit of fleeting pleasure, he had traded something genuine and beautiful for a moment of meaningless thrill. The sense of guilt and remorse within him was momentarily overwhelming. Thomas wondered if he subconsciously pushed people away to protect himself. He had always strived for perfection, thinking that if he was just good enough, or responsible enough, that people would love him. But now, he felt that even his *best* efforts were too little, too late.

Thomas looked around at the people in the park, seemingly so carefree and happy. He envied them, and wondered why he couldn't just be like everyone else, why did *his* mistakes seemed to have bigger consequences than others?

As he sat there, lost in his thoughts, his heart suddenly hardened with purpose. He consciously built an emotional wall around himself, thinking it was better not to let anyone inside that wall rather than to face the pain of losing them. The idea that he had to be perfect to be loved, to be worthy of someone's time and affection, was exhausting to him.

The sun began to set, casting long shadows across the park. Thomas stood up, feeling his new resolve take root within him. He decided that he would no longer let his past dictate his future and wouldn't let her absence define him any further.

As he walked back towards the darkening city streets, the lights began to twinkle on. Thomas felt determined. He would find a way to break the cycle of abandonment he had personally experienced in his life, and he would somehow learn to be vulnerable, yet strong, imperfect, yet still worthy of anyone's love. His stride reflected the shift in him. The world just better get out of his way, he decided.

Chapter 57

Godspeed

As the weeks went by, Thomas found himself increasingly caught up in the routine of simple, everyday life. Work kept him busy, and he spent most of his evenings alone, watching TV or reading a book. Thanksgiving was a welcome break from the monotony, and he spent that day with his family, catching up on news and sharing a delicious feast together. His mother had not lost her touch! He enjoyed the time spent with his loved ones but, as the day came to an end, he felt a sense of loneliness creeping up on him once more. Christmas turned out to be no different. On Christmas Day, he sipped hot cocoa and listened to Christmas carols with his family. As the day wore on, he felt that same emptiness within him growing even stronger. Despite his attempts to move on from Gabrielle, he couldn't forget about her. The memory of her lingered in his mind, acting as a constant reminder of his past mistakes. He longed to reach out to her, to apologize and make things right, but he feared it was too late for that. He had lost her trust over the phone that fateful day in Oviedo, Spain, and he didn't know how to get it or her back again. He considered the fact that he seemed to be so good at fixing problems on a *professional* level, but not on a personal one.

This day, Thomas was determined to focus on work and put his personal life on hold. He threw himself into his job, taking on extra assignments and working late into the night. However, no matter how hard he tried, he couldn't shake off the feeling of being disconnected from the things that really mattered in Life. He remembered the conversation he had pursued with Darius that night at their favorite dive about what was important in Life, but he felt no closer to an answer yet.

He wondered what the future held for him. Would he ever be lucky enough to find someone like Gabby to share his life with again? Or was he destined to be forever alone, trapped in everyday drudgery? Only time would tell but, for now, he had to keep moving forward, one step and one day at a time.

The early morning of December 28th, just a few days later, was clear and cool in Phoenix. Thomas had woken early, feeling restless and groggy. He checked the time on his phone, and it read 6:00 AM. He knew he wouldn't be able to fall back asleep, so he got out of bed and stretched, feeling the stiffness of his muscles from a poor night's sleep.

The apartment was chilly, so he chose his favorite hoodie sweatshirt and headed to the kitchen to make a cup or three of coffee. As he waited for it to brew, he looked out the window at the clear, starry morning sky above. It was a peaceful and serene sight, but it only served to deepen the loneliness that had been weighing on him.

As he finished his coffee, he went for a walk. He put on sneakers and headed outside, feeling the cool air brush against his cheeks. The sun was just starting to rise, casting a warm golden glow over the landscape.

As he walked, thinking about the past *and* the future, Thomas concluded that he couldn't change what had transpired with Gabrielle. He could only resolve to work even harder, to be more disciplined, and to never give up. The walk wasn't long, but it was enough to reset his mind and give him a working perspective.

After he returned to his apartment, he felt a peace and optimism that he hadn't felt in quite a while. Maybe the future wasn't so bleak after all?

He took a quick shower, enjoying the warm water cascading over his body. As he exited the shower, he lit a cigarette and put on music by Mozart, and felt the music fill him with energy and vitality. He dressed meticulously, putting on a black suit with a raspberry sorbet dress shirt. After picking the watch that best suited his outfit for that day, he used a bit of his favorite cologne.

He looked in the mirror and pronounced himself ready to go. It was time to reclaim himself!

Thomas grabbed his luggage, which was already packed and waiting by the door, and headed to his car. He had a long drive ahead of him to the Phoenix airport, but he didn't mind. The early morning traffic was light, and he enjoyed the peaceful solitude of the empty roads. He arrived at the airport early for his flight and made it through security with plenty of time to spare. As he waited for his flight, he reviewed his notes, mentally preparing himself for the job ahead.

After getting settled into his first-class seat on the plane, he felt calm and focused. He leaned back and stretched his legs, enjoying the comfort of his surroundings. The flight attendant, who had already taken his order, handed him his drink and he took a sip, relishing the taste.

As he relaxed, he sent a text to Nouvel, "En route to meet Francesco Ajello. Will update once I connect with him." he typed. He hit 'Send' and leaned back again, feeling a sense of purpose.

Nouvel, unsurprisingly, responded quickly with a single word: "Godspeed." Thomas put his phone away and closed his eyes, the soft hum of the engines and the gentle vibrations of the plane soothing him. He closed his eyes, letting his mind drift at 35,000 feet.

Many hours later, when the plane began its descent, Thomas felt a jolt that woke him from his drowsiness. He opened his eyes and peered out the window, watching as the landscape below grew closer. The sight of the Italian countryside was breathtaking, with rolling hills and quaint towns nestled in the valleys.

As the plane landed, Thomas felt anticipation building within him. He retrieved his luggage from the baggage claim and made his way to the airport exit. *"Time's a'wastin'!"* he thought cheerfully.

Chapter 58

Grow Up, Francesco!

Thomas Rene stepped out of the taxi and walked up to the entrance of the old building, admiring the ornate stonework and its faded elegance. He found the elevator and rode it up to the sixth floor where his target was located, room 612. As he walked down the hallway, he noticed the intricate design of the wallpaper and the plush carpeting beneath his feet. He felt good knowing that he was close to completing the mission. When he arrived at room 612, he paused for a moment outside the door. He knocked twice and waited for a response.

"Come in," a familiar voice called from inside.

Thomas turned the doorknob and stepped inside to see Francesco Ajello standing by the window, his arms crossed tightly across his chest. Thomas could see that Ajello was visibly nervous, his eyes a bit panicky. In fact, Francesco barely acknowledged his arrival, seeming quite preoccupied.

As Thomas stepped further into the room, he noticed that the mini-bar was open, and several empty bottles were scattered about. He couldn't help but feel a pang of worry in his chest. It was clear that Ajello was under a lot of stress and the alcohol had failed to soothe him. Instead, Ajello seemed to be on edge.

"Francesco, is everything alright?" Thomas asked, not trying to hide the concern in his voice.

Ajello finally turned to face Thomas, his expression dark. "I don't know if I can *do* this," he said, his voice cracking.

Thomas had assumed that this was probably not going to be an easy job, but he had hoped that Ajello would be able to handle the pressure. He walked over to him, trying to assess the situation. As

241

he got closer, he could smell the expected alcohol on Ajello's breath.

"Francesco, I need you to focus. We're counting on you," Thomas said, trying to sound encouraging.

Francesco sighed heavily, his shoulders slumping. "I know, I know. It's just that...it's just that this feels wrong. It feels like we're doing something wrong, you know what I mean?" he said, his voice trembling.

Thomas could sense the fear in Ajello's voice. He took a deep breath and tried to keep his voice calm. "Francesco, we're doing this for a good reason. Heck, you'll be a hero if this all works the way we think it will!" he said, trying to give the shaky man strength.

Ajello's demeanor slowly began to shift. "Mr. Rene, I really don't know if I can go through with this," Francesco said honestly.

Thomas kept his voice steady, "Francesco, we *need* it. We have no choice."

Ajello stubbornly shook his head, "I'm sorry, Mr. Rene. I can't do this. It's too risky."

Thomas felt his heart sink, realizing that this moment would not be as smooth as he hoped. "Francesco, you promised me that you would do whatever it takes to get the item."

The man took a deep breath, holding it a moment then explosively letting it out, "I know, but I can't. I *thought* I could, but being here now I realize I can't."

Thomas could feel the frustration building inside him. They had a job to do, and he *needed* this idiot to complete it. "Francesco, please think about this. Consider the consequences if we don't get this item."

Ajello looked at him, his eyes filled with fear. "I'm scared, Mr. Rene."

This last admission was the final straw for Thomas. His mind starting racing. Suddenly, a thought occurred to him. Ajello had said before that he thought he could go through with the plan *until* the moment he got to the hotel room. That meant that he *must* have the item with him. Thomas looked around the room, trying to figure out where this fool could have hidden the item. His eyes settled on the mini-fridge, and he remembered the empty bottles on the coffee table. It clicked. Ajello had been drinking to calm his nerves, so the item most likely was in the mini-fridge. He probably had thought he was being very clever to hide it there, but he had not considered the quick wits of one Thomas Rene. Thomas walked over to the fridge, his heart racing. He opened the door and there it was, a small rectangular metal case. He picked it up and turned back to the horrified Francesco who had just realized he no longer held the winning hand.

Ajello's eyes widened, and he quickly ran towards Thomas, his drunken movements unsteady and erratic. He reached out to grab the metal case from Thomas's hand, his fingers closing around Thomas's arm instead. Thomas quickly defended himself by using his other arm to blast the fool in the face with his fist. Ajello stumbled backwards, crying out as his body crashed into the surprisingly fragile window. The glass shattered, spraying sharp shards everywhere.

For a moment, everything was still. Then, Ajello groaned in defeat, his body slumping to the floor. Blood oozed from a gash on the man's forehead, and he began to sob, crying like a child after the school bully had beaten him.

Thomas hadn't meant to hurt Francesco beyond the bare necessity of his own self-defense, but he couldn't let him take the item back. He took a deep breath and looked around the room, taking in the shattered glass and blood on the carpet. This was certainly not the meeting he had planned! But he knew that he had to keep moving forward.

He knelt next to the still sobbing Francesco and slapped him across the face, trying to snap him out of his funk. After a couple of healthy swats, Ajello started muttering to himself. "Ok, ok! I'm sorry! I know what they're planning to do with it!" Francesco said, his voice slurred and still husky with tears.

Thomas looked down at him with anger. "I don't care what *Turner Research* is planning to do with it and it's certainly none of *your* fucking business, either! My job is to retrieve the item and deliver it. End of story. Now, grow a pair and pull yourself together! We need to come up with a story for the mess inside this room."

The broken man nodded, wiping his tears with his arm. Grudgingly, he said, "I'll say that I accidentally fell into the window."

Thomas thought for a moment. "Yes, say you drank too much and accidentally fell into the window. It's a believable story." With that, Thomas stood up, said goodbye to Ajello, and turned to leave when the man grabbed at Thomas' pant leg.

"Please, Mr. Rene, don't do this. You must understand, there's too much of a chance it will all go wrong!" Ajello pleaded with him.

Thomas looked down at him with a cold expression. "Grow up, Francesco! We were hired to get this, and now we've done it. It'll be fine, so quit your crying!" He said disgustedly. Thomas detested whiney men. *"No self-respect!"* he thought to himself as he left.

Chapter 59

I'm Sorry, Daddy!

Thomas sank down into the plush first-class seat of his plane and tried to relax. He ordered a drink and sipped it slowly, letting the alcohol numb his senses. He still needed to unwind after the unpleasant encounter with Francesco Ajello back at the hotel, but he couldn't shake a nagging feeling lurking in the back of his mind.

He started to eat his meal, a juicy steak that was cooked to perfection, oddly enough, considering this was an airplane meal, but he just couldn't enjoy it. His mind kept wandering back to the small metal case that he had retrieved from the hotel room mini-fridge. It was the second time he had been sent after such a thing by Nouvel. He took it out of his pocket and stared at it curiously, turning it over in his hands.

So many questions were running through his mind. What was in the case? Why was it so important? Thomas truly yearned to open it, both to satisfy his curiosity and put his mind at ease. Despite this, he knew that he shouldn't. He had been hired to *obtain* the item and deliver it to Nouvel at *Turner Research*, not to open it. He wouldn't willingly betray that professional trust. He just had to keep the case safe, no matter how curious he was about its contents.

His internal struggle continued even though he had a few more drinks in the attempt to numb his mind and to help him resist the temptation in front of him. But, no matter how drinks, he couldn't shake the growing feeling that he was missing something very important. He felt like he *needed* to know what was in that case, and this was probably his only opportunity.

Thomas made his way to the in-flight restroom. Once inside, he splashed some water on his face to sober up a bit and tried again to shake that nagging feeling he truly needed to know what was in the small metal case. He was beginning to accept that his "feeling" wasn't going to go away, with or without alcohol.

Thomas had learned the hard way in his life that ignoring those strong feelings of his was inevitably a mistake. Conversely, every time he paid attention to them, things worked out for the best. Replaying such past key moments in his head only served to deepen his conviction that *this* was the time to consider the bigger picture.

Thomas thought back to Archbishop Rodriguez. Rodriguez had also entrusted Thomas with a small brass box. Thomas had felt a driving curiosity then but had delivered that box without opening it. He had regretted not piercing the heart of that mystery but had been satisfied with himself as a professional that he had not done so. So, why was this time even harder to ignore? Was this a second chance at the very same mystery? If so, Thomas wasn't sure he should pass this opportunity up. And why did he feel so driven to violate his standing protocols? This was unusual, to say the least!

Another moment that was replaying in his mind was the confrontation he had had with Ruth Weber and David Kim. He had felt some internal pressure then, too, but he had stood his ground and not violated his client's confidentiality request by not looking at what was on the zip drive.

Finally, he thought back to the fight in the hotel room with Ajello. He had found and taken the small metal case, but he had resisted the urge to open it.

Sighing, Thomas left the restroom and returned to his seat. He settled back into the plush first-class accommodations and tried to push the small metal case to the back of his mind. He switched to soda, and he took a swig from his drink while he loosened his tie and tried to relax. He knew that he couldn't let his curiosity get the best of him. He had a job to do, and he had to do it right.

Thomas tried to get some rest as the plane soared through the night. He closed his eyes and took a deep breath, letting it out slowly to quiet his mind and drift off to sleep.

Thomas found himself dreaming of when he was a young child, around four years old, and his father was standing over him, looking stern and disappointed. It seemed so real. In the dream, Thomas had opened his father's guitar case, curious about the shiny objects inside. In the process, he had caused all his father's guitar picks and extra strings to fall out and scatter across the floor. "I'm sorry, Daddy!" young Thomas had said, tears welling up in his eyes.

His father had only looked at him in mild disappointment, telling him to never open other people's things. He quickly picked up the scattered items and calmly closed the guitar case, which left young Thomas feeling guilty as he sat alone on the floor. The dream faded, and the older Thomas woke up feeling restless and uneasy. He couldn't shake the feeling that something was wrong. What was his mind trying to tell him?

Thomas tried again to settle into his seat, his thoughts weighing heavily on him. He changed his mind about the relative merits of alcohol and ordered a Jack Daniels, hoping to drown out the questions that were plaguing him. But, even as the fine whiskey coursed through his veins, he couldn't shake the feeling that he was about to either make a grave mistake or find out something momentous. He pulled out the metal case once more, holding it delicately in his hands. *"Now or never,"* he thought to himself.

With shaky hands, Thomas finally did it. He opened the metal case. The hinges creaked softly as the small lid swung open, only to reveal a tiny piece of stained tan fabric suspended between two slides of glass. *"What the hell?!"* he thought, surprised.

He stared at the fabric between the slides, not sure what to make of it. It appeared very old and had clearly come from a larger piece of the same material. More was at stake here than Thomas knew. He had no idea what it was or why it was so important, but something inside him still urged him onwards, to keep looking, to try and uncover the truth.

As he examined the fabric, Thomas noticed that one of the glass slides had a slight crack. A wave of guilt washed over him, and he wondered if he had damaged it somehow.

Even as he felt the guilt, he couldn't help but be intensely curious. What *was* this stuff? Why was it important to *Turner Research*? What secrets did it hold? He stared at it for what felt like an eternity, lost in his thoughts.

Suddenly, the flight attendant interrupted his reverie, offering him another drink. He shook his head, realizing he had already had too much. She glanced casually at what was in his hands but didn't ask him what it was. Thomas was relieved. As she walked away down the aisle, Thomas quickly closed the metal case and tucked it safely in his pocket, deciding to put the thoughts of the strange sample of fabric out of his mind for the time being. Maybe a nap would help, he hoped. *"God knows I'm not getting anywhere being awake!"* he thought to himself with a feeble attempt at humor, but it didn't cheer him up.

Chapter 60

I Can't Keep Doing This

Thomas sat in his dark apartment, illuminated only by the flickering light coming from the logs in the fireplace. The smooth notes of the Bach cantata, *Sleepers Awake*, drifted through the air, filling the room with a sense of beautiful melancholy. He held a glass of whiskey in one hand while feeling the warmth of the liquid seep through his veins. However, it did little to dull the constant pangs of guilt he felt in his chest. He felt guilt for having betrayed his fragile trust with Gabrielle by fooling around with Perdita on that trip they had taken. He felt guilt for opening the metal box, and guilt for breaking his oath. He couldn't deny that he had violated trust by opening it. He understood that he had been hired to do the job of acquiring that mysterious item, but he had crossed a line, professionally speaking.

As he sat there, lost in his various regrets, he took a puff from his cigar, letting the smoke curl around his face. He could hear the soft crackling of the fire and the mournful notes of the cantata, but his mind was elsewhere. He couldn't help but wonder what secrets that tiny piece of fabric held, and whether he would ever find out what they were.

Thomas took another sip of whiskey, feeling it burn down his throat. He closed his eyes and tried to focus on the music, to let it carry him away, but even the beautiful melody couldn't erase the concerns in his mind.

At that moment, Thomas heard a knock on his door and got up quickly from the couch, feeling a small spark of hope ignite in his chest that it just might be Gabrielle returning. Unfortunately, as he looked through the peephole, he saw that it was only Evelyn Perdita, who was standing confidently wearing a one-piece mini dress. He hesitated for a moment, knowing all too well what might happen if he let her in. *"What the hell is she doing here?!"* he thought sourly. After taking a large final gulp of whiskey, he grudgingly opened the door, his expression guarded. Evelyn swept in, her dark hair cascading down her back, her olive skin glowing in the soft light of the fireplace.

"Hey, Baby," she said, her voice low and sultry.

Thomas felt his resolve to resist her slipping away as he looked at her. Evelyn's extraordinary beauty and the whiskey he had drunk made it difficult for him to take his eyes off of her.

"Evelyn, *what* are you doing here?" he asks, keeping his tone neutral.

"Well, I was worried because we haven't spoken in a while, and I decided to check on you. *Ta-daa!*" she said, curtseying with demurely downcast eyes.

Thomas had to admit that he enjoyed her style, but he tamped it down. He knew this was a mistake an inch away from happening. "Evelyn, it's late, and I don't feel like company right now. I appreciate your concern, but it's probably best that you go. Thanks for stopping by." He gestured ineffectually towards the door. "I can't keep doing this." He muttered.

Instead, Evelyn moved a little closer to him, and Thomas took an unsteady step backwards, feeling a bit wobbly from that last slug of whiskey. She came even closer, her hand reaching out to touch his arm. Her scent and her touch sent shivers down his spine, and he felt his resistance already beginning to crumble. Thomas tried again to back away, but she followed him inexorably, pinning him against the wall with her bra-less breasts as her lips and tongue traced a nibbling path up to his ear.

Thomas let out a low groan, his body betraying him once again despite his semi-heroic attempts to resist. He muttered in protest, but his voice was weak, barely audible over the sound of the music. Evelyn took this as a cue for action and moved in for a kiss. Thomas felt the last of his resistance crumble completely as he reluctantly surrendered to her well executed seduction. The taste of her lips and the feel of her body pressed against his sent him spiraling over the edge into a world of desire. All that mattered in that moment was pleasure.

The room was still dark, illuminated only by the glow from the fireplace. Even so, Thomas could see that Evelyn was somehow miraculously naked. She pulled him towards the couch, and Thomas knew he had lost. He could feel his heart race as she pressed her lips to his, her hands busily removing his own clothes. He tried to resist, to focus on the reasons why he shouldn't allow this, but Evelyn was relentless, her sensual presence driving him beyond the brink of madness.

In a flurry of passion, they collapsed onto the couch, their bodies entwined. Thomas could feel the heat of her skin against his as the rhythms of their breathing became one. He pounded her into the couch, and all he could think of was how good it felt. It had been so long since he had been this way with a woman.

Afterwards, once their breathing returned to normal, Evelyn went to freshen up. She was not a 'cuddler,' for which Thomas was truly grateful. He lit a cigarette and took a long drag as he lay there on the couch, realizing he'd just been screwed. Ironically, the worst part was that the guilt he'd been attempting to escape was back again and, this time, was even louder. He stubbed out the cigarette and headed for his bedroom to sleep, hoping against all reasonable hope that she would take the chance to leave.

Chapter 61

Better Late Than Never!

Thomas woke up the next morning with a pounding headache, feeling the aftermath of too much whiskey the night before. As he rubbed his temples, he realized that Evelyn was still there. He could hear her in the kitchen doing something noisy and irritating. Apparently, she had stayed despite him being asleep by the time she had finished freshening up the night before. He sat up slowly, his head spinning, and heard a sizzling noise coming from the kitchen. Then the aroma of bacon and eggs filled his nostrils. He was forced to flee to the bathroom to pray for mercy at the feet of the porcelain god. After throwing up, he considered himself a true penitent. *"Never again!"* he thought woozily as he rinsed out his mouth, but he was unsure if he meant Evelyn, the booze, or both.

He looked at himself in the mirror, his eyes bloodshot and his hair sticking up in all directions. He splashed some water on his face, hoping it would help clear his head. When he finally made it to the kitchen, he saw Evelyn standing over the stove, wearing only his dress shirt from the night before. She turned to him and smiled, her eyes sparkling with sly humor.

"Rough start to the morning, huh?" she said, handing him a cup of black coffee.

Thomas barely managed to grunt before he took a sip. It was strong and bitter, just the way he liked it.

As he nuzzled his coffee, he noticed that the metal box he had brought back from Spain was on the kitchen island, not where he had left it on his desk. He walked over to the island, his head still pounding, and picked up the box. It felt heavy in his hand, and it reminded him he could still feel a weight of guilt pressing down on him. He looked over at Evelyn, who was busy flipping the bacon, and wondered if she knew what was inside the box. Did she look inside it while he was asleep?

He didn't want to think about it yet. He set the box back down on the island and realized that he was starting to get hungry. Maybe some food would help at this point. He turned his attention back to breakfast, hoping that the bacon and eggs would distract him from his woes.

He took a tentative bite of the eggs, chewing slowly as he surreptitiously studied Evelyn's body language. She seemed relaxed to him. Casually, he asked, "Hey, did you happen to move that metal box from my desk to the island?"

Evelyn paused, raising a finger to her mouth, and pretending to think. "I don't know, did I?" she said, flirting with him.

His hangover made it difficult for him to hide his frustration, but he tried to remain calm. "Come on, Evelyn," he demanded, his voice tinged with irritation. "I *know* you moved it, but did you *open* it?"

Evelyn's smile disappeared and she looked away. "Maybe I did, and maybe I didn't," she said reluctantly, still not meeting his gaze.

Thomas put down his fork, his frustration mounting in equal ratio to the headache. "Why would you do that?" he asked with an edge to his voice.

Evelyn shrugged nonchalantly. "I was curious. Didn't *you* open it to look for yourself?"

Thomas looked at Evelyn *hard*, his eyes narrowing slightly. He knew that she was aware of his strict code of confidentiality when it came to such things, but her on-point question and her casualness about it still made him uncomfortable. After all, she worked for *Turner Research* the same as he did. They might listen to her if she said something! *"This is not good"* he thought through the mental haze. He desperately wanted more coffee. "I don't *need* to know what's in it." he replied, which was an evasion of the truth rather than a direct answer.

Evelyn looked at him with another sly smile. "But don't you *want* to know?" she asked, refusing to let it drop.

Thomas hesitated, unsure of what to say. He had already opened the box, but he wasn't sure if he should admit it. Evelyn's question still hung in the air, tempting him to share his secret. However, he couldn't take the chance. Thomas sighed and shook his head. "No, I truly *don't* want to know," he said firmly.

Evelyn shrugged and took a bite of her bacon. "Suit yourself," she said with a grin. "But you know, sometimes the things we don't want to know are the things that drive us the craziest."

After breakfast was finished, Thomas decided to get ready for the day. After he emerged from the bedroom, freshly showered and dressed, he struggled with his tie. When he entered the kitchen, his eyes were immediately drawn to the metal box which was in Evelyn's hands. "What are you *doing*?" he barked, the frustration and anger clear in his voice.

Evelyn just turned to look at him, an odd look on her face. "Relax, Thomas," she said, waving the box in his direction as though that would reassure him. "I just wanted to take another look. No harm, no foul."

"But you shouldn't be looking at it at *all*," Thomas replied, his tone harsh. "We could get into *serious* trouble if anyone finds out."

Evelyn shrugged off his concerns, a glint in her eye. "Sometimes rules are meant to be broken, don't you think?" she said, gesturing at the box.

Thomas took a deep breath, trying to quell his rising frustration. "That's not the point," he said, his voice strained. "I have a responsibility to my clients to keep their secrets safe."

Evelyn rolled her eyes dismissively, clearly not taking his concerns seriously. "Oh, lighten up, Thomas," she said. "You worry too much." Evelyn approached him, still holding the box in her hands. "Come on, Thomas," she urged. "I *know* there's something important in here, no matter how it looks. Let's figure it out together! Thomas, look, I just want to understand. What *is* that piece of cloth? What's so important about it?"

Thomas realized in that moment that Evelyn had *already* looked inside the box. How else could she know it was a piece of old fabric? The only good thing about this revelation was that she didn't know that *he* knew.

She sidled closer to him, tilting up her lips for an expected kiss and letting his dress shirt she was wearing fall open as though by accident. It was an obvious manipulation on her part, and Thomas shuddered internally. Rather than being swayed by her sexual allure, he found himself repulsed, but he tried not to show it. Her tricks weren't working anymore on him, and he took some small comfort in admitting to himself. *"Better late than never!"*

"I don't think so, Evelyn." he said and took the box back for safekeeping. He was not letting this thing out of his sight until he safely delivered it to *Turner Research.*

Evelyn seemed a bit shocked at her failure to convince him, but she rebounded quickly enough to fool many other men under similar circumstances by smiling and laughing as though she didn't really care. Fortunately, Thomas was no longer one of them. He knew better, and he wanted his shirt back.

Chapter 62

You've Earned It

Thomas arrived at the *Turner Research* building on Monday morning, slightly earlier than his scheduled 9:00am meeting with Dr. Crane. As he approached the entrance, he saw the protesters were once again gathered in front of the building with their signs and chanting of slogans. Despite the noise, he was greeted cordially by the security guard at the door who checked his ID and let him enter. *"Business as usual!"* thought Thomas.

As he walked towards Dr. Crane's office, he noticed that the people in the building seemed more hectic than usual. They were rushing around with papers and folders tucked under their arms, and there was a buzz of activity in the air. When he arrived at Crane's door, he knocked and heard the familiar voice say "Come in."

Upon entering the office, Thomas was surprised to find Nouvel there as well. He asserted that he had flown in especially for this meeting, and both men seemed excited to see him. Thomas opined it was most likely because of what he had brought to the meeting this day. They greeted him with uncharacteristic enthusiasm, but Thomas could sense the underlying urgency in their voices even as they all exchanged pleasantries.

When the meeting commenced, Nouvel's eyes fixed on Thomas as Nouvel asked for the box with eagerness in his voice. Thomas stood up, reached into his jacket and brought out the small, metal box for Nouvel who quickly took it from him. Thomas thought privately that Nouvel seemed like the character, Gollum, from *The Lord of the Rings*, when he put on the ring of Sauron.

With a look of anticipation on his face, Nouvel slowly opened the box and peered inside. Thomas couldn't see inside the box due to the way Nouvel was holding it, though he knew the contents within.

After a moment of silence, Nouvel looked up briefly at Thomas and then back at the box, his expression blank. "Thomas, did you drop this?" he asked, cocking his head oddly like a shrew about to gobble a tasty worm.

Thomas felt his blood pressure suddenly rise rapidly, though he let none of that show on his face. "No, Samuel. It's been protected. Why? What's wrong?"

Instead of answering directly, Nouvel then closed the box and handed it to Dr. Crane, who peered inside with a big smile. "Why does everything seem to come in small, metal boxes these days?" he joked. He turned back to Nouvel. "Don't worry about it, Samuel. It's just a glass slide. It was probably cracked before Thomas received it from our contact. The most important thing is that the sample is fine!"

Nouvel nodded, then ceremoniously stood up and walked over to the desk drawer, pulling out a bottle of whiskey and a few glasses. "Anyone want a drink to celebrate?" he asked, pouring the amber liquid into each glass. As he handed out the drinks, Nouvel turned to Thomas and said with a small smirk. "So, did you enjoy Evelyn's company on your trip to Spain?" he asked, his voice dripping with innuendo and one eyebrow raised archly.

Thomas immediately knew what he was getting at since Nouvel was the one who had told Evelyn to surprise Thomas there. Thomas hesitated for a moment before responding a bit harshly. "It was a *business* trip, Samuel. I had no idea Evelyn was going to be there and, frankly, I didn't appreciate the lack of a 'head's up' from *you* about it!" Thomas glared at him, knowing that Dr. Crane was watching this interaction.

Nouvel laughed derisively, shaking his head. "I sent her to *help* you, my boy! Believe me, I don't care a whit about your personal life, Thomas. All I care about are results!"

Having expressed his disdain, Thomas could do little other than to accept Nouvel's answer and move on.

Nouvel's demeanor became more aggressive, and he leaned forward in his chair to look challengingly at Thomas.

"Mr. Rene," he began abruptly, "I need to know if you're aware of what's inside that box." His voice firm and direct, leaving no room for evasion or misinterpretation.

Thomas felt a bead of sweat trickle down the back of his neck. He knew that this was a pivotal moment and that the answer he gave could have far-reaching consequences. He took a deep breath and considered his options, aware that Nouvel and Crane were carefully watching him.

Thomas was about to answer in his usual manner---"the truth, nothing but the truth, so help ye, God" when he suddenly remembered his maternal grandfather giving him some hard-won advice as a boy. Gramps had said in response to a question asked by young Thomas, "Grandson, I don't hold with lying whatsoever. You know that. But, if you're gonna lie, make it a whopper!". Thomas realized in that moment, sometimes, a convenient lie can successfully lead to an even greater truth. Telling the truth without proper preparation could also alienate people to the degree that they would reject that greater truth out of hand. Thomas realized that this was such a moment. He had to decide whether to stick to his normal 'tell the truth, no matter what' mentality or to protect his own ability to choose the future. If he told the simple truth, that he had felt compelled to open the box on the airplane, then he would likely lose his job and his reputation. If he denied opening it, he would be only telling them what they expected to hear and they would be likely to allow him further access to the mystery. The fact was that he didn't understand yet what was going on, and he felt strongly that he needed to know. He didn't know *why* he needed to know, but he trusted his gut instincts. There was a reason, but he'd have to figure it out using whatever clues he could assemble. *"Thanks, Gramps!"* he thought to himself.

It had only been a moment while all this furious thinking had gone on. Thomas looked them in the eyes and answered, "No," and said no more. The die was cast. The universe waited for what was to happen next. It wasn't long in coming.

"I told you!" burst out of Crane as he turned to Nouvel. "You owe me $100."

Nouvel looked upset, but he acknowledged that he did, indeed, owe the money.

Thomas, while relieved, was nonplussed at their response. "$100?" he asked.

Dr. Crane laughed and explained to the mystified Thomas. "What Samuel doesn't want to admit is that he already talked to Evelyn about you, and she stated for the record that she did not believe that you had looked at the object in question. Sammy here bet that you did. I took the bet!" finished Crane triumphantly, clearly pleased with himself.

Samuel turned to Crane and said, "You know, I've been thinking. Perhaps we should consider bringing Thomas in further. He's been a clear asset to *Turner Research*, and he's completed every assignment we've asked of him in exemplary fashion." He looked at Thomas with a smile that seemed more like a grimace to Thomas.

Crane and Nouvel had obviously discussed this beforehand. "That's an interesting possibility," Crane said with a grin. "Thomas *has* proven himself consistently invaluable."

At that moment, Nouvel reached into his briefcase and pulled out an envelope. He handed it to Thomas, "Speaking of the matter in Italy, we wanted to give you a little something to show our appreciation. Consider it a Christmas bonus."

Thomas didn't hesitate in taking the envelope. He assumed it was more than just a simple card. Crane gestured for him to open it, and Thomas did so with some alacrity.

As he pulled out the check, his eyes widened in disbelief. He stared at the amount, "A hundred thousand dollars?" he stammered, almost not believing it.

Dr. Crane chuckled and patted Thomas on the back. "You've earned it. Your effort and honesty have not gone unnoticed. We hope you'll consider this a token of our appreciation and an investment in you. We have much to discuss."

Thomas looked from one man to the other, the impact of the moment sinking in. He knew his life had just changed, and not just because of the money. Thomas was every bit his Gramps' grandson. He knew people didn't throw around that kind of money without expecting something in exchange. The question Thomas had was whether he'd be willing to pay it.

Chapter 63

Son Of Science

Thomas followed Nouvel and Crane as they led him through the pristine laboratory wing. The long-hallway was lined with glass walls and doors that gave glimpses into research and various experiments. Thomas had been there before, but today felt different.

As they approached the end of the hallway, Thomas couldn't help but feel a sense of awe. The large double doors loomed ahead, a barrier that had always been off-limits to him. He had often wondered what lay beyond them, but until now, the secrets held within had remained elusive.

Crane turned to Thomas, noticing his curiosity. "You've visited this wing before, Thomas, but today is going to be special. Today, we're going to share something with you that we've never shown anyone else outside of those doors."

Nouvel nodded in agreement with the scientist, his face solemn. "We believe you're now ready to be a part of something much bigger than any of us individually." With that cryptic statement still hanging in the air, they reached the double doors. Crane swiped his access card and the doors swung open with a soft 'whoosh' sound. Thomas' heart raced as he finally entered the room beyond. The space was enormous, filled with state-of-the-art equipment, and illuminated by a soft, sterile glow. Scientists in white coats moved between workstations, focused intently on their tasks. The atmosphere was a curious mix of determination and, oddly enough, *reverence*. Thomas found that combination very strange.

Nouvel leaned against one of the workstations, his gaze intense. "You see, Thomas, the *idea* of God or gods has been the foundation of human civilization for all of recorded history. These ideas have shaped our values, our culture, and even our understanding of the world around us. At the same time, the concept of divinity has also been a source of conflict, division, and eventual stagnation."

Dr. Crane added to the explanation, "Throughout history, religion has too often stood in opposition to scientific progress. Examples of this would include the Church's persecution of Galileo, the suppression of medical research during the Dark Ages, and even the modern-day clashes between religious fundamentalists and the advocates of science—all of these are symptoms of a deeper issue."

Thomas was intrigued by the conversation. "So, what is the 'deeper issue'? Are you saying that religion and science are fundamentally incompatible?"

Nouvel shook his head. "Not necessarily. There have been religious minded scientists who have made great contributions to human knowledge. The deeper issue Dr. Crane is referring to is the way religious institutions can discourage questioning, stifle curiosity, and promote dogmatic thinking that refuses to test the boundaries of our experience and understanding. When we unquestioningly accept the dictates of a religious institution, we are likely to limit our own ability to explore and understand the true nature of the universe."

Crane interjected at this point, "Our goal here is not to attack people's *faith*. We understand that belief in a higher power than our own can bring comfort and a sense of purpose to those who believe. However, we are determined to challenge the concept of God itself—the idea that there is an omnipotent, omniscient deity who created and still controls the universe."

Thomas listened, fascinated by the direction they were taking. "How do you propose to do that? How can you possibly prove God *doesn't* exist?"

Samuel Nouvel smiled mirthlessly. "We submit that the ultimate proof of God's existence, or not, lies in the very figure that billions of people today still revere as the divine incarnate: Jesus

Christ. By using the tools of science, we can analyze a sample of blood believed to contain his DNA. We intend to demonstrate that Jesus was a man like any other. We further posit that Jesus was subject to the same natural laws as the rest of us and possessed no special abilities."

Dr. Crane elaborated, "If we can demonstrate that Jesus was only human and that his recorded miraculous deeds can be explained in other ways, then we will usher in a new era of enlightened scientific inquiry, one that is not subject to the constraints of religious dogma."

Thomas considered their words, aware of the significance of this conversation. "It's an ambitious undertaking, to say the least, but don't you ever worry about the consequences? Even if you can find a way to accomplish this, what if proving that God *doesn't* exist leads to a world without morals or meaning? Couldn't it trigger Armageddon in the form of anarchy and chaos?"

Nouvel's face wore a solemn expression, "Those are valid concerns, Thomas. Anything is possible, but we think the pursuit of Truth is the highest calling. Also, as we continue to advance our understanding of the universe, we can develop *new* ethical frameworks that are based on empathy, compassion, and reason, rather than the old dogmatic beliefs."

Thomas wasn't quite as starstruck by all of this as he might have appeared, felt obliged to offer a comment. "Yeah, about that. Those "old, dogmatic beliefs" *are* based on caring about your fellow man and use reason to support that belief system. I don't necessarily have to be a Christian to know *that*."

Crane responded, "Ultimately, it's about empowering humanity to explore the true potential of science so as to build a better future for ourselves without arbitrary limits."

Thomas, still processing the magnitude of the conversation, shifted his focus to the two different metal boxes he had retrieved for his clients. "So, what's so important about the boxes I brought you? What do they have to do with all of this?"

263

Nouvel exchanged a meaningful glance with Crane before replying. "The boxes you retrieved for us hold the key to unlocking the 'mysteries' we've been discussing. They contain invaluable artifacts that we believe carry the DNA of Jesus Christ."

Dr. Crane continued, "The first box contained scrapings from the Shroud of Oviedo, also known as the Sudarium of Oviedo. It is a bloodstained cloth that is believed to have been wrapped around Jesus's head after his crucifixion. That cloth has been preserved for centuries and, although it is not as well-known as the Shroud of Turin, is considered one of the most important relics of Christendom."

Nouvel jumped back in and elaborated further, "It is said to have been used to cover his face before He was laid to rest in the tomb. The scrapings you brought us contain traces of the blood that we believe holds Jesus' genetic material."

Thomas's eyes widened with shock as he absorbed this information. "And the second box?"

This time, Crane responded, "The second metal box holds another significant artifact—a small piece of the Shroud of Turin. This is a linen cloth that bears the faint image of a man who appears to have been crucified. Many believe it is the actual burial cloth of Jesus Christ. The cloth has been the subject of intense scientific study and debate for decades, and its authenticity remains a point of contention among scholars."

Nouvel added, "Despite the controversies surrounding the Shroud of Turin, we believe that the piece has immense value for our research. If we can extract DNA from the fibers of the cloth, we can compare it to the sample obtained from the Shroud of Oviedo, potentially verifying that both relics indeed carry the same genetic material. Hopefully, of Jesus Christ. Unfortunately, the only way to know if it is actually Jesus is to clone and test an embryo."

Thomas stared at them in near disbelief, realizing the enormity of his role in obtaining these priceless relics. "So, by analyzing the

DNA from both artifacts, you hope to prove that Jesus was just an ordinary man and not divine?"

Nouvel nodded in affirmation. "Exactly, Thomas. Our research here aims to demonstrate that Jesus was subject to natural laws. We hope to dispel the myth of his divinity and open the door for a revitalized era of scientific exploration."

As the significance of the artifacts and their implications for the project sank in, Thomas felt justified for denying having opened one of the boxes. To the contrary, he knew now that he was an integral part of something that could change the course of history. The journey ahead was uncharted territory, filled with challenges and uncertainties, but Thomas realized that he was right where he belonged. *"Someone's got to keep an eye on this pair of mad scientists!"* he thought.

The three men walked around the room observing the various scientists at work, each absorbed in their respective tasks. The laboratory was filled with advanced equipment that hummed and beeped, a testament to the cutting-edge research taking place within its walls. As they strolled between the workstations, Thomas became mesmerized by a particular machine filled with lights and gizmos. As Thomas stared at the flashing lights, contemplating the extent of the technology before him, he asked Dr. Crane, "So, how exactly does the cloning process work? How do you plan to use the DNA from these artifacts to create a clone of Jesus?"

Crane was pleased by Thomas' interest and began to explain the process in some detail. "First, we need to extract the DNA from the samples you provided. This is a delicate procedure, as we must take care not to damage the genetic material. Once we have successfully isolated the DNA, we'll analyze its sequence to ensure its integrity." He gestured to a high-tech machine in one corner of the room. "Next, we'll use a technique called *somatic cell nuclear transfer*. We'll take an unfertilized human egg cell and remove its nucleus, which contains the egg's own genetic material. Then, we'll replace the egg's nucleus with the genetic material we've extracted from the artifacts."

Nouvel, hating being left out, chimed in, "After the transfer is complete, we'll stimulate the egg to begin dividing and developing as it would in a normal fertilization process. Eventually, the egg will develop into an embryo, genetically identical to the individual from whom we obtained the DNA—in this case, hopefully, Jesus Christ."

Thomas had been listening intently in the attempt to grasp the complexity of the procedure. "And once the embryo has developed, what happens then?"

Dr. Crane replied, but it was not difficult to see that he was a little irritated by Nouvel's horning in on Crane's area of expertise. "We'll implant the embryo into a surrogate mother who will carry the pregnancy to term. Once the child is born, we'll have a living, breathing individual who is a genetic copy of Jesus."

Thomas frowned as he considered the ethical implications of Crane's statement. "Even if the clone has the same DNA as Jesus, he wouldn't be the same, would he? He'd be the Son of Science rather than the Son of God, correct?"

Crane nodded, acknowledging Thomas' point. "That's true. While the clone would *genetically* be identical to Jesus, his experiences, upbringing, and environment would be entirely different. The purpose of this project is not to recreate the *historical* figure of Jesus, which would include his apparent miracles, but to demonstrate that, genetically speaking, Jesus was a normal human being."

They left the laboratory and began walking back toward Crane's office. Thomas finally broke the silence. "I have to ask—why are you sharing all of this with me *now*? I've been working for you for a while and never had any inkling of what you were really doing."

Nouvel responded carefully. "There are a few reasons, Thomas. First, you have been an important contributor to this project so far, and we expect to need you even more in the time to come. And, given your intelligence, it's only a matter of time before you'd start putting the pieces together. Lastly, we'd rather have you fully informed and able to protect us, rather than wasting time trying to figure things out on your own."

Dr. Crane chimed in, happy to have the chance to finally horn in on Nouvel's area of expertise, "Also, as you continue to work with us, you'll inevitably discover even more about the project. It's better to prepare you now with the information you need and ensure that you understand the importance of your own role in this huge endeavor."

Nouvel nodded, although he clearly didn't enjoy the shoe being on the other foot. "And finally, we think we can trust you, Thomas, at least up to a point." He glanced meaningfully over at Crane who had the good grace to look a bit embarrassed. "It's *my* job to determine what that point is. To accomplish something of this magnitude, we need *everyone* on board, working together as a cohesive unit. Your skills and resourcefulness have proven invaluable to us already and we believe that you still have a crucial part to play in the success of our project."

Thomas had listened carefully, taking in their words. Frankly, he was still in shock from the size of the check they had given him earlier. He was determined to stay involved and see where this was going. To do that, he realized there were two things he must do---he needed some cool jazz and a great steak, then all would be well with the world!

Chapter 64

Just Stay Away From Me

Thomas entered the restaurant he loved and was greeted by the familiar, luxurious atmosphere that brought him comfort. When he was escorted to his table, he noticed the same singer from the last time he'd been there, her voice weaving through the air in perfect rapport with the piano player's harmonies. He took a seat and soaked in the music, allowing it to clear his mind. The waiter came and Thomas ordered the same Wagyu steak he'd enjoyed previously. This time, he decided to splurge on a bottle of wine, selecting a 2009 Romanée-Saint-Vivant Grand, priced at $3,200. The wine was a renowned, elegant Pinot Noir with a complex flavor profile—soft, dense, floral, with seductive notes of violets, blackberries, green tea and woodsmoke.

He sipped the wine and savored it while reflecting on the recent revelations and his new, expanded role in the ambitious project of cloning Jesus. He felt a mixture of excitement and trepidation when he considered the stakes.

Evelyn arrived during his moment of inattention, preoccupied as he was between the music and his musings. Her dark hair framed her olive-skinned face, her eyes sparkling with seductive allure. She wore an elegant, yet revealing, sleek black dress that accentuated her figure and certainly drew interest from both the men and the women in the crowd, just not from Thomas. She slid into the seat across from him, "I hope you don't mind me joining you," she purred, her voice like velvet. Thomas had heard it all before and was profoundly disinterested.

Thomas looked up, only mildly surprised to see her. "How did you know I'd be here?" he asked.

She smiled somewhat triumphantly as she adjusted her seat. "Thomas, I *know* what you like. When I heard that you mentioned grabbing a steak and enjoying some live jazz earlier, I had a feeling you'd be here."

He forced himself to be polite and invited her to order something for herself to eat, though she declined and instead asked if she could share in the wine. Thomas begrudgingly nodded in the affirmative and signaled the waiter for another glass.

With Evelyn seated across from him, Thomas realized he just felt empty. He felt a sudden yearning for the simple grace of Gabrielle flash through him. He looked at the beautiful woman in front of him and realized he felt nothing. She just held no allure for him any longer, attractive as she was. The sultry voice of the singer filled the room, accompanied by the skillful support of the piano, but the ambience was shattered for Thomas by his internal revelation about Evelyn Perdita. In fact, he wasn't even sure whether he *liked* her or not at this point. After all, she had informed on him with Nouvel, and Thomas didn't care if she *did* work for *Turner Research.* In his mind, you don't do that to a friend.

The singer's voice filled the air, her rendition of "La Vie en Rose" added a romantic undertone to the evening. Her voice was superb, and her passion for the music was easy to see as she effortlessly navigated the song's emotional nuances. As Thomas tried to lose himself in the song, to no avail, the waiter delivered the food. The wine's subtle tannins and velvety finish perfectly complemented the tender, melt-in-your-mouth Wagyu steak, each bite *would* be a sensory delight except for tonight.

Evelyn leaned in closer to Thomas, her dark eyes sparkling with mischief. "You know, Thomas, you really should relax and enjoy yourself tonight. You deserve it." She reached across the table and gently brushed her fingertips against his hand, but her touch meant nothing to him. He pulled back a bit but realized that she was staying.

As the evening progressed, the waiter approached and asked if they would enjoy another bottle of wine. Thomas decided that Evelyn was not worth *that* level of cost and opted, instead, for a more moderately priced wine, the 2010 Château Margaux, valued at $1,100. Evelyn seemed surprised by the extravagance, her eyes narrowing as she said, "Thomas, is something wrong? You don't normally do this."

"No, I just want to celebrate my bonus I got from *Turner Research*. No big deal." answered Thomas somewhat gruffly. *"It's weird,"* he thought, *"but every guy in this restaurant would kill to be sitting in my place with this woman right now, and I just don't care!"*

As their awkward meal ended, Thomas decided to indulge in a luxurious dessert, a chocolate soufflé. While they waited for the dessert to arrive, Evelyn moved to sit beside Thomas, her intention being to snuggle up to him as they listened to the music, but Thomas gave her the stink-eye and she just sat in the chair next to him, instead.

Frankly, Evelyn's unannounced visit was not going as she had envisioned. She was getting angry that he wasn't hanging on her every word or gesture the way men normally did. He just seemed cold and distant, as though he was barely tolerating her presence.

When the dessert finally arrived, it was a sight to behold—the soufflé had risen beautifully, its top dusted with powdered sugar, and the raspberry coulis drizzled artfully on the plate. They both ate the decadent dessert, but Thomas stubbornly refused to respond beyond a grunt or two as she chit-chatted. Instead, he ate the rich, gooey chocolate soufflé with grim determination.

After they finished the dessert, Evelyn's hand found its way to Thomas's thigh under the table. She gently rubbed his inner thigh, hoping her touch would inspire him to be more receptive. Normally, this would have the desired effect, but tonight all it did was to provoke him to firmly move her hand away.

In the dim romantic light of the restaurant, Evelyn decided to gamble. She had to do something to regain control of the situation. Something was *badly* off. She deliberately softened her voice and made a carefully calculated confession. "Thomas, I have something to tell you. It's probably hard for you to believe this, but I've known about the Jesus project from the very beginning—before I even took you to that seminar where Dr. Crane was speaking."

Thomas listened, sitting silently as he heard what she had to say. The gravity of her calculated confession hung in the air between them.

Evelyn's hand returned to even higher up Thomas's thigh, her fingers trying to tease him. She artfully turned her face towards him, her lips mere inches away. "I don't want any secrets between us any longer," she whispered, her breath warm on his skin. With that, she leaned in and placed a slow, seductive kiss on the corner of his lips, the contact sending shivers down his spine. As she pulled away, Thomas realized he had enough.

"So, you don't want any more secrets, huh? I appreciate that. I really do." He once again removed her unwelcome hand, this time just before it reached its final destination. "Look, I know you talk about me with Nouvel all the time. In fact, he probably thinks you've got me wrapped around your little finger, doesn't he? Well, you don't. I'm not stupid, Evelyn. Eventually, I catch on!" He took a deep breath, trying to keep his cool.

Evelyn Perdita looked horrified. She had sworn to Nouvel that she could handle Thomas. Her boss was not going to be pleased at all. She stammered, "Nooo, Baby! It's not what you think! I'm just trying to help you!"

But Thomas did not back down, and he certainly didn't believe her. He signaled the waiter for the check by holding up his card in the air. The waiter quickly approached the table, taking the card in hand and scurried off to complete the transaction.

Thomas felt so stupid that he had fallen for this crap. Much less, that he had let this woman come *between* him and Gabrielle! At that moment, the waiter conveniently appeared with the check in hand. Thomas quickly scribbled a tip and signed for the balance. The waiter did a polite bow at the size of the tip and bid him a good evening.

Thomas turned back to her. "Look, Evelyn, we may have to *work* together, but we *don't* have to sleep together. Go back to Nouvel, just stay away from me, ok?!" That said, Thomas stood up and headed for the door.

Evelyn just watched him leave, but she was already thinking of her next move, predictably enough. She finished the expensive wine Thomas had paid for and reluctantly admitted to herself she would have to tell Nouvel that the dog was off the leash. She shuddered. Nouvel could be *very* unforgiving to those who failed him.

Chapter 65

Vanilla Shake

Over the next two months, Thomas found himself increasingly entangled in the web of *Turner Research*'s clandestine operations. His role within the company had evolved beyond a trusted enforcer/problem solver to a confidant that handled a variety of matters. He still ensured that both current and former employees maintained their silence regarding the company's secret projects. There were times when a simple conversation over coffee was enough to keep employees in line. Thomas would casually mention the potential consequences of breaching their contracts, and most would take the hint without further effort on his part. However, there *were* instances where a more forceful approach became necessary.

Because of the often dark and morally ambiguous nature of his work, Thomas found solace in the little things, such as a great steak, wine, and some amazing jazz. These palliatives helped him survive the murky world he was immersed in, though the need of them seemed to grow stronger as time went on. Regardless of these cherished moments of relative peace, Thomas couldn't shake the unease that gnawed at him. The project he was now fully aware of weighed heavily on his conscience, leaving him restless and questioning his *own* morality. "*Sometimes, ignorance is bliss.*" He would occasionally think in retrospect.

As the end of March approached, a cold front moved into the city, mirroring the growing chill in Thomas' heart. The once-clear lines between right and wrong had begun to blur, and he found himself caught in a moral storm of his own making. The totality of his actions over the past two months had left him with doubts. He wondered to himself when his conscience kicked up, what had changed? He didn't used to be so concerned over the consequences of doing his job.

This particular cold night in March, Thomas and Darius met at their favorite local bar to shoot pool and catch up after weeks of limited contact with each other. The dimly lit establishment was filled with the hum of conversations barely heard over the sound of classic rock playing in the background, and the clatter of billiard balls.

The two friends each sipped on their drinks as they waited for their turn to play. Fortunately, they each took their turn quickly. Darius, always observant, noticed that Thomas seemed more distant than usual. He glanced over at his friend with concern. "Yo, Dude," Darius said, lining up his shot, "You been mad hard to get ahold of, lately. What's been goin' on?"

Thomas looked up, his expression guarded. "You know I can't discuss my work, Big D. But, overall, things are okay, I guess." He paused, weighing his words carefully. "Just been busy, that's all."

Darius nodded, but knew, as good friends will, that there was more. He took his shot, sinking a solid ball into the corner pocket. "Alright, I get it," he replied, moving around the table for the next one. "So, what about that smokin' hot babe, Evelyn? You see her lately?"

Thomas shook his head, focusing on the table as he positioned his next shot. "No, I've moved on. Turns out she was narcing on me with one of the bosses. So, I cut the bitch off."

Darius frowned, clearly concerned. "I don't know, man. I already worried about you with that chick since you work for the same place. Maybe that's for the best that you axed her. I just think maybe you should holla at Gabrielle. You know, see how she's doing?"

Thomas let out a sigh, his pool cue hovering above the table as he thought about it. "Maybe," he conceded, finally taking his shot. "But I haven't heard from her, and I don't know where she is. I wish I *could* call her." he said wistfully.

Darius leaned against the pool table, looking at his friend with a gimlet eye. "Don't lose sight of who *you* are, man. You got a good heart. Just make sure you're making the right moves for the right reasons."

Thomas grunted and took a slug of his beer, grateful for his friend's support, even if he didn't say it out loud. The familiar atmosphere of the bar and the camaraderie with Darius provided a temporary escape from the crazier sides of his life.

Darius lined up his shot, aiming for the eight-ball, when his gaze caught sight of a man sitting at the bar he'd seen before. "Hey, Thomas," he said, smirking. "Looks like your lover boy's back. Are you wanting some action, huh?"

Thomas glanced over at the older man Darius was looking at and recognized him as the same guy who had been watching Thomas multiple times before. He narrowed his eyes, feeling a surge of annoyance. "Yeah, we keep seeing him around. What's his deal?"

Darius chuckled, sinking the eight-ball with ease. "Maybe he's got a crush on you, man. That's what I keep sayin."

Thomas decided not to continue with the humorous exchange. He had enough stress on his plate already. Instead, he decided to ignore the stranger and go grab a fresh round of beers at the bar.

As Darius waited for Thomas to return with the 'brewskies,' he surreptitiously watched the older man. He had become very good at doing this during his stay in prison. Survival there was tough, and being caught looking at the wrong person at the wrong time could be hazardous to your health. Darius decided to take matters into his own hands. He knew Thomas was going through a lot these days, and he figured he could put a smile on his buddy's face by finding out who the man was. Darius knew he was a large, imposing figure, and his presence alone was usually enough to intimidate most people. As a point of fact, he counted on it. As he saw the man head towards the restroom, Darius saw his chance and followed the man, a determined scowl on his face.

Darius waited just outside the closed and locked bathroom door, his arms crossed as he leaned against the wall. He looked like any other patron just waiting for his turn to use the bathroom. A few minutes went by, then Darius heard the lock disengage. As the man opened the door to leave, Darius quickly pushed him back inside and locked the door. The older man stumbled backwards, surprise flashing across his face.

"Who are you, and what do you want with my buddy?" Darius demanded, his deep voice echoing off the bathroom tiles.

The man, shocked at the situation, tried to throw a punch at Darius' chin, but Darius was too quick for him, despite being the bigger man. He blocked the punch effortlessly and grabbed the man by the throat, slamming him against the wall. "I just want to *talk* to you, dammit!" Darius yelled, his face inches from the man's panicked visage. The man, in his 50s and clearly outmatched, spat out, "Let me go, nigger!" his voice partly choked by Darius' forearm now pushing on his Adam's apple.

Darius' eyes narrowed, and he pushed a little harder, his anger rising. "Oh, Nigga, is it? *That's* how we gonna do this?!" His voice rose. "Oh, I got ya nigga dangling between my legs, little man. Matter a fact, I haven't had a good piece of vanilla shake since prison. " The man attempted to knee Darius in the groin, but Darius could feel the shift and turned his hips to counter. He flipped the man around to face the mirror over the filthy sink and held him there by the neck. He growled as he unbuckled the man's pants while holding the man's head pinned. Darius rumbled deep in his throat, "You want to treat me like some street nigga, I'm gonna show you a *prison* nigga, instead."

In a moment that seemed to unfold in slow motion, the man's pants suddenly dropped down to his ankles. The sudden movement released something that had been hidden at the man's waist---A snub-nosed .38 revolver had fallen out and clattered loudly on the tile floor. It spun a few times as it skittered across the stained tiles only to come to a stop against the wall.

Darius' eyes widened as he took in the sight of the gun. "Oh shit… you out to play, huh, bitch?" he asked, but his voice was now menacing. Darius let go of his neck and grabbed both of his wrists to pull them behind the man's back where he could hold them upwards to the point of breaking with one big hand. At the same time, he shoved his own hips forward, pinning the man's front against the sink. Satisfied that he was now fully in control, Darius reached around and grasped the man's genitals with his other hand. The pressure he exerted caused the man to shudder in agony.

"You know, there's this scene in 'Deliverance' I'm quite fond of," Darius said, his voice now cheerfully conversational. "It's about making someone *squeal* like a pig. You ever seen that movie?"

The man's eyes widened in fear, and he attempted to wriggle out of the hold he was in, but it accomplished nothing except to amuse Darius. "Okay, okay!" he cried out. "I'm a private investigator. I was hired to keep tabs on your friend."

Darius' iron grip remained unyielding. "Who hired you?" he demanded.

The man hesitated, but another painful squeeze elicited a high-pitched squeal from him. "It was a guy named Nouvel!" he blurted out desperately.

Darius gave his new toy one more squeeze as a warning of his seriousness. "Good boy, you're doing better." he said mockingly. "Is there anything *else* you want to tell me? Cause I got me a hankering right now for some vanilla shake, ya know?" And he gave his new toy a mild twist just to help the shaking man's motivation.

"Vanilla shake? I'll *buy* you a shake. Just let me go!" the man pleaded, but Darius noticed that this time, he didn't struggle. Apparently, *he* valued his toy, too. Darius approved, snickering to himself. "Nah, you don't get it. It's called a "vanilla shake" when a cracker like you is getting' fucked in the ass."

The man broke, volunteering, "Ok, ok! There was a woman with him. A real good looker, too. Don't know what her name was. Never said. Now, let me go! Please!"

"You know, you shouldn't play games you're not prepared to finish." Releasing the man, Darius patted him on his butt condescendingly. "Got a business card?" he asked casually.

The man, still shaking from the ordeal, muttered, "In my pants pocket. Just a second." With trembling hands, he pulled up his pants to buckle his belt. While he was doing that, Darius picked up the gun. The man's eyes widened, and he hurriedly searched himself for a business card which he promptly gave to the large, black man in front of him.

Darius held the card in hand, his gaze still fixed on the private investigator. "You're *lucky* I'm letting you walk out of here after what you called me," he said in a low, stern voice. "And stay away from my friend. Or you and I be havin' another friendly conversation."

That said, Darius didn't want to linger in the bathroom. He spared no further glance at the shaken investigator, who was still reeling from their encounter. Darius had what he needed and now his focus was on safety and discretion. He paused briefly to empty the .38 snub-nosed ammunition into his pocket, then placed the unloaded gun in the sink, where it clattered briefly again, its sound a stark contrast to the tense silence that now filled the small bathroom.

Darius exited the bathroom, keeping his expression carefully neutral just in case. He walked with a relaxed gait to not draw any attention to himself. His eyes, however, remained sharp, scanning the bar area for other potential threats, including possible witnesses that may have overheard the scuffle in the bathroom.

Thomas looked up from his beer as Darius approached, immediately noticing the subtle shift in his friend's demeanor. "What's up?" he asked curiously.

Darius smirked, fighting back the temptation to laugh as he handed the business card to Thomas. "Your man is a private investigator, working for some cat named Nouvel or something like that. He told me he was hired to keep tabs on you."

Thomas stood there for a moment, stunned by the simultaneous realities of Nouvel hiring someone to watch him coupled with the fact that Darius had just gotten involved in a big way. "How in the heavens did you get him to talk?" he asked in amazement.

Darius recounted the bathroom scuffle, not sparing any details, laughing periodically during the story.

"Vanilla shake?" Thomas muttered while cocking his head in disbelief. "Were you really going to do it if he didn't talk?"

Darius laughed harder than Thomas had heard him laugh in a long time. "Nah, man, it's just some fucked up shit to say. When a white boy hears a brotha say that shit, it makes him *real* open to anything you need. By the way, he also said there was some hot babe with this guy Nouvel, for what that's worth. Didn't know her name, though. "

"Darius, my brother, you didn't *have* to do that! But I've got to admit, it *is* hilarious."

Darius grinned at him, his single gold tooth gleaming in the lights, and shrugged nonchalantly as though he did this sort of thing every day. "Hey, I've got your back, Bro. No one messes with my friends."

Thomas thought about that for a second. Maybe Darius *did* do this every day?

Chapter 66

Desire And Sacrifice

Thomas sat in his dimly lit apartment, the heavy rain outside casting eerie shadows on the walls. He poured himself another glass of whiskey, the amber liquid sloshing against the sides of the glass. The room was filled with the rich scent of cigar smoke, as he took a deep puff and exhaled slowly. He was alone, the quiet emptiness of his apartment weighing heavily on him.

His laptop screen illuminated his face, casting a harsh blue glow on his features as he stared at his bank account. His balance now read $560,000 – more money than he'd ever had before in his life. Debt-free, with a small fortune at his disposal, he couldn't help but feel a mixture of pride and discomfort. He downed the whiskey in a single gulp, feeling the familiar burn as it slid down his throat.

He staggered to his feet, the alcohol making him unsteady. As he paced around his apartment, he couldn't shake the feeling of being lost, angry, and lonely. The money should have brought him a sense of freedom and security, but instead, it seemed to only amplify his negative emotions.

Thomas felt a growing contempt for people he worked with, the very people he once sought to help. They seemed shallow and selfish, so far removed from the lofty goals they aspired to achieve.

He walked over to the window, the rain pelting against the glass, and stared out into the dark, stormy night. The city lights flickered in the distance, like the fading dreams of his past. He took another long drag from his cigar, the smoke swirling around him like the chaotic thoughts in his mind.

In the depths of his despair, Thomas wondered what had brought him to this point. He had sacrificed so much in pursuit of success, but now he was left questioning the price he had paid. As he downed another glass of whiskey, the rain continued to fall outside, echoing the turmoil raging within.

Thomas stumbled around his apartment, his head swimming from the alcohol and cigar smoke. He had just caught sight of his phone lighting up on the counter when it began to ring. Squinting at the screen, he saw the name "Saint Joseph's Hospital" displayed, and his heart leapt into his throat. It was 1:19am in the morning, why would they be calling him? For a moment, he hesitated, unsure if this was some drunken hallucination or reality. Taking a deep breath, he answered the call, his voice stoic and guarded, not knowing what to expect. "Hello?"

A man's voice asked, "Hello, this is Dr. Harrison at Saint Joseph's Hospital. May I speak to Mr. Thomas Rene?"

Thomas assured him that he was Thomas Rene. "What is this about?"

The doctor said, "I'm sorry to have to tell you this, Mr. Rene, but we have a patient here by the name of Gabrielle Amadeo. Would it be possible for you to come over here now? We promised her we would contact you. We can talk more when you get here. Just ask for me at the front desk. My name, again, is Dr. Harrison."

Thomas was sobering up quickly. Adrenalin has that effect, he supposed. "Of course! I'll be right there. Is Gabby alright?"

Dr. Harrison answered cautiously. "I think it's best to discuss that here at the hospital, if you don't mind."

"No problem. I'm on my way right now. Tell her I'm coming!" Thomas blurted as he ran about the apartment looking for his keys and a jacket. The doctor hung up, satisfied that Thomas was on his way. Panic surged through Thomas as he hurriedly grabbed the keys and dashed out of the apartment, lighting a cigarette in the car to calm his nerves.

His thoughts raced wildly as he sped through the rain-slicked streets, the wipers working furiously to clear his windshield. What could have happened? Was she hurt? What had brought her to the point of reaching out to him after months of silence?

Arriving at the hospital, Thomas burst through the doors, his face pale, and his breathing ragged. He approached the Front Desk, his voice crackling with desperation. " Dr. Harrison is expecting me. Could you please tell him Thomas Rene is here?"

The receptionist was one of those rare ones who could tell that time was of the essence and immediately picked up her phone to make an announcement over the loudspeaker, "Paging Dr. Harrison. You have a visitor in the Main Lobby." She repeated the announcement again, then heard the intercom buzz. She picked it up. "Front Desk here, Julie speaking. Aah, Doctor Harrison, a Mr. Thomas Rene is here to see you. Shall I tell him you're coming down?" The doctor answered affirmatively, then hung up. The receptionist told Thomas the doctor would be right with him and to please hold his questions until the doctor arrived.

Thomas anxiously awaited the doctor near the Front Desk, wondering what was going on with Gabrielle. A couple of minutes later, a middle-aged doctor approached him. He had a kind face, but the somber expression he wore spoke volumes.

"Mr. Rene?" the doctor asked, extending a hand. "I'm Dr. Harrison. I've been overseeing Gabrielle."

Thomas shook the doctor's hand, his eyes searching for answers. "How *is* she, Doctor? What's going on?"

Dr. Harrison sighed, and his eyes filled with sympathy. "I'm afraid Gabrielle has suffered from a rare complication during childbirth. It's called *amniotic fluid embolism*, and it has caused her vital organs to fail. We did everything we could to stabilize her, but her condition was critical, and I'm afraid it was a case of 'too little, too late'. I'm sorry to have to tell you this, but she died 20 minutes ago."

Thomas felt his heart drop, and he struggled to breathe. He couldn't believe what he had just heard. "She's gone? She was

282

pregnant?!" He was stunned. His brain felt like mush. He couldn't think straight.

"Yes. She just gave birth at precisely 1:00am. The good news is that the baby is in excellent health, and it's a boy. Congratulations, you're a father!" The doctor said with a kind pat on Thomas' shoulder.

Thomas, still letting the reality of the situation hit him, muttered "I have a son?" The doctor simply nodded in the affirmative, though after a few moments of silence, he realized Thomas needed to be alone and excused himself to attend to other patients.

As Thomas stood in the sterile, white corridor of the hospital, Dr. Harrison's words reverberated through his mind like a death knell: Gabrielle was *gone*. The finality of her absence, a void that could never be filled, enveloped him. There was no conversation, no letter, no farewell message of any kind - just the deafening silence of a future that would never be. Memories flooded in. He could not stop them. Gabrielle's laughter, the warmth of her touch, and the sharp sting of the bitter memory of his betrayal with Evelyn Perdita, a decision that now seemed not just foolish, but tragically consequential.

Thomas leaned against the wall, feeling the weight of his own remorse like cold iron chains around his heart. He closed his eyes, wishing he could turn back time to a moment before the choices that led him here. He remembered the pain in Gabrielle's voice, the way it had broken when she discovered Evelyn had spent the night in his hotel room. Thomas knew the pain he had caused in that moment, yet he hadn't comprehended the depth of that pain, not until now, when any chance of reconciliation or apology had just been cruelly snatched away.

The hospital's incessant buzz felt like a different world as Thomas sank into an emotional abyss. He thought about the child Gabrielle had carried, *his* child. This realization struck him hard with a paralyzing mix of grief and guilt. In his mind, he saw the future that might have been - a family with Gabrielle, first steps and birthdays - all seemed to vanish like smoke.

Thomas's thoughts turned inward, reflecting on the impermanence of life and the irreversible nature of choices. His relationship with Gabrielle, once full of promise, had been irrevocably altered by his own actions. He understood, with a clarity that cut to his core, that every decision carved a path, not just in *his* life, but in the lives of all those he touched along the way. In the quiet of his solitude, Thomas grappled with a torrent of 'what ifs.' What if he had been faithful to Gabby? What if he had resisted temptation? The answers were like ghosts, both haunting and taunting him with a sense of loss too profound for tears.

He stood there, an almost broken man amidst the indifferent hospital halls, and he realized the bitter truth that we *never* truly know what tomorrow will bring. Our actions, big and small, cast ripples in the pond of time, ripples that we often cannot foresee or control. He was learning *this* lesson in the hardest way possible, and its cost was immeasurable. In this moment of painful introspection, Thomas found resolve, not for redemption – that path was closed to him now – but for *awareness*. He now had a greater appreciation of the preciousness of these pivotal moments, of the impact of decisions, and of how fragile the thread was that Life hangs upon. Gabrielle's death, and the life of the child he would soon meet, would be constant reminders of this profound truth.

This new understanding and resolve, though born from tragedy, would shape the rest of Thomas' days. It would be his burden and his guide, a poignant memory of the love that could have been. It would forever remind him of the importance of decisions and the delicate balance between desire and sacrifice.

Chapter 67

I Will Always Be There For You

Thomas sat quietly in the waiting room. His mind awash with emotions he hadn't dealt with since he was a child, and now he felt as if the floodgates had been opened. His heart ached-and the enormity of what had just transpired weighed heavily on him.

After what felt like an eternity, the nurse entered the waiting room, her face sympathetic. "Mr. Rene," she said softly, "would you please come with me? It's time to meet your son!"

Thomas nodded, snapping out of the fog he was in as he rose shakily to his feet. He followed the nurse down the quiet hospital corridor, his heart pounding in his chest. As they approached the nursery, he felt a growing sense of responsibility and trepidation washing over him.

The nurse led him to a small, glass-walled room where tiny babies lay swaddled in warm blankets. She gently picked up one of the infants, cradling him in her arms as she turned to Thomas. "Mr. Rene, meet your son, Thomas," she said, the tenderness in her voice unmistakable. "Miss Amadeo chose his name before she passed..." Her voice trailed off, which allowed the significance of the name to register with Thomas. He felt a lump form in his throat as he realized he now had his own Thomas, just like his father before him.

Thomas stared at the tiny, fragile form in the nurse's arms, and his heart swelled with love and protectiveness for the child almost immediately. The baby's eyes were closed, and his delicate features were a testament to the miracle of Life. Carefully, the nurse handed the infant to Thomas, guiding his hands to ensure he held the baby securely.

As he cradled his namesake for the first time, the weight of the baby in his arms was daunting and humbling to Thomas. He looked down at the child, an overwhelming wave of emotion washing over him. This was his *son*, his own flesh and blood, the living embodiment of Love.

Tears welled up in Thomas's eyes as he gazed upon his child. It was the first time Thomas had cried since he was a child himself. He felt the tremendous connection between them. In that instant, he grasped, as fully as any new father ever could, the reality of his new role. He vowed to be the best father he could possibly be and to protect this child with all his ability.

The nurse stepped back, giving Thomas a moment to be alone with his son. The quiet of the nursery amplified the sound of the baby's soft, peaceful breathing. Thomas leaned down and whispered softly to the baby, "I promise you, my boy. I will always be there for you unlike like *my* father. I love you more than words can say, and I will make sure you grow up knowing that." As he whispered those words, Thomas felt the powerful bond between father and son solidify, forever tying their lives together. And, in that moment, amidst the quiet of the nursery, the overwhelming love for his son coupled with the sorrow of Gabrielle's absence, Thomas Rene was forever transformed.

Later, as Thomas began to become drowsy with the new little Thomas lying comfortably on his chest, he felt a gentle touch on his shoulder. Opening his eyes, he found his mother, standing over him. Her face was etched with concern and a hint of disbelief at the fact her son was now a father. She was still processing the news Thomas had shared with her earlier on the phone. She leaned down and kissed him on the forehead, saying gently, "I'm here for you, Thomas. Don't worry. I'll help you."

Sitting up, Thomas rubbed his eyes and glanced at the clock. It was 10 am. He hadn't slept much, but his mother's presence was truly a comfort. She cooed over the baby and was delighted to hold him, sharing stories of Big Thomas when he had been a child. For the babe's part, he seemed quite happy in her arms. Of course, seeing them like this gave Thomas another reason for welling up, so he had to swallow deep to manfully hold back from a further emotional display.

At this point, his mother suggested that he go home, shower, and prepare himself for the day. She assured him that she would stay at the hospital to watch over Little Thomas while he did whatever he needed to do. She was not going anywhere.

Thomas was disheveled and emotionally drained. He couldn't help but shed a few tears as he confided in his mother that the reality of losing Gabrielle and simultaneously having a newborn son was still too much for him to fully comprehend, much less talk about to a great extent. His mother listened quietly and understood, but her heart ached for her son's loss and confusion. He eventually managed to leave the baby, his mother, and the hospital to return to his apartment. He needed a shower, fresh clothes, and some coffee. As he tiredly stepped out into the morning sun, he accepted that his life had just changed forever in only a matter of hours. It had been night when he arrived, and it was day when he was leaving.

He finally reached his apartment and headed straight for the bathroom, stripping off his clothes on the way into the shower. The water cascaded over him like a warm waterfall, providing a moment of relief from the stupor that had engulfed him earlier. After the shower, Thomas dried himself off and put on a fresh set of dress clothes. He felt the need to look presentable as this was a means to regain at least some semblance of control over his life. As he buttoned his shirt, he caught sight of the crucifix hanging on his mirror. He paused, staring at the symbol of his faith, feeling a mix of guilt, fear, and sadness.

Standing there lost in thought, with his tie still unfinished, he glanced at his phone and realized the date: *April 5th*. A premonitory dread flooded his senses as he suddenly remembered an additional significance to this day besides his son's birth– this was the day the cloning procedure was scheduled to finish! The moral implications of the project came crashing down on him, and he felt a surge of panic.

The awful thoughts swirling in his mind consumed him. He couldn't shake the feeling that the birth of his son would now be tainted by this monstrous crime against humanity set to take place on the very same day. He imagined the world's reaction once the truth came to light. The fact was, by Thomas' way of thinking, the day *his* son had been born would forever be linked to this terrible transgression about to occur.

Thomas's breathing became ragged, and he leaned against the wall for support, his eyes still locked on the crucifix which had reminded him of the impending attempt to clone Jesus. He was torn between his nascent love for his son, his determination to be a good father, and the overwhelming guilt he was feeling for his own part in the cloning project. The weight of it all threatened to crush him, and he closed his eyes, desperately searching for clarity and understanding of what was ahead.

He stood there staring at his own reflection in the mirror, searching for something deep inside himself, summoning up the courage to make this difficult decision. Suddenly, something within him hardened with purpose – a moment of determination that surged through his entire being. He knew now what he was going to do.

His eyes locked once more onto his reflection, and now he saw a man with purpose. It was as if a fire had been ignited within him, and he knew there was no turning back now. The time had come to take a stand. *"Damn the torpedoes! Full speed ahead!"* he thought bravely.

Thomas picked up his phone and called his mother. His voice was serious and steady as he spoke to her. "Mom, I need you to watch Little Thomas for me today. There's something important I must do. Do you mind?"

She was clearly besotted with the infant. "Of course not, Son! We're doing fine. He is such a handsome boy!" she cooed. "I'm really enjoying spending time with him. He keeps grabbing my finger. He's so cute!"

He could hear the joy in his mother's voice, but he doggedly continued, "I want you to know how much I love you and how grateful I am for everything you've done for me throughout my life."

His mother came out of her baby-haze, sensing Thomas' seriousness, and gave him her full attention. "Well, Thomas, you know I love you, too, and you've got nothing to worry about. We'll be fine right here. Do whatever it is you need to do, sweetheart. We'll be waiting for you!" she said cheerfully.

Thomas swallowed the lump in his throat, feeling his love and concern swell to almost choking levels for his son. This was going to be difficult, and he wished he could pray for God to watch over them. However, he had lost the habit long ago. With grim resolve, he hung up the phone and prepared himself to face the challenge ahead, driven by the need to protect his son and to do what Thomas thought was right.

Chapter 68

I Need Your Help

Thomas pulled up to *Turner Research*. His jaw was clenched, and his eyes were fixed on the entry to the imposing building. When he exited the car, shouts of protesters still filled the air, but he hardly noticed them anymore. He strode through the crowd with cold determination, his rapid pace carving through them like a hot knife through butter.

The security guards at the entrance recognized him and opened the door. They exchanged an odd glance with each other, taking note of Thomas' stoic expression and singular focus.

Once inside, Thomas made his way to Crane's office. He knocked on the door, and a voice from inside beckoned him to enter. As he pushed the door open, he was surprised to see Samuel Nouvel sitting in the office alone, casually sipping whiskey from an ornate glass.

"Ah, Thomas, you caught me celebrating." Samuel greeted him with a perfunctory smile, but his smile quickly vanished as he took in Thomas' serious demeanor. "You look like hell, Thomas. What's the matter?" Nouvel's voice was calm, but there was an edge to it. He clearly was not interested in anything other than the successful completion of his precious project.

"Samuel, you *must* halt this cloning project," Thomas implored, his voice a potent mix of urgency and frustration. "It's not about whether God exists or not. That's irrelevant. It's about having hope, the kind of hope that sustains people through the seemingly unbearable hardships of Life."

To Nouvel, this was exactly the sort of nonsense he hated with a passion. He responded with a dismissive sneer. "Hope? You mean those comforting illusions they cling to? Thomas, I'm about to

dispel the greatest myth of all time---the idea of a divine Jesus."
Samuel spread his arms out, the whiskey glass still in one hand,
and bowed his head in a mockery of Jesus on the cross.

Thomas, and not for the first time, thought Nouvel was a total ass.
His hands clenched into fists while his voice rose in an answering
challenge. "And what will *that* achieve, Samuel? Why rip away
from people the one thing that gives them the strength to face yet
another day? People are out there battling pain, loneliness, and
loss. If believing in a Heaven, something beyond this mortal life,
gives them some scrap of comfort, why strip that away?"

"Because it's a *lie*," Nouvel spat out, his tone laced with chilling
certainty. "And the truth, however harsh, is *always* preferable to
self-serving lies." He poured another shot because he was
beginning to enjoy himself. It wasn't often he got the chance to be
open about these things.

Thomas shook his head and stepped closer, attempting to make
Nouvel see reason. "Life is cruel *enough*, Samuel! It's filled with
plenty of despair already. Why take away this small solace? Why
condemn people to *your* reality where the only certainty is
suffering and *still* dying afterwards?"

Nouvel's eyes gleamed with a feverish intensity as he began to
speak, his voice convicted but laced with a venomous disdain for
everyone that didn't agree with his point of view. "Thomas, you
speak of hope in the form of faith. Let me illuminate for you the
grand fallacy of this millennia-old delusion: This isn't just about
disproving the existence of a deity. It's about *liberating* humanity
from the shackles of a baseless and archaic belief-system." He
leaned forward, his words seeming to slice through the air like a
knife. "Consider the evidence, or rather, the glaring lack thereof.
Historical records, when stripped of their inherent religious bias,
offer no concrete proof of this so-called Savior. Miracles,
resurrection, divine birth – they are all fabrications built upon a
frail foundation of human fear and ignorance." Samuel's voice
grew even harsher, even more fervent. "And what of the *moral*
inconsistencies, the blatant contradictions within the very
scriptures that people cling to? Think about it. A benevolent god

who sanctions wars, condones slavery, and demands blind obedience? *This* isn't divinity, Thomas! It's tyranny, a tyranny of the *mind*." His disgust was almost palpable as he continued. "People spend their entire lives groveling in prayer, seeking favor from an invisible overseer, sacrificing their rationality on the altar of Faith. And for what? The promise of an afterlife? A celestial kingdom that has no more evidence of its existence than fairy tales?"

Samuel's fist slammed onto the table, his eyes burning with a zealot's fierce conviction. "I'm seeking to not just disprove the existence of *Jesus*, Thomas, I'm aiming to dismantle the entire edifice of religious dogma that has plagued human growth for millennia. I intend to show the world that God and Jesus are nothing more than figments of the human imagination made up by people grasping at straws." He stood up, the whiskey fueling his pacing like a predator circling its prey. "You speak of the comfort that faith provides. *I* see the chains it *forges*. I see the wars that have been waged in its name, the persecutions, the subjugation of entire peoples under the guise of Divine command. It's a poison, Thomas, a sweet, seductive poison that dulls the mind and shackles the spirit." His voice dropped to a venomous whisper. "And *if,* in my attempt to reveal this truth, I must tear down *everything* they hold dear, so be it. Better to live with harsh truth than a comforting lie. I will expose this Jesus myth for what it really is and, in doing so, I will free all of humanity from its long bondage." Samuel's expression was self-congratulatory as he neatly dismissed any value to other ways of thinking than his own. "Let them hate me for it. Let them rage against the destruction of their mass delusion." He paused and thought for a moment, then pronounced smugly, "In the end, they will *thank* me for saving them!"

Thomas' face filled with anguish as his eyes filled with tears. "Today, my son was born, Samuel. A new life. A new beginning. I refuse to let his birth be tarnished by this atrocity of a cloning project. I won't allow his future to be ruined by the day we shattered the world!"

The room seemed to hold its breath and Thomas' words hung in the air. It was more than a clash of ideologies; it was a true struggle for the soul of humanity, a fight for its right to believe, to hope.

Nouvel paused as he gazed off into an imagined glorious future that only he could see as he took yet another sip of his drink. "Thomas, you see before you a project, but you fail to grasp the depth, the sheer magnitude of what I've embarked upon. This is not a mere whim. It's the culmination of years, decades, more than you could possibly comprehend." Samuel turned, his eyes dark with a passion that bordered on obsession. "I have poured not just millions, but *billions* of dollars into this endeavor. Every resource at my disposal, every waking moment of my existence, have been dedicated to this cause. You must understand, Thomas! It's not about the money. It's about the *principle*, the real truth that must be revealed." Samuel's voice was imploring as it took on an almost hypnotic cadence. "You see, while others were content with their lives, basking in their own colossal ignorance, I was already working to expose the lies that hamstring humanity." He leaned closer and owlishly eyed Thomas, "This project is *my* legacy. It will be my gift to humanity – a revelation so profound that it will shatter the very foundations of their collective faith. And, when that happens, when the world awakens to the reality I've exposed, they will see that I was right all along." Nouvel settled back into the comfortable chair.

There was a brief, unsettling silence as Nouvel's eyes slowly drifted shut for a moment, then they snapped open again and seemed to pierce through the very soul of Thomas. Nouvel spoke in almost a whisper the final words he felt impelled to share, "Imagine the effort it takes to challenge centuries of belief, to stand against the tide of religious fervor. It's a task that demanded a will of iron and a heart unencumbered by the frivolities of faith and hope, let alone the birth of *your* bastard child!"

Thomas felt a surge of anger at this self-important, little twit calling his son a 'bastard', but he clung to his last vestiges of control. "No, I won't let you do this, Samuel. Not today." Thomas declared, his voice resolute, echoing the power of his conviction. "I will *fight* to preserve that hope, not only for my son, but for everyone."

"You've lost it, Thomas. You've *always* thought you were more important than you really are!" Nouvel sneered pityingly as he subtly reached for the emergency button under the desk, but Thomas was aware of its existence and was even faster to react. He lunged across the desk, pinning Nouvel's hand against the smaller man's chest. The two men struggled, inadvertently knocking Nouvel's whiskey glass to the floor where it shattered loudly. With blurring speed, Thomas grabbed the bronze desk lamp and swung it at Nouvel's head. The blow landed with a sickening crack, and Nouvel crumpled to the floor, out like a light.

Thomas stood over Nouvel's unconscious body, his chest heaving. It had all happened so fast! He looked down at the blood pooling on the carpet, the gravity of his actions sinking in. However, this was no time for remorse. He snatched Nouvel's security pass laying on the desk and bolted from the office.

The corridor was a blur as he raced towards the labs. He rounded the last corner and nearly collided with the security guard, a towering figure with an imposing grasp of proper posture. The name 'Dave' was emblazoned on his badge which seemed to barely hold on to the large pectoral muscle underneath. His eyes, sharp and assessing, focused entirely on one Thomas Rene.

"Sorry, Sir," Dave forestalled Thomas, his voice possessing the deep rumble of authority. "No unauthorized personnel are allowed in the labs today. Strict orders."

Thomas' mind raced. He needed to get past this human obstacle, but how? He could sense Dave's unwavering commitment to his duty. The guard's hands were relaxed but ready, his posture unyielding, yet alert.

"I *am* authorized." Thomas responded with all the certainty he could muster. Dave, though doubtful, reached over and picked up a clipboard from his desk, searching diligently for 'Thomas

Rene.' He did not find it. Before the guard could say anything, Thomas said, "Dave, listen," mustering all the charm and persuasiveness he could. "I *really* need to get in there, now. Nouvel sent me. It's critical I speak with Dr. Crane!"

The security guard's eyes narrowed slightly, assessing Thomas's urgency, trying to discern truth from deception. He shook his head. "I'm sorry, Sir," he repeated firmly. "My orders are very clear. No one gets through unless they are on the list, and you are not on it."

Thomas could feel the clock ticking, each second was a hammer blow to the face of his chances. In a desperate gambit, he stepped back from the guard, a look of resignation on his face. "Okay, I understand. I'll just wait for Dr. Crane then. Mind if I grab a coffee from the break room?"

Dave relaxed slightly, relieved that Thomas was not being confrontational, and nodded. "Sure, go ahead."

As Thomas turned towards the break room, his mind was a whirlwind of possible strategies. He needed a distraction, something to throw the guard off balance. The break room was quiet, its usual bustle absent, even the hallways were empty. His eyes swept over the room, landing on the coffee machine, then the microwave, then steak knives near the sink, and finally settled on the fire alarm.

Thomas' heart pounded as he reached a decision. He walked towards the alarm with a casual gait. With a quick glance around to ensure that he was unobserved, he pulled the lever down sharply. An alarm blared, a piercing sound that echoed through the hallways. The muscular guard burst into the room, his face showing concern and confusion in equal measure.

"Fire!" Thomas yelled, pointing to the microwave. "I think I saw sparks!"

As the panicked guard rushed past him to investigate, Thomas suddenly made his move. He stuck out his foot and tripped the guard so that the man landed face first on the hard, concrete floor. This stunned him just long enough for Thomas to leap onto his wide back, knees first. His arm snaked around the man's bodybuilder neck in a crushing chokehold. The guard's bulging muscles tensed as he tried to resist the unexpected assault.

In the frantic struggle, Dave's hand flailed about, searching for something, anything, to gain the upper hand on his attacker. His fingers closed around one of the steak knives that had fallen to the floor. With a swift, almost reflexive motion, the guard swung back over his shoulder and plunged the knife into Thomas just below his left breast near his armpit.

A sharp, searing pain exploded through Thomas's body. He screamed, a raw, primal sound of agony and shock, but the pain also triggered a surge of adrenaline, flooding his system and enabling a fierce, almost inhuman strength. He twisted away from the sudden pain, ripping the knife free from the security guard's hand, and then tossing it across the floor. Gritting his teeth against the pain, Thomas tightened his grip around the thick neck of the guard. His vision blurred, a red haze clouding his sight, but he held on. Every fiber of his being screamed in protest, the knife wound burning like fire, but Thomas' resolve was unflinching.

The hapless guard's struggles weakened, and his attempts to break free were growing more and more feeble. Seconds stretched into eternity as Thomas poured every ounce of his remaining strength into the chokehold. Finally, with a last, desperate twitch, Dave's body went limp as he succumbed to the darkness of unconsciousness.

Thomas finally released his grip, panting heavily. He rolled off the guard onto his back, his hand clutching the wound on his chest. Blood seeped through his fingers, warm and sticky. The pain was intense, almost unbearable. However, he couldn't stop now. The mission was all that mattered. With a grimace of pain and determination, he stumbled to his feet and headed towards the lab entrance, each step fueled by pure adrenaline. The alarm continued to scream in the background, BEEP... BEEP... BEEP, but Thomas barely heard it. His focus was singular – to stop this heinous act at any cost.

Chapter 69

Its Warm Embrace...

Thomas stood at the threshold of the lab, his heart racing like a trapped bird, acutely aware of the monumental consequences of what he had to do next. His hand hovered above the security card reader as he drew a deep, steadying breath to tame his turbulent thoughts.

In this fleeting moment, memories of his son enveloped him — the gentle heft of his newborn in his embrace, the exquisite details of his tiny face, and the tidal wave of love that had washed over Thomas. Driven by promises whispered to Little Thomas earlier, Big Thomas had a fierce determination to shield his son from the repercussions from this project which straddled the fine line between science and divinity.

As Thomas wrestled with the uncertainty of what lay ahead, poignant images of his son's future milestones tormented him. The thought of not being there for his son — to not see his first steps, to not hear his first words — and he feared his child growing up unaware of the depth of his father's love. These things gnawed relentlessly at his heart. The ache of his pain, both beautiful and excruciating, threatened to overpower him. As he stood there, memories of his own childhood emerged, shadows of a past marked by his own father's departure when he was just four years old. This abandonment had left an indelible scar, a deep, aching void that had shaped every corner of Thomas' life. It had taught him harsh lessons of solitude, embedding in him an unrelenting fear of trust, and a reluctance to form deep connections with others.

Now, facing a moment that mirrored his deepest fears, the possibility of his own son experiencing a similar heartbreak was an agony far greater than any physical pain. The thought of his son enduring such loss and living under the same shadow that had haunted Thomas' every step as a child, sent shivers down his spine. Tears, unbidden, welled in his eyes, each unshed tear a silent testament to the years of loneliness and the unhealed wounds of a child abandoned by a father.

With his voice quivering with emotion, barely a whisper backdropped by the chaos around him, Thomas made a solemn vow, "No matter what happens, my son, hold onto my love. What I do today, I do for you." His words were also a fervent plea to God, a desperate hope that God's love would build a bridge over the chasm of abandonment that had cast such a shadow over his own childhood.

In that moment, Thomas' love was like a beacon in the darkness, a balm to the old wounds that time alone had failed to heal. This love, deep and unyielding, was both his gift and his promise, a path illuminated by the unwavering light of a father's love.

Gathering his resolve, Thomas swiped the security card, and swung the doors open. The lab was chaotic, and the alarm blared incessantly. BEEP… BEEP… BEEP. He noticed a security guard with a phone pressed to his ear while, at the same time, trying to pacify the agitated crowd in white lab coats. The guard's eyes locked on Thomas as he burst through, although the realization of his intent dawned too late.

"Hey! Stop!" the guard shouted, scrambling to give chase, but Thomas was already a blur and his initial burst of speed, unmatchable. Thomas' sprint down the hallway was a whirlwind of motion, his shoes squeaking their purchase against the polished floor. The alarm still blared. His breaths became labored-as everything around him seemed to slow down, yet he remained a constant force of speed and determination. Lab technicians, clad entirely in white, were a blur as they swirled around him. Thomas pushed the bodies aside while documents fluttered in the air in his wake.

A familiar voice pierced the cacophony of sound. "Thomas, stop!" It was Evelyn, emerging from a nearby lab. Her eyes widened in shock at the sight of Thomas covered in blood and with a determined look etched on his face. Her pleas were lost in the commotion, drowned out by the panicked group of scientists who were acting like geese frantically winging their way to safety.

Thomas' mind was completely focused, every thought centered on the task in front of him. The adrenaline coursing through him grew even stronger as the double doors at the end of the hallway loomed closer with each stride.

The alarm's piercing BEEP... BEEP... BEEP continued as he neared his objective. The weight of time, his son's future, and the fate of the world bore down on him with crushing intensity. With a last burst of speed, Thomas broke through the final barrier of white coated bodies, their confused cries merging into the symphony of alarm and chaos that filled the hallway.

As he neared the double doors, Thomas noticed a bright light beginning to shine through the cracks around the door frame. The light grew stronger and more intense with each stride, casting an ethereal glow over the hallway. The stark contrast between the sterile walls of the corridor and the mysterious, otherworldly light emanating from the door cracks only intensified the urgency of the situation.

Upon reaching the doors, Thomas quickly swiped the security badge through the terminal and heard a reassuring clicking sound as the doors unlocked. His heart pounded in his chest as he grasped both sets of handles, feeling the cold metal beneath his bloodied hands. With a deep breath, he pushed the handles down and pulled the doors open. As they swung wide, the brilliant, white light from within the room radiated outwards, enveloping him in its radiant embrace. For a moment, time seemed to stand still as Thomas was engulfed by the dazzling light. The chaos of the hallway, the screams, and the blaring alarm all faded away and were replaced by a profound sense of resolve. This was the moment everything had been leading to, the culmination of all his cumulative choices.

Thomas felt an immense power surge through him, fueled by the love for his son and the future he had vowed to protect. He was ready to step into the unknown, ready to face whatever challenges awaited him on the other side of the open doors, and he knew he would not stop.

Despite the blinding light, Thomas was able to see a solitary figure standing before him. The serene presence of the man was unmistakable – it was Jesus, His gentle eyes filled with compassion and understanding. Bathed in the radiance of divine light, Jesus stood tall and strong, yet He also seemed tender and caring. The brightness of the light surrounding Him was so intense that Thomas had to struggle to keep his gaze on the figure. Despite his tearing eyes, Thomas felt a powerful sense of awe and reverence wash over him as he was humbled by the inspiring, yet somehow calming presence. The love and grace emanating from Him touched Thomas' very soul, filling him with a profound sense of peace. As he stood there, captivated by the divine encounter, the light brighter and brighter, eventually enveloping Thomas in its warm embrace...

Chapter 70

You Are The Light Of My Life

In the heart of an ethereal brilliance, Thomas found himself alone and cradled by a light that seemed to pulse with life. It was a cocoon of serenity, a sanctuary bathed in a glow reminiscent of the first gentle rays of dawn. The world beyond this celestial embrace faded into the background, leaving a canvas painted with nothing but radiance that began to envelope him.

In this profound stillness, where even the passage of time seemed hushed, a delicate sound emerged—a baby's cry, soft, yet clear, and it cut through the silence that surrounded him. It was a sound that resonated within his soul, stirring waves of love and recognition in Thomas. He reached into the heart of the light, guided by invisible threads of connection. His hands were trembling, but they found what they sought and emerged with a precious burden—his son, little Thomas.

As he pressed the infant to his chest, a surge of shared warmth connected them. Thomas felt the baby's tiny heart beating rapidly, a rhythmic drumming that synchronized perfectly with his own. In this sacred communion they shared, their heartbeats harmonized, singing a comforting lullaby of connection.

Lowering his head, Thomas brushed his cheek against the velvety softness of his son's skin. He inhaled deeply, savoring the scent unique to newborns—a fragrance of innocence and new beginnings. A flood of emotions welled up within him and tears cascaded down Thomas' cheeks as he experienced an overwhelming sense of purpose.

Thomas whispered to his son in a voice choked with emotion, words that were more felt than heard. "I love you, my little Thomas. You are the light of my life. You are the answer to *my* deepest cries of loneliness, a redemption of my lost years of fatherly love. The silence of my father's absence left a void in me where his love should have echoed, but *you* fill that void. With every fiber of my being, I promise you will experience the love that I begged for, to be the father I needed, and the father you deserve." Thomas had a revelation at that moment, almost like someone or something was putting the idea in his head, that unconditional love is a bond that transcends the very fabric of reality.

Around them, the light intensified, its brilliance bearing witness to Thomas' oath until it seemed to consume all that existed. It was as if the universe itself was acknowledging the timeless and unbreakable connection between them. In that moment, they were the only two beings in existence, and they were wrapped in an all-encompassing blanket of light that symbolized the importance of hope, the purity of purpose, and the unyielding strength of Love. They were now intertwined in the luminous tapestry of their shared existence for all eternity.

THE END